MUSTARD SEEDS

Modern Parables

ISBN 978-1-950034-71-0 (Paperback)
Mustard Seeds: Modern Parables
Copyright © 2020 by Melissa Levi

Author photo credit: Angela Fields.

For permission requests, write to the publisher at the address below.

Yorkshire Publishing
4613 E. 91st St,
Tulsa, OK 74137
www.YorkshirePublishing.com
918.394.2665

Printed in the USA

MUSTARD SEEDS

Modern Parables

Melissa Levi

TULSA

Everyone has a Ministry

> *As every man hath received the gift, [even so] minister the same one to another, as good stewards of the manifold grace of God. If any man speak, [let him speak] as the oracles of God; if any man minister, [let him do it] as of the ability which God giveth: that God in all things may be glorified through Jesus Christ, to whom be praise and dominion for ever and ever. Amen.*
> *1 Peter 4:10-11*

I never wanted to be a Christian writer. I wanted to be like *Stephen King or Michael Crichton.* I wanted to wow people with my imagination. Bring you to tears. Make the hair stand up on your neck and your skin crawl. I wanted the reader to be awed by *me.*

When I wrote my Christian Sci-Fi thriller, it was still just for me. I thought that if I changed it to a Christian based storyline, I would finally be successful in my writing. Well it got me published, but satisfaction was fleeting and glory very short lived.

Even so, I craved writing. It was like breathing to me, and not one day passed that I did not scribble an idea on paper or build a character in my head. I knew beyond a doubt that I was meant to write. Nevertheless, my writing lacked something.

Over the years, my mother has advised me to write about my life and my experiences. Every time she said that I would think,

"Why would anyone want to read about my life my experiences?
I don't want everyone to know what a loser I am!

I did not give it another thought because I was sure that I, personally, had nothing to write about. I felt that for my writing to be effective I would have to be capable of writing plots that were so beyond anything anyone had written, read or experienced. I was afraid that if I tried to write what *I believed* God wanted that I would no longer enjoy writing. I wanted the writing to be for me. I wanted the credit fully.

One night, my teacher in Bible class suggested that maybe I could write a couple of devotionals for the website. He left it open for me to think about. I thought about it a lot. Back and forth, the tug of war continued for nearly two weeks, until one evening in class I heard something that shifted my perspective. The lecture was focusing on the men that had written the New Testament. This handful of men had been chosen to write the most important compilation of writings man has ever read. We were looking at the personalities of the writers. Each author, Matthew, Mark, Luke, James and Paul, each different men with diverse backgrounds, stations in life— and they brought that to their writing. God was not using these men as mere scribes but inspiring them to reveal to the world the true character of God through their hearts by how Jesus had impacted their lives and how they through faith and obedience were dedicated to reaching everyone with the Gospel of Christ. In their writing, His Love, His sacrifice, His greatness and the vastness of His Grace was being expressed by the pens of men willing to open themselves up to receive the message of God to His children.

I was so worried about losing myself that I was missing out on a blessing that I was designed to complete. God did not want to lessen me; He wanted to add to me. Now, I am more fulfilled in my writing than I have ever been. Why? Because when I surrendered to His Will in my writing, He revealed to me much more than I had ever expected. He opened my eyes to His wonders daily, He guided my focus from meaningless trivial matters of the world to the real workings of His Hands in the lives of all those around me. I have been humbled by emails, cards and letters from people that relate to the day to day struggle and victory of a life through Christ. I have been honored by being asked to pray for people, some I have never met. No amount of money or best seller list could ever compare to knowing that God in all my imperfections and failures uses me to speak to His called.

When you offer yourself for His use, you are fulfilling the plan you were specifically designed to accomplish. He has no desire to take from you but to quench you and build you in His Glory. Within that act of surrender is the beginning of a closer relationship with Jesus. He has a mission for you. A specific mission that can only be fulfilled by you, but only if you are willing.

If you are reading these words, know that you have a gift, talent or ability that was given specifically to you to fulfill the ministry designated for you.

Because everyone has a ministry.

The Rise of Fear

This weekend I watched **Rise of the Guardians** with my girls. No matter how old I get I will always love animation. We settled under the blankets and with ice cream bowls filled, we started the DVD. As I watched the movie, I was inspired by the parallel in the story and this world.

In the movie the struggle for the future of the children between the Guardians and Pitch Black with his "Night Mares" was an excellent example of the struggle that exist in the unseen world. The villain, Pitch was determined to fill the dreams of the children with fear. With the brush of his fingertip the black fright devoured joy, faith, and love. With nothing left to believe in, the children began to sink into lives ruled by foreboding and dread of the darkness. Their laughter ended and everything seemed bleak.

Their faith in the Guardians waned and one by one the sentinels could no longer be seen or felt by the children. Darkness began to reign.

But one child remained faithful and refused to give into the fear. It was his faith that gave the Guardians the ability to crush Pitch leaving him impotent and consumed by his own Night Mares.

It is much the same in our lives when fear creeps into our dreams. As fear swallows us, the darkness seems to be all we can see. We lose sight of the cross; we forget the battle has been won. Our imagination runs amuck and soon the fear draws doubt, anger, guilt and shame.

Many times in our lives, we are touched by trepidation maybe by a bad diagnosis, loss of a job, trouble in the marriage, low bank account or loneliness. Whatever it may be, it quickly consumes our thoughts, fuels our imaginations and clouds our eyes. Our focus is compromised and all we see is the darkness and all we feel is the anxiety.

Recently, I have been dealing with a fear. My mind plays out scenarios and my anxiety mounts. My imagination runs wild and the fear grows. I lose sleep, my stomach churns and I struggle. Fear is a ruthless opponent it has no pity and is determined to bind you with alarm and darkness within your mind. But it is not supposed to be that way. You have the power, the ability to be freed from the fears that lurk in your thoughts.

2 Corinthians 10:4-5 tells us that it is the Might of God that cast aside the strongholds; His spirit gives us the power to control the imaginations and recognize the things that are contrary to God. It is the faith in the Power of God and the Blood that overcomes the threat of the consuming fear.

> *"For God gave us a spirit <u>not of fear</u> but of power and love and self-control." 2 Timothy 1:7*

Age is a High Price to Pay for Wisdom

*For the fruit of the Spirit is in all goodness
and righteousness and truth.*
Ephesians 5:9

A fresh faced young man came into my office the other day. He was well mannered and inundated me with "Yes and No ma'ams. Once he left, I realized that his politeness was more about my age than his upbringing. After some calculations, I realized I could be his mother! Where had the time gone? It didn't seem like that long ago that young men wanted my phone number! Ego bruised I returned to my task at hand. I twisted the idea over in my brain a few times and wondered,

> *"Was my relationship with Christ as evident as
> the grays poking out around my temples?"*

It was an interesting question. It was clear to this young man that I was a mature woman by my appearance and maybe my actions. But could anyone know my relationship with Christ by my appearance and words? Did my demeanor and my language reflect a connection to the spirit? In everything that we do, we should be a reflection of Christ. From our words, what we choose to watch on TV and movies, the books we read, the friends we congregate with to even our clothing.

As we mature in life we recognize the errors of our youth. Our ideals and priorities change, and inevitably, so does our appearance. It is the same in our maturing in Christ. As our walk with Him becomes closer, our standards and how we look to others change. We recognize the folly of our lives before we become recipients of the grace of God through the shedding of Jesus' blood. Our priorities change and we are compelled to share our wisdom with others and the good news of salvation.

As you pray this week, take a look at your reflection in Christ. Take stock of the things in your life. Does your choice of movies, friends, vocabulary and clothing reflect Jesus? When you choose an outfit do you think about whether or not it is attractive to the world or an expression of your commitment to Christ? When choosing a movie do you think about what the contents of that movie will say to others about your witness for Christ?

My relationship with Christ should be as obvious as the gray hair on my head. My hope for you is *"**That you might walk worthy of the Lord, fully pleasing, being fruitful in every good work, and increasing in the knowledge of God." Colossians 1:10**

Sneak Attack

Be sober, be vigilant; because your adversary the devil walks about like a roaring lion, seeking whom he may devour.
1 Peter 5:8

One day as I spoke to a new baby in Christ about the many problems she faced, I reminded her that the enemy would oppose her at every turn and that she needed to be ready and understand who she was up against.

She lifted her face and through her tears she laughed. "You aren't talking about devils and demons are you?"

"Yes." I confidently answered.

"You have got to be kidding me!" she laughed again. "You are an educated, intelligent woman and you are telling me that there are these monsters out after us. I know you really don't believe that!"

I do.

Most of my redeemed life I have sat on the sideline in the spiritual battle that rages all around us. I have been content to say my prayers, go to church and declare that I was a Christian. I did children's VBS, taught a women's study group and did three tours of duty on

Jamaica mission trips. I pray in public at restaurants and make sure my Christmas cards are about Christ and not Santa.

That was enough until I came to college. I came to take a class titled **_The Chemistry of the Blood_** by Dr. MR DeHaan. I thought I would take a few classes and learn more. Catch some of the Bible stories that I might have missed. Now, as my second year at Old Bethel is in full swing all that I mentioned above is no longer enough. In fact, as time passes I have ventured out more moving toward the front line.

As I revealed a couple of weeks ago, I told God I was ready to move forward. I was ready to take that next step. He took me by the hand and guided me through some of the things He wanted cleared out. With reluctance on my part, we worked through it.

This past weekend I received news that truly knocked me off balance and while I was vulnerable our enemy struck and struck hard. I will tell you that I was shocked and really very put off that he would strike when I wasn't ready. I was naïve to think that his weapons and strategy would stay the same that he wouldn't up the game when I did, but he did. I might have been knocked down a peg—maybe two—but I regained balance and moved forward.

I took what I have been learning and I fired back. I kept in mind that this wasn't a fight for the victory as my teacher, had pointed out last week this was a fight against a foe that knew he was defeated but wouldn't stop.

Just because he is defeated doesn't mean that his attacks are any less malicious or that there are not casualties along the way. But Praise God, we have the victory and the tools to fight.

If I had not made the decision that I wanted to learn all I could and store it up in my heart, I would not have withstood the attack of this past weekend.

We do have a foe, an enemy that has one goal: to take all that he can before his time runs out. He has been conquered and he knows it but he will not quit until the bitter end. In order to stand up to him you will need the full armor. (Eph 6:10-17)

<u>Ephesians 6:10-18</u>

[The Whole Armor of God] Finally, my brethren, be strong in the Lord and in the power of His might. Put on the whole armor of God, that you may be able to stand against the wiles of the devil. For we do not wrestle against flesh and blood, but against principalities, against powers, against the rulers of the darkness of this age, against spiritual hosts of wickedness in the heavenly places.

Imitation is the Most Sincere Form of Flattery

Be ye therefore followers (or imitators) of God, as dear children; And walk in love, as Christ also hath loved us, and hath given himself for us an offering and a sacrifice to God for a sweet-smelling savour.
Ephesians 5:1-2

This morning I got up and began getting ready for my day. The girls are on spring break so I slept in and planned on eating breakfast at work. Over the scent of shampoo I detected coffee. My youngest daughter had gotten up and started coffee and breakfast. She had two fried eggs, toast and coffee waiting for me. It was a wonderful surprise.

Once I was ready, my daughter dressed in my old bathrobe, accompanied me to the porch to hand me a coffee refill and kiss me goodbye.

I giggled, "What do you want?"

"Nothing, mom, I just wanted to wish you a good day like you do for us." Her green eyes were wide and innocent.

As I drove to work the saying *"Imitation is the most sincere form of flattery",* came to mind. My daughter was imitating me even as far as the kiss and the old bathrobe. Her act of sacrifice of getting up when she didn't have to was precious to me.

Our children are great imitators of us, even our bad behavior. As Christians, we are to be imitators of Christ for people that we interact with every day, our families, friends, coworkers and even the cashier at the grocery store. Our behavior, whether good or bad, is witnessed and taken in by all those around us. My day was brightened and my heart filled with love and a smile. God is the same when we sacrifice to show others His amazing love; we bring happiness and a smile to His face.

Through the Word we are exhorted to follow as children. Like my daughter's eyes were on me our eyes should be on God. Unless we see Him as the Father, and have the same dependence and devotion of a child, we can never follow him in the purity of a child.

We need to be more than imitators of Christ, we need to **resemble** Christ. We were created in His image, given the example of Christ and filled with the Holy Spirit. Our actions should be more than imitations but reflection of Christ to those around us.

Have you resemble Christ today?

If all Else Fails, Read the Directions

This morning the request for breakfast was pancakes. I confess that I have been using prepared mixes to conserve time in the morning. Unfortunately, I was out of mix. I began pulling out the ingredients, we would go scratch today. Using memory I began to dump in the flour, sugar, egg, and vanilla.

When the pancakes hit the table, they were more *"flatcakes"* than pancakes. My youngest, always has something to say and hasn't learned the art of when to be quiet.

"What happened? Did you scrape them up off the road?" Her sister joined in the teasing. Raucous laughter peeled throughout the house.

What happened was that I didn't consult the cookbook! I didn't take time to check my method against the standard. So many times in our lives, we fail to check the standard given to us by God in His Word.

If I had taken the time to read over the recipe my pancakes would have been fluffy and tasty, but I chose to rely on myself and got flat in taste and in presentation. It was not a very appetizing breakfast! A life lived without the Word being applied is much the same, **"flat"** and not very appetizing to those unsaved that are watching.

Do you consult the Word on a daily basis? There are many books with yearlong plans, online plans, small groups, and, of course, you can just pick the Bible up and start with your favorite story.

Get started today!

Storms Come and They Go

*But when you ask, you must believe and not
doubt, because the one who doubts is like a wave
of the sea, blown and tossed by the wind.*
James 1:6

Every morning after breakfast and the girls leave, I get ready. That's my 35 minutes of silence and preparation for the day. My two little felines, Vlad and Dante, follow me silently from room to room, waiting patiently for their bowl of milk. Sometimes, they curl up on the bed and snooze. Other times they will sit on the dresser and watch with interest as I go through my wardrobe, but they never get excited or impatient. They never worry that I will forget or neglect them. They believe and trust that I will provide the milk and they wait however long it may take.

This past weekend my car broke down. I freaked! My car is my livelihood. Without it, I am toast. I prayed and then wrung my hands, sent out text, prayed again, whined, pitched a fit and lay awake most of the night worrying about what I should do in between prayers.

The next morning my best friend picked me up for work. Throughout the morning my mind worked in overtime between fretting on how I would get the car fixed and if this would have a negative impact on my job. The more I rode the waves of worry the sicker and more anxious I became. By lunch I was positive I would be without the car for weeks and my job was in jeopardy. I was mentally and emotionally zapped.

Later that day, three gentlemen came to my aid. They mobilized and took over and in a matter of two hours they had fixed the car and brought it to my job. I was floored. Their generosity and kindness filled me with joy and thanksgiving.

I would have never dreamed that was the way that God would have worked it out. In all the scenarios that had played through my mind, this had not been one of them. I got more than just my car fixed I got a lesson in trust and faith. I should have waited patiently after my prayer was breathed. I should have trusted and slept. Whether I stayed up wringing my hands or sleeping peacefully the plan was already in motion. Before the car coughed its last, the way was being made. The "what if's" kept me churning. Like many of us, I was trying to handle the situation, trying to take control and all it got me was bags under my eyes.

Is there a situation in your life that you are praying about? Do you whisper your prayer and then begin trying to work out a solution?

God has his own timeline and it rarely coincides with ours. Without faith in your prayers and in God's ability you find yourself like the *waves of the sea, blown and tossed by the wind.* Your faith and trust is your anchor. It may take a while for the storm to pass, but it will pass.

No Appetite for God

…Whose end is destruction, whose god is their belly, and whose glory is in their shame— who set their mind on earthly things.
Philippians 3:19

Every six months I have to have a blood pressure recheck. I don't enjoy doctor visits, but I do enjoy seeing my health care professional and my sister in Christ. I was particularly looking forward to talking to her about her recent mission trip to Buenos Aires, Argentina.

As she began to share her experience with me, I was taken aback at her passion and broken heart for the people of Buenos Aires. Her mission began on the flight. The lady next to her, on her way back home, asked her why she was going to Buenos Aires. When she replied it was a mission trip the woman seemed confused and asked, "Why? We are not hungry."

Little did she know that was to be the theme of her mission trip.

Buenos Aires is the capital and largest city of Argentina, and the second-largest metropolitan area in South America, after Greater São Paulo. It has a population of 2.891 million. It is a beautiful and busy metropolis, much like our own New York City and it is full of satiated people. They are filled with every comfort, food, technology, jobs, money and opportunities.

As she talked to people her heart was broken over and over. The people were kind, hospitable and gracious listening to her, but they had no hunger. Time and time again, she spoke, passionately giving them the Good News. They congratulated her on her faith and even thanked her for sharing the joy she had but they had no need of it. With a smile they faded into the throngs of people that went on their way. Looking out over the square and the thousands that moved by she was broken because she could never speak to each of them.

Like the people of Buenos Aires, we are a satiated people stuffed with flat screen TV's supersized value meals, grocery stores with pre-chopped onions, and microwavable dinners. We sprint from our jobs to ball games, through drive throughs, online bill pay, Redbox, Smartphone apps and I could go on and on.

Our bellies are satisfied by the technological advantages that leave us stuffed but empty. We are not hungry.

As I left her office and passed by all the houses in my neighborhood, I thought of how many of them are not hungry as they dine on what the world has to give them. Though Buenos Aires is a small fraction of the world's population, they are a very accurate representation of the world's attitude. If you don't know you need saving, you don't know you need a savior. As the days pass, we come closer to the glorious return of Christ Jesus.

19 Go therefore and make disciples of all the nations, baptizing them in the name of the Father and of the Son and of the Holy Spirit, 20 teaching them to observe all

things that I have commanded you; and lo, I am with you always, even to the end of the age." Matthew 28:19-20

It is a sobering statistic that of the 7.082 billion people on the Earth right now, 4.882 billion lonely lost souls are on their way to Hell. Two thirds of the world is dying and going to an eternity of misery and pain we can never fathom with our human minds and they don't know it!

You don't have to travel around the world to share the Good News just go outside your house. My mother always told me that your first mission field is your own backyard and she wasn't kidding, of the 15 houses on my block, 5 are involved professing Christian homes.

This week I want to challenge you to pray for your neighbors. If you don't know their names then write down the color of the house, God knows who you are talking about. Pray for them and the next time a neighbor waves or comes your way, invite them to church. For some people we are the only example of Christ they see. Two or three times a week my neighbor and I walk the street in front of the 15 houses and we pray about those souls. You may think that isn't much compared to the 4.882 billion lost and dying, but if everyone that read this did the same and passed it on, what kind of difference our prayers could make. What souls could be brought to Jesus with the simple act of inviting someone to church or to come over and share the joy that lives in you.

I encourage you to take up my challenge and pray for those families in your neighborhood. Do more than wave or smile; share that wonderful gift of salvation.

Making the Grade

A couple of weeks ago I had lunch with my mom at Mt Vernon Restaurant. I wasn't just excited because of the Amaretto Pie (yum) but because this was the first time my mom and I had met for lunch. I would have her to myself. No brother or sister or most importantly grandkids to vie for her attention. I wanted to look good, exude professionalism and be everything that she would want me to be. I changed outfits three times before I made the decision of what I would wear.

We met outside the Chattanooga landmark and once seated we enjoyed catching up on what was going on with everyone. We giggled and I made her roll her eyes, which is always fun. I shared with her about my studies at Old Bethel. I attempted to dazzle her with my newfound knowledge and good grades. As any good mom would, she nodded and smiled and took it all in.

When I finally took time for a breath, she said. "You know I think that what you are doing is great and you don't need to worry about keeping 4.0 you have a lot going on with your job and the girls."

She paused and took a bite of her salad; I followed eagerly chewing waiting for her next words.

She continued. "Mostly, you need to remember that all the classes and the test and the grades will never take the place of faith. Don't get so caught up in the studies that you forget that God is a mystery and you will never be able to comprehend Him or understand His ways. You were never meant to because it is about faith in Him and Jesus' sacrifice."

We talked about many more things after that. We laughed more and then the pie came, our favorite part. I took what she said with me, and I thought about it. Had I become so focused on the grade and spouting the facts I had learned that I was missing the whole point of my classes.

I began to pray and look inward to see what had become my motivation. I think she was right; I was more worried about the grade than the lesson. I was focused on the number and not the message. I worried what the teacher, the other students, my family and my friends would think if I did not score high on every test.

College isn't about the degree or the grade. It is about the knowledge and understanding to be the best we can be in the Lord's army. It's training and conditioning for the daily warfare that we meet every time our feet touch the floor.

Every class is more than facts or history it is a deeper understanding of the grand plan that God has set in motion and my role in it. The classes are spiritual and filled with fellowship as together we search what lessons and treasures the Lord's Word has for us.

I think we get caught up in the rating. We think that the grade somehow defines us as a person, assigns some sort of value to us and when we do not meet that perceived idea of intelligence we allow ourselves to doubt. Doubt our worth, question our abilities and worse we let Satan creep into that crack and tell us we couldn't possibly be wanted or used for God's glory. After all, we couldn't pass with a good grade.

Throughout life there are grades to be made, deadlines to meet, people to impress and images to be polished. But not in God's eyes. He does not assign your worth by your grades, your image or whether or not you've impressed HIM. Rather, your worth can not be defined or measured, nor is your value proved by a diploma, but by the precious blood spilt for you. Before you opened your first reader or learned your first Bible verse, you were worth the sacrifice of His Son.

Don't worry about the grade, your image or the "sheep skin". Take the lesson of the class with you that cannot be measured or proved by a test. ***But God commendeth his love toward us, in that, while we were yet sinners, Christ died for us. Romans 5:8***

Under New Management

> **Therefore, if anyone *is* in Christ, *he is* a**
> **new creation; old things have passed away;**
> **behold, all things have become new.**
> **2 Corinthians 5:17**

While studying for my class, *New Testament Survey*, I was reading about Paul's letter to the Ephesians. Paul was instructing the new Christians that had come out of Idolatry about what was acceptable and not acceptable as Christians concerning different rituals and whether or not meat sacrificed to idols was fit to eat. On my way to work the next day I saw a sign in front of a well-known restaurant that read, "Under New Management." Workers were busy painting and cleaning up the outside, and I wondered, would they do anything to the inside? As I drove on, I thought about that sign and the work being done as the new owners tried to give the old restaurant a new and appealing look. I thought about the work that is done in our lives when Christ comes into our hearts and we are *under new management*. Except Jesus doesn't worry about the paint and spackle on the outside, He is only interested in the inside.

Just like the Ephesians of the first century, today we are challenged to be set apart from the world. The Ephesians were surrounded by temples to pagan gods and goddess and they had no idea how to be different, so they needed all the instruction they could get. We are the same. Paul wanted to teach them so that they could grow and become stronger through Christ. In order for that to happen they had to be changed on the inside first. Their attitudes and ideals that they had developed from the pagan world around them had to be cleared out. We are surrounded by a world as pagan as Ephesus was then and we have to undergo some internal renovations ourselves.

If the new owners of the restaurant only paint the outside and don't clear away the 30 plus years of grease and grime, revamp the menu, is it really a new establishment? No. In order to be new in Christ you must allow the new owner to completely renew you from the inside out.

This week as you pray, ask God to clear out the rubbish and old attitudes and equip you with His new and improved reformation.

> [25] *Then I will sprinkle clean water on you, and you shall be clean; I will cleanse you from all your filthiness and from all your idols.* [26] *I will give you a new heart and put a new spirit within you; I will take the heart of stone out of your flesh and give you a heart of flesh.* [27] *I will put My Spirit within you and cause you to walk in My statutes, and you will keep My judgments and do them. Ezekiel 36:25-27*

Is there an APP for That?

I have just returned from vacation with my friend and her family. It is hard to leave behind the smell of Hawaiian Tropic, eating too much at Joe's Crab Shack, sunburns, chlorine tainted hair and the freedom of not having a schedule.

Things have changed a lot since I was a kid traveling with my brother and sister fighting for every inch of my third of the back seat. We played games like counting cows, red cars or license plates. We sat on the side of the road as mom passed out sandwiches and Dad consulted the map. We talked to each other, laughed, fought, and marveled at the scenery, but not today. Today my girls sat in the back listening to music on headphones and texting wildly to three sometimes four friends at a time. The GPS barked instructions in Ronald Reagan's voice while my android brought up *Points of Interest* and Sirius radio kept us tuned to our choice of music. The car was silent except for the "Hit list of the 80's".

So when the GPS failed, the radio became scrambled and my android lost its feed outside of Bryson City, NC. I was not really that upset. We stopped at a welcome center and got a map. Yes, they still have them! Together we plotted our route and we were off again. The winding roads of the Carolina Mountains made it essential for the girls to look up and away from their Smartphones to avoid motion sickness. The scenery was breathtaking. We got out of the van and walked along a trail to see a waterfall. Along the way we saw two water moccasins and about ran over each other to get up the incline; then laughed wildly as we relived our *brush with death* with one another. Back in the van the chatter of excited teens and tweens filled the air.

Now, we were vacationing!

As we pulled into our hotel I noticed a family in the hot tub. The father was reading on his Kindle and each of his girls had a Smartphone tethered to them and his wife was adjacent on her iPad. What a sad view of today's American Family, together yet never so far apart.

We are playing right into the hands of our enemy.

Today, the world is more connected than ever before. There is texting, Skype, email, you name it there is a way to get a message to anyone and everyone. The internet has knitted nation to nation and people to people all across the globe, but the suicide rate, divorce rate, broken homes and the number of people popping anti-depressants is the highest it has ever been and rises daily. We are isolating ourselves more and more. There are iPhones, iPads, iPods iTunes, iCal, iChat, iSync, iPhoto, iMovie, iDVD, etc. We have become an I-people, all about me. What I want, when I want it, how I want!

Everything is at your fingertips and just a "*google*" away.

As I read back over what I have just written, I am reminded of the "five I will's" of Satan. Satan is all about the "I" as seen in Isaiah 14:12-15.

> *__12__. How art thou fallen from heaven, O Lucifer, son of the morning! How art thou cut down to the ground, which didst weaken the nations!*

> *__13__ For thou hast said in thine heart, I will ascend into heaven,*
> *I will exalt my throne above the stars of God: I will sit also*
> *upon the mount of the congregation, in the sides of the north:*
> *__14__ I will ascend above the heights of the clouds;*
> *I will be like the most High. __15__ Yet thou shalt be*
> *brought down to hell, to the sides of the pit.*

When Satan forgot his place and focused on his "I", destruction was right on his heels. When we forget that we are here not for ourselves, but for others. Destruction is close. As born again, professing Christians, we are to put away the "I" and look to the Son. Jesus stepped down from Glory. Removed His robes of white, took off his crown and his feet touched earth as a baby. He put away everything for you. There was no "I" when Jesus bled it was about you. And it was about your neighbor, co-worker, friend, cashier, doctor, dry cleaner, and the person next to you at the bank. Jesus did not take up the cross for himself. He had no need of the saving grace his blood provided. The whole cross was for you. There could be nothing more important to share with all those around you. Make the face to face communication with those that are in need.

Show them a face filled with the light of the loving Lord. Depart from the norm and reach out with a warm hand.

Your challenge:

Take time this week to pick up a pen and write a card, stamp it and mail it. Dial a new number on your phone and speak to someone that maybe wasn't in church this week or someone you haven't seen in a while. Forgo the email or text and knock on someone's door.

Take the "I" out and put the Son in.

Prayer Can Change the Heart

I used to have the worst attitude before I was *under new management*. Nothing was my fault. *I* was a victim. The odds were stacked against me, and everyone, including God, was in opposition to me.

I spent every day in that mind set. I woke up mad and blaming everyone for my troubles. If things didn't go well at work, it was my co-workers' fault or the personnel department, the car broke down the electric was shut off, I couldn't buy groceries somehow it was always someone else's fault. I accepted absolutely no responsibility for my life. I would pray by complaining.

That is all I did at the throne was complain and whine. I just wanted God to fix it, fix my husband, fix my finances, fix my situation, but I didn't want to make the adjustments needed in my life, heart and mind, I didn't want to take responsibility.

It was a sad, wasted time in my life.

That lack of responsibility in my choices blocked the relationships between God and I, my family and my friends. I lived in this slum of self-pity for years; until I found out I was pregnant. Once I realized I had a life in me, growing, fully dependent on me, I began to take better care of myself and worry about the future of this tiny being. Finally, my eyes had been diverted from just myself. That was the awakening for me. Soon after the birth of my first, I was pregnant again. Now two lives depended on me.

The journey was underway.

God rarely acts immediately. Instead, He has carefully orchestrated everything to work together for your good and His Glory. He has begun the restoration before you realize it.

The Israelites' cried out to God for 400 hundred years to be delivered from the slavery of the Egyptians. Generation after generation passed, but God was working. There could be only one man, Moses to lead the people. He would be reared in the house of Pharaoh—he would understand the customs, the way of the Egyptian thinking. He was groomed for that moment when he would be the instrument of God on behalf of the people.

It would take 5 more years after giving birth before I would relinquish and begin taking up responsibility for my past actions. Three more years after that to begin trying to mend relationships through acknowledging my mistakes, and still today I continue to live the consequences of my past choices. Taking up responsibility is not easy, nor is it glamorous.

Being responsible for your actions takes courage and character. Both of which I had traded for the easy path. I had to start from square one. It took time, a lot of time to build up courage to do the hard things in my life that needed to be done, courage that would have been impossible without the Holy Spirit. It took time to develop the character which had been corrupted by my selfish pursuits. It took years to rebuild trust with the people I had hurt and time to heal and forgive those that hurt me and to forgive myself.

If it had not been for the prayers of my mother, father, grandmothers and friends, who knows what could have happened to me? They did not waver in their prayers. I imagine in time as the years rolled by they must have thought I was lost forever but they kept praying. I am very thankful they loved me enough to pray without ceasing.

Is there a situation in your life that you have been praying about, but day after day there is no answer? Be assured that God is working on that petition. Know that though your human eyes or ears sense no evidence of change, it is happening. God hears your prayer, He feels the despair you feel, His heart breaks when yours breaks.

Trust that your earnest prayers still live in the Father's ears. Your prayer is eternal because it was offered up to the Eternal Almighty. That prayer lives on and God is working on your behalf. I will always regret that my grandmothers never knew that I was returned to my earthly as well as Heavenly family, but I am renewed knowing that even as they left this world their prayers, though their lips were stilled, lived on in the eternal throne room.

Pray without ceasing.

And those who know your name put their trust in you, for you, O Lord, have not forsaken those who seek you. _Psalm 9:10_

Out On A Limb

But your iniquities have separated between you and your God, and your sins have hid his face from you, that he will not hear.
Isaiah 59:2

I was not a bad kid growing up. Mischievous, sure, sneaky, of course, but not bad. My biggest fault was my smart mouth. I just never did seem to grasp the art of shutting up when it was good for me. I confess I still can have a smart mouth; the *last word* is just so sweet.

My parents were strong supporters of Proverbs 13:24 and 23:13. They enthusiastically exercised their God given rights often, but not without provocation. Today, I thank God they were parents that cared enough to discipline myself and my siblings. Raising my own children I have come to realize that it would be so much easier to just let them be sometimes but that is not what I was called as a parent to do.

Discipline is never pleasant it is the least favorite part of my responsibilities as a parent.

One suffocating afternoon in late July, when I was 8 or 9, my mouth got me in trouble ...*again*. I knew this because my mom's beautiful olive green eyes dilated into black ink blots and her lips disappeared into a thin white line. I was well acquainted with this reaction, and as she reached for me I ducked, faked left and cleared the back steps. Across the yard, I ran—my legs pumping literally for my life. Swiftly dodging the scattered toys and wading pool, I hit the tree at full speed, digging my toes into the bark; I went to the tallest part, hoping the spindly limbs would hold me. I wedged my foot in the fork and rested my rump against the opposing branch. I was, at least for the moment free.

Of course, my mom was no slouch she had been close on my heels and there she stood, white knuckled fist dug into her hips, staring at me from the base of the tree. In that moment as our eyes locked, I wondered what would happen next. Would she shake me from my perch like a ripe apple or come up after me? Either was possible. For a moment we simply stared at one another.

She turned and headed back, the slap of her flip flops fading as she disappeared into the house. I exhaled the breath I had been holding and relaxed. As I began to negotiate my descent; the slap of flip flops cracked me to attention. Back up the tree I clawed and reclaimed my temporary refuge. Marching across the yard, magazines tucked under her arm and a folding chair bouncing violently behind her, she placed the lounger below the tree and stretched out in the shade. From her short's pocket she withdrew a Tab cola, its condensation twinkling in the sun teased me. Popping the top, she selected a magazine and there she sat thumbing through recipes and articles as I clung to the limb battling insects, heat and fatigue.

Have you ever found yourself out on a limb? Stranded in the heat, nowhere to go, alone with your sin? Have you stepped off the path? Lost your focus?

It was a long, breezeless afternoon. The late sun, orange with angry heat, bore down on me zapping my strength. Eventually I had to come down and face the consequences of my behavior. It was hard to come out of the tree and stand next to her knowing that punishment was inevitable. But your sin, your punishment has been commuted by the blood of Christ Jesus.

God is waiting. He is waiting for you to come to Him. He is waiting to forgive you and rid you of the sin that has separated you from Him. Through the sacrifice of Christ Jesus, He has made a way to close that gap that was created by sin.

Do not wait; come to the Father through the Son. He waits for you.

The Lord is not slack concerning his promise, as some men count slackness; but is longsuffering to us- ward, not willing that any should perish, but that all should come to repentance. 2 Peter 3:9

Looking For That
Pat on the Back

*For do I now persuade men, or God? Or do I
seek to please men? For if I still pleased men,
I would not be a bondservant of Christ.*
Galatians 1:10

Sometimes these "seeds" come easy to me, other times they are stubborn. There are times I know exactly what I am going to write and then other times I haven't a clue. Still, there are some that press to be written and I am reluctant because I know that God wants me to share something of myself that goes beyond my comfort. _#13 Prayer Can Change the Heart_ was such a difficult one to write. I know that I am not that person anymore, but that does not remove the pain that was caused to my family and friends. Revisiting those times is difficult and I am still ashamed.

God, however, was insistent that this should be written and shared, and with much fussing, whining, fit pitching and sulking I surrendered myself to HIS Will.

When it was done, I felt that I had completed what HE had asked of me.

The "Seed" was published on the site, copies mailed to those without email and posted on Facebook. There were not the usual encouraging emails, phone calls or comments on Facebook that I had become accustomed. Instead, silence echoed from all media. I began to question whether or not I had done what I should have. Did I miss the message? Had I failed to deliver the point that I had felt certain had been given by God? I began to obsess about it. I reread the article several times. I began to panic and worry. My mind started whirling the possibilities. As my emotions continued to lather I went to God and I asked. "Why has no one commented?"

In between the clatter of my thoughts came a voice so sweet and low. "Why do you worry what others say? Why do you crave their validation? Am I not enough?"

I am the worse for wanting the approval of those around me. My parents, my siblings, my friends, neighbors, my children, coworkers, church members and strangers, I want them all to think of me as good, special or smart. I will bend over backwards to satisfy what they want of me, but how often do I consider what God desires of me? When do I ever just say, "He loved me enough that Jesus died for me? Why do I need man's validation, when I have saving Grace?"

Reflecting back on <u>Prayer Can Change the Heart,</u> I realized that was how I landed in that mess to start with. I was searching for validation and acceptance everywhere but the cross. I looked to men for my validation, my sense of worth and found neither. I wanted so badly to have someone look at me and tell me I was special, beautiful and worthy. No matter where I looked I did not find it. I would pray and beg God to send that special one, the one that would think all those things.

How I must have grieved HIM as He watched me run from place to place, person to person, job to job, friend to friend, weight loss programs to program, denomination to denomination, exhausting myself when all the time He hung there, arms outstretched, tears, blood dripping to the thirsty ground, and smeared with my sins. Everything that I ever asked for in a man was right there in Jesus. Jesus loved me unconditionally. He loved me, not my body, my possessions or what I could give Him but just me. To Jesus I am beautiful, I am special, I am wanted and loved. He chose me. That was all I ever sought to be chosen, wanted and loved.

Me. Just me.

Maybe no one commented because it had been written not so much for them, but for me—of where my validation comes from and obedience without hindrance from worrying about what people may think.

Your validation comes through Christ Jesus.

For God sent not his Son into the world not to condemn the world; but that the world through him might be saved. John 3:17

French Toast Flop

In 1987 I moved into my first apartment with my best friend. Infused with youthful invincibility I wanted to go, try and do everything I could. I had big dreams and hopes for my life.

It was a wonderful time, full of so many firsts like laundry and using a dishwasher. I learned quickly that dish washing liquid and automatic dish detergent are two separate entities. Dishwashing liquid in a dishwasher produces enough bubbles to fill a kitchen completely!

Up until this point my culinary skills had been very limited, but I was ready to conquer the kitchen. I tried a lot of things and failed at some.

One Saturday morning I decided to try my spatula at French toast. A personal favorite and seemingly simple recipe, I got everything together and began.

Moments later I presented my roommate with a plate of French toast, I was anxious to see what she thought. Cautiously, she inspected my offering. After all, there had been some pretty friend testing entrees set before her thus far.

The toast was dark brown—some may call it black—but it was more brown, really. The center was golden yellow with veins of brown though it. Little grains of sugar artfully sparkled adding to the appeal. The scent of cinnamon and sugar clashed in the air with maple syrup. I poured her a cold glass of milk and settled across from her my fork at the ready. Pride shone like morning sun from my face. I couldn't take my eyes from her. This would be the one. Finally, a meal of satisfaction. She took a pat of butter and dropped it on the top. The pat disappeared. Leaning forward, we peered in the crater that had opened up to swallow the butter. It had fallen through the stack and hit the plate beneath. Raw egg mixture slowly spread around the blackened edges of the toast.

Failure.

Failure like that French toast is never easy to swallow, but it is a necessary part of growth. That includes your walk with Christ. Sometimes failure is necessary to help you understand someone else's feelings or maybe even your own. Failure is humbling and brings us into submission with God. As well failure can encourage growth in character.

Today, my French toast is revered (ok revered is a little extreme, but they really do like it) in my home along with most of my other offerings. But it took time, practice, patience and faith to be able to say I am a good cook. It was worth the work.

Don't be afraid to try. If you fail, get up, dust off and do it again.

Damsel in Distress.....NOT!

When I first got divorced, I spent a lot of time daydreaming of the man that would come to save me, my knight in proverbial shining armor. He would ride in, take over and life would be *"Happily Ever After"*. A couple of unsuccessful relationships later, I realized that there were plenty of jokers out there but knights weren't so easy to find. That did not douse my hopes. I was sure someone would show up to save me.

I wasted valuable time waiting. I just didn't want to deal with life's problems myself to be honest. It was hard. I believed I couldn't do it. I shrank in fear of making decisions. At least before in my marriage there had been another to blame. Good or bad, I would have to deal with the fallout. It was all on me, and frankly, I was paralyzed at times, afraid of making the wrong choices. After all, my track record had been pretty lousy.

Turning a blind eye became my M.O.

I had just moved into my own apartment with my daughters. Since the split I had shared a residence with best friend and her daughter. With my new roommates I never felt alone and we shared the responsibilities of the bills and house. It was a scary change. I had never been solely on my own. Now it was just me. Singular responsibility rested on my shoulders.

It was Father's Day. Hot, sticky and miserable was the forecast. I was getting ready to go to my parent's to celebrate my mom's birthday and Father's Day. It was special because after years of estrangement we were rebuilding relationships and I was excited to be back in the fold.

The girls had whined, not wanting ponytails and frills, but I was not relenting. I was determined that nothing would ruin this day. Finally the three of us appeared presentable and ready to go. Down the steps I bounced my excitement mounting and then evaporating as I looked at the Maxima leaning to the right. She had a flat tire. I told the girls to run back upstairs and watch TV. It was the first time they compiled without complaining.

What was I going to do now? I did the only thing I *thought* I could. I sat on the bottom step and cried. Fat, hot tears streaked my face, leaving rivulets in the makeup.

The parking lot was empty, there was not a soul was on the basketball court, and no one was on their deck. Not even a bird tweeting! I was alone.

I called to give my parents the news that I would be at best late and that I would do all I could to get there. My father, ever the sweetest Daddy offered to drive 30 minutes to fix it and then back. I could not allow that. No, I would figure out something. But what?

I manned my station at the bottom of the steps and stared at the tire. As I stared at the brake- dust coated, bald as Montel tire a crazy idea formed in my head, what if I changed the tire? I was smarter than some, relatively strong, definitely clever.

I would try.

I ran upstairs and changed, and then with determination, I went back to the car. I popped the trunk and unloaded the necessary equipment.

I would like to tell you it was a smooth operation, but it wasn't. There was a lot of praying, skinned bleeding knuckles, smudged mascara, several broken nails and at least one tantrum, but I got it done.

Sometimes, God doesn't ride in. Sometimes He doesn't send a knight. Sometimes it's up to the Damsel. God gave us grace. Grace to endure what comes our way. God gave us intellect, strength and Jesus.

> *Sometimes God doesn't act because it is you that*
> *needs to step out so He can act through you.*

In Exodus 2, we see Jochebed stepping out. She knew that Moses was important not just to her, but to God's plan and that she needed to take action. She used the intellect that the Lord had given her to devise a way to save Moses. She did not sit back and cry, she stood up and acted. Because she was willing to act the Lord used her and worked through her to bring Moses to the Pharaoh's house. Jochebed was willing and had faith in God, so her plan was successful. I am sure that Jochebed prayed. As a mom, I am sure that Jochebed fell on her face before God and begged God to save her son. Then her mind filled with an idea and on faith she set about making that idea a reality. God was with Jochebed and Moses but she had to be willing to act. As Moses floated out of her hands she had to give it all to God.

Jesus was with me that Sunday afternoon. He was on the steps next to me when I cried. He was crouched on the pavement next to me as I took all I had and lifted the donut to the wheel.

He was there all the way, cheering me on. I tackled a job that just a couple of hours before had seemed overwhelming and impossible. Circumstances that I felt I was too weak to face. God didn't send in someone to fix it because that flat tire wasn't about the nail in the tread but the nail in Jesus' hand. It was about the opening of my eyes to my strength, and intellect, but mostly my relationship with Him through Christ Jesus. I don't need a man to rescue me; I have already been saved by Jesus. I needed to quit looking for the knight and accept the Son, because only Jesus can fulfill all my needs. He strengthens me in difficult times and he instructs me, I just have to listen.

Would Moses have made it to the Pharaoh's daughter if Jochebed had done nothing? Yes. But because she took initiative God allowed her to have her son a few years more as his wet nurse, safe in her arms before he was sent to live in the shadow of the Pharaoh, to learn the Egyptian ways and someday be the instrument of God.

Would my tire have been fixed? Definitely, but I would have continued to live under the guise that I was at the mercy of my situation.

I made it to mom and dad's not too late and it was an awesome day! I learned an important lesson on that Sunday and it had nothing to do with a lug wrench. I learned something about me. I believed the lie that I was a weak victim of my circumstances. That I needed someone to take care of me and that God wasn't enough. I cowered from life and my blessings. I cheated myself of the gift of an intimate relationship with Jesus. So often, we allow ourselves to believe the enemy's lies, and we miss out on beautiful blessings.

I was a strong woman saved by grace capable of wonderful things with Jesus. I had been equipped with everything I needed to face and be victorious over whatever came my way through the relationship with Jesus.

That day I realized that I didn't need a knight to save me. Covered in brake dust, sweaty and smiling I looked at the tire. I had done it. Though it was a small thing, it was the beginning of a wonderful journey that I no longer traveled alone. What else could I do, I wondered. I looked forward to finding out.

I still get scared dealing with life. But I remember that day. I think of the heat, the sweat in my eyes the filth of the job the weight of the tire, Jesus next to me and I smile. Since that incident, I have had the confidence to face many more trials because I know that I am not alone and that by fully trusting in God I can do anything through Him.

We need to be a people of action. Put faith in God and ask for His guidance. Step out boldly and know that with Him you cannot fail.

You are of God, little children, and have overcome them, because He who is in you is greater than he who is in the world. 1 John 4:4

Repurposed

I sat on the floor of the living room, staring at the loveseat. It had seen better days. The left arm hung slackly, the cushions were crushed and it sat forlorn and forgotten in the corner. Now an eyesore in the crowded room, I contemplated the feat of dragging it to the road to be hauled away and destroyed. As I looked at it longer, as strange as it may be, I pitied the tattered piece of furniture. Maybe I would tow it to the sunroom and use it there; I knew better, it would have the same fate. I stood, ready to begin the task.

As I gripped the arm and began to yank an idea sprang into my mind. I looked from the loveseat to the couch and back again.

I wondered if my crazy idea would work.

I went to the laundry room and rummaged through my toolbox. I returned to the living room with my jigsaw, power cord and safety glasses.

The jigsaw hungrily munched through the wood of the loveseat. Sawdust spilled out onto the floor and swirled in the air tickling my nose. Finally, I cut the last bit and the arm hit the floor with a thud. I knelt and looked inside. It seemed that everything else was sound. I pushed the maimed seat to the couch, using the flap of material left by the dissected arm; I wrapped the stump and guided the two pieces together.

Success! Now I had a sectional sofa.

Repurposing items is something I have come to enjoy quite a bit. There is so much beauty, joy and satisfaction in taking an old, discarded piece of furniture and giving it new life and purpose. Much like what God through His Son did for me. I was lost, damaged, crushed; some may have thought I was beyond help or use, but not God. Just like that loveseat, He saw a purpose for me. He excised the broken part, healed me, forgave me and brought me to join with the body of Christ. Once that loveseat joined with the couch, it became a new piece of furniture.

I became repurposed for God through the restoration of Christ's blood.

No matter the damage, condition, age, or even the appearance will deter the Master from the desire to give new purpose and life to any that ask. You can never be beyond the help of the Master Carpenter's hand.

Come As You Are

*1. Let not your heart be troubled: you
believe in God, believe also in me.
2. In my Father's house are many mansions: if it were not
so, I would have told you. I go to prepare a place for you.
3. And if I go and prepare a place for you, I
will come again, and receive you unto myself;
that where I am, there you may be also.
4. And where I go you know, and the way you know.
John 14:1-4*

This weekend my friends and I hosted a Luau for the neighborhood. It was an awesome opportunity to meet more of our neighbors and grow our ministry. We started early that day; there were food preparations, decorations and logistics to consider. As the sun rose higher the humidity, like a wet blanket, swaddled us in sweat. We worked all day to turn Kim's front yard into a Hawaiian paradise. Palm trees and Tiki torches lined the yard, streamers and decorations surrounded the one long table in the center. It waited eagerly for the guest.

We have a diverse neighborhood, families, singles, retirees and ethnicities. Next door to me is a sweet Vietnamese family. They have four children. One is in college, two in high school and one in middle school. I have watched these children grow into beautiful young men and women. I have prayed for the family since I moved in because they are Buddhist. The mother is very devout to the Buddha.

The youngest of the Vietnamese family, Nam, was working in a neighbor's yard and came up to me. He looked concerned.

"Neighbor?" He addressed me. (I consider this my honorary title since the entire family calls me this.)

"I have nothing to bring as a side dish, but I really want to come."

I assured him that would be fine. I was making plenty.

A few minutes later.

"But Neighbor, I have nothing to wear to a Luau."

I assured him that would be fine; I had extra leis and skirts.

A little bit later.

"Neighbor? If I work for you, can that be my payment for the Luau?"
"You do not have to work to come, you are welcome."

Again the young man approached me. "Neighbor, I don't know what to do at a Luau."

"Nam, there is nothing special to know or to do. Just come as you are and join my family."

It put me in mind of our Father's table. He doesn't want you to bring a side dish, or wear something special. You don't have to work for your place at the table He just wants you to join His family.

There is a table prepared for you.

All that the Father gives me will come to me, and whoever comes to me I will never cast out. John 6:37

What's the Point in Praying?

*"Delight thyself also in the LORD; and he shall give
thee the desires of thine heart. Commit thy way unto the
LORD; trust also in him; and he shall bring it to pass."*
Psalms 37:4-5

I was speaking with a lovely woman with whom I am building a friendship. She is very intelligent, kindhearted and yet there is something sad about her. It is in her eyes and the very air about her. Maybe it is more like defeat. She seems to have given up and surrendered to being a victim. This lovely woman has just stopped. Stopped trying, stopped trusting, and stopped living.

After one of our discussions, I reminded her that I would continue to pray about a particular situation that burdens her heart. Usually she nods and thanks me, but this time was different.

"I wish I believed in prayer like you, I quit praying a long time ago. What's the point? God does what he wants. It's His Will."

I will tell you that I was stunned. I did not know what to say. Yet, at the same time, so much became clear. This woman had lost all hope. No wonder sadness clung to her. She had traded living a life of hope and joy for existing.

It brought back memories of a difficult time in my spiritual life. I had become so frustrated with God. I wanted certain things, but He did not open the doors or present the opportunities. In my fit I told Him that I just would not waste my time praying. So I did not. I refused to pray for anything except forgiveness of sins. This tantrum wore on for months. The longer it wore on, the more alone and hopeless I felt.

I sat back down and began to share my experience. I told her that at one time I had given up on prayer.

Prayer is not about rubbing the genie bottle. Prayer is sharing and fellowshipping with God. I have written a couple of thoughts on prayer before and I will tell you that I believe in the power of Prayer. Does that mean that every prayer I offer up is answered the way I want? No. However, through prayer and fellowship with God, I am able to have peace when my prayer is not answered the way I had hoped.

Sometimes they are answered in a much better way than I could have imagined. Sometimes in ways that are painful and disappointing, but I know it is for the good. Prayer is about sharing your troubles, fear and pain. It is about opening yourself up to get to know God and his character. Prayer is about building a relationship.

Throughout Jesus' traveling, the Bible cites how Jesus always found a way to get away and engage in prayer with the Father.

> **23 And when He had sent the multitudes away, He went up on the mountain by Himself to pray. Now when evening came, He was alone there. Matthew 14:23**

**[12] Now it came to pass in those days that He went
out to the mountain to pray, and continued
all night in prayer to God. Luke 6:12
[28] Now it came to pass, about eight days after these
sayings, that He took Peter, John, and James and
went up on the mountain to pray. Luke 9:28**

Jesus, though He was the Son, knew the importance and necessity in seeking the Father in prayer. Prayer is not just about asking for His favor in matters, but it the strengthening of the spirit to give us the ability through His grace to withstand the trials that life has for each of us. Prayer affords us grace to face the doctor when he gives the diagnosis, the confidence when we go on a job interview and the faith that our needs will be met. It is the strengthening of your relationship with God that brings you peace. Jesus knew this as he went to the garden in chapter 26 of Matthew. He knew that His death was now only a few hours away. Jesus knew what was to come. He asked, **"O My Father, if it is possible, let this cup pass from Me; nevertheless, not as I will, but as You *will*." Matthew 26:39.** Jesus took the strength that He was given by His communion with God to face the betrayal of Judas and the torture by the Romans. He took the love that He had for you, me and my friend to the cross.

**[16] Rejoice evermore.
[17] Pray without ceasing.
[18] In everything give thanks: for this is the will of God in
Christ Jesus concerning you. 1 Thessalonians 5:16-18**

Maintaining Your Focus
When in the Storm

I just got the Prom pictures back of my daughters' night out. They were so lovely and I was proud to see them enjoying themselves. As I scrolled through the pictures I thought of the joy they have brought to my life and how thankful I was for them.

Until.........I saw the picture of the three of us.

There I was tired and fading nestled between the full blooms of youth. I immediately began to focus on the negatives, my weight, my tired skin and less than perfect teeth. Suddenly I did not want anyone to look at that picture. I was embarrassed. In that moment my focus had been diverted and my joy was drained. All I saw were my flaws and not the full picture.

I think several of us get our attention taken from the big picture and focus on the flaws. The old adage "The devil's in the details" is probably spot on. As my attention was focused on the negative I was missing out on what that picture was really about. It was about my joy as a mother and my daughters' excitement of the evening. When I pulled back and really looked at that photo is was a moment of pride and happiness.

It is so easy to get our focus derailed. Just ask Peter. I always felt sorry for Peter. This big strong fisherman wanted so badly to serve God and follow Jesus but he kept letting his focus get compromised. He tried so hard but lost his center and got scared. I really identify with him. That's me in a nutshell.

One evening after Jesus had taught and then fed the multitude, He went to pray. He had asked the disciples to rent a boat. He told them to take it out and He would meet them later.

Well into the night Jesus dwelt with His Father in prayer. I imagine after all that traveling, teaching and performing miracles, Jesus knew He needed to strengthen His focus and did so by communing with the Father. It was now just before dawn and a storm was on the sea. The ship the disciples had procured was struggling being tossed by waves and the wind blowing against it. (Matthew 14:24-25) You can imagine that the disciples and the sailors were struggling to keep the ship upright. I have no doubt they were scared and worried. I cannot fathom what went through their minds when they saw Jesus coming to them **walking**.

Matthew tells us they thought it might have been a spirit. (14:26)

Now I can just see Peter clinging to the ropes, rain pelting him, the wind ripping at his clothes, the thunder clashing and the rhythmic flashes of lightning revealing a figure. I am sure that after all they had witnessed and been a part of in their travels with Jesus that they had come to expect the unusual. The storm raged, but the figure came closer. It was then that Jesus told them to not be scared, *"It is I"*. (14:27)

Now Peter was transfixed on the form of Jesus calmly coming to him. "Lord, if it be thou, bid me come unto thee on the water."

Jesus said, "Come."

The Bible says that Peter *came down out of the ship*. I take from that that it was a large vessel and not a little dingy. Peter climbed out, then once out Peter with his gaze fixed on Jesus *walked on water*.

Can you imagine that moment? Eyes locked on the Savior of all men, the waves crashing, the sky black before the dawn, the howl of the wind, the taste of salt and Peter is defying everything he had ever known by simply keeping his focus on Jesus. Though all those things were going on around Peter he was walking. The Bible does not say that he struggled against the wind, or that he ran or stumbled, it says he walked.

Until...........

"But when he saw the wind boisterous, he was afraid; and began to sink, he cried, saying, Lord, save me." Matthew 14:30

"and *immediately* Jesus stretched forth *His* hand, and caught him, and said unto him. O thou of little faith, wherefore didst thou doubt?" Matthew 14:31

Once Peter allowed His focus to be compromised, he became afraid and began to sink. He failed to hold on to his faith in Jesus. There have been times like that in my life. I let my focus on Jesus be stolen by my fears of what this world was slinging at me. I begin to doubt and then I begin to sink.

However, when Peter called out over the thunder and gale "Lord save me" Jesus does not hesitate to reach for him and lift him out of the sea. Verse 31 says *"immediately"* Jesus stretched His hand to Peter.

When you are caught in the storm, your focus compromised, your thoughts consumed with fear, call out to Jesus. Without hesitation HE WILL lift you from the storm.

Be Careful What You Pray For

> *13 Let every soul be subject unto the higher powers. For there is no power but of God: the powers that be are ordained of God.² Whosoever therefore resisteth the power, resisteth the ordinance of God: and they that resist shall receive to themselves damnation.³ For rulers are not a terror to good works, but to the evil. Wilt thou then not be afraid of the power? do that which is good, and thou shalt have praise of the same:⁴ For he is the minister of God to thee for good. But if thou do that which is evil, be afraid; for he beareth not the sword in vain: for he is the minister of God, a revenger to execute wrath upon him that doeth evil.⁵ Wherefore ye must needs be subject, not only for wrath, but also for conscience sake.*
>
> *Romans 13:1-5*

I had my idea for this week's Mustard Seed all worked out. It was to be a warm and fuzzy, to be honest, but something happened today that has so impressed me that I feel I should share this instead. I would much rather coax your mouth into a smile with lovable Emma antics, but instead, you're getting poultry. I hope you understand, I made a promise to God that He was the author of this column and not me. He speaks, I type.

I have been skirting around a decision that I just did not want to make. I just knew that if I ignored it long enough, it would fade away and I could carry on without the discomfort of a hard decision. Some decisions are easy. Some not so much—when it has to do with the heart of your child. My daughter wants to bring home chickens from school to care for over the summer. After checking with East Ridge, I learned that farm animals are prohibited in the city limits. She has grown so attached to these feathered creatures that telling her no is hard to think of. I have been bouncing it around in my head trying to figure out what I should do.

I know you have heard the adage, "be careful what you wish for" the same can be said for what you pray for. When you bring a prayer before the Lord you better be sure you are ready for the answer. I have been praying that God will flush out the sin in me. When I prayed this I was thinking of my financial decisions, prejudices and other assorted vices. Nothing major, I mean I am a pretty good person. Right? However, I never knew it would trickle down to the disappointment of my child.

I shamefully will admit to you I had decided to bend the rules in order to make her happy. I was fully prepared to do it too. Until God brought the answer that I had been praying for front and center.

Now on the big scheme of things this bending of the rules seemed very minor to be truthful. In the end it probably would not have made a hill of beans of a difference if two chickens spent 7 weeks in East Ridge was what I thought.

However, in that moment I saw clearly how this seemingly insignificant slight could have cost a king's ransom, literally. This decision could have caused damage to my testimony to my children, to the six Buddhist next door and to the woman down the street who has given up hope in God and prayer. It could have been the difference between someone choosing to accept Jesus as savior and continuing a life without him. How am I to speak to others about a life in Christ, about being set apart if I am not willing to do it myself?

I had to choose between making my daughter happy and serving the Lord to the letter. I realized in that instant that I do not have the right to pick and choose how I will serve God. I will either serve Him completely, or I do not serve Him at all. If His word tells me that it is wrong, then it is wrong and I am to uphold His word even in the face of my child, my friend, my co-workers and this world. It was a sobering moment in my walk with Christ. This past two weeks as I have prayed for the discernment and clarity and I must tell you that this prayer has brought to light that I am not completely off the fence. I am guilty of meandering around the seemingly insignificant rules to make my life easier or to please another.

There is no commandment any less than another. They may be in a numerical order, but they are in no way arranged in degrees. When I chose to bend a rule, ignore a commandment or justify my choice in not upholding an edict, I am passing on the idea to my children that my relationship with God and with them is conditional on what is comfortable, popular or easy for me.

I made the decision that I should have made in the beginning. Tonight I will go home and take out the Bible and show my child why I did not condone what had been asked for and then I will ask her to forgive me for not being steadfast and committed to my walk with Christ.

This Mustard Seed is dedicated to my precious
friend Bronna, who keeps me straight.

Are You In or Out?

Remember summers running wild in the neighborhood or in the woods? Climbing trees, riding bikes, playing Bionic Man/Woman and the big adventure every summer brought? I had wonderful summers. I drove my mom crazy running in and out of the house asking if I could go to the pool or get a drink or take out a toy to play.

Finally, she would block the doorway and say, "Missy, you are either in or out! Stop running back and forth you're letting the cool air out and the flies in!"

"But Mom, just one more time." I'd whine. "Donna wants me to bring out my Princess Leia doll."

She would sigh and let me in to get the doll. Of course, it would not be long before I was running back in the house.

I found myself yelling the same thing the other day as my daughters and some neighborhood kids were wearing out the back door. In and out they came for drinks and bathroom breaks.

"Girls, you are either in or out!"

Over the past quarter of school, I have been struggling with Debate classes. I am not fond of debating at all. I get all nervous, my stomach hurts and I worry that I cannot do the job. I decided I would begin polling people to get their thoughts on certain debate topics. What I learned is that a number of people claiming to be Christians do not believe the Bible is the inspired Word of God. They do not believe in Jonah and the Whale or Noah's worldwide flood. Yet in the same breath claim Christ as savior. How do you claim Christ and discredit the rest of His word?

You may be sitting there in front of your computer reading this and wondering to yourself: *does it really matter to your salvation if you do not think that the flood was worldwide or that Jonah got swallowed and three days later vomited on the beach?*

Yes, it does.

As Christians, we are either in or out. You either believe the **entire** Word of God or you believe none of it.

To say you do not believe in the worldwide flood or the whale is the same as saying you do not believe in the life-giving Blood of Christ on that cross. Where do you draw the line? Is the fact that Jesus was born of a virgin any less fantastic that the story of Jonah, the sun standing still, the wet fleeces, the parting of the Red Sea?

I believe every word in the Bible from Genesis to Revelations. I believe the worldwide flood, the day the sun stood still, the pillar of fire and the wall of Jericho. I believe that God planned a way of salvation for you and I. I believe that Jesus was born in a stable amid the straw and that he grew into a man, a man that was fully human and fully God. I believe that he went to the cross for the sins of all that would accept the blood.

There are many arguments to discredit the Bible. There are scientist and theories galore that give you many explanations. However, all their proof means nothing to me. My belief and faith is not in a theory or an explanation. My belief is in Christ Jesus.

My mom told me something soon after I started to study at Old Bethel. She told me not to lose faith. I thought that it was a strange thing to say to someone in Bible school. However, I understand it now. All the understanding and education is in no way a substitute for faith. There are many mysteries in this world that we were never to understand. Because understanding how the entire world was submerged for 371 days is not how you get to heaven, it's the faith that it happened because His word tells you.

Hebrews 11:1- Now faith is the substance of things hoped for, the evidence of things not seen.

My question for you is "are you in or out?"

Rotten Fruit

I was in the grocery store after work one day. There is always something we need. I really dislike going to the store after work. It is always crowded and they never have enough people on the cash registers.

As I perused the cereal aisle with my daughter, saying no to every overpriced, sugar coated, gaily colored box of pre-diabetic breakfast offerings, I saw a woman that I had known for more than twenty years. Twenty five years ago, we spent plenty of time together. She had witnessed and encouraged me through some of my lowest moments. When I saw her, I ducked down another aisle. I found myself creeping down the infant section, hoping she would get far enough ahead that I could get out of the store without being spotted.

It was not to be. I had not gotten past her radar. I resigned myself; I was going to have to speak with her.

As she plunged headlong into filling me in on all of her woes, I found myself growing more and more uneasy. My daughter stood next to me and switched glances between me and her. She had been fired, had to file bankruptcy, could not find another job, had run up massive credit card debit and in all of it she never once assumed responsibility for any part of it. She was being ganged up on by the world. The county were against her, the school had wronged her son, her employer cheated her and on and on she went. I politely nodded and expressed my sympathy concerning her difficulties. She moved on to complaining about her ex-husband and what she had gone through with him eighteen years ago when he was out of work. She bounced from present to past troubles for at least twenty minutes.

I realized as I listened to her that not only had her life of drama continued just as it had been twenty five years ago, moreover she had not changed anything about herself. Her hair was the same length and color it had always been. She was dressed as I had always seen her in jeans and a T-shirt. Even her eye shadow was the same. It was as if nothing had changed for her.

Throughout the evening the thought rolled around in my brain; why had she chosen to stay stagnant?

I think it started with her not letting go of the past. It seemed that for the past twenty five years, this woman had been riding a loop of drama, assuming the role of victim and shunning all responsibilities. She spewed negativity.

It was her words that kept her riding the loop. Nothing out of her mouth was positive. She seemed to ooze the negative.

I am guilty of this at times as well. Sometimes my words are laced with toxicity. I allow myself to speak defeat rather than victory. In order to stop speaking death you have to adjust your way of thinking. Everything begins with the way we think. Our attitude is the difference between defeat and victory and sometimes it can mean the difference to those around us. If our speech is negative and defeatist then that is what we emit to those around us. Family and friends will begin to adopt our speech, and that in turn will infect their attitude. A bad attitude is like rotten fruit it infects the good.

When I spent a lot of time around this woman my speech and then my attitude was poisoned. It took a while to rid myself of her way of thinking and reacting. She saw everything as a problem, not an opportunity. She believed that everything that had happened to her was uncontrollable circumstance rather the consequences of the choices she had made.

Whereas it is true that there are circumstances that are out of control how we choose to face them is wholly ours. Your attitude in any situation is the key to whether you have victory or defeat. As believers, our attitude and our speech should reflect our trust in God.

I encourage you to examine your words. Your words have the power to spread life and death, not just to you, but to those around you.

Proverbs 18:21 says that we will shall eat the fruit thereof. I'd rather eat the sweet and skip the bitter.

Dig A Little Deeper

And ye shall seek me, and find me, when ye shall search for me with all your heart.
Jeremiah 29:13

A couple of weeks ago a co-worker walked passed me in the hallway. I did not receive hello much less a smile. Immediately I began the frantic mental search for anything that I may have done to upset this person. However, there was nothing I could think of that could have been considered even a mild injury. Later the same day this co-worker walked by me again, again no acknowledgment. Bothered I turned around and addressed them.

Would you like to know what had caused this slight? My hair.

Yep, my hair. I had worn it straight that day. For those of you who do not know me personally, I have naturally curly wild hair. I would say that it is probably one of the first things that people notice about me; the thick unruly curls. Because my hair was sleek and smooth that day, this person did not recognize me.

I was first relieved that everything was ok between us and then I began to examine the situation. This individual recognized me by this physical characteristic. Was it all that people saw when they looked at me the rowdy tresses?

The more I thought about it, the more I realized that it was simply an example of how surface minded we all are. We tend to only look at the shell and neglect what is inside. We do it in relationships, choosing mates and making friends. We also do it to ourselves. Nice clothes, coiffed hair, shiny car and big house. We fix up the outside and ignore what is within. We present what we want the world to believe about us.

We also do it in our relationship with God. It is so much easier to stick to the surface isn't it? Go to church, hit up Sunday school a couple of times a month and pray before dinner. We mutter prayers before we go to sleep asking for forgiveness and strength, but what about the deeper prayers? What about the opening of our hearts for His dissection and improvement?

God cares nothing for your shiny veneer. He cares about what's inside. He cares about the condition of your heart. God wants to know the real you and wants you to know the real Him. We can never know the awesome power of our God by only dealing with the surface. We can never feel the fullness of His love, the caress of the spirit or understand the sacrifice of Jesus by only concerning ourselves with the outside.

Seek the Lord by digging a little deeper.

Emma the Terrible
Felled by a Shoe

There hath no temptation taken you but such as is common to man: but God is faithful, who will not suffer you to be tempted above that ye are able; but will with the temptation also make a way to escape, that ye may be able to bear it.

1 Corinthians 10:13

Emma the Terrible has so much energy. She wants to play all the time. Last night she stood at the back door barking. She had her ducky with her, a favorite toy good for chewing and fetching. It had rained shortly before and the yard was in no state for duck hunting. However, Emma saw it differently and refused to give up her plea. I snatched the duck from her and returned to the living room where the girls and I interested her in a game of keep away. From couch to loveseat to chair, she ran panting and tail wagging, it was without a doubt good fun for all involved. After a few revolutions we decided we would change up on Emma and reverse the flow. Now love seat to couch to chair. I began the toss and Emma launched from my lap with the zeal we have come to expect from her—up on top of the couch, across the back, down to the arm, and an impressive leap to the chair. Now down my daughter's leg to the ottoman and to the floor. Gaining some traction from the area rug, she prepared for her leap to my lap on the love seat, but not this time. Off the ottoman she came, and in full run, she headed for me. But just as she was about to grab some air, her hind legs clipped a lone tennis shoe. She flipped and belly flopped on the hardwood and skidded to a stop with the front portion of her body under the love seat. Only her hind legs sprawled and her limp tail was visible. The air was sliced with a collective scream befitting a house full of females as we scrambled to rescue our Emma. We extricated her from the underside of the love seat and beset her with kisses and pets.

Poor Emma. Everything was going so well. She had her people, her duck and a good game going—until the shoe.

I can relate.

Whether an old flame, the opportunity to knock back a cold one, peer pressure, depression, financial woes or well you got the idea, some of the most benign items and situations can be a stumbling block in your walk with Jesus. Often times, we do not notice them until it is too late and we have belly flopped.

Throughout the word, we are warned to be vigilant and reminded that Satan roams about looking for whom he may devour.

> ***Be sober, be vigilant; because your adversary
> the devil, as a roaring lion, walketh about,
> seeking whom he may devour 1 Peter 5:8***

I think the first line of defense would be to evaluate yourself, your weaknesses your areas of temptation and avoid venues and people that could erode your resolve.

> ***But each person is tempted when he is lured and
> enticed by his own desire. James 1:14***

It is unfortunate that we have to at times remove people from our lives. It is a hard and sometimes painful process, but less painful compared to the pain of allowing them to remain.

> ***Be not deceived: evil communications corrupt
> good manners. 1 Corinthians 15:33***

Is there a situation, person or venue that is a ***shoe*** in your life? Now is the time to remove it.

Not All That Glitters is Gold

> But the LORD said unto Samuel, Look not on his countenance, or on the height of his stature; because I have refused him: for [the LORD seeth] not as man seeth; for man looketh on the outward appearance, but the LORD looketh on the heart.
> 1 Samuel 16:7

I always enjoy a good laugh on my way to work it seems to lessen the drudgery of the morning commute. I was not disappointed this morning as I fell in line behind a motorcycle. I admit I don't know much about motorcycles and even less about the biker culture, but there are some things that I think would be glaringly obvious.

The bike, rather small in size, was bedazzled with grinning skulls and chrome. Its rider was painted with tattoos and clad in ragged jeans and a sleeveless denim jacket. Atop the rider's head was a Pickelhaube. (I don't know about you, but the sight of the spiked topped helmet on anyone is pretty funny.)

He played the part to perfection, revving the engine and leaning deep into the curves as if he was really the Dragon's Tail. It was obvious that this rider was at least in his mind a menace to society in general.

I followed this cycle through the tunnels, down the incline to the red light. As we slowed to a stop he switched lanes and with all the macho he could muster he poised himself. I glanced over to take one more look before I went my way and he his. As I did I noticed that beneath the chrome and cross bones he was riding a **Honda**. He turned his well-rehearsed scowl and knitted eyebrows to me and stared in the hope of intimidating.

Intimidation? No.

Peals of laughter? Oh yes!

This Honda riding wannabe was much less intimidating and more humorous than he ever wanted to be.

I admit there have been times that I have tried to be someone I was not. I am sure it was apparent to everyone around me, but unfortunately not to me.

Sometimes, we spend so much time trying to convince others of who we are we get lost in the charade.

God, however, is not interested in the shell, but His focus is on the heart. When Samuel was sent to anoint the new king that would take Saul place, he was told what to look for in Samuel 16:7

> **But the LORD said unto Samuel, Look not on his countenance, or on the height of his stature; because I have refused him: for [the LORD seeth] not as man seeth; for man looketh on the outward appearance, but the LORD looketh on the heart. 1 Samuel 16:7**

Samuel went to the house of Jesse as directed by God to find this new king of Israel. Jesse paraded all seven of his sons before Samuel but they were not who God wanted. Finally, Samuel asked Jesse if there were any more sons and he answered.

"Yes, David is out with the sheep".

David was a shepherd and the youngest. Probably a bit scrawny and still wet behind the ear, but he loved God. Jesse forgot about him. He figured that the kid in no way looked like a king. I am sure that if we saw him out in the field, dirty, smelly and chasing lambs, "king" would be the last word to cross our minds.

However, what God saw was a heart that loved Him.

As a society we spend money and time making the outside look good. We work hard to promote how we want the world to see us but spend very little time on what really matters and that is the heart.

Whether it is teen boys sporting drooping pants or adults struggling to keep up with the credit card payments, we lend most of our focus to the outward appearances. Where is your focus? Is it on the latest fashions and what is trending? Or is it on the heart and how you can grow in your relationship with God? Do you as much time grooming your heart with prayer and Bible reading as you do your coif?

Even so ye also outwardly appear righteous unto men, but within ye are full of hypocrisy and iniquity. Matthew 23:28

The Long, Long
Bumpy Ride of Life

- Have not I commanded thee? Be strong and of a good courage; be not afraid, neither be thou dismayed: for the LORD thy God [is] with thee whithersoever thou goest
Joshua 1:9

There hath no temptation taken you but such as is common to man: but God is faithful, who will not suffer you to be tempted above that ye are able; but will with the temptation also make a way to escape, that ye may be able to bear it.
I Corinthians 10:13

I like old movies, whether they are comedies, action or romance. I enjoy the simplicity of the older films. Actors had to really act and viewers had to use their imagination rather than depend on the efforts of CG effects.

One movie in particular has been coming to my mind lately. I think I will force the girls to watch it with me this weekend.

The movie is a 1954 classic entitled, "The Long, Long Trailer" with Lucille Ball and Desi Arnez. This movie is characteristic Lucy with all the physical humor you can pack into a flick. Lucy and Desi play newlyweds embarking on their life together by buying a 36 foot travel trailer to tour the United States. My favorite part is when Tracy (Lucy) decides that to save time, she'll ride in the travel trailer, and cook dinner while Nicky (Desi) traverses the winding roads leading to their next campsite. Dressed in a beautiful green frock, hair and makeup perfected, Tracy plans to prepare a romantic dinner. However, things turn dicey pretty quick.

Tracy runs herself ragged trying to cook while dishes, pots and pans roll around and burst out of the cabinets, as Desi negotiates hairpin turns and too close for comfort steep drop offs. Try as she might, Tracy simply cannot keep up with all that is going on around her. She stirs the pot on the stove and runs to catch the mixing bowl as the trailer is slung around a curve, the tire nimbly riding the edge. Then the trailer shifts and the oven burst open and a roast flies out skidding across the black and white checkered floor. Flour flying, cans rolling and constant shifting of the land whale leave Tracy off balance. Finally, she begins to yell out the front window for Nicky to stop, but he cannot hear her because he is babalu-ing too loudly to hear anything. Finally, they make it to the campsite.

Nicky parks and comes to check on dinner. Ready for a hearty meal with his lovely wife, he flings open the door and is met with a pie in the face by his food smeared ticked off bride. Things go from bad to worse during the trip and Nicky leaves Tracey squalling in usual Lucy style. (I encourage watching it to find out how the story ends.)

Though things are not as drastic as trying to cook in a moving trailer, life does seem to throw as many curves and roasts at you. When the ride gets bumpy it is hard to keep a cool head. Things are said, anger flashes and the damage is done. I often feel like I am dealing with life in a moving trailer, chasing my job, my family, school, writing, cleaning house, teens to corral, bills to be paid, lawn to mow, leaking ceiling. On and on I could go! It is exhausting trying to juggle everything on uneven ground.

The truth is that none of us will escape problems, trials, temptations and woes. However, it is important to remember that what you face is in no way uncommon or unprecedented nor do you face it alone. Unlike Tracy when we call out for help, God hears our plea and is faithful to answer.

If you have been feeling like your cooking dinner in a moving trailer, take heart, smooth roads are to come. Let your concerns be known in your prayers to our Father. He is anxious to hear from you.

Pursued By a Perfect Love

I pray for them: I pray not for the world, but for them which thou hast given me; for they are thine.
John 17:9

It was 10 am; recess time. The yellow sun had crept above the tree line and beamed down on the dry grass of the third grade playground. The air smelled of pear trees and sweet honeysuckle. Spring was slipping away to summer. From the side door of the brick building, gangly knock kneed boys and girls screamed and giggled as they ran across the pavement to line up on the grass. The teachers shouted commands to the children and they quickly lined up as the teachers chose captains.

It was kickball day.

I did not share the enthusiasm of my classmates. I nervously twisted my hands and dug the toe of my shoe into the dust. Sweat began to pop out on my brow. I felt the butterflies of anxiety as the kids grouped into their cliques. I hated kickball day. It was the day that your peers either endorsed you with an invitation to their team or rejected you with the refusal to include you in the lineup. It seemed to take forever as I waited for the giggling pig tailed girls and freckle splattered boys to whisper among themselves to choose the next players. There were times when I was chosen rather quickly other times I was left last, tears welling, sweaty palmed and red faced.

The fickle kids of Ms. Wilson's third grade class kept me in a constant state of worry. I was always afraid to not be chosen. To not be considered good enough to kick the orange ball and claim a base. Not be chosen by the boys as a competent player or by the girls as being popular enough. I dreaded Tuesday and Thursday recess. My stomach churned with the panic of being passed over and rejected.

Things don't change much as you continue to move through the years. We find that we are missing party invitations, not being asked to prom, not getting the job, the interest of the handsome guy, or winning the promotion. Life is a constant popularity contest and struggle to fit in, be accepted and liked.

I can tell you that my anxiety on the kick ball field did not stay there. It has followed me throughout my life, and I have made some bad choices in the pursuit of quelling my fear of rejection. I spent years upon years striving for the endorsement of my friends, society, coworkers, men and those I strived to be like. I played the part, used the lingo and tried to conform to what I thought they wanted me to be. I was miserable and desperate. Finally, I no longer knew who I was. I did not know what I liked, what I enjoyed what I wanted out of my life.

Years of trying to be what I thought people wanted me to be left me a stranger to myself.

It took a long time to get to know who I was. In the beginning I did not like Melissa Levi and believed no one else would like the real me much less love me.

Yet the whole time I was being pursued by a love that I wanted no part of. If no one wanted me or chose me here on earth, then why in the world would God have use for me? I rejected Christ and stubbornly held to the idea that I was unlovable, unwanted and worthless.

However, Jesus never tired in His quest of my soul. I was the one of the ninety- nine sheep and He followed me into the wilderness.

Even as I turned back to church, Jesus, my family; I continued to believe only in my unworthiness.

Then there was a verse that I had read and heard many times in my life, yet this time it meant something very personal to me.

> **I pray for them: I pray not for the world, but for them which thou hast given me; for they are thine. John 17:9**

Jesus as He prepared for His death on the cross, He also prepared His disciples for the time to come. He also prayed for you and me.

> **Neither pray I for these alone (only), but for them also <u>which shall believe on</u> me <u>through their word (message)</u> John 17:20**

Two thousand years ago, He knew me and He knew you. He knew that you would have the message brought to you of His boundless love and desire to include us in the family of God and He prayed you would believe. If Christ, facing a horrible death, removed from God himself by the sins of the world, prayed for me, how could I consider myself unwanted and unloved?

He pursued me with a perfect love. He pursues you too.

Life Isn't Fair

For they being ignorant of God's righteousness, and going about to establish their own righteousness, have not submitted themselves unto the righteousness of God.
Romans 10:3

It was Thursday afternoon and the freeway was backed up and so was every road leading north of the city. I decided that I would go up through the tunnels home. Bumper to bumper and inch by Inch, traffic slowly clawed up the hill leading to the tunnels.

My Altima was not pleased to be idling with the air on so I conceded, turned off the air and rolled down the windows to allow the moisture saturated air of late July into my vehicle.

Immediately, the swirl of humidity encased me in a swaddle of sweat and discomfort. I stole glances at my road mates. Just like me, they reluctantly withstood the aggravation of the rush time traffic snarl under the oppression of mid-summer heat.

It seemed like hours rather than minutes as we lurched forward, then idled, and lurched again sluggishly tracking to the top of the hill.

I was now only five cars from the roundabout and I craved the freedom that the other side of the tunnel promised. I heaved a sigh of relief. However, before I moved one more car length, a rather large gray pickup rumbling up the emergency lane roared past me, and the four cars in front. Perched at the summit, it began to muscle its way in front of the leading car. A choir of horn blasts filled the air. Mine included. Hot temps led quickly to hot tempers. Every driver in front of me bunched their sedans together to push out this upstart. Fist and fingers waved dissatisfaction and the chorus of horns rose up filling my ears. The woman in the leading car, a small white Sentra, screamed and stomped her gas pedal to thwart the advances of the line breaking Dodge. The woman in the truck shrieked in response and roared the truck forward to counter the Sentra.

People began to hang out windows, screaming and wailing obscenities to the driver of the truck.

Nonetheless, this line breaking Dodge refused to heed the show of solidarity of drivers, and nearly crushing the leading car refused to back down. Nosing the truck forward the truck rolled over the divider and plunged into traffic disappearing into the black hole of the tunnel. The little white car whizzed around the roundabout and vanished into the burrow right behind the bold intruder. All the way down the road the white sedan chased the gray truck, weaving and speeding through the town. I clenched the steering wheel at every light as each ignored the safety of others. The pursuit continued up the highway and I was happy to be taking my turn down my street.

I thought about that incident throughout the night and how angry the drivers were to be pushed out of admittedly an earned position in the line of weary workers seeking the refuge of their homes. I questioned the audacity of the truck driver to deliberately and without remorse cheat the motorists of their turn.

I thought of other aspects of our lives that we viciously protect our interest, our rights and the fairness of the situation. If we have heard it, felt it or shouted it ourselves, we know how much being slighted and treated with unfairness infuriates not just the adults but everyone down to the toddler.

My mother, when I would whine of the unfairness of a situation was quick to tell me, "Life, is not fair."

I can tell you that without a doubt my experiences have proved her correct more times than I can remember. Life is indeed not fair. We see it every day in the hospital, the boardroom, the roadways, the ball fields and right in our own homes.

Fairness is a very human concept. It is not biblical and nowhere that I have found does the Word intimate that God is "fair." We, however, have evolved into a society that believes that fairness is due. In today's society, children do not fail, no one loses, and everyone gets a trophy. We bring gifts to the siblings of the birthday child so as not to make the other children feel left out.

People get all lathered up when they think they, or a group is being treated unfairly. In our world today, evil is not treating everyone with the same "fair" standards. Everyone has to be treated equally. This idea breeds the concept of entitlement, and the excuse not to do anything for anybody because we cannot do it for everyone.

Nowhere that I have found in the Bible are we guaranteed a "fair" deal here on earth. In fact, the Bible instructs us in our fair behavior toward others with no guarantee of the same being returned to us. (See Deut 25:15, 2 Cor 8:13-14 and Col 4:1)

What is and is not fair has been determined by the world.

Instead of wasting our time and energy worrying about what is fair and how we have been treated, we should try focusing on how we deal with others and serve God.

God is not fair, He is just.

He Prepares a Home for Us

About 4 months ago, I was awakened by the frenzied barking of Emma. She was racing around the house from my bed to the living room back and forth over and over again.

Finally, I got up and stomped to the living room where Emma was perched on the back of the chair, her muzzle pushed through the blinds. As I reached for her neck, there was a sudden boom and the roof of the house down the street erupted in flames.

I grabbed my bathrobe and shoes and ran out the door. As I grabbed up blankets my heart raced I was scared for the family in the house. I wasn't the only one awakened. People began to come out of their houses. The mother of the house screamed for her daughter and her husband who were still inside.

Her sons stood behind her mesmerized by the yellow licks of flame that reached into the darkness. Finally, the father emerged with the blonde girl in his arms. They were sooty, scared, but alive.

The police showed up then, three cars squealing down our street, lights flickering. The officers jumped out and asked was anyone else inside. Thankfully, no was the answer.

It seemed like a lifetime before the distant sounds of the fire trucks and ambulances were heard. As we waited the flames hungrily devoured the house and smoke black as the dark skies behind it billowed out of the windows. Glass broke, and the house moaned as it was eaten alive by the fire. It was like watching a death. While the neighborhood stood in little pods around the scene, the family stood in a tight formation like a wadded up fist. Tears streamed down faces and their bodies shook with the chill of the night air.

It was not the lights of the fire trucks or the noise of the equipment that kept me up that night after I returned to the house. It was the frantic cries of the mother echoing in my brain. Her cry was saturated with pain, fear and the realization that everything they had, had been destroyed in just a few minutes. It was a long night.

Yesterday, as I watered the plants on the front porch I noticed the same family standing on the sidewalk enjoying the site of the new house that is being built. It is an impressive house, much larger than the one before. They walked around the perimeter pointing to the different aspects of the house. It was a joy to see this family together and looking at a bright future.

The family soon left, but I remained on the porch. No, I was not dwelling on that terrible night; instead, I was enjoying a glimpse into the future of us all.

Life is full of heartache, pain, loss, uncertainty and despair. However, our future is bright in Christ. As that family stood in front of the house, they were not thinking of the past, that night or the tragedy that brought them there. They were focused on what was to come. To them that house was hope, it was peace and happiness. Jesus in John 14 comforted His disciples and us by letting us know that we would soon be in His Father's house.

Despite the tragedy of that night there was hope ahead.

Farsighted

Well, school is back in session. That means I am back to getting up at 530 and cooking breakfast for the girls.

This morning I stumbled to the kitchen and began to gather from the refrigerator the staples for packing lunches and fixing breakfast.

I reached for the mayo, lunch meat, tomato, lettuce…maybe an avocado…the sausage…butter of course…ah yes, we'll need the jelly…I will need the creamer.

I spread everything out onto the counter. Firstly, I would need to get the oven on to heat up, but to what temperature? I whirled the can biscuits around to the direction side and stared at the wrap. I pulled the container closer and then to arm's length. I am sure I looked like I was trying to play the trombone! Back and forth I adjusted the biscuits to different distances hoping I could read the temperature needed to bake them. However, no matter how I tried the package looked as if I was peering through a kaleidoscope.

I looked through my purse, looked in the living room on the desk and I finally found my reading glasses. I adjusted temperatures and began my morning duties.

As I built sandwiches to explicit specifications, I thought about my vision and people's vision in general.

I have no trouble seeing for miles. The leaves in the trees are clear, street signs, the TV all easily seen. However, when it comes to the up close things, I have a handicap.

I think most of us do when it comes to personal up close things in our lives. I have no trouble seeing what I think are faults in other people.

"Why did she wear that?"
"Why doesn't he just divorce her?" "How can she stand to live like that?"
"I can't believe they spent their money on...... "

And it is not just confined to friends, family and coworkers! Oh no, I can go through the gamut with a complete stranger in the grocery line.

However, after you read Matthew 7:1-5 and Luke 6:41-42, you see it is certainly nothing new. It is effortless to spot and criticize another's blunders and ignore our own. After all it is much easier to give an opinion rather than working through our own shortcomings. Correcting ill behavior in ourselves is no easy task. It takes courage to take a hard and honest look inside our heart and then take responsibility.

Jesus' parable was directed to the Pharisees. They spent their time working on new rules and passing judgment on their people, but the lesson is for us still today. We spend a lot of our time comparing ourselves to others. By pointing out where they are lacking, we make ourselves feel better.

Yet, when our time is come and we face the Father, he will not compare us to any other. Instead, we will answer for our own failures. Matthew 7:2 and Luke 6:37 warn us that the measure we use to gauge others will be used against us.

That is pretty sobering; I know that often I can be very harsh in my appraisal of others. So the next time I am examining the motives, actions or words of another, I think I will first see what I can do about my beam.

> **"For all have sinned, and come short of
> the glory of God," Romans 3:23**

What a Blessing is a Friend

"Ye are my friends."
John 15:14 (a)

Well, I am here on the side of the road again. The girls missed the bus and the tire blew as we got off the interstate. Luckily the girls got a ride with a classmate that drove by us. Now it is time for me to get to work on this tire.

I took off the balding tire and inspected the hole in the worn radial. I lugged out the spare. It was flat too.

I leaned against the car and watched motorist scurry like ants up and down the pike.

What to do now?

As I was formulating a plan, my phone buzzed. "You ok?" my friend texted. "The spare is flat too! LOL!" I sent back.

"I am on the way." She replied.

Just like that, she dropped what she was doing, told her boss she had to help her friend and drove across town. She came to drive me to Walmart to purchase another tire and return to the car to put in on.

Why? Because that is what a friend does.

As I sat in my car waiting for her and watching the morning sun's creeping fingers stretch over the landscape, I thought about friendship for a moment. I thought of the times precious friends held me when I cried, listened to me as I whined, rebuked me when I was straying, and laughed with me, sometimes when there seemed to be nothing to laugh about and I was impressed with how important friends really are. The blessing of friendships is a wonderful gift from our Father.

While I waited, I got out my Bible and found a *friend* in the concordance. As I read Chapter 15 of John, I really saw the importance of friendship to Christ, not just with the disciples but with you and me today.

When Jesus came to the understanding of who he was and what his purpose was, he did not rush out into the world to judge, point fingers or condemn. Instead, he shared the love of God, as a friend would share good news with another.

In verse 14 of John 15, it begins with ***"Ye are my friends."*** That statement was not exclusive to those that were present; it was to all of us. Jesus came as a friend into this world, to share the love of his father and to lay down his life so that we could have everlasting life.

> ***Greater love hath no man than this, that a man lay down his life for his friends. John 15:13***

Jesus is not asking us to lay down our lives. He is asking us to be a friend to those that are lost, in need and hurting. Friendship is a choice. We choose who to treat as a friend and who not.

> ***Ye have not chosen me, but I have chosen you, and
> ordained you, that ye should go and bring forth fruit,
> and that your fruit should remain: John 15:16 (a)***

Jesus chose to be my friend. Through that expression of friendship and sacrifice he pierced my heart and drew me close. I believe that he choose me to be a friend to those in my life that are lost and lonely, so that I can introduce them to Jesus.

Do you count Jesus as your friend? Do you share his love and concern with those in your life?

All you have to do is be a friend.

The Show Must Go On

All three first grade classes crowded into Miss Milligan's classroom excited to hear the decisions for the roles in the upcoming PTA Parent's night play. I sat on the rug, legs folded beneath me, fingers crossed and sweaty with excitement. I hoped that this time I would be chosen for a real role, I was done with being trees, daffodils and rocks. I was ready for a part with meat! Finally, the forest fauna and animals had been cast. Would I be banished to the chorus, or was there a role for me this time? I squeezed my already blood starved fingers tighter in their cross and repeated my mental mantra, *"Let me get a part, let me get a part!"*

My heart pounded as the excitement mounted.

Then the teacher announced. "The part of the "Ugly Duckling" goes to Missy Levi.

"Yes! Yes!" I screamed in my brain. Finally, I had a real part! I would stand center stage before the entire PTA. My character would morph from the ugly duckling to the beautiful swan. I would strip away the yellow mundane costume of the duckling and expose the pristine white feathers of the swan. There before the whole elementary *I would be the Swan!* The sole occupant of the spotlight! They would gasp at my beauty and the auditorium would erupt with applause as people scrambled to their feet. Roses would pile up around me and the cheers would ring for me. My mom would be so proud the other girls would weep in jealousy it would be the greatest production of The Ugly Duckling my elementary or any elementary had ever seen!

"And finally the part of the Beautiful Swan goes to Stephanie Warner!"

What? What did she mean the beautiful swan would be Stephanie Warner? I was the star! Me! I was the duckling that got to become the swan, me not Stephanie Warner!

I cried a lot over that play. I did not want to do it. I tried to get my mom to tell Miss Milligan I could not do it. I did not want to participate at all. In fact, I asked mom if I could change schools. I would have done anything to keep from having to be the ugly duck of the first grade.

Miss Milligan's first grade class was a long time ago, but the lesson from that experience has stuck with me. More than once through the years I have had a path chosen for myself and it was disrupted. Loss of loved one, loss of job, dissolved marriage, illnesses, foreclosure, lost pregnancy, lack of money, broken relationships and I could just keep typing the tragedies. Tragedies many of you have endured as well.

It is not easy to accept alterations of our plans. We are disappointed, angry, and sad, confused and bitter sometimes. However, we must continue on through the tears, through the insomnia, the embarrassment, the ridicule of others and frustration.

The show must go on.

My mom made me do the play. Even if I did not understand why she did at the time she knew that if I could not handle doing the play how I would ever be able to stand up to a life that is full of disappointment. She put together a cute duckling outfit with a huge orange bill that strapped to my face. I sat in the plastic pool in front of the assembly with kids dressed in tree and flower costumes behind me, the chorus kids to the left and I quacked as the narrator read the story. I left the stage and Stephanie Warner burst forth in her swan outfit.

It may not have been my debut, but it was a lesson that I think of now and again. We may have grand plans for ourselves, but that is not always the plan of our Father. He knows the paths and plans that are best for us. His paths lead us to a closer relationship with Him, people we may have never met along our own trail and opportunities to share His love and mercy with others.

Though times can be painful and we just do not want to face them, we must with the assurance that He is there with us, guiding us and making something great through it all.

Marcia, Marcia, Marcia

> *Not that I speak in respect of want: for I have learned,*
> *in whatsoever state I am, therewith to be content.*
> *Philippians 4:11*

I was in the restroom at work the other day. I was trying to make some sense of my hair. One curl fell between my eyes and another stood tall and proud at the top of my head. As my frustration grew with the unruly locks, I was transported back to the late seventies. Back when everyone wanted to look like Marcia Brady: tan, lean and blonde. Nothing like me: freckled, chubby and frizzy. I have countless memories of screaming into my pillow, tears and afternoons with my head on the ironing board as my grandmother attempted home straightening. I really did hate my hair.

Yet it seems I might have been the only one. I have had complete strangers ask to touch my hair. I worked with one lady years ago that would bury her face in my hair and breathe it in. I have gotten some really strange requests and comments over the years concerning my mop. I never could understand how they would covet this mess that adorns the top of my head, but many do.

I was also reminded of a morning back in junior high when my friend Donna got on the bus. She had straight blonde hair and could have been a look alike for Marcia Brady. This particular morning, she sat down beside me with limp curls all through her hair.

"What have you done to your hair?" I exclaimed. "Do you like it? I wanted curls like you."

Donna had slept all night on rollers trying to get her hair to curl... like mine. I could not believe that she would want my unruly locks. By the time we got to school, her curls had fallen out and her hair was almost as straight as always. She cried for the entire morning with disappointment.

I guess that is just human nature, we always want what someone else has, or what we cannot have. Contentment is a foreign concept to so many of us. The lack of contentment can lead to a very unhappy life. It is easy to look at what others have and ask why we don't have the same, why do they have it and I do not. This attitude cheats us of the enjoyment of what we do have and breeds ungrateful insolence.

Paul understood the danger of this kind of thinking. He wrote about it to the believers. If anyone had the right to question and ask why, it was Paul. He was hated, pursued, imprisoned, shipwrecked, snake bit, beaten and much more throughout his career. However, through it all, he exercised contentment and thanksgiving for what he did have.

I do not mind telling you that if I had been in his situation, I do not know that I could have maintained contentment and gratefulness. I would have been asking a lot of whys.

And I do, but they are the wrong whys and whens. I should be think-ing of what God wants me to learn from particular circumstances or what I am to share with others. I am sure that Paul could have asked: *why I am I being subjected to imprisonment and beatings God if I am working for you?* Instead, Paul knew that his circumstances were to be for the glory of the Lord and the extension of the Good News of Christ. It is the same in our lives. Our particular trials are not to be viewed as punishments or persecutions but an opportunity to learn something about ourselves, gain a new perspective or gain the empathy to help others in their time of need.

Contentment in all situations allows us to take the focus off of the condition and place it on Christ.

Home Invasion

This morning I went about my usual routine of flipping on lights, starting the coffee and turning on the TV to listen to the news. Then, as was customary, I opened the front door, unlatched the storm door and pushed it open. I expected to see the outdoor cats run in single file and head for their bowl just inside the kitchen.

However, this morning they did not.

"Kitty, Kitty!" My shrill invitation went out into the pre-dawn gloom.

Yet, Dot nor Henry answered the call. Instead, from the darkness a form moved into the pale light, and crossing over the threshold he sauntered into my home. I stared in disbelief, my jaw slack, my knees weak and my heart pounding in my ears. He turned his head and then rolled his black orbs to look at me. His mouth spread wide into a grin and he panted from recent exertion. I backed away, my knees banging on the corner of the loveseat. As I did, he moved further into the house.

My mind reeled as I played out possible scenarios. Would the girls awake and come into the living room and incite him to attack? Would Emma the Terrible finish her breakfast and come from the back of the house and irritate him with her barking?

As my thoughts faded and I focused on him, he moved closer to me. I stood rigid, fixed on his eyes, trying to read his intent.

Closer he moved, nostrils flaring, as he took in the scent. Finally, I felt his hot breath on my hand and I trembled. He nudged me. I stifled a cry by biting my lip and felt my calf muscles press into the couch. He pressed closer and I had nowhere to go.

Then, I remembered the treats in my bathrobe pocket for Emma and the Assassins. I slipped my hand into the pocket and three little morsels dotted my palm. It took all my strength to extend my hand before him. His muzzle, soft and hot took my meager offering, his eyes never left mine. I swallowed hard and side stepped him, pushing the storm door open. He disappeared as stealthy as he came back into the blackness.

I fell back onto the loveseat and covered my face with quivering hands. I began to laugh the nervous laugh we do when we know how close to a real danger we have been. I had trouble grasping the event that had just happened. How or why had this pit bull found his way to my front door and then into my house?

He had just entered into the house, brazenly without any sense of fear. The door was open and he walked inside.

As I sat on the couch willing my heart to return to normal rhythm, I thought about the audacity of this act. The sheer audacity reminded me of how sin boldly enters into our lives. All it takes is a crack, a gap in the door and it is inside.

Maybe it started as a harmless flirtation on Facebook. Possibly, just a five-dollar bill from the till went unnoticed, and before you knew It, you had taken several fives. Possibly it was just a case of venting frustration that became malicious gossip against a friend. Perhaps that injury has healed, but the sweet oblivion of the pain pills is too hard to resist. The heat of numbness as the alcohol spreads through your blood dulls the regrets and blurs the pain of yesterday. Whatever gap may be at your door, Jesus knows how to close it. All you have to do is ask.

Jesus is ready and waiting for you to turn it all over to Him.

Blind Panic

"You are far from my plea and the cry of my distress. O my God, I call by day and you give no reply; I call by night and I find no peace."
(Ps. 22 1-2)

Sometimes writing Mustard Seeds is not always that simple. At times everything comes together with ease other times it is a struggle to get the words down with some semblance of order. This week I have all sorts of thoughts, but finding the central theme to focus on has been eluding me. I expressed this to my friend. She reminded me of an incident that happened probably 13 years ago.

This memory we shared would be the *seed* I had been looking for.

I got divorced close to the same time as my friend so we decided that sharing an apartment would be economically better as well as logistically beneficial with day care, work and school schedules.

We moved into a rather large three bedroom apartment. Moving day is in itself is very stressful, but mix in three little girls ages 4, 5 & 5, my family, her family and you have a whole new meaning of stress.

Most everyone had left and it was just us girls. We still had a few things in the cars and we wanted to get them in before dark. There were two ways into our hallway, the front entrance and then a rear door that had a path leading to the lower parking lot. I corralled the girls and told them we were going out to get more boxes. I warned them not to leave the apartment, we would just be outside and right back. We started out the back door to get another load. With arms full we trudged up the path. It was then that we heard the familiar cry of my child.

Out of the front of the building ran my youngest, at that time 4 years old, screaming "Momma!" She was hysterically crying and wailing. She was in such a panic that she did not look when she stepped off the curb for cars, she did not stop to look around for me. Instead, she ran down the walkway and into the parking lot. Across the black top in and out of parked cars her little legs pumped, propelling her further and further from me.

I dropped my boxes and began running screaming her name, tears welling in my eyes, my heart thumping and a chill of fear spreading throughout my body. I too ignored the possibility of traffic or danger because I had one focus and that was getting to her before something terrible happened. Finally, she heard my voice and ran back across the pavement to me. I scooped her up and squeezed her so hard she asked me to let go of her so she could breathe.

As I carried her in the building I inquired, "Why did you come outside? I told you to stay in the apartment because I was going to get boxes out of the car."

"I know Momma, but I couldn't see you anymore."

There are times in my own life that I find myself in a panic because I cannot see God.

I do not understand why God chooses to be silent at times and quick to respond at others. I guess I forget that God is not a mere man, but the Sovereign God of all. He can do what He wants, whenever He gets ready. That's hard to take for an impatient woman like me.

When I think of His silence I think of Mary and Martha, two very real women in a heartbreaking situation.

Mary and Martha had a brother named Lazarus and they lived in Bethany. The trio were very good friends with Jesus. They always opened their home to him and his disciples when they came through the area.

Unfortunately, Lazarus became ill. It became apparent that Lazarus may die so the sisters sent word to Jesus. They knew that Jesus could heal their brother. However, upon receiving the message, Jesus stayed for two more days where he was. He did not send back a message or go right away, he waited. He remained silent. (John 11:6) Mary and Martha could not see him. They did not hear from him, but they waited on him.

While they waited, Lazarus died.

As I read this I feel a little pang because I think about the pain and worry the sisters had been going through, the suffering of Lazarus and I have a bit of trouble reconciling this passage. I imagine that they watched together for Jesus to come. Neighbors and friends watched the horizon. By night they lit the oil lamp and waited, but Jesus did not come.

They endured the silence.

By the time Jesus came, Lazarus had been in the grave for 4 days.

So why did Jesus not come? Why had he remained silent? The Bible says that he loved them. (John 11:5). They demonstrated their faith but still no answer in this time of need.

The answer is in John 11:4, "This sickness is not unto death, but for the glory of God, that the Son of God might be glorified thereby." Jesus told the disciples that this situation was for one purpose. Lazarus' death was the opportunity to glorify God and the Son. Many Jews had gathered at the home of Mary and Martha and they had followed the sisters to meet Jesus at the grave. When Jesus called Lazarus from the grave there were many there to see it. On that day many believed.

Do not panic when you do not see God. When He's silent, He's working on a miracle.

Groomer Assaulted, Emma the Terrible Banned from PetSmart

And he shall sit as a refiner and purifier of silver:
and he shall purify the sons of Levi, and purge
them as gold and silver, that they may offer unto
the LORD an offering in righteousness.
Malachi 3:3

The smell of wet dog and shampoo tickled my nose as I waited my turn at the PetSmart groomers. I had brought Emma for a much needed nail trim. Emma hugged close to me. Her eyes were wide and her tiny body trembled. I cooed reassurances into her velvet ears. Finally, it was our turn.

I moved to the counter and handled over my little friend. She whined and leaned back toward me. I walked back to the corner with a guilty heart.

I no more than seated myself when I heard the familiar yipping of Emma. The groomer, an obvious rookie, tried to reassure the distrustful canine. However, Emma was having none of it. She twisted her body and swung her legs to get free of the young lady. This went on for several minutes and I soon noticed the entire waiting room was focused on the snarling, snapping five pound demon. Even the other groomers and pets seemed mesmerized by the scene playing out.

Having pity on the new recruit, a veteran of the doggie spa came to help. As the young lady held Emma, the experienced groomer grabbed a paw and gripped the nail with the clipper. The snap of the cuticle rang out in the waiting room.

Emma's eyes bulged, revealing the white of her eyeballs. In a split second she became a whirl of fur and teeth, incensed by this infraction on her body. Emma was not going to let this go unpunished.

Realizing that the entire establishment had come to a halt and the windows became filled with curious spectators, the groomers turned away, their backs shielding the drama from prying eyes.

It was then that I heard the horrified squeal of the young groomer. I jumped up from my seat and rushed to the counter, fearing the worst for this young lady.

Surprise, disgust and anger was the only way to describe the look the groomer had on her face. I followed her gaze and saw what the cause of her outburst was. Emma had wet on her and her scrubs turned dark with the trail of urine.

Gasps from fellow groomers and well as the spectators rang out. Holding Emma at arm's length the groomer handed her to me and asked us to leave. I stepped outside the enclosure and clipped on the pale pink lead.

I took the walk of shame past my fellow dog lovers following behind Emma, who bounced with great triumph across the parking lot to the waiting car.

Just like Emma, I am not too fond of being groomed. However, to be at our best for Christ, we have to endure the grooming to become better than we were.

God allows or withholds situations, illness, trials, and tribulations in order to groom us in our service to Him and others. Being groomed for service is sometimes a very unpleasant part of our lives. However, it is necessary to bring the best out of us to benefit those around us as well as ourselves. In order to grow and mature in our relationship with Christ, we need at times to endure terrible and heartbreaking circumstances.

Just like the silver smelter, God applies heat to our life to refine us. As the silver heats the slag or impurities come to the top and are skimmed off. Once all the impurities are removed, the smelter can see his reflection. That is what God is doing when he applies the heat to your life. He is working to remove the impurities and sin from your life so that His reflection can be seen in you.

What reflection is seen in your life?

Double Take

But even the very hairs of your head are all numbered.
Luke 12:7a

My daughters go to a Conservation high school. They really enjoy it. It gives them the opportunity to be themselves. However, this year, the school has made some changes as the enrollment has increased. There a few more rules and they have added a Headmaster.

My oldest daughter is not overly keen on this new educator. Why? The Headmaster cannot tell my daughter's apart. It infuriates both but the eldest has been very vocal to me, the Headmaster, and the teachers that it is not appreciated. She wants to be seen as an individual.

Whether the eldest's hair is up or down, even if they are wearing different clothes he cannot tell which one is which. When I had my parent teacher meetings he came up to me and began telling me how they looked exactly alike and he asked if they were twins.

"No," I replied. "They are seventeen months apart." "I really thought they were twins." He added.

Over the years I have heard that a lot. However, to me, my daughters are very much different. I know that the youngest eyes are hazel, but the oldest is light green.

One's nose has a splatter of freckles and the other has a mole at the hairline. One girl is shorter, their body styles different. The way they stand—their expressions are all different. To me they are two young ladies with many differences. Each has a wonderful personality, ideals and thoughts. They are dear each one in their own special way to me.

Thankfully, the Master knows us individually. He knows our strength and weakness. His knowledge of us is intimate. Beyond the shell, we travel this world within. I think that we forget that we are prized by God. You are very much an individual in God's eye.

I will praise thee; for I am fearfully and wonderfully
made: marvelous are thy works; and that my
soul knoweth right well. Psalms 139:14

You were fearfully and wonderfully made in your mother's womb by His hands.

But even the very hairs of your head are
all numbered. Luke 12:7a

Even the hair on your head is numbered and God knows each one because He placed it there.

You are precious and unique to Him.

In the Pit

He brought me up also out of an horrible pit, out of the miry clay, and set my feet upon a rock, and *established my goings.*
Psalms 40:2

The long dry grass crunched as I swam through the hay field on my belly to the small white fence enclosure. There I and my fellow compatriots froze, listening for the howl of the dogs. Satisfied that we had made it without detection, we slid underneath the old weathered boards.

Four tombstones, worn, crumbling, and silent stood. The grass closely shorn around the markers left us feeling hidden, in our own private hideaway. I scooted back and leaned against the fence. Donna dug in her cut off jean pockets and withdrew what we had met for. She dumped her pockets on the crispy grass of the tiny civil war graveyard. Scott did the same, pouring his offering over the top of Donna's pile. As soon as everyone contributed, we formed a tight circle and picked out our favorites. As for me, anything with chocolate was all I was interested in procuring.

The breeze rattled the dry leaves that clung to the branches, leaves that were reluctant to let go and ride the wind to the ground. I could feel the chill of fall on nature's breath and in the cool dirt beneath me. We soon settled ourselves on the ground, our bellies full of candy, and chattered about the onset of the new school year, which teachers we wanted and lamented at the idea of others. We giggled and pointed out the shapes in the clouds. We talked about who was cute and who was not. It was a great afternoon.

As the sun began to dip behind the pines, we heard the familiar sound of tire on gravel. We knew that the owner was home. Peering over the fence and through the hay we watched him creep up the driveway. He hung out of the car window and stared in our direction. We dared not move, knowing that he would see the grass stir. On our knees we watched and waited. Beyond we could hear the dogs, excited that the master had come home. Suddenly, he hit the gas and the car's back tires spun, spraying out a clatter of rocks and dirt.

We had been made.

I did not waste time with a covert retreat; instead, I bounded through the tall razors of grass, ignoring the blades slicing across my face. Behind me the howl and whooping barks of the owner's Dalmatians filled my ears and pricked my skin.

Beyond the grass was a deep ditch. I knew that once I reached it, I would have to be prepared to jump. Once over the ditch I would be safe, the Dalmatians never crossed the ditch or left the property. Arms above my head, I used my torso to mow through the thick hay. I knew the ditch was close now. I heard the yowl of the approaching dogs and looked back over my shoulder.

It was a mistake. I fell in the trench, rocks and dirt tumbled around me.

The other kids had mounted their bikes and were frantically peddling down Julian Road. I gripped the earth and dug my toes into the soft dirt and struggled to climb out of the pit. Behind me the dogs were getting louder. Tears streamed down my face and I clawed at the soil. Panic, fear, and terror circled me pushing my heart to pound louder in my ears and my tears to drip from my chin. The hay wildly waved as the dogs came closer. I did not cry out, I was afraid the dogs or worse the man would find me. I jumped and grabbed another handful of soil and as the attempts before they crumbled and showered down on my feet. Again and again, I clawed at the dirt and struggled to find a foothold, but it was no use. The dogs were close enough that I heard the sound of their sniffing of the air and ground. I shook, and pressed against the dirt wall, willing the spotted sentries not to find me. I squeezed my eyes shut and waited.

"Hey!" I heard the whisper. I looked above and a hand clumsily swatted the air above my head. I grabbed it. Another hand descended and I took it too.

Once out of the pit I ran as fast as I could down Julian Road and straight home.

That adventure was a couple of decades plus some ago. Yet, I find myself thrashing around in pits all the time. Of course, I am not talking about the real ones like this, but just as deep and equally hard to get out of.

There are so many pits we run across that threaten to keep us captive. There is drinking, drugs, sex, depression, pornography, money, destructive relationships, self-pity, hatred, and stubborn rebellion to name just the most notable. Just like this pit, it took the hand of a friend to get me out.

Are you in a pit? Do you struggle to lift yourself out? No matter how hard you try you just cannot get out. That's because you need the help of a friend. You need Jesus. Call upon Him, take His nail scarred hand and allow him to pull you from the muck and filth of your pit. His hand is extended, He waits only for you to reach out and accept it.

So Long Old Friend

For as we have many members in one body, and all members have not the same office: So we being many, are one body in Christ, and everyone one members one of another.
Romans 12:4:5

Today is a surgical day for me. My gall bladder and I will soon part ways. Up until this past year, we've been friends—not so close it is true. I did my thing, and she did hers. It was not until recently I realized that my gall bladder had it in for me. I guess I can understand why, I never gave her credit for the work she did and admittedly I was very ignorant of her exact job. I took advantage of her contribution to the intimate operations of my internal workings.

Now our working relationship will come to an end; she will go her way and leave a void just under my liver. The doctor says that in a few weeks my body will adjust and the liver will assume full control of the bile injection process. There will be food that I will have to avoid, time of healing and a couple of days out of work. This unknown sac of bile will make a bigger impression on her way out, much more than she did while she was here.

Though I was ignorant of her role, it was important, nonetheless. As I lay here pencil and paper in hand, open backed gown and stylish footsies, I think of how we as the body of Christ think that sometimes our role in the body is insignificant but it is not. Many times we think that if we do not have the high profile job we are not important. We are sorely misguided in this way of thinking. Each and every one of us is necessary to the healthy and active body of Christ.

As part of the whole we must take our role with enthusiasm and dedication no matter what it may be. Additionally, we should recognize and respect the position of others by acknowledging them.

You are a very important piece of the workings of the Body of Christ.

Knowledge Really
is the Power

> **For God hath not given us the spirit of fear; but of power, and of love, and of a sound mind.**
> *2 Timothy 1:7*

I have a younger brother, Russ. He is 4-1/2 years my junior. I will tell you that as a 4 almost 5 year old little girl I was never receptive to this addition to our family. To say that I exhibited some jealousy would probably be a gross understatement. I remained resentful for a long time. I saw no reason to share my momma or daddy. After all, they were mine first.

I remember the day they brought the pink squirmy kid home. He happily cooed in the bassinet and everyone talked about how handsome and sweet he was.

Well, what about me? I was cute and sweet long before he got here. Obviously, there was only one thing to do. While they chattered over coffee cake and other refreshments, I reached into the bassinet and twisted his little toe. He scowled more in surprise than pain.

I jumped back.

The room of relatives, church members and neighbors about ran over each other to see what was wrong with the new heir. Momma came quickly to check on her precious.

I blurted out, *"He cries too much. You should take him back to the hospital."*

With little notice of me she lifted him and began to soothe the wailing infant.

Today, I love my brother his wife and beautiful daughters very much, but in the beginning love was the last thing I felt for this perceived trespasser.

Throughout the Bible we see where jealousy pushed some to devious acts. Cain committed the first murder by killing his brother Abel, Jacob deceived his father for Esau's blessing, and Joseph's brothers sold him into slavery. That's just the beginning of Genesis! Jealousy is in no way anything new to the human race.

I still deal with jealousy. Sometimes it is over someone else's blessing, promotion, new car, spouse, smooth hair, youth or well I guess most anything can be coveted. Jealousy is always an ugly thing.

Recently, I had a very bad bout with some jealousy. I knew that my feelings were wrong. I knew that they were unfounded and if not put into check, they would become sinful. When I prayed and reasoned it out, I knew that it was silly. However, in the back of my mind I was turning those thoughts over and they were festering.

I decided I needed to do a bit of research on my enemy. I am not referring to the individual that I was coveting. I needed to understand jealousy. Jealousy is a demonic force. We know this because in Numbers 5:14 and Numbers 5:30 *"and the spirit of jealousy come upon him..."* The Bible calls jealousy a spirit meaning it is part of or is a principality or demon. So what is the root or cause of jealousy?

Jealousy comes from our insecurities. This individual made me feel insecure in myself. This insecurity lead to paranoia and fear. It was the principality of fear that was fueling my jealousy. 2 Timothy 1:7 tells us that the spirit of fear is **NOT** from God.

Once I identified the root of my jealousy I was able to fight it and not allow it to consume my thoughts and my actions.

As Christians, it is important for us to understand our enemy and our reasons for behavior. I believe many of us suffer under the lies and deception of Satan because of our ignorance to the Word of God. Through the study of God's Word the spiritual laws that govern the supernatural realm are revealed to us. To inherit the blessings the Lord has for us, we must abide within the spiritual laws that God has ordained.

I encourage you to study the Word everyday in some form. There are many study plans online, in guided study books, and of course my favorite just opening the Bible with an open heart to what He wants so dearly to share with us in His Word.

"My people are destroyed for lack of knowledge..." Hosea 4:6

There is No Victory without Sacrifice

I have fought a good fight, I have finished
my course, I have kept the faith:
2 Timothy 4:7

One summer while I was in elementary school, my Daddy decided that he would start running. Every evening as the sun's final rays clung to the horizon, my dad would lace up his tennis shoes and prepare for his run. He would stretch, run down the driveway, turn right and start up the hill. He ran through the summer and into fall and even most days in the winter. I would ride my bike zooming past him turn around and back I would come. He tolerated me until he passed my boundary and then I would watch him run until I could see him no more.

Every evening as he took the crown of the hill he was met by Bill. Bill would stand in his driveway, beer in hand and survey the neighborhood. As Daddy passed, Bill would raise his beer in a toast and my dad would nod, take a right and continue his run. Weeks become months and my father continued running, adding to his goal and before long he was doing 3 to 5 miles a night. Without fail, Bill would wait to toast my daddy as he ran by.

One night my father came by Bill's house, but he was not standing in the driveway with his beverage, but next to the mailbox. He wore a white t-shirt stretched over his generous middle; cut off blue jeans, athletic socks tucked under is knobby knees and army boots. As my daddy passed, Bill fell in beside him, head up and boots slapping the pavement as they continued down James Street. One block, then two, Bill began to struggle to keep pace with Dad.

"Bill?" My dad breathed, "Do you think the boots are a good idea?"

He puffed up and replied between gasps, "Wore these very boots in the army. Ran and marched for miles!"

A couple more blocks and now Bill was floundering. He had moved from gasping for air to gulping it.

"How far you run, Levi?"

"I have a three mile loop." My dad answered.

The thwack slap of the boots became more disorganized. Bill could not keep up with the steady pace that my Dad had accomplished. He soon quit and limped home holding the stitch in his side.

Bill never waited to toast my daddy again nor did he offer to run with him.

Do you know a Bill? I know that I have been "Bill" in my life before. I didn't want to invest the time, endure the sweat, the possible failure, the pain or the sacrifice needed to reach goals. My father put in months to get to the point that he was able to complete the miles. He had to sacrifice his time and chose to trade possibly a favorite show or just the opportunity to relax to obtain the end result. Unfortunately, Bill was not willing to make the sacrifice and invest. He just wanted to cut to the end.

Do you have a circumstance or situation in your life that you are trying to cut to the end of? Do not cheat yourself, the blessing and the victory lie in the journey.

Great Expectations

I was crocheting a hat the other night. I lifted it up to take a look. There it was, misshapen looking much more like a mushroom cap than a hat. Somehow, I had double stitched. I let out a long sigh of frustration and began pulling the stitches out. As it unraveled I felt a wash of annoyance.

My daughter was sitting opposite of me. She had been watching me mutter as I dismantled all my hard work.

"Mom, why are you taking it apart?"

"Well, sometimes you have to take things apart to make them right." I replied as I started the row again.

Three days later I was in my car pouring my heart out to God about a situation that is weighing heavy on me. I put it all out there, threw up my hands and surrendered it all to God. The very next day, my life seemed to be unraveling as easily as the crocheted loops had.

"God," I implored, "Why Lord are these things happening? I prayed for your help and guidance and now everything is worse! I do not understand."

Tears began to well up in my eyes when the memory of the little hat returned to my thoughts. That is when I understood why my life seemed to be unraveling. Sometimes things have to be rearranged and unraveled for the Lord to make them better.

Often we pray and we anticipate a quick, painless, and immediate answer. However, it does not always work out that way, sometimes God has to make some changes to get you where you need to be.

I am guilty of fearing God's design at times. We anticipate evil although God's entire plan is for the good. That is hard to remember when you seem to be spinning in uncertainty.

In Matthew Henry's Jeremiah Chapter 29 Bible commentary, he makes this statement concerning verse 11.

"...but the Lord is never at an uncertainty. We are sometimes ready to fear that God's designs are all against us; but as to his own people, even that which seems evil, is for good. He will give them, not the expectations of their fears, or the expectations of their fancies, but the expectations of their faith; the end he has promised, which will be the best for them."

Expect.....great things.

The Lost Highway

One thing that I dreaded in my marriage was the yearly trek to visit with his parents in Indiana. After spending a couple of days with my in-laws, it was glaringly obvious where he had gotten his boorish behavior.

On one such trip we ran into a little problem along the way. We were ¾ through Kentucky when my husband decided that he needed a nap. We switched out at the next rest area. He quickly fell asleep and I began enjoying the peace and quiet. With the radio filling the air with soft music and the darkness of night quickly gobbling up the light, I settled back in the seat and enjoyed the ride.

After a couple of hours of driving I was nearing the Kentucky Indiana border. I had been told that when I got close the border to wake him so he could navigate to the family home just outside of Bloomington.

As I saw the signs announcing the border cross, I made a decision to not wake him. I would take us into Indiana and wake him before we got to Bloomington. I just wanted a bit more time to drive.

I drove on into the night. Hours passed, and finally he awoke stretching and yawning. "What time is it?"

"Nearly midnight." I answered.

"Midnight? We should be there. Where are we?"

I told him how many miles outside of Bloomington we were. He looked at me, confused. "Pull over!" He demanded and I complied.

After much investigation, we realized that I was on my way to Bloomington, Illinois not Indiana. I was headed 200 miles away from our destination.

There was much exchange of heated words and anger on the 100 plus miles back across the state to our original destination. If only he had stayed in Illinois.

"How did you get lost? Why didn't you just wake me?" He yelled.

Yet, the truth was that the entire time I was driving, I had no idea I was lost. How was I to know there were two Bloomington's?

There are millions of people on this earth right now that are traveling in the wrong direction and have no idea they are lost. They obey the rules, pay their taxes, give to the charities and raise their kids to be kind and responsible yet the whole time they are on the road to Hell. It is a terrible thing to think about. I detest thinking of anyone that might be on their way to Hell but there are many. The Bible is very explicit. There is only one way to Heaven and that is through Christ Jesus and the acceptance of His atoning blood. Have you truly accepted Christ as your Savior? Are you on the right road?

Loose Pickles

> **Let no corrupt communication proceed out of your mouth, but that which is good to the use of edifying, that it may minister grace unto the hearers.**
> **Ephesians 4:29**

On one particular day many years ago when I was a vivacious toddler, my mom and dad took me to the Piggly Wiggly for our weekly shopping trip. As mom looked for bargains my daddy was put on "*corral Missy duty*". Marching up and down the aisles I went, never tiring, little shoes slapping on the tile of the old store, and strawberry pigtails bouncing. Behind me my father walked never a step or two away.

Down one particular aisle, my attention was stolen by the jars of pickles lined up neatly on the shelving. I then and even now, find a crunchy pickle to be a treat. I began to examine these jars with pickles crammed in them and decided I needed one. However, when my request was denied, I began to pitch a fit and run my bottom lip out. Budding with independence even then, I reached for a jar and tried to lift it. The result was I dropped it. Pickle juice splattered and dills rolled about the floor.

My daddy began scolding me and bent to lift me out of the briny mess. As he reached for me, I reached for a pickle. It was, after all a shame to leave them there.

"No!" Daddy bellowed and smacked the pickle from my grasp.

I shouted, "Daddy, don't beat me!" and plopped myself amid the broken glass and puddles of green juice. Lip run out as far as it could go, chunky little arms folded across my chest and tears swelling from my eyes, I intended to sit it out until I got my pickle!

A middle aged woman had stood just out a few feet away with a smirk as she watched this young man try to deal with a toddler. However, her smirk became a frightful look of disgust and anger when the darling little child plead for mercy.

Wham! Her purse landed on my dad's head. Again she reared back and the leather bag fell between his shoulder blades. She pulled back, ready to level another blow, but Daddy lifted me up and headed away from the attacker. The lady shrieked and yelled as she followed him to the front of the store, never missing an opportunity to weld her dissatisfaction at him with her handbag.

The manager of the store ran to intercept the vigilante housewife, mid rage. A curious crowd had begun to form at the front of the establishment. Whispers and questions mingled. Though no one knew exactly what had happened, they were sure this young man had been up to something heinous.

Why had I said such an outrageous thing? Leveled such a horrible thing at my gentle father?

Well, my grandmother would tease and ask me if my mommy and daddy were beating me? If I answered yes, hugs, kisses and a treat would be mine. It was a harmless game, just a bit of fun. She'd tickle and gnaw on my ear and call me her baby. My grandmother had never dreamed her harmless words would have created such a fuss.

Often, we do not guard what we say. It may be a harmless statement taken out of context. Maybe we are just sharing the news with a neighbor. No malice in our thoughts, just talking. Yet unguarded words can have damaging repercussions. Being careful with your words can spare a good deal of grief.

Dancing with the Son

I have what some may call a "bucket list". I make out a new list every five years on my birthday. First, I open the previous five year's list. I check off what I have completed and then make a new one. On one five year list I had, "...to learn to dance". I really wanted to learn how to perform real dance steps, not just jerk around the floor. I found a dance instructor and excitedly signed up.

As time came closer for me to begin my classes, my anticipation grew. I was determined and eager to add a checkmark to this item. Early to the session, I seated myself out of the way and watched as my classmates came in the studio. It did not take long for me to realize I was easily 20 years the junior of all my classmates and the instructor. In addition, they were all women.

The first class was very basic; we stood in front of the wall mirror and practiced our steps. At home, I practiced those moves every night in expectation of the next lesson. The week finally came that we would be paired and put those steps to the test.

My partner was an older gentleman, dressed impeccably, and sporting a fedora. He was a regular stand in for the classes. Just watching him dance with the other pupils, it was obvious, this man loved to dance.

I was nervous when my turn came. Sweaty palmed and trembling, I took his hand. "Relax now and just follow me." He said into my ear as the music began.

I stepped on his foot. Not once, not even twice, but repeatedly. I even kicked him in the shin. I was absolutely terrible. I went back to my position in the line as the next pupil took my place. I felt like a supreme failure. I was embarrassed, ashamed and I felt so bad for this gentleman. I just wanted to quit.

Before long, it was my turn again. I hesitated. He came to me and offered his hand. We tried again. It went much the same.

"Melissa, do not look at your feet. Look at me. Focus on me."

I nodded as the music began. I stepped on his foot immediately. He lifted my chin, "Follow me. Let me do what I should. Let me lead."

The music started and he began to ask me questions about my daughters, my job, and my life. As I answered him, I began to relax and I forgot to count the steps or even try to think ahead to the next move.

I was dancing.

After class this dear sweet man came to me. "Melissa", he said. "You got to learn to let the leader lead. There cannot be two leaders."

He was right, and his words went much further than the dance floor. I kept tripping all over the place because I could not relinquish the lead. When I finally relaxed, ignored the room of people and allowed the artiste to lead, we glided. We moved as one across the floor.

In our relationship with Christ, we have to let Him lead. Trust Him and follow. I find that when I focus on Jesus and not my feet, we glide.

Entertainment World

Love not the world, neither the things *that* are in the world. If any man love the world, the love of the Father is not in him.
1 John 2:15

A couple of Saturdays ago I was out doing my weekend errands. I had stopped for my weekly fill up at the gas station. As I filled my tank, I realized that I was staring at the TV screen in the pump. I looked up, and everyone else stood still, watching the screen with its advertisements and news snippets.

I went on to get the oil changed. Again, I found myself mesmerized by a TV screen strategically placed just a couple of feet from the driver's window. I looked across the bay, and every driver was staring at the TV screen.

I drove down the road and noticed the billboards that continually rotated advertisements to drivers. In the grocery I stood in line as a TV screen hung from the ceiling with commercials scrolling.

On the way home, I was almost hit in an intersection by a woman so busy texting that she ran the light.

Finally, at home I sat in the living room on my tablet looking for suitable Christmas gifts for my girls. I looked up and saw one child on the laptop playing a game and the other reading on her tablet. There we were all together in the same house, the same room, but in different worlds.

We have become a people that believe they have to be entertained all the time. Gone is the time that my parents and grandparents enjoyed on the porch being outside and together. Today everyone is connected but never so far apart. Relationships are made and maintained on Social Media. Information is constantly streamed so we do not have to think, or form our own opinions. Those too are canned and presented to us neatly and efficiently. No wonder this world suffers from extreme disconnect. While you and I are drawn into the Candy Crush, YouTube and Facebook worlds we cannot see those that are hurting around us. Our eyes, ears and minds are hypnotized by the colors and challenges of the cyber world, leaving us shrinking opportunities to share the Good News of Christ, help the needy and minister to the sick and dying.

We, and in this I mean me, needs to get out from behind the cell phones, tablets, and computers and reach out to the dying that are all around us. As long as we are "entertained" and "engaged" in worldly offerings, we are missing out on the opportunity to minister to those in need.

You cannot reach out to the homeless on the internet. You have to go to the place where they are and offer a hand, not an email address. You cannot minister to the elderly in the nursing home on *Twitter,* you have given more than *PayPal* information. These people need the eye to eye, hand to hand warmth that can only be given by you in person.

An app is no substitution to the tenderness of a smile and a heart willing to give.

We are Called to Walk in the Light

> But if we walk in the light, as he is in the light, we have fellowship one with another, and the blood of Jesus Christ his Son cleanseth us from all sin.
> *1 John 1:7*

Years ago, my parents had a house with woods in the front. At night, to be honest, it was very spooky. In the interest of safety, my father installed motion detection lights around the house. The first night, as everyone slumbered, the lights unexpectedly came on, flooding the front of the house in brilliant illumination. My father was awakened. He left his bed to peer out the window. He strained to see what had tripped the monitor, but he saw nothing. The lights faded and he went back to bed. However, before he could pull the covers over himself, the lights came on. On and off the lights continued for thirty minutes or more. Finally, they went off and stayed off.

The next day, Daddy checked the wiring and connections to make sure everything was hooked up correctly. He could find no fault. The very next night, about the same time as the previous incident, the lights came on waking my father from his sleep. This time he was determined to see what was causing the sensors to trip. Unfortunately, before he could descend the staircase the lights were extinguished.

He stood poised on the steps in the gloom waiting for several minutes, but nothing happened. Irritated, he stomped back to the bedroom. Just as he crossed to the bed, the lights flooded the yard and the bedroom. He took off down the stairs, stumbling down the steps and landing in the foyer. He reached for the knob and flung open the front door. The yard was illuminated like Fort Knox, and as he stood, his hand shielding his eyes, he scanned the trees for any movement. The lights faded, leaving him surrounded by the night's chill. Daddy stood on the stoop listening and peering into the black. Yet, all he heard was the silence and intermittent giggles from the leaves tickled by the breeze.

He waited, his senses eager and his heart pounding in his chest. The trees, bent and twisted, loomed around the driveway. The moon hid his face behind the gauzy gray of clouds.

Inky black night closed in on him. Yet, he continued to linger and listen. Then he heard it: a rustle of leaves. It was faint at first. So faint that perhaps, he thought, he had imagined it. But then the crunch came again, and it was louder. In response, the lights came on. That is when daddy saw what had been causing all the problems. Just a few feet beyond the driveway, the stark light revealed the white face of the villain. It was an opossum, frozen, mid step in the front yard. The lights went off, rustle of leaves, lights on and there stood the opossum just a few feet further across the yard. This chain of events continued until finally the opossum was out of range of the motion detectors.

The light scared that opossum. He felt comfortable in the dark, hidden and unseen. If he chose to move in the light, he knew everything would be laid bare. He retreated from the radiance and lived his life in the gloomy chill of night always in fear of the revealing light.

However, we have no reason to fear the light because we are forgiven and saved by the Grace of God through His Son Christ Jesus. Jesus is the Light, the Hope, and the Salvation of all that choose to step into the light.

Do you hide in the darkness? You do not have to. Come into the light.

His Stripes Have Healed You

Who his own self bare our sins in his own body on
the tree, that we, being dead to sins, should live unto
righteousness: by whose stripes ye were healed.
1 Peter 2:24

In the neighborhood that I grew up in was surrounded by pine trees. Ugly, spindly trees that were only good for dropping needles and cones. Every yard, up and down the streets had the giant prickly trees. They towered above the one story ranchers, dropping their hateful cones on yards, cars and homes. Not one yard was spared the rain of debris.

One day as I ran through the yard, barefoot and carefree, I stepped on a cone. It flattened under my foot, but not before its sharp spines penetrated my flesh. I fell to the ground, cradling my foot and wailing. Five spots ripe with blood oozed just inside my arch. I wiped away the debris and saw that 2 of the 5 bristles were still lodged in my skin. Wiping away my tears I returned to my play, limping.

Every day, my foot hurt more than the day before, but I did not want to tell my mom because I knew that she would want to dig out the spines. I did not want to submit to the painful removal of the thorns.

Instead, I endured the pain, keeping it silent. I ignored the hurt, waiting and hoping it would simply go away. I was willing to tolerate the discomfort. I accepted the limitations that the injury to my foot imposed on my life, refraining from my normal tree climbing and raucous play that I enjoyed so much.

Finally, on Sunday morning I was dressing for church and could not bear to wear my dressy shoe over my swollen and painful foot. Tearfully, I limped to my mom's room carrying my shoe. Removing my lacy sock I showed her the red puffed wounds left by the cone. She examined my infirmity and then set about cleaning and removing the spines.

It was painful. My foot was tender and I cried as she reached her tweezers into my flesh. Hot salty tears streamed down my face as my mom struggled to hold me still long enough to remove the infected pine bristles. It was a painful experience made worse by my choosing to hide it from my mother. If I had brought it to her when it had happened, then the pain would have been minimal compared to what I had forced myself to experience.

My mom asked me why I had waited so long to let her help me. My only answer was that I was afraid of the pain.

Many of us endure pain day in and day out. We limp along in our lives, choosing to push the nagging spines and thorns that affect our flesh aside. We allow our hearts to become infected rather than turn and face the discomfort. You do not have to endure the pain. You do not have to carry the thorns of betrayal, the spines of fear or the bristles of a broken heart. Instead, go to the Father and pour out your hurt, give him your pain and relinquish the fear that you carry. Allow

Him to heal your brokenness. To mend your wounds and remove the thorns that plagues you.

......by whose stripes ye were healed

Post-Christmas Grinch

I am writing something that may not be very popular, but I think several are thinking the same thing. I am glad that the Holidays are over. What a terrible thing to say, feel or even share, but it is the truth. I have stuffed so much ham, pumpkin pie, Cole slaw and chocolate covered things in my face that I am honestly sick of eating. I have juggled schedules and taken so many side dishes that if I see another green bean casserole I may lose my already strained brain.

I am sick of Christmas.

Christmas has become a contest of whose house is decorated the best, most beautiful wrapping paper and most expensive presents given. It really has become a constant revolving door of parties, luncheons and covered dish dinners. I have spent so much time running from function to function; that I have not spent my time reflecting on what all of the season is really about. I have not taken the time to read Luke 2 or meditate on the babe whose birth, life and death is really what the point of Christmas is supposed to be about.

In all my celebrating, I have lost my bearings. I worried more about getting a gift, getting to the party on time and what I will wear that I forgot to share the real gift. I lost my grip; I got caught up in the hoopla.

It is easy to lose your focus. To be distracted to the point that you forget why you are even where you are. Paul knew that. He reminded the congregation at Colossae to not spotlight the earthly things, but keep the light on Christ.

Though the trees have been thrown to the side of the road and the wreaths packed up for another year, we can continue to experience and share the hope and joy of Christmas throughout the year. Let us start this new year with our hearts tuned into Christ.

Happy New Year to all.

There is Always A
Silver Lining

When I was 15 we moved. This meant that my school zone changed and I would have to go to a new school. I was not happy to be leaving behind friends that I had known since kindergarten. My neighborhood and our neighbors I had known my entire life. It was difficult. I was resentful, angry and soon became bitter about the move. I attended the new school and carried all those feelings with me. Needless to say, I did not make a lot of friends, very little, in fact, during my tenure. I did not enjoy my high school years. I did not go to the dances, date or get involved. I just could not shake my feelings of anger at having to change schools. I allowed myself to dwell on the resentment and indulge the pity party that I seemed to be living in every day. I was not just angry at the new school, and my parents, I was angry that I did not have a say in it. I was mad because I could not control the situation. I was moved to a new neighborhood and new school and I had absolutely no say in the matter.

That move could have been something great. I could have made new friends, experienced new things, but I did not. All because I choose to concentrate my energy on being mad at the circumstance.

Throughout life, we are subjected to many changes. Changes that we would have never chosen for ourselves. It is hard not to become bitter when people in our lives, companies, health changes, and even the government makes alterations that we have no control over. Suddenly a situation modifies your entire life and you feel hopeless and trapped. You find yourself angry that you have been pushed into a position that you do not want.

When you find yourself somewhere you never wanted to be, read the story of Joseph in the Bible. (Genesis 37)

Joseph, the favorite son of a sheik, was dropped in a hole by his brothers. He was sold as a slave, serving as a house boy. He was also sentenced to life in prison for a crime he did not commit. Joseph never wanted these things to happen, but he did not spend his time wallowing in self-pity, instead, Joseph glorified God and worked as if for God rather than as a man's slave. Through it all, Joseph trusted that God was ultimately in control. He believed that he was where he was, not because of a mistake but because God had a purpose.

I find that as I get older and closer in my walk with Christ, that many of the disappointments, and suffering I experienced was not in vain. God can take any circumstances and bring good out of it and glory for Him. When you find yourself in those situations, focus not on the loss or the pain, but what will soon be gained and how the experience will be a benefit to you or someone else in your life. Know without doubt, that each and every one of our painful incidents has a purpose. Know that God, the ultimate author of your life and life itself has a plan.

Son Block

Back in the summer I went camping with another family. I love to camp. I love the smell of the fire early in the morning with the taste of coffee. Nothing beats being lulled to sleep by sounds of cicadas and the breeze in the trees. Watching the deer graze and listening to the kids scream and play in the lake. Camping has always been something I really enjoy.

This time I thought it would be fun to make some snacks and watch a movie one evening. We stretched out a bed sheet, lined up the camp chairs, got the Jiffy Pop going and passed out colas.

While everyone was searching for a prime locale, I worked to set up the projector and laptop. Of course, electronics and nature do not always mesh and I found myself struggling with the projector, smoke in my eyes and the quickly closing daylight. Finally, things were properly tethered and I started the movie. Disappointingly, the projector was projecting the picture into the trees. I got up and began to adjust the equipment. As I did so, all the kids began yelling that

I was blocking the movie. I was in the way of the projector and the screen was dark. Only the campfire lit the area.

Someone hollered. "Your daddy wasn't a glass maker, move out of the way!"

Everyone, including neighboring campers who decided to join us, began to laugh and join in hurling abuse and popcorn. I made a final adjustment and returned to my seat. The movie began.

Sometimes in my life, I find myself blocking the Light. I get busy with all the details, presentation and how I might be viewed that I stand in front of Christ and obstruct His light from reaching those around me. It is easy to do. Sometimes I do not realize that I am doing it. I forget because I lose sight of what is really important and begin thinking of myself.

In John 8:12, Jesus clearly says, "*he that followeth me shall not walk in darkness*." He says nothing of me standing in front, or leading the way. Instead, He tells me that in order for His light to eliminate the darkness in my life and those that I come in contact with, I must follow.

Do you follow the Light?

Emma the Terrible Rides Again

Emma the Terrible loves to ride in cars. She does not care where we go as long as she can see out the window. The other night I had to go to the pharmacy and Emma was doing her "*dancing bear act*" at the front door. How could I resist? We got into the car; she took her place in the crook of my arm and shook with anticipation of where our evening adventure may take her.

Once in the drive thru we waited patiently. Well, I waited patiently. Emma ran from window to window to bark at the other cars.

"Oh, how cute!" Many exclaimed as Emma tried to convey her vicious side. People pointed and smiled. Emma was not amused. Could they not see that she was doing her job; defending her mistress? Did they not tremble in the shadow of her fierceness?

Finally, our time had come. I pulled up to the window ready to tell the pharmacy tech my needs, when Emma went bananas at the sight of the man in the window. I pushed her back to the passenger's seat and holding her collar, gave my request.

He left to get the prescription and Emma went to the opposite window to bark at the other patrons. Upon his return, he extended the drawer to take my payment. When Emma saw that he had returned and had the audacity to employ this villainous drawer toward our car, she went completely berserk. Lunging at the drawer she snarled and bared her teeth, determined that the evil pharmacy tech know that she meant business.

He took the payment and placed the reason for our trek in the drawer.

The drawer slowly extended from the building, closing the gap between our car and the pharmacy. Emma had decided enough was enough and flung herself at the invader, catching the edge in her teeth, she began tug of war with the metal box. The gentleman in the window laughed and called over other co-workers who joined in his amusement. He dropped a dog treat in the drawer. I took the treat hoping that it would entice her attention away from the intruding drawer. I offered it, but her full attention was on the task of protecting me. I pried her loose and pulled forward and out into the darkness.

Emma would have nothing to do with the treat; she moved into the back seat still barking. She was determined to have the last word.

I often feel like Emma. I feel like I am jumping up and down. Trying to get someone's attention, to be taken seriously and heard. I think we all feel like that from time to time. Feel like Emma, small, insignificant in the big scheme. However, Emma does not let it stop her. Despite the laughing, the "cute" remarks and the bribe of a treat, Emma remains true to who she is and her duty. So should we. People may laugh when you share the Good News of Christ. They may ignore your offer to pray for or with them. They may not appreciate your gift. And that is ok. You keep telling people about Jesus and His sacrifice because the Word shall not return void.

A Picture is worth a Thousand Words

This week when I prayed for direction in writing the next Mustard Seed, I saw a picture in my mind. It was a photo that I had not thought of for a couple of years and one that puzzled me. Why would this photograph need to be the subject of a Seed?

The photograph in question is not a pleasant photo. It is in fact the only hard evidence I ever possessed of my husband's infidelities during our marriage. However, this photo represented much more than his sin, but more of mine.

I carried this picture for years in my wallet. When I changed wallets, I made sure it was transferred to the new one. Later, I moved the image to my jewelry box and there it stayed several more years. During a cleaning out I once again found the Polaroid and upon unfolding it found myself sliced with the knife of humiliation once more. I knew that holding on to this picture was wrong. Why was I so attached to it? I threw the picture in the trash and went on with my chores.

I am ashamed to tell you that I dug that picture back out of the trash and replaced it in the jewelry box. I just could not let it go. Eventually, I did destroy the photo and it is now gone but it did not go easy. I had to step back and really examine why I was refusing to let it go.

That picture was not so much about his injury to me but was more about me not forgiving him fully. I do not know about you, but forgiveness is not so easy for me at times. Oh I try. I pray and I say it out loud to the person but I can become angry all over again later.

Forgiveness is more than prayers and words, it is a deliberate action. You have to release the anger and humiliation. You have to or there is nothing to back up the words.

Jesus knew this. He did not just announce us forgiven; he paid the price and with deliberate action hung on that cross for you and me.

Do you hold on to the injury? Do you refuse to let it go? Release it and carry it around no more.

The Original Gossip Girl

> "A talebearer revealeth secrets: but he that is of
> a faithful spirit concealeth the matter."
> **Proverbs 11:13**

At a previous job years ago, I was hopelessly and eagerly hooked on gossip. I loved it. I craved it. It was a large portion of my attention each and every day. Nothing made me happier than hearing and dealing the daily dirt on those I worked with. I reveled in the drama of it all.

One particular day, a rather juicy tidbit had reached my ears. A manager was said to have been cavorting with a subordinate. My one and only goal was to find out who was the subordinate. Disappointingly, no one wanted to share that morsel with me. From contact to contact I went relentlessly questioning. As the workday was ending, in a last-ditch effort, I went to the one that would know, if anyone did. She was the information guru with her finger on the pulse of the company's trash.

I entered her office almost salivating at the impending possibility of learning the name of the secondary player in the affair. I began my interrogation.

You can imagine my frustration when she refused to share the name. I was not about to allow this to deprive me of my prize. I pushed a bit more.

"Fine!" She raised her voice. "It is you. Ok, you are the woman in the rumor."

I doubt that I could relay to you the cocktail of emotions that flooded me at that moment. However, I will tell you about one realization that felt like a stab. It was the name and faces of everyone that I had breathed out my malicious rumors about. I had no particular consideration for what my words may do to them. In that moment I was humiliated knowing that my coworkers and some I considered friends were spreading this lie about me. There was also some fear, what if somehow this lie made it to my husband or personnel.

It was this incident that brought the full weight of what I had been doing to others on my shoulders. Often times, we talk about co-workers, friends, neighbors, church members and others without examining what we are about to say and how these words can impact others. As Christians, we are called upon to be a source of encouragement to others in our lives. We are fully responsible for the words that pass over our lips. Let us remember to choose our words carefully and with what Jesus would find pleasing to hear from us.

> *"Set a guard, O Lord, over my mouth; keep watch over the door of my lips." Psalms 141:3*

Five More Minutes...Please!

In the morning the first alarm goes off at 5:20. Emma comes crawling out of the burrow she has made in the blankets and begins growling at the clock. I lift my leg and lower my heel on the snooze button. Emma returns to her burrow and I drift into the twilight. Nine minutes later, we replay the scene. On any given day, we may perform that act three, four or more times.

I just do not like getting up. Never have. You can ask my mom. In and out of my bedroom she would storm, and I, fully conscious, would lie there unwilling to relent and accept it was time to get the day going.

Today, however, as I lay in bed, drifting in semi-sleep, I thought about how much time I squander and the anxiety I put myself through with rushing about the house because I will not get up.

Procrastinators Anonymous has a reserved seat for me.

While thinking more on the subject I began to consider all the opportunities I may have wasted during my life due to simple laziness. How many chances I have missed to help people? How many hours did I flitter away that could have been spent encouraging and lifting people up? How much of my time is really wasted?

The Bible is explicit. We do not know when Jesus comes again, when we may be taken home or when the opportunity may no longer be there. God does not promise that you and I have tomorrow or even the next hour. Therefore, we should seize every moment of the day given to us to help one another. Treat others with kindness, share the Good News and seek out the Lord through His Word and in Prayer.

Let's not get caught sleeping.

A Table for One

I usually eat lunch at my desk. However, today I decided to go out.
It was beautiful; the sky so clear and blue for as far as you could see.
I got my lunch found a table in the window and began to eat. As I
watched the cars and people go about their business, I began to think
about me sitting in that restaurant, alone, enjoying my lunch with
just my thoughts.

You may be wondering what the big deal is. So you had lunch alone.
So What?

Well, there was a time not too long ago when I would have never
walked into a restaurant and ate alone. And that was not all. I never
wanted to be alone. In my home, at my job, going to the grocery
store, you name it. I did not want to be alone. I would do anything
to keep from being alone with my thoughts.

When you are alone, that is when the demons come. We all have
them. Whispering into our ears, winding doubt through the convo-
lutions of our brains. They are good, they've had a couple thousand

years to know just where to hit, where it hurts the most. Before I could not sit in a restaurant because all I could think about was what I *thought* people were thinking about me. I projected my insecurities and fears on them.

> *"Poor girl, she must have no friends."*
> *"What is wrong with her that no one wants to dine with her?"*

Many of us deal with insecurity in our lives. It is not exclusive to teenagers. It is also not just a woman's problem. Men deal with it too. It can, at times, be debilitating.

This epidemic of insecurity comes from people, like me, that measure themselves against the world. What does the world find attractive and desirable? I was so busy worrying about what complete strangers thought of me and trying to conform to a flawed standard that I was left empty, terrified and truly alone.

Once Jesus entered into my heart and loved me just the way I was, I began to see how I was looking to the wrong measure. It took time, quite a bit of time to squelch the destructive whispers that plagued me. Every time I thought negative things about myself and worried what people thought, I had to refuse to allow it to continue. In my thoughts I would immediately say, "I refuse to go back down that road." And I would focus on Jesus. In time, I trained myself to rebuke the harmful thoughts and look to Jesus for the positive and correct way of thinking of myself, and I also learned to see people as God sees them. Not as the world.

I challenge you to stop allowing those whispers, maybe of past sins or the abuse of someone in your life, continue to invade and rule your thoughts. Seek out the truth and accept it. You are a precious treasure of the Lord and He paid handsomely for your freedom.

I enjoyed my lunch today. Not what I ate, but the fact that Jesus set me free of the lies and destructive way of thinking that held me in its grip for so long.

He set me free and He wants to free you too.

Hit and Run

The sun had begun to fade, but not her heat—and sweat beads clung
to the curls that twisted from my head. Mom stood at the end of the
house, watering the parched flowers. Dad was to my right; he was
putting up the screen door on the porch.

I was bored. I had circled the house many times on my bike. I had
jumped and defeated every obstacle I had built. I needed a new challenge. I fiddled with my streamers, and I tried to think of something
else I could race, jump or run over.

However, as I scanned the back yard, I was disappointed.

My little brother was running all around the yard. I watched, waiting for something to happen. My eyes roved from my brother, to
mom, then dad. All three were completely involved in what they
were doing. Then it happened, my brother fell, smack down in the
grass. He lay in the lawn stunned by the fall. This is what I had been
waiting for. I stood up on the bike pedals and thrust my foot down

with all my might. The back tire spun before traction was captured and I shot down the pathway with every bit of steam I could muster!

However, I was disappointed. Unfortunately, a five year old really did not offer much of a speed bump or an opportunity to snatch some air. Dad came to my brother's aid. I dropped off my bike and ran to see his condition and declare my innocence. He was fine, a bit dazed, but fine. As daddy led him away the clear imprint of my tire was on his shirt.

It happens all the time. Brothers and Sisters stumble and fall. They get themselves in a bind, in trouble, in jail, in divorce court or the unemployment line. Just when they need someone to come alongside to help them, to lift them up, they get someone anxious to run them down.

As Christians, we are to come alongside each other. We are not to judge or spout the "I told you so" speeches. Galatians 6:1 is certainly a model for how we should help one another. We are to come alongside to help restore them, and to do so in a spirit of meekness.

Of course, that is not so easy. However, the Bible tells me to address it with meekness; to be gentle and mild.

The next time a brother or sister in Christ falls, do not be so quick to run them down. Instead, come along side and lift them up.

The Shoelace Express

Driving home in the rain the other night, I had a memory pop up in my mind. I began to giggle, and then I laughed as I remembered. I knew these two guys probably more than twenty years ago now. These two came up with some of the craziest ideas I had ever heard. It was always some sort of get rich quick scheme.

One day they went in together and bought this rusted out, pitiful excuse for a car. They had worked out how they could fix it up and sell it for a huge profit. Somehow they believed they could make this rattletrap a pot of gold.

Surprisingly, they got it to run. Enthused with this triumph, they decided that they would drive it around the city one afternoon. Often, as it does in the summer, a storm blew in just as they were driving back from their jaunt. Fat, warm rain drops plummeted the city, and the car.

While inventorying the car's working versus non-working items, they had both failed to check the condition of the windshield wipers. They did not work.

There was only one thing to do, wait out the rain. Well, that's what I would have done.

Instead, each man unlaced both their shoes and used the laces to tie to the windshield wipers. They stood under the overpass and practiced the rhythm they would need to imitate the wipers. Confident they could work together and get home, they started out on the highway.

"Pull." The first man yelled. "Pull." The second man echoed.

The first half mile things worked ok, except that the laces were too short to pull from the comfort of their seats. Instead, each man leaned out of the car windows to be able to pull their wiper. Back and forth, they struggled as the warm, stinging rain pelted their faces. There was pulling and tugging, cussing and cursing, but they kept yanking on those shoelaces. However, soon they began to pull out of the turn and argue. Finally, a lace broke and now only one man struggled to pull the wipers. Under the strain the second lace broke as well.

There was no other choice but to pull to the side of the road where they continued to argue. Finally, the passenger got out of the car and began to walk down the highway in the pouring rain his shoes flopping after him.

There is nothing easy about working together, especially in the face of adversity. Yet, Paul pleads with the Church at Corinth to be of like mind, speaking the same thing to protect against division. Just like in the time of Paul, today, Christians still find it hard to be of like mind and joined together in the same purpose. As a follower of Jesus, we should be burdened for the poor and needy, compassionate to the sick, kind to the friendless bold in sharing Christ's love to a dying world. However, working in unison in the church is as hard as it was for these two men.

In order for us to share the common goal, we have to have the mind of Christ. What is important to Jesus should be important to us. What he taught us during His time here on earth should be our collective goal and what we pass to those we meet.

Don't let it Skew Your View

Do you ever feel like screaming? Falling down on the floor and kicking like a two year old? I hope at least some of you are thinking "yes" or I must look pretty silly. This has been an awful week. One irritation after another, I have a sick child, work has been hectic, the house is a mess, I have a neighbor that has become a thorn in my side and I do not have enough money to pay all the bills due this week. I just seem to be spinning in circles trying to handle each catastrophe after another. I am being attacked from every direction. Every time something else happens, I just want to scream and run away! I think if one more person, child, neighbor or coworkers presents another issue for me to handle, well I may just blow into a million pieces.

I have been working hard at keeping a positive attitude. I have been praising the Lord through it all. However, today, well, I could hear the moan of my hull. I was beginning to buckle under the onslaught.

So I prayed, "God, help me hold on! Give me the grace to muddle through." I put on a smile and strolled across the parking lot. I sat at my desk, distracted and worry kept my brow furrowed. I was determined not to let these problems tear me down.

I breathed more prayers.

Suddenly, my phone buzzed. It was a text message. Oh dear, what would it be now? With apprehension I tapped the text app and read.

It is funny how one thing can adjust our attitude or our mood. You see, someone so dear to me texted me that they were cancer free. Boy, that put it all in perspective. Praise God, He's in control. He's in charge no matter what is going on. He has me, He has you and we are going to be ok. We just have to keep it in perspective.

This life is full of pressure, problems, heartache, pain and disappointment, but that's not the big picture. That's just a small piece and we have to back up and take it all in view.

If you seem to be plagued with issues and problems, do not allow it to skew your view! Keep your eyes fixed on the Lord.

Resting the Soil

My grandmother always had the most beautiful and prosperous garden in our community. She spent many hours in the garden before the sun came up and into the dusk, tending, watering and nurturing the plot. I enjoyed helping her as much as I could and I think she enjoyed it too.

One season as planting time was quickly approaching, Nanny was preparing the ground. However, there was one piece of the garden that she had not measured out. It was a section that usually had wonderful sweet corn. I asked her why she was not planting in that area. She replied, because it is time to let the soil rest. Why, I wondered, would dirt need a nap?

Over the years, I watched her rotate crops and at times allow some plots to stay bare for a season. Nanny knew that the key to a good crop was how she prepared, nurtured and rested the soil.

The same is true of us. In order to produce good fruit, we must take care of the soil of our hearts. We must nurture it with God's Word and we must take time to rest. Lately, I have been running myself beyond what I should. I have been missing sleep, not eating like I ought to and finding myself so busy I have neglected to take time to read my Bible. In doing so, I have found myself ill-tempered and physically drained. The fruit in my life is suffering. My soil had been leached and I am producing bad fruit.

As I prayed about my dilemma my mind was filled with the memories of my grandmother's lush garden and the years of fruit and vegetables that we enjoyed from it. Particularly the memory of the napping soil lingered in my thoughts. In order for us to produce good fruits for others to see and enjoy, we must first take care of the soil.

As we enter into a new season, I ask that each one of you take the time to nurture your soil in prayer, Bible study and rest.

Loves Me, Loves Me Not

And why call ye me, Lord, Lord, and
do not the things which I say?
Luke 6:46

I asked my daughter to do the laundry while I was working over the last couple of days. The next morning when I went to get my shower there were no towels. I had to dig out a beach towel. I was irritated and that was putting it mildly. Later that evening when my daughter went to take a shower, I waited for the inevitable holler.

The water went off, a pause and then the *"momma"* shout. "Momma! I need a towel!"

I went to the bathroom door, a dripping hand extended out. I handed her a roll of paper towels.

I know that my daughter loves me, yet sometimes I question it. I ask her to do certain things and she does not do it.

Why?

Well, I assume the same reason I do not do what God wants me to do. Because I have things on my mind, I forget, I get focused on other stuff and then frankly, sometimes I just do not want to.

When my daughter was confronted with the opportunity to go to a friend's house to play video games or stay home and help mom out, she took the video game. She also paid the price and dealt with the consequences. Her actions also impacted her sister and I.

Though a day without clean towels is rather mild, the same principle applies to other incidents in our lives when we chose to not adhere to the commandments and be diligent in doing what the Lord has asked us to do.

Throughout the New Testament, Jesus made a point of asking the disciples if they loved Him. He also reiterated that *if we love him, we will obey him.*

I think that Jesus stressed the love, because He knew that if we truly loved Him it would be our desire to be obedient. Not out of fear of retribution but out of our love and devotion to Christ. If we are obedient but do it out of obligation, guilt or fear, then our actions mean nothing to the Lord. However, the act of obedience with a heart of love is certainly sweet to the Father.

If we love the Lord, then let us be obedient in all things.

Down But Not Out

My parents have a crepe myrtle in their yard. It is not your ordinary myrtle. This tree is over 100 years old. She is massive, and her boughs curtsy with copious clusters of magenta blooms. Her fragrance wafts on the warm summer breezes. She stands proudly at the edge of the woods, her leaves unfurled to capture the nurturing light.

This beautiful giant has weathered time, been through storms, had limbs break under the weight of snow and ice, suffered drought, and enjoyed times of abundance. She has seen the land change, people come and go, yet she remains.

In the aftermath of the 2011 tornado, this titan was found on her side, motionless, not even a breeze to ruffle her boughs; she seemed suspended in the piercing silence. Limbs broken, root ball exposed, it seemed that she would never sway to the music of the wind or offer her blooms for food and shelter to the insects and birds of the valley. It was distressing to see her lay beneath my shadow after the years of enjoying her shade.

In the days that followed, mom and dad were busy with the task of cleaning up after the twister. Up and down the road, smoke boiled from offering pyres as they consumed splintered and shredded wood. The sky above the valley was a haze and the sound of chainsaws and trucks rumbled well into the night.

On hope, my mom asked if the dozer guy could upright the fallen giant. He righted her and mom and dad staked her. Only time would tell if she would survive.

Summer came, fall followed, and winter held the valley in icy suspension. The myrtle remained tall, staked to the ground and we waited.

In early spring, the myrtle presented shiny green new leaves from the tips of the limbs. There was hope.

Late spring passed into summer and though her blooms were not as robust, she bloomed. The bees, hummingbirds and insects came to drink the nectar, and she welcomed them with her brilliant petals.

This tree survived because her roots were deep. She was anchored, and she had held on to the ground with her fingers dug deep into the soil and though she was blown over, her roots held fast. She was knocked down, but she was not out.

We are much the same. If we do not have our roots built up in Christ Jesus we have nothing to hold on to when storms and trials come our way. Jesus is the constant, no matter what we face; we know that He is with us always. Storms come and go, people drift in and out of our lives, but God is the same yesterday, today and tomorrow.

What are you rooted to?

Almost Swept Away

I saw the ocean for the first time when I was four. Though, I had no idea of the magnitude of the sea that stretched out before me, I fell in love with it.

Even if my recollections of that first encounter are hazy and more of emotion rather than actual memories, I had an experience that never left me.

I do not know how long my daddy and I had been playing in the waves. I do not know when the waves began to charge upon the sand in quicker succession.

White foam rushed, as if chased, so quickly that I swooned with dizziness. As the sky boiled with an incoming storm my daddy said we had to go. I know I was disappointed; I never wanted to leave the beach. As we turned to walk out of the water, a wave reached out of the sea and grasped me.

I remember the gritty sand that scraped my skin and my face as the wave pressed me down. I can close my eyes even now and see the swirl of white foam, green sea water and sand. Mostly, I remember the suspension of thought and the loss of all control. My body rolled, water filled my nostrils as I was spun in the surf. I was helpless, unable to right myself, and nothing to grab on to. I was at the mercy of the sea unable to influence the waves that had swept me away.

What I am sure was a split second in reality, for me seemed like several moments of turmoil and uncertainty as I twisted, helpless, in the churning surf. Then, as it seemed I would spin away into the depths, my ankle was clasped and my daddy lifted me out of the waves. I coughed, water spewed and the back of my head burned as the water drained from my nostrils. I flung my arms around his neck and he carried me out of the breakers.

Often I feel like that in my life today. I feel as though I have been swept up and out by sudden waves. I am suddenly lost in the swirl, helpless and drowning.

However, God, our Father is there. He is there to reach into the depths of our trouble, our pain, our confusion and the darkness we have sunk to. He reaches for us and HE WILL CARRY YOU OUT OF THE WAVES.

Never doubt, no matter how fast or deep the sea of your problem, pain, despair, and worry, His hand can find you!

Papa and the Lawnmower

**But God shows his love for us in that while
we were still sinners, Christ died for us.**
<u>Romans 5:8</u>

I would imagine that one of the best perks of retirement is sleeping late and the time you have to spend with your family. My dad is new to retirement, but one thing he really enjoys is spending time with his three year old grandson. It is evident that these two love each other very much.

When I was growing up, my dad played with us, whether it was board games, riding bikes or just wrestling on the floor. It appears that has not changed. Unfortunately, one thing has changed. My dad does not get up and down as easily out of the floor.

Just like the rest of us.

One afternoon, my dad and nephew were playing around the house. My nephew wanted to play cars. He asked my dad to bend over and push the cars with him. The energetic youngster took off, hands on the cars, bent at waist and running on his feet around the coffee table. As much as my dad wanted to join in, his back and knees protested loudly and he had to sit the race out.

It was immediately apparent that the three year old was very disappointed that Papa could not play cars with him. My father tried to interest him in sitting on the floor and pushing the cars around but it would not do. He wanted Papa to join him in the race.

After a few minutes of expressing his frustration, my nephew took Papa by the hand and asked him to go upstairs.

"Where are we going Buddy?" Papa asked. "To play race car," my nephew answered. "Papa can't play. His knee hurts."

"I know." That was all he said as he led Papa into the room. Once inside, the youngster pointed to a toy in the corner. "Papa you have that."

"Oh, you want to play lawnmower?"

"No Papa. That is your race car."

He wanted my dad to play with him so much, he found him something that Daddy did not have to bend over to race. For the next couple of hours, Papa raced his lawn mower against the cars.

When my dad told me this story as we sat on the porch together on Easter I knew that this was a Mustard Seed. Just like my nephew loves and desires to be with my dad, God loves and desires to be with you. That child was willing to meet my dad where he was. God is the same with you and me. He meets you where you are.

Often in my past, I would think:

I will go to church when I quit smoking.
I will go to church when I get out of this relationship.

We always seem to think we can make ourselves good enough to be accepted.

Just like this child exhibited, you are acceptable the way you are. God wants to meet you; wherever that may be. You may be dealing with an addiction; you may be wrapped in depression, you may be stuck in a sin and do not know how to get out of it.

I think of the woman at the well. (John Chapter 4) Jesus did not wait for her to leave the man she was living with; instead, He came to her in the midst of her sin and offered the living water that only He can give.

No matter where you may be; He is ready to meet you right where you are.

Gutter Ball

I slid out of the front seat of my friend's van proudly toting my new acquisitions from the thrift store. I had a new dish drainer and a bowling ball. Swinging the ball beside me, I bounced up the front steps. My eldest daughter met me at the door. She glanced from the globe that hung from my fingers to my face.

"Mom? What is that?"

I raised my hand to eye level and announced with great enthusiasm, "It's a bowling ball."

"Yeah. What are you going to do with a bowling ball?"

"I saw on the internet, the cutest garden ladybugs made from bowling balls!"

"Isn't that what you said about the other bowling ball?"

"Yes." I answered. I had completely forgotten about the ball that sat in the corner of the barn. "Now I can have a bee and a ladybug!" I smiled as if it had been part of my grand plan the entire time.

"Mom how many projects have your started? That bowling ball has been in the outbuilding for a couple of years! Don't bring home anything else until you finish something."

"I'm gonna work on them this weekend." I replied, as I unloaded spray paint from a plastic bag that hung causally from my elbow.

She groaned and walked back into the house. I dropped the bowling ball in the garden next to the porch. It is still there.

As I passed the purple orb this morning I noticed that it was partially hidden by growth that was quickly working to swallow it into the weeds. I thought back on my daughter's inquisition of the use and fate of extraneous bowling balls around the property. Could she have a point? I scanned the yard. I had bags of dirt, potted plants and some bricks on the sidewalk; pallets in the barn a pile of bamboo from a neighbor's yard and a healthy assortment of empty pots at the gate. I realized that I was full of plans and ideas, yet I was getting nothing done. I had not dedicated the necessary time to each project to complete.

Naturally, as I wrote this I was thinking of procrastination. Yet afterward, I asked God what the message of this story was. He took me in a different direction. Commitment is the underlying theme. We as human find it hard to commit, whether it is a diet, a project, a spouse or our relationship with Christ. Being fully committed to Christ means sacrifice, devotion, fearlessness and courage. That's a tall order in the world we live in today.

In Galatians 2:20, Paul stated that he had been crucified with Christ; meaning that he had put away everything contrary to Jesus and committed himself fully to his service and the spreading of the good news of Salvation. He vowed to live in Christ and by faith, not just speaking of the salvation but alive in it.

Are we to be less committed in this time that we live? No, if anything we should be more committed; faithful to fearlessly sharing the Word with the lost and dying in this world. I cannot help but wonder if I cannot commit to complete a yard project, how can God trust me to be committed enough to fearlessly present the truth to those around me. Our lives should be lives of commitment to the principles and commandments that Jesus taught in his time here. If we are not committed how can we presume to win others to Christ? Without a full and unwavering dedication, we have nothing.

Do you live a life of commitment to Christ, to the needy, to the dying and the lost?

Sometimes, It's Just Not about You

Now ye are the body of Christ, and members in particular
1 Co 12:27

Earlier this week, I had a business lunch. As I entered the restaurant I spied a couple that I knew. In fact, it has been 26 years since I had seen them. I was nervous, I wanted to speak to them and tell them how much I had benefited from my time that I was employed with them. I stood in the foyer and struggled with the decision should I go on to the table or address the couple.

I crossed the room, timidly approaching their table. I introduced myself. They looked from me to each other and then back. They returned no smile and held me in suspicion. Nervously, I told them that I had worked for them over 25 years ago and that I wanted to thank them for everything I learned. Still, they did not seem to know me.

I addressed the gentlemen and thanked him for teaching me how to be professional and do my work with diligence. He removed his hat and tears began to become visible behind his glasses.

"You've made my day, young lady."

I turned my attention to the lady and thanked her for her kindness and the book she had given me. I still had it and had read it several times. I told her it had been a very big help in my life and I cherished her inscription. She stood and hugged me.

Even after I said these things, neither seemed to be able to place me, however, both thanked me for sharing with them. Over my shoulder as I went to join my party, I saw them smile one to another, and the wife patted the husband's hand.

I had the business lunch. However, in the back of my brain the idea that they had not remembered me kept nagging.

As the afternoon wore on, I found myself returning to the disappointment of not being known again and again. I will tell you that I was bothered by it. I was bordering on being offended. I just could not let it go. So I mentioned it to my friend.

"Well," she said. "Maybe it doesn't matter. I mean you said what you needed to say and I bet that they needed to hear it. You said that the gentleman seemed truly touched."

Yes, I thought to myself, maybe it was not important that I was not recognized. Maybe that chance meeting was about them and not me.

Often times, it is hard to remove ourselves from a situation. Let's face it; we all want to be acknowledged. We all want the recognition and credit we feel is due. Yet, well sometimes it has absolutely nothing to do with us. I venture that the chance meeting and the overwhelming desire to share my thoughts and feelings with this couple was more about an encouragement from God for them rather than about me getting validation by being recognized after 25 plus years.

Sometimes you are just the mouthpiece, an instrument of God. We are all called to be used by God to reach out to those in need, pain and lost. We are the hands, the feet, and yes, even the mouth of Christ. As the body of Christ, we are to be ready to deliver comfort, hugs, smiles, acts of kindness, share wisdom, provide food, give money, speak encouragement and never miss an opportunity to thank those in our lives.

I think that if we thought more about the benefit to the other person by our willingness to share of ourselves, we may be less worried about our own compensation. Unfortunately, that is one of today's biggest issues among Christians. Many of us are looking for the acknowledgment rather than releasing ourselves to be used by Jesus. I have heard it many times that we are to be Jesus with skin on. That is exactly what we should strive for because sometimes it just isn't about you.

The 360 View

"Examine yourselves, whether ye be in
the faith; prove your own selves.
II Corinthians 13:5

Ah, summer. Pool parties, cookouts, sunburns, sandals and swimsuits. It is a great time! Well, except for the swimsuit search.

Last Saturday, I was out searching for a bathing suit. Gone are the days I worried about what suit would leave the least tan lines and what was cute, now I worry about getting the most spandex psi, (pounds per square inch). I found what I thought would be suitable and with great trepidation made my way to the dressing room.

As I fought with the springy fabric, I wished that I had brought a shoehorn or maybe a crowbar. Finally, I squeezed into the spandex maiden, and while drawing in shallow breaths I gawked at the reflection before me. As I stood in the middle of the dressing area, my eyes roved from mirror to mirror to yet another mirror. I was presented a 360 degree view. There is something very sobering about seeing yourself **all** at the same time.

I am about to share something with you that is a bit delicate but nonetheless important to this illustration. I am fully aware that I am a robust woman, yet my mental self-image did not compare to the reflection before me. Because I had not had the view of the multiple mirrors I was oblivious of my true proportions.

As the afternoon wore on, I gave up and headed home. As I drove, I found myself questioning how I could have not been fully cognizant of my body. Until I had stood before the mirror and seen myself from all angles I was unaware.

I continued to mull over this revelation and as I did so I realized that many of us may be unaware of our shortcomings especially in our spiritual and Christian lives. As a Christian I have professed a belief in Jesus, but does my life match my profession? Do people see the image of Christ in me? If my life does not conform to the gospel, it negates any claim to standing firm in the faith.

In 2 Corinthians, Paul tells the congregation to "***Examine yourselves, whether ye be in the faith; prove your own selves.***" When Paul said examine, he used the Greek verb peirazo, meaning to tempt, try or test. Paul was challenging the Corinthians to test themselves to see whether they are in the faith. The kind of testing Paul envisioned was that which proves the worth or genuineness of something

We are to prove ourselves daily. We have to be willing to look at the 360 view. It is not always pleasant to take full stock of ourselves but we must. In doing so, you and I can become more in tune with the needs of others and more open to the guidance of the Holy Spirit.

The challenge of introspection sounds foreboding and frankly not very much fun. Yet true profession of faith should be characterized by "love, joy, peace, patience, kindness, goodness, faithfulness, gentleness and self-control" (Gal 5:22). As Paul challenged the church at Corinth, I want to challenge you to test yourself. Does your faith produce the fruit of Galatians 5:22? Examine your heart and how you live your life before others.

The Lunch Hour

> [34] *A new commandment I give unto you, That ye love one another; as I have loved you, that ye also love one another.* [35] *By this shall all men know that ye are my disciples, if ye have love one to another.*
> *John 13:34-35*

I have been anxious over the last few weeks. In fact, as my closest friends read this opening line, they are rolling their eyes and nodding. Each one of them have listened to me whine. Why, you are wondering? Because my oldest daughter is spreading her wings. She has a car, a job, a debit card and is ready to get out into the world. I, however, want to tuck her back under my wing.

The other day she called me at work. She asked me to go to lunch and came by to pick me up. As we sat across the table from each other I smiled. My first born had become a beautiful young woman.

I enjoyed our lunch. We talked about trivial things, and she asked my advice and opinion on some other things. We laughed and shared. I was thankful that out of all the choices she had that day, she chose me. She could have gone and done anything but she chose a lunch hour with mom.

I returned to work, a mix of sadness for the child lost and joy for the woman found. As I thought about the happiness that lunch brought to me, I thought about how God must feel. He is there day after day waiting for us to choose time with Him. Waiting for us to turn off the TV, slow down, and forego the many social events we go to, the rush of our lives. He just waits.

I imagine the joy that I felt is the same that God feels when His children slow down and look up. When we forego what the entire world has to offer to find a quiet moment to just talk with Him. Tell him about our day, ask for his advice and then listen.

Jesus while he was here on earth, had to remove himself from the world, the crowds the disciples and all the demands that he faced so that he could share with God. It was this time of fellowship that gave him the strength and direction. We also need to find those quiet times when we can come before the Lord and fellowship.

Being a Christian is not about rules, robes and rituals. It is about relationships; a relationship with God, relationship with family and friends. It is about fellowshipping and being there when you are needed whether by a friend or a stranger. It is sharing love. We get so worried about the rules and our image we miss the point. Do we follow the commandments and live upright lives? Yes. But not as the Jews did under the Law of Moses, but as His redeemed. No longer are we under legalism of the Pharisees.

At the Last Supper Jesus said, *"**A new commandment I give unto you, That ye love one another; as I have loved you, that ye also love one another.**"*

If we as Christian took this **New** commandment and truly committed to following it, then all the other commandments would be followed also. If we loved one another, there would be no adultery, murder, lying or stealing.

Above all things love one another, as Christ loved you. Find time to fellowship; fellowship with God, with friends, family and those in need. Live the new commandment.

GPS-Gone Past Stop

I am suffering from what I call *Vacation Hangover.* It is where I stayed up late every night, ate rich foods, rode roller coasters I should have reconsidered and consumed too much caffeine, sugar and gravies.

I have been lying in my bed waiting for the Tylenol, ibuprofen and Kaopectate cocktail to take effect. To entertain myself, I have been reflecting on the past week. I truly enjoyed my vacation. I can say with confidence that it was a smooth experience, except for the GPS. I have renamed it; Gone Past Stop.

Before we took to the highway, we synchronized our GPS and launched our vacation. Up I-75 I led our convoy. We took 75 to I-40 and then the 407 exit to Gatlinburg and Pigeon Forge. Smooth sailing until my GPS barked instructions to take a left on 411. I pulled into the turn lane and waited for the green arrow. As I did so, my phone began to ring.

"Hello."

"What are you doing?" "My GPS said turn here." "Mine says go straight."

We got the green arrow and with flasher on we pulled to the side of the busy street and conferred. Back and forth we went. "But the GPS says…"

Finally, I decided to follow her. She had driven to Gatlinburg many more times than I. We continued to follow the instructions from the little box to a dead-end road when we were trying to find our condo. After a kind passerby set us straight we found our way to our lodgings.

On the way home we had decided to stop off in Knoxville to enjoy an Egyptian exhibit. On the advice of the GPS, we found ourselves at the wrong hotel and I was in the parking lot of the new Walmart. This piece of technology was anything but helpful.

We ditched the GPS and took the map as our guide.

As I lay here I am thinking about how everyone is trying to get somewhere. All humans at some time in their life question their purpose, their origins and a desire to find truth. Some search for it in other people, others in alcohol, drugs, money or power and still more look to a more spiritual plane. Even in spirituality some search in Buddhism, Hinduism, Islam, and Judaism, mysticism, and tarot cards. Some rely on psychology and education for the answers.

While many search, going from place to place and person to person, we have the direct path. In John 14, Jesus is comforting His disciples after He has told them of His impending departure.

Naturally, they are upset, and distraught at the thought of being separated from Jesus. In verse 5, Thomas asked: "Lord, we know not whither thou goest; and how can we know the way?"

And Jesus answered: "I am the way, the truth and the life; no man cometh unto the Father but by me."

There is only one way to enter into heaven and into the presence of God and that is through Christ Jesus. It is His sacrifice that leads the way to salvation.

This world is full of people searching for the peace and salvation that can only be satisfied by Jesus.

Will you show them the way?

You, Me and the Bear Makes Three

The fear of the LORD *is* the beginning of knowledge: *but* fools despise wisdom and instruction.
Proverbs 1:7

After a long day of travel, GPS snafus and loading and unloading cars I was ready for a bit of relaxation. I climbed between the cool sheets and took out my new book. I had not the opportunity to even warm the covers when someone began pounding on the door.

Cautiously, I peered out the window to see a woman standing at our condo door. I left my room and tiptoed down the hall. My eldest daughter stood in the threshold listening as the woman's excited words flew from her mouth. Upon seeing me, she seized the opportunity to tell the story again with equal enthusiasm.

I trailed behind the animated woman out onto the walkway and followed the direction of her finger. That is when I saw what all her fuss was about. As darkness crowded in on the last streak of light, a lone black bear was eagerly working to get his paw into the animal proof dumpster. It was easy to see he was determined to dine. I ran back in and banged on my friend's door, I knew she would want to see it too.

Returning to the breezeway, I found a spot on the railing with the other spectators. Oblivious, or more accurately unconcerned by us, he continued to dig into the garbage until he found the remnants of pizza. Once the pizza had been devoured he climbed down and strolled across the parking lot, weaving between cars and trucks.

As I watched this powerful animal silently move into the woods and evaporate to darkness I felt the hollow of my gut move. I feared this beast.

Later, as I spoke with my daughter about it, I attempted to explain that the fear I spoke of was not one of me being afraid of the animal but rather being cognizant of his power and potential. I respected the bear and acknowledged his power.

In Proverbs, and several other references in the Bible, we are told *"to fear the Lord"*. However, the word fear in this context refers to respecting and revering the Lord. Unfortunately, fewer and fewer people fear the Lord. They, including many proclaiming Christians, have lost respect for our Almighty Father. They fail to acknowledge His majesty and greatness.

I am guilty of this too. Most nights I do not make it to my knees, rather I lay in the bed offering lazy prayers. I fail to come before the King in the manner my King deserves. I fail to acknowledge Him as God the Almighty.

We see it in our churches that concentrate their message on His love and friendship, yet fail to teach of His majesty, Omnipotence, Justice and as the all-powerful I AM.

It has become a sad part of our society as respect for God, His people and Word is reduced to being just another religion and Jesus no more than an icon. The more I thought about it the more convicted and sad I became. Maybe the world views our Lord and Savior with such a trivial manner because we do too.

I encourage you to take time this week and examine how you recognize our Lord. How do you treat the savior of your soul? Is it with reverence that He deserves or is with the casual attitude of the world?

Evidence of Things Unseen

I have been attempting to declutter my kitchen. I do not like to part with things as you may remember from a previous Mustard Seed. So today I have agonized over which skillets to keep because I have eight.

Who needs eight skillets?

I began to shake as I compared roasters. I have two roasters, but only one oven. Logically, it seems simple. But the emotional side, the insecure part, is reluctant to even consider parting with the extra roaster or skillets.

As I sat on the stool in the middle of my kitchen looking at all the pots, pans, roasters, kitchen appliances and dishes it occurred to me how easily as humans we attach to inanimate objects. I can tell you where I got almost all of my dishes and cookware, or who gave them to me. Many like my grandmother's casserole have dear memories attached. And, as strange as it may be, I find comfort in having my things around me. I can see them, touch them and I know exactly where they are.

I think that is why faith is so hard for most. As humans, we feel a need to have something to hold, something that gives us a sense of comfort and security. It begins with the pacifier and continues from there. We just seem to believe we need something to physically have and hold.

I never really understood why the Israelites in Exodus freaked out and fashioned a calf to worship while Moses was on the mountain speaking with God. (Exodus 32:1-6.) Why would they do something like that after God brought them out of Egypt? He defeated the Pharaoh, parted the sea, fed them manna, and provided water. They were led by a cloud by day and a fire by night and yet when it became silent, they literally freaked out. Unfortunately, I am no better. God has brought me through many things. Intervened when I thought all was lost, however, when my prayers go unanswered, I tremble. I go to the Bible, more prayer, and then a friend and so on. I get freaked out when I have to wait on the Lord to respond.

However, that is what faith is, isn't it? Hebrews 11: 1, "Now faith is the substance of things hoped for, the evidence of things not seen." It isn't the things that we can touch or look at. It isn't the eight skillets, its faith. It is faith in the dark hours. Faith believes when everyone else has given up. It is knowing that God is in control, that God has not forgotten us. That is what you and I need to hold on to. Not the things of this world. Not the trappings that turn our heads so easily.

If you are going through something right now that is pressing on you, hold on to your faith in God. I know that you are tired, maybe confused. However, please know that this "affliction, which is but for a moment", God is working to deliver you. Your faith, if in God, is not misplaced.

Root-Bound Rupert

*[13] Those that be planted in the house of the LORD shall flourish in the courts of our God.
[14] They shall still bring forth fruit in old age; they shall be fat and flourishing;*
Psalm 92:13-14

I am sure this will come as no surprise to any of you that I name all my plants. In fact, our story today is about Rupert. Rupert is a Chamaedorea Elegans, but you probably know him better as a Parlor Palm. Rupert is a grumpy palm and has been for several seasons.

On my way out the door the other day, I noticed that Rupert had offered no new growth this season. However, Bert, the Cat palm was flourishing.

Once I got home, I checked Rupert over. He appeared healthy. However, he was not thriving. He had become stagnant. I got out my books; Rupert was suffering from being root bound.

Early Saturday morning I got my potting table out, my garden tools and gloves. I took Rupert to the table. I tapped his pot, smacked the bottom and then gripped the palm at the base and pulled. I pulled again, but Rupert held fast. I tucked the pot under my arm and really gave it a tug, but still the pot remained unyielding. Frustrated, I sat down on the steps and placed Rupert's pot between my knees and using two hands pulled with all I had. Finally, the pot relented and hit the concrete with a hollow thud.

I lifted him up on the table and marveled at the naked Rupert. No dirt fell from him and his roots held the form of the pot. Knobby fingered roots tangled back on themselves, and twisted into a mass void of dirt. Rupert was not producing new growth because he had exhausted the nutrients of the soil and was effectively just being sustained by water.

Christians get like Rupert sometimes. We get root bound. We go to church on Sunday and park in the same slot, we sit in the same pew we talk to the same people, the plate comes round we drop our ten percent and then go home, content to wait to do it again next week.

However, just like Rupert, root bound Christians fail to produce new growth. A Christian life was never to be a stationary life.

In John 15, Jesus is talking to the disciples. He uses the illustration of the vine. "I am the true vine, and my father is the husbandman."

By using the term husbandman or the Greek term, georgos, the land worker or farmer, Jesus makes it known that he is not speaking of wild vines but rather the cultivated vines of a prized vineyard. This illustrates that God is in care of the vine and all the branches. He plants and He waters, He gives the increase because we are His husbandry. Jesus is the root or vine that all the branches extend because new life is found only through Christ. In this illustration, Jesus shows his submission to the Father by being the root. God watches over the root and the branches to protect and nurture them. The Lord prunes the branches when needed to coax growth and fruit. He also removes the branches that bear not fruit.

> *Every branch in me that beareth not fruit he taketh away: and every branch that beareth fruit, he purgeth it, that it may bring forth more fruit. John 15:2*

We all at times must undergo the purge or pruning of the Master. Sometimes, the process is not pleasant, but it is necessary for our growth. I am hopeful that Rupert will take to the nutrient soil and soon produce shiny green foliage. However, it is ultimately up to Rupert whether he will reach out his roots.

You are part of a prized vineyard, a vineyard that God tirelessly lavishes love, discipline and care. God has selectively and carefully chose exactly where to plant you, now it is up to you to reach out.

Don't be a Root Bound Rupert!

Anger Management

My God, my God, why hast thou forsaken
me? Why art thou so far from helping me,
and from the words of my roaring?
O my God, I cry in the daytime, but thou hearest
not; and in the night season, and am not silent.
Psalms 22:1-2

Recently I spoke with a gentleman that has just come through a horrible medical ordeal. It was really touch and go for a bit and honestly, most of his family, friends and others had just about resigned to accepting his death. However, as quickly as he sunk into the coma, he awoke one afternoon to the relief of his wife and family.

That, of course, was not his only battle; it would take weeks for him to recover and be strong enough to return to work and a normal life.

I was walking Emma one evening and he came down his driveway to meet me. We started with the pleasantries and trivial chatter when he said, "Thank you for praying for me. I know that it was everyone's prayers that saved me."

I smiled. "So now that God has spared you and given you a second chance what are you going to do with it?"

He drew on his cigarette and let the smoke slowly escape his nostrils. "I don't know. Twenty years ago, I was in church, I prayed, I believed and I tried to live a Christian life.." His voice trailed off and we stood in silence.

I decided to invite him to share more. "What happened?"

"It is what didn't happen. I was so angry. I quit praying and going to church. I didn't want anything to do with God or the church."

"What about now? Have you prayed? Did you thank God for sparing you?"

It seemed like forever as he mulled over the questions, drawing in on his cigarette and casting his eyes on the fading sun. Finally, he turned to me, "I don't think He would hear me now after all this time."

"I disagree; I know He is eager to hear from you. You should at least try."

He crushed his cigarette on the pavement and turned to go up his driveway. He paused and looked back. "I might."

As I watched him disappear into his house, I thought about how many people have been and may be in his situation right now. I have been angry with God, and I too choose to sulk. I have turned my back on God and walked away because something did not go my way, or maybe I was unwilling to go the way He had instructed me. Either way, I understood how he felt.

There are many examples in Psalms of David expressing his anger with God. Though being mad at God may not be the best idea, it is after all part of being a human. The difference is that David chose to express his anger with God in the Psalms. He shared his angst with the Lord and in doing so, he continued to keep the communication open, hence allowing the spirit to teach and comfort David.

Maybe you have some anger or disappointment you are harboring toward God. Why? Do you not know that He knows your heart? It is not disrespectful to share your disappointment or anger with God.

Nonetheless, do not allow the anger to cause you to sin. Do not turn from God in anger, but like David, turn to Him and share your feelings. He is eager to hear from you

A Unique Life

*"and who knoweth whether thou art come to
the kingdom for such a time as this?*
Esther 4:14

I received an email a couple of weeks ago. It was from an old friend I had not seen in 32 years. I was pretty excited that she wanted to reconnect. I responded right away, eager to speak with her.

As I waited for a reply, I decided to google her. If you google my name, you get about 15 Melissa's, but when I put in her name she came up with a very impressive resume and list of accomplishments. She had done exactly what she had always wanted and said she would. However, those dreams I had shared on the trampoline in her backyard 30 plus years ago, had never come to fruition. I was immediately ashamed of my simple life.

Her email came back with a number for me to call. I did not call. The thoughts of speaking with her horrified me. How could I compare to her extensive and impressive life?

Days passed and still I did not call.

I brought my feelings of inadequacy before God. I was not jealous of my friend, but I was very much embarrassed of myself. I needed God to help me sort out my thoughts.

As I prayed, God opened my heart and gently revealed something to me. My work, my life, my relationship with God through Jesus, is not to be compared or judged against another. My experiences, my circumstances are unique to me. I am exactly where I am supposed to be, to fulfill the purpose of my life for God. My friend is exactly where she should be so that she too may use her situation to touch lives for Jesus.

One of my favorite Bible stories is of Esther. Esther was a Jew and a small town girl. In a moment she entered into a world that was alien to her, and she trusted God. Through her trust and willingness to follow God, she found that a teenager plucked from the town streets could save a nation, charm a king and assume the title of a beloved queen.

> *For if thou altogether holdest thy peace at this time, then shall there enlargement and deliverance arise to the Jews from another place; but thou and thy father's house shall be destroyed: and who knoweth whether thou art come to the kingdom for such a time as this? Esther 4:14*

Esther was reminded by her uncle Mordecai that ultimately it was her choice whether to "holdest thy peace". However, he was quick to remind her that she was placed in the palace for "such a time as this".

Each and every one of us no matter who we are, where we work, our titles or positions in life, we are exactly where we are supposed to be. You were created "for such a time as this."

I received another email. The same number was given. I called. We talked well after midnight. The difference in education, our careers and 30 plus years melted like snow. She had experienced heartache, failure, pain and disappointment. She had also had victory in Jesus, hope in dark times, joy in her family and peace. The most joyous part of our conversation was sharing how God was using our unique lives for His Glory.

It Takes a Village

*There is neither Jew nor Greek, there is neither
bond nor free, there is neither male nor
female: for ye are all one in Christ Jesus.*
Galatians 3:28

Well, life has been happening to me lately. I am more than sure you know exactly what I mean.

My youngest called me at work in a panic. The house was filled with smoke, especially in her sister's room. I instructed her to leave the house immediately and call 911, I was on the way.

You never want to drive up on your house and see fire trucks, rescue squad or officers milling around your yard, however, when I got home that was what I faced.

I am happy to report the damage was minimal and can be rectified with some rewiring and paint. I was fortunate and I believe God's angels were there and protected my family and home.

However, the blessing did not end there. My neighborhood, aka *The Village* as I affectionately call them mobilized. One precious neighbor was at my home to console my daughter and protect my interest as the firemen did their job in my absence. Another neighbor knew somebody who knew somebody and got an electrician to the house to secure it immediately without cost. Still others offered their support calling to check and see what was needed.

After the firemen and neighbors left I sat on my porch with lemonade and I counted my blessings. One blessing in particular touched me; I had experienced community in action.

Community in action is a marvel to behold. The overwhelming comfort I found in my village was priceless. With their support I was able to face this, though relatively minor incident, with confidence. I was not alone as I dealt with the aftermath.

I think many people misunderstand what the Christian Community embodies. Some people get nervous when you begin to talk about Christian community, fearing they will be urged to sell everything and move to a commune somewhere. However, that is not what community was meant to be in the body of Christ. Community is sharing a common life in Jesus. It challenges us to commit ourselves to being the people of God. When we share our burdens, pain and failures with other Christ minded people, it lightens the load. We are given courage, strength and the ability to face the challenges that meet each of us.

Within the community, we are not only uplifted, but are held accountable, taught and have the opportunity to teach one another. We are to watch over one another for good and be a beacon to those that are without Christ.

That ye may be blameless and harmless, the sons of God, without rebuke, in the midst of a crooked and perverse nation, among whom ye shine as lights in the world; Philippians 2:15

The abilities and resources of the community should not be only designated to the believer but to the lost. A Christian community, as one body should reach out to those in need; such as families in crisis, children in need, the broken and the forgotten.

My own experiences within ***my village*** lifted me up, strengthen me and gave me comfort in an emotional and frightening situation. As Christians, we should work together in the spirit of community to all those in need.

Emma the Terrible Gets a Pal, Whether She Wants Him or Not

Wherefore receive ye one another, as Christ
also received us to the glory of God.
Romans 15:7

A couple of weeks ago, I introduced you to Senor Bryan, our bilingual pup. He has settled into the household quickly. Eager to learn and ready to play, he has already brought so many laughs. He is a mixed breed, solid white with freckles on his muzzle. At five months old, he is already over twenty pounds and full of rambunctious energy.

This morning as I stood on the back deck looking over the yard with Emma at my feet, I watched Senor Bryan playing fetch with my daughter. Up and down the yard, he ran with great enthusiasm chasing the stuffed toy. Emma watched intently. She shook with excitement and panted. It was obvious she wanted to get into the game, but it would mean sharing with Bryan. However, Emma was not ready to welcome Bryan fully. Finally, she decided that maybe the grudge she had been harboring against this pup was really not necessary. Down the steps she bounced, her high pitched yip announcing her intention to join in the fun. Back and forth the odd couple dashed for the toy and quickly returned it for another run.

Emma might be only five pounds, but she made every pound count as she ran between Bryan's legs to snatch the toy and bring it to my daughter. Bryan was elated to have someone to play with and together they chased the stuff animals, sometimes returning it together. For a good 30 minutes they tracked the toys and each other. Finally collapsing in exhausted bliss, these two very different pooches lay just inches apart from one another.

Sometimes it is hard to include someone new into the family. Even Christians are guilty of closing ranks. We get comfortable with our group, our Sunday school, the choir maybe even the pew. It is a normal human response to protect our position. However, just as we were fully accepted into the Family of God through Christ, we too need to welcome new brothers and sisters into our churches, our circle of friends and into our community.

Let us open our hearts to those around us and share the Good News of Christ to all.

Co-Laborers with Christ

For we are labourers together with God: ye are
God's husbandry, ye are God's building.
1 Corinthians 3:9

I was saved when I was in the third grade at age 8. I was very excited about it. I felt wonderful, happy, invincible and special. I wanted my friends and everyone to know that feeling too. I wanted to share the gift with someone.

Not long after a girl joined my homeroom class from out of state. I just knew that this little girl would need to know about Jesus and hopefully she and her family would come to church.

She was a very pretty girl. Her name was Melody and she had long, smooth brown hair gathered up into a navy bow that matched her navy dress. She wore white knee socks and buckled brown shoes.

I rehearsed my speech in my mind all morning. I had planned to talk to her at recess. Unfortunately, all the girls had the same thought and had gathered around her on the tether ball court. I inched my way through the curious giggling girls.

"Hi." I smiled as big as I could. "My name is Missy. Would you like to come to church with me?" I was so very proud of myself. I puffed up, still grinning, eyes shining waiting for the obvious acceptance of my invitation.

Melody looked me up, then down. "What makes you think that I need to go to church, or would want to?" The girls around us laughed. She raked me over with her stinging blue eyes one more time before she turned to walk away.

Needless to say, I was crushed. I ran crying to the bathroom, my face on the cool wall tiles, inconsolable by even my favorite teacher. I could not understand why she would reject church, or me.

Before you get mad at Melody and come by my desk to pet me that is the risk you run when you chose to share Jesus with others. Often times, when we share Jesus it seems to fall on deaf ears or hardened hearts. As difficult as it is to accept, that is how it often plays out. But what is harder to accept, is that you are not here to save them. **Jesus is the Savior, we are the messengers.** You and I plant the seeds; water them with acts of kindness, forgiveness and love. However, it is the Son that will draw the seed to open.

Ultimately, whether that seed takes root, is up to the individual.

It may be 2 weeks or twenty years, but our efforts will make a difference. People over the years have planted seeds in me that frankly I rejected. But later, when the time was right and my heart ready, it made all the difference.

Paul told the congregation at Corinth, *"I have planted, Apollos watered; but God gave the increase.. 1 Corinthians 3:6*

Share the love of God confidently. It will, when the time and the heart is right, open those seeds planted by you.

Senòr Bryan is Afraid of...............EVERYTHING!

Poor Senòr Bryan is without a doubt a lover and not a fighter. He is afraid of rain, his reflection in the oven door, the Assassins (which is wise) and the shower curtain. Emma and the twins relentlessly torture him. He spends a lot of time sitting on me or my daughters.

This morning Bryan did not want to go out to potty. Instead, he stood pressing against the back door whining into the predawn darkness of the yard. I do not know what he saw or sensed but he was indisputably fearful.

It is difficult to see this 30 lb. animal, with all his potential and abilities, recoil. He could whip all the pets easily. Instead, he cowers because he does not know the power he possesses.

There are plenty of Christians, including myself, that are unaware of our potential. Just like Bryan many do not know how much power they possess. Likewise, I did not realize the potential for my life through Christ Jesus for many years. I continue to experience new facets of His authority daily.

> *But ye shall receive power, after that the Holy Ghost is come upon you: and ye shall be witnesses unto me both in Jerusalem, and in all Judaea, and in Samaria, and unto the uttermost part of the earth. <u>Acts 1:8</u> -*

Notice that this verse says that "ye shall **receive**". In order to receive you must accept what is being given. Many of us fail to accept the power given to us by Jesus through the Holy Spirit. It is not a temporal power but a spiritual and moral power. We allow ourselves to believe that we are powerless. However, as a Christian, you are anything but powerless and nothing of this earth or the enemy can hurt you.

> *Behold, I give unto you power to tread on serpents and scorpions, and over all the power of the enemy: and nothing shall by any means hurt you. <u>Luke 10:19</u>*

You possess a marvelous and absolute power through Christ Jesus. All you have to do is accept it.

Party Line

My grandmother had an old black phone that sat on the corner of the dining room table. It took two hands for me to lift the receiver and it had a rotary dial on the front. However, these were not the things that made this phone so compelling. My fascination was for the fact that it was a party line. There are some of you that are wondering what a party line is and others that are nodding their heads and smiling. A party line is basically a shared phone line with several other households. If you needed to make a call you would lift the receiver and if you heard voices, you knew you'd have to wait. I was forever lifting that receiver as gently as I could to listen for the conversations of other ladies in the community. I loved listening in on them. Sometimes I would get caught and my grandmother would snatch the phone from me and scold me for eavesdropping. Of course, as you can guess, I was always waiting on the opportunity to sneak a listen.

I was reminded of my grandmother's party line when I was asked to pray for someone. They told me they knew I had the inside line.

I laughed, "You got the same line. We aren't on a party line, you know!"

Through Jesus' intercession, you have a direct line to the throne. No waiting, no tolls, no answering machines. God is ready and eager to hear from you.

When Jesus ascended into heaven, His role became as the eternal Shepherd of the elect. He is seated at the right hand of God and He advocates for you and I.

> *"If ye then be risen with Christ, seek those things which are above, where Christ sitteth on the right hand of God." Colossians 3:1*

You won't get a busy signal because the line is always open!

> *And all things, whatsoever ye shall ask in prayer, believing, ye shall receive. Matthew 21:22*

Beware of the Knockoffs

I stopped off at the store on the way home from work the other
day. I needed some cleaning supplies. Particularly, I needed a new
sponge, mine was so old and germy that scientists have declared it a
new species!

As I looked for a sponge to fit my needs, I was struck at the number
of brands and choices that we have of *sponges*.

Sponges folks!

Seriously, there were 9 different brands/types of sponges on one aisle!
However, what I found to be the most interesting was the fact that
for every "name brand" sponge there was a knockoff. These knockoffs promised to be just as good as the brand. They were colored and
packaged the same as the counterpart. For all intents and purposes,
they seemed to be every bit as good, but with a lower price.

A big problem today is that humanity is offered alternatives to Christ that seem like they may be just as good. Many are looking for a savior, something to fill the void in their souls and they find the knockoffs.

However, there is only one way to grace and redemption and that is Christ Jesus. Jesus paid the full price for your sins.

> *"For there is one God, and there is one mediator between God and men, the man Christ Jesus, who gave himself as a ransom." Timothy 2:5*

He paid the price that you could not.

> *None of them can by any means redeem his brother, nor give to God a ransom for him. Psalm 49:7*

Jesus is the only way of salvation. Beware of the knockoffs.

Spiritual Clog

But your iniquities have separated between you and your God, and your sins have hid his face from you, that he will not hear.
Isaiah 59:2

This morning as I was in the shower, I noticed that the drain seemed slow and a puddle began to form. By the time I completed my bathing, I was standing ankle deep in water. It took some time for the tub to drain and I stomped around the house angry that I had another issue to deal with. I was angry with the situation, the tub, the guy I bought the house from and anyone in eyesight. In my anger, I did not behave as I should.

As I huffed up and down the grocery store aisles for a drain cleaner, I began to think about how easily the pipeline can be blocked. Not just in my in my 76 year old bath plumbing, but in my spiritual pipes too.

My pipes under the tub were without a doubt clogged with any number of usual culprits and unfortunately in my rant, I was choking up my spiritual pipes. There are times in my life when I allow things to influence me. Be it my pride or just plain stubbornness, I allow sin to congest the plumbing.

As long as I was stomping around, mumbling under my breath, glaring at fellow shoppers and losing control, I was filling my own spiritual pipeline with garbage and strangling out God's influence. I imagine that I was anything but a good example for Christ as I muttered to myself and stamped around.

It is easy to allow situations, people, circumstance and sin to get in the way of a close relationship with Jesus. If these things are between us and the Lord, our prayers become impeded. Likewise, you cannot receive His counsel, peace and guidance in your walk.

Through confession of our sins to God, forgiveness of others, resisting sin and seeking God in all things through prayer and His word, you can avoid the spiritual clog.

If you are having trouble with spiritual clogged pipes, I urge you to take a moment to step back and examine what is in the way of a flowing relationship with Jesus. If it is sin, confess it. If it is non- forgiveness, forgive. Whatever it may be; you must address it, or your clog will never be removed.

Core Strength

> *It is* God that girdeth me with strength,
> and maketh my way perfect.
> *Psalms 18:32*

One day I saw a young woman on a paddle board. There she stood, relaxed and gazing over the waters. It was at that moment I decided I wanted to try it. However, I was worried that I would not be able to do the paddle board because, well frankly, I am out of shape. Well, that's not entirely true. I have a shape; it is just that it is *really* round. So I enlisted the help of a precious friend of mine. She committed to getting me in better proportions, so for the past six weeks she's been cracking the whip. I will admit, reluctantly, that I have not been dedicated to the regimen.

Finally, the day of reckoning came and I nervously walked into the establishment to rent the paddle board. I was given a standard issue life jacket, paddle and guided to the river for my quick lesson. As the reedy built college boy with obvious ADD issues quickly ran through the principals of paddle board, I began to realize I may have overestimated my abilities.

Out I glided on a three foot wide piece of fiberglass, nothing between me and the river but air. The overpowering odor of the waterway filled my nostrils and I felt a bit of nausea. Following my friend's lead, I paddled out a safe distance on my knees.

It was now time to stand. I ran the instruction through my mind and began the arduous battle with gravity and balance to raise my body upright. What a sight I must have been. There I was poised on a piece of fiberglass in the middle of the Tennessee with only my tail high, dry and pointing skyward. Time after time, I tried to raise myself, yet each time I found myself stuck with my tail up, yet nothing else.

Each attempt left me shaken, sweating and exhausted. Finally, I made it upright and for maybe 45 seconds I stood on the board. A boat passed by, the water became choppy and I folded to my knees.

As much as I tried, I could not stand on the board and paddle. I was disappointed, embarrassed and acutely aware that I was in no shape for this sport. As my friend explained my core was weak, and without core strength, I could not maintain the balance needed to stand and paddle.

I think that I would be correct in saying that many of us find it hard to stand spiritually and against the issues that plague every human because our core is weak. Without balance in our lives, we have no hope to stand against the assaults that we each face daily. As much as I tried, truly giving it all I had to give, I simply could not stand. Without Christ as our core, there is no strength. We find ourselves languishing in bad relationships, in an addiction, struggling in depression and spiraling out of control without anything to hold on to.

Just like exercise strengthens my physical core, prayer, reading the Word and actively choosing to make Jesus first in my life will strengthen my spiritual core. It is this strength that I will draw from to face what life sends my way. It is this strength that will give me peace. What strengthens your core?

You Never Have to go it Alone

I was in the grocery earlier today doing my weekly shopping. As I went through my mental grocery list, I realized that I had forgotten a can of corn. I stepped back a few feet and bent to get the can from the bottom shelf. As I returned to my cart a lady in her early 60's stood with her hand on hip and her face in the unmistakable disappointed momma look.

"Young lady, she began, don't walk off from your purse! You don't know me. I'm broke and you don't know how desperate I may be." She punctuated her statement with twisted lips and piercing eyes.

"Yes, ma'am." I stammered and quickly closed the gap between me and my cart. I zipped up the gaping purse and moved on to the produce.

"You have to be more careful. You don't know these people." She said over her shoulder as she turned to go down the next aisle.

I will admit I was a little shaken as I continued my shopping. As I compared prices and nutrition values, I thought about what this outspoken lady had said.

It is true that none of us actually know what is in the heart of another. We do not know the pain and difficulties that those around us are experiencing. Many of you that are reading this right now are dealing with difficult issues, from personal health, to the loss of a loved one, financial issues, marriage problems and other personal matters. However, there is one that knows. God knows what you are dealing with. He knows what keeps you awake and he knows what has bruised your heart.

More importantly, He cares. *1 Peter 5:7 - **Casting all your care upon him; for he careth for you.***

Often we feel that we are alone in our pain, but we are not. God knows your heart. He understands. How, you may ask? Because Jesus came to earth as a man. He experienced life as we do. He got tired and had to rest, he thirst and drank.

> *Now Jacob's well was there. Jesus, therefore, being*
> *wearied with his journey, sat thus on the well:*
> *and it was about the sixth hour. John 4:6*

He wept at the death of Lazarus

> ***Jesus wept.*** (John 11:35).

What you are going through is important to the Lord. You are not going through it alone.

Two Edged Blessings

A sweet friend and I were talking the other day. Our conversation had developed into a discussion about a particular person that was dealing with a handicap.

My friend said, "It makes you mindful of your blessings." "Yes." I quickly agreed.

A strange look passed over her face. "I'm not saying that they aren't blessed too."

After the conversation and my friend had left, her statement rolled around in my head. *"I'm not saying that they aren't blessed too."*

We have equated the word *blessing* with only good things. We see blessings as answered prayers, healing of sickness, financial gain and good health. However, blessings are not always what **we perceive** as good.

God knows what is best for me and for you. It is not always pleasant. It is many times painful. And most times it is contrary to what you want. Nonetheless, God, like a parent, does what is best for His children.

Sometimes we are **blessed** with an adverse event or circumstances, not as a punishment but as a growth opportunity. You may not like troubles, I don't. However, if you are to be strong in your faith, close to Jesus, a beacon for the lost, these tests and trials are necessary.

Rejoice in all blessings.

The Donkey and the Turtle

Abigail is a donkey. She has long dark lashes and a frilly mane. She has a wonderfully soft nose and long fuzzy ears that swing like radar dishes, taking in the noise of the farm.

One day, Abagail noticed something moving across her field and being a rather nosey donkey, she went to investigate. A large turtle was making his way across the field to the pond. He moved with slow determination through the grass. Step after deliberate step, he followed the route to the pond.

Unfortunately, Abigail had not extended a right of way to this trespasser. She charged at the turtle, her hoofs thundered around him and the turtle retreated into his shell. Yet after a moment he extended his head from his mobile home and resumed his trek toward the pond. Time after time, Abagail stomped and brayed at the determined reptile. However, no matter how much of a fit Abigail threw, the turtle refused to alter his path. He continued his plodding toward the fishpond.

Finally, the turtle decided that he had enough of this rude donkey. As Abigail dropped her head to nudge the turtle he did not recoil into his carapace but rather snapped his beak shut on her tender pink nose. A high pitched bray peeled through the valley and Abigail leapt skyward. All four hooves launched her two feet off the ground. As Abigail retreated, the turtle continued his journey home.

Throughout our lives, we find that people, circumstances and our own poor choices can cause us to veer from the path. We should be as determined as this turtle in our journey. He knew the way to the cool waters of the pond. He knew that the pool held safety and sustenance.

Daily we are faced with temptations, choices and difficulties. These can cause us to lose focus and veer from the path that God has set before us. It is easy to lose sight and lose our way.

Though you find yourself inundated with distractions, do not lose sight of Jesus.

> ***Order my steps in thy word: and let not any iniquity have dominion over me. Psalm 119:133***

He Knows Your Name

> *"But now thus saith the LORD that created
> thee, O Jacob, and he that formed thee, O
> Israel, Fear not: for I have redeemed thee, I have
> called thee by thy name; thou art mine."*
> **Isaiah 43:1**

When I was in the first grade I met a girl named Missy. I was upset. I began to cry and beg her to not to say that Missy was her name. She responded by yelling it repeatedly at me. I began screaming at the little girl not to say it again. It was my name!

The teacher came to see what the ruckus was about.

Between tears and hiccups, I explained that she said that her name was Missy but that was my name and not hers.

I remember feeling fear. Not that this little girl would do anything to me, but that if she had the same name then I may be forgotten. She may get something that was mine. In my first grade mind, I had equated my name with my identity, and I feared that it was in jeopardy. I could not understand how there could be two Missys. What if I was forgotten? How would anyone know me if there were two?

I think that sometimes we think it is the same with God. We feel that we might be just part of the masses, just another nameless face in this world, plodding along the path of life. However, God knows exactly where you are, He knows what you are going through and He knows how you feel about it.

In Isaiah 49:15-16, the Lord says: ***Can a woman forget her sucking child, that she should not have compassion on the son of her womb? Yeah, they may forget, yet will I not forget thee. Behold, I have graven thee upon the palms of my hands; thy walls are continually before me.***

Your name is engraved in the palm of the Almighty God because you are His and He cares for you.

Red Rover, Red Rover

The sun was still a pale yellow and the air crisp with the breath of fall. The dew had my toes wet and brown grass stuck to my shoes. I shook with excitement as the 5th grade class formed the Red Rover scrimmage lines. Name after name was called as the teams invited the other to bust through the ranks.

My team was losing badly. Somehow every bully, overweight and abnormally tall kid in the fifth grade had ended up on our opponent's line. Nervously, we rocked holding sweating hands and waiting for the name to be hurled from the other side.

"Red rover, Red rover, send Missy right over!"

I was up! It was me that had been called. I nodded to the kids on either side and focused on the task ahead. Fists waded up, teeth clenched and eyes narrowed (for maximum psych out). I took off, my legs pumping so fast I thought my corduroys would catch fire. I hit the line between Ben Edwin and Stacy Cole.

For the rest of recess, I laid on the ground next to Ms. Austin with an ice pack on the ripening knot on my forehead. I did not make it through the line, only as far as Ben Edwin's knuckles.

We seem to only measure success, well by *success*. However, there is a lot to be said for giving it all you got and doing it the best way you can.

I did not break the opponent's line but I did answer the call and I did my best.

When you answer God's call and you give it all you have and do your best, you please God. We are called to be bold and to step out in faith. It does not matter if we do not do everything just right, it matters that we try. It matters that you stepped out in faith, believing that God is going to help you.

If you are living your life afraid to step out, afraid to heed His call, then you are not living a life fully in Jesus.

You and I have been called to live boldly, confidently in Christ.

Three, Four, Maybe One More

And they heard the voice of the LORD God walking in the garden in the cool of the day: and Adam and his wife hid themselves from the presence of the LORD God amongst the trees of the garden.
Genesis 3:8

"Mom said three Oreos each!" I announced to my little brother as I opened the package. He shoved me to the side and took his three cookies. Scurrying away, he went to hide in his room and savor his prize. I took my three and poured a glass of milk. Unfortunately the pleasure of the treat was short lived and I found myself staring at the package on the counter.

"*Maybe just one more*", whispered in my thoughts.

I knew that my mother would know if we took more than was allotted. However, the craving for the creamy center and crunchy cookie teased me. I took the package, intending to put it away, when an idea struck me. I slid the tray out and took three from the end of the package. I slid the tray back in place, put the cookies on the shelf and consumed my extra three.

The next day after school, the setup was much the same. However, this time, I took more than an extra three, I took five.

The next day, again I took more than my share from the back of the tray. The thought of the cookies plagued me. I had easily taken what I wanted and no one was the wiser. I snuck to the cabinet several times and took a cookie still no one had noticed. Well, until day four, when my mother went to get herself a chocolatey treat.

Busted.

Just like I thought I could hide my disobedience from my mom, we often try to conceal our sins from our family, friends and others in our life. We think that we can keep these indiscretions hidden from even God. However, nothing is secreted from God. We sometimes try to hide from our sins, but trying to run from your sin is equivalent to running from your shadow. "Hidden" sins are dangerous. Unconfessed sin blocks us from God, denying us His fellowship and blessings.

If you have an unconfessed sin, now is the time to bring it before God. Through Jesus' sacrifice on the cross, His blood covers our sins when we confess them.

Your Heart's Desires

When I was eight years old, all I wanted for Christmas was a bike. Oh, not just any bike. I wanted a blue one with streamers, a bell, and a banana seat. I told my mom and dad, my grandparents, my teachers and basically anybody that would listen. I had pictures cut out of catalogs on the refrigerator, left on my parent's bed, casually lying about the kitchen counter. Every guy that even remotely resembled a Santa was quickly instructed on exactly what the bicycle should look like. I left no avenue unexplored; I wanted a blue bike, with streamers, a bell and a banana seat, very badly.

On Christmas Eve the tree still did not have any gifts that looked big enough for a bike. I looked behind the tree, the furniture and even in the closets. However, I did not find the bike I so desperately yearned.

Sometime in the pre-dawn hours of Christmas I awoke. Something shiny caught my attention and I sat up to see in the dimness the outline of a bicycle at the end of my bed. I sat staring at it, peering afraid to believe that it was the bike. I laid back down, pulling the covers under my chin and stared into the darkness. Was it the blue bike with streamers, bell and banana seat? Was it really here?

I could not sleep and kept peering over the covers to see if it was still there. I was almost afraid of morning, fearing the bike would be gone when the light came.

Have you ever prayed for something? Was it something so precious that your heart yearned? Did you bring it before God in faith and in hope? When it was answered, were you ever afraid to accept it?

You may find these questions to be strange, or like me, you are nodding your head. Before I sat down to write this, I asked some people these same questions. I got basically the same response from all.

"I just couldn't believe he answered it."
"I was literally blown away when it happened."

I have to tell you, I have felt the same way. Why is that? Why after we take our petitions to God, do we faint with surprise when they are answered?

Truthfully, I often feel unworthy for God to bless me so tremendously. However, as the verse in Matthew 7:11 above tells us, we should expect only good gifts from God. Even as imperfect and flawed parents, we desire only the best for our children and we wish to give them good things. It is no different for our heavenly Father. He also desires to bless us with good things.

Do not fear accepting the good gifts of our Father. You are worthy of the gifts and answered prayers through Christ Jesus' sacrifice. You are God's precious child, His treasured possession. (Deut. 7:6)

God wants to give you the desires of your heart. Do not hesitate to receive them.

> ***Delight thyself also in the Lord: and he shall give thee the desires of thine heart Psalms 37:4***

Lift Up Your Ebenezers

Then Samuel took a stone, and set [it] between
Mizpeh and Shen, and called the name of it Ebenezer,
saying, Hitherto hath the LORD helped us.
I Samuel 7:12

I have a jewelry box that sits on my dresser. It actually does not have jewelry in it. There are pictures of me as a baby with all four of my grandparents, a love letter from high school, a broken key that once started my first car. There is a newspaper article about me, my daughter's baby teeth, a picture of my mom and dad's prom. This jewelry box is more a treasure chest of memories and reminders. As I looked through it tonight, I held my grandmother's delicate handkerchief against my face and I drew in the scent. The smell of her hand cream was still on it and it filled me with a sense of peace. I smiled at her memory and teared up at the pang of missing her.

A smell, a taste or a simple object can revive vivid memories. It can be the same in our spiritual life and relationship with God. Throughout my life, God has intervened, and brought me through things that I thought I would not be delivered.

Just like I keep special memories in my chest on my dresser, the Israelites built stone altars to commemorate the miracles and deliverances that God accomplished on their behalf. These altars were the reminders for the people of God's grace and love.

Just like the Israelites stacked stone altars, we should take the time to recognize the Lord and the miracles that He has performed in our lives. These stone altars were not just to commemorate a time in Jewish history; it was also a reminder of the power of God. Every time the stones were looked upon the memory of the event was revived.

Often times, I find myself in a situation that I take to the Lord, and as soon as I utter my "amen" I find myself wondering if the prayer will be answered. Will I be delivered by the Lord's mighty hand? It is this moment that I need to look to the Ebenezer stones that mark the work of God in my life.

If you are in prayer about a situation and you find yourself wavering in faith that this circumstance will be handled, hold up your Ebenezer and give thanks for what God has done for you. Reflect and remember that God has acted on your behalf before and He will again.

God's Place at God's Pace

*For ye have need of patience, that, after ye have done
the will of God, ye might receive the promise.*
Hebrews 10:36

The plan was simple. All I had to do was stand on the sidewalk and wait. Mike was going to unlock the car, return with an umbrella and escort me. That was it, a simple, efficient plan.

For those of you that know me and know me well, I am not patient. Yes, you probably already guessed it. I did not wait. Instead, as soon as he unlocked the car, I stepped off the curb. I stepped down, my ankle turned and I landed in a puddle, in the rain on all fours. I scrambled to get up and into the car.

Beside my skinned knee and throbbing wrist my ego had taken a good hit. I was embarrassed, if only I had just waited.

I cannot help but wonder how many blessings and opportunities I have missed because I did not exercise control and patience.

As I was looking up scripture for this piece, I was taken in a very different direction than I anticipated. I knew that it would be focused on patience, or rather lack of patience. As I read scripture and commentaries, I learned that impatience is a form of unbelief. Impatience is what I feel when I begin to doubt the wisdom, guidance and goodness of God. It happens when things don't happen as I think they should or in what I think is a reasonable time.

I found my study of impatience to be eye opening. I had never thought that my spirit of impatience was in fact, my doubt and lack of faith in God's plan for my life. Now that I am aware, I can battle the unbelief. In doing so, I must employ the opposite of impatience. The opposite of impatience is a willingness to wait for God where you are in obedience or to persevere at the pace he allows on the road of obedience.

It is learning to wait in God's Place at God's Pace.

RSVP

> *"A man once gave a great banquet and invited many. And at the time for the banquet he sent his servants to say to those who had been invited, 'Come, for everything is now ready.' But they all alike began to make excuses. The first said to him, 'I have bought a field, and I must go out and see it. Please have me excused.' And another said, 'I have bought five yoke of oxen, and I go to examine them. Please have me excused.' And another said, 'I have married a wife, and therefore I cannot come.' So the servant came and reported these things to his master. Then the master of the house became angry and said to his servant, 'Go out quickly to the streets and lanes of the city, and bring in the poor and crippled and blind and lame.' And the servant said, 'Sir, what you commanded has been done, and still there is room.' And the master said to the servant, 'Go out to the highways and hedges and compel people to come in, that my house may be filled. For I tell you, none of those men who were invited shall taste my banquet.'"*
>
> *Luke 14:16-24*

The table was set, the candles lit and the aroma of turkey filled every room of the house. I had everything just so and I was ready for my guest. I waited with anticipation, eager for my invitees to come and sit at my table, to partake of my offerings and share in the spirit of thanksgiving. I had spared no expense, buying only the best ingredients for my dishes. I wanted to make sure that everything was perfect. Soon the house was filled with laughter, the feast had begun.

As I was tidying up after the meal, I thought about the planning and care that is lavished on the preparations of the Thanksgiving dinners throughout America. These thoughts put me in mind of the feast Jesus told as a parable in Luke 14:16-24.

In the parable, invitations were sent out for the banquet, however, when the meal was prepared, the invitees made poor excuses for missing the feast and all declined the call. I imagine that many of them thought that there would be another invitation, another opportunity. However, their seats were filled and servants sent to find more to attend and fill the Master's house.

Many are called yet few will answer the appeal, by doing so they have missed out. Their choice is respected and made permanent. ***For I tell you, none of those men who were invited shall taste my banquet.***

So it will be with God's judgment on those who choose to reject Christ: they will have their choice confirmed, and they will never taste the joys of heaven.

The invitation of salvation has been extended to all. Will you answer the call?

The commandment to go to ***the highways and hedges and compel people to come in, that my house may be filled*** has been handed down. Do you offer God's invitation to those in your life?

The feast is close at hand and as His servants we need to be extending the invitation to all. Now is the time to prepare for the feast.

Re-Born Free

It was 1:00am, and I was awakened by the dinging of the bell at the back door. Bryan was anxious to get outside. I padded to the back and opened the door to let him out. As I stood just inside the door, my robe wrapped about myself, I waited for him to come back inside. As I waited a blur scurried past me. It was Vlad, the grumpier of the assassin twins. I ran down the steps, barefoot and robe flapping behind me like a cape, but I was no contest for Vlad and he sprinted across the yard and up a tree. He perched high in the branches, his black fur blending in the night backdrop.

Back to the house I ran to get some help from the girls. My oldest and I stood beneath the tree, waving cans of tuna and shaking bags of treats, however, the cat was in no way moved by our attempts. Finally, we gave up and went in the house.

"Mom, why does the cat want to be outside so bad when it is warm inside and there is plenty of food?"

"Because, sweetheart, the cat's nature is to climb trees, chase birds, pounce and stalk. You cannot blame him for being what he is, a cat."

We too, have to contend with our nature. We were born into flesh, yet when we accept Jesus as our savior, we die to the flesh.

> ***Therefore if any man be in Christ, he is a new creature: old things are passed away; behold, all things are become new. 2 Corinthians 5:17***

Daily life is a struggle between the flesh we were and the new creature we have become in Christ. I often find myself in the tussle between who I was and who I have become.

Being a new creature is much more than just a new name or a new dress, but we now have a new heart and new nature. Our old thoughts, old principles and practices are passed away. Rejuvenating grace creates a new reality in the soul. We are now reborn and our renewed soul acts from new principles and rules.

You are a new creature in Christ. You are no longer subject to nature but are set free through redeeming grace.

Three Held Hostage
by Masked Bandit

Living in a more rural area tends to expose one to a bit of the unusual. That is exactly what happened to a couple that purchased an old farm. They were fortunate to make quick friends with the neighbors and settled into the vicinity comfortably. One evening as the couple prepared for bed, they received a hysterical call from one of the neighbors. She had come out to check why her dog was barking and soon found herself cornered in her basement by a rabid raccoon. She had managed to get the door closed, but now she was afraid to come out because the raccoon was pacing and growling. There was no way into the house from the basement and she was stuck.

The husband pulled on his jeans and got a flashlight. He decided that he would walk across the street and see what was going on. Surely the animal would escape to the woods once he saw someone approaching. As the husband came up the drive he heard the frantic barks of the small dog and when he got closer, he saw that two eyes glowed from beneath the doghouse. Shining his flashlight into the pen, he realized the eyes staring back were not those of the dog. The canine was perched atop his house, bug eyed and teeth bared. As the husband realized that the eyes belonged to that of the raccoon, the beast shot out from the tunnel and climbed the fence with great dexterity. The husband turned to run. Seeing what was unfolding the neighbor threw open the basement door and yelled for the man to come to her.

Soon the wife received a phone call and the husband reported that now he and the neighbor were trapped in the basement and the raccoon was head butting the door. The husband gave instruction for the wife to come in the truck, bring the rifle, ammo and no matter what stay in the truck.

The wife complied and came to the neighbor's house in the truck with the rifle and ammo, yet when she pulled into the drive all was quiet so she got out of the truck and called to her husband leaving the rifle in the seat.

Now the wife also stood in the basement along with her husband and neighbor staring out the window at the pacing animal. After a few minutes the husband knew what he had to do, so summoning up all his courage he burst from the basement and ran to the truck, the raccoon close on his heels. The husband sat in the truck for several minutes waiting for the raccoon to settle down.

With rifle at the ready, the husband threw open the door. The ringed beast shot out from under the doghouse and scaled the chain link again, however, this time he was unable to finish his charge as the husband ended his ailing. The wife ran out and stood next to her husband.

"Is he dead?" The wife asked.

With the air still heavy with gun smoke and fur the husband looked at the wife incredibly.

"I mean he's not suffering is he? Maybe you should shoot him again to make sure." She peered at the lifeless fiend.

So the husband fired the weapon again and looked at wife. "He's definitely dead now."

Many times, as Christians, we become so complacent, we fail to give situations the attention and preparations that are needed. Whereas, the husband's willingness to aid the neighbor is good, he came unprepared to deal with the situation. We should always be armed with the full body of armor when we endeavor to help another.

The wife came armed, but she failed to listen which essentially left her unprotected and vulnerable. The full armor is most effective when we spend time in communication with God. When we are willing and eager to hear His word and store it up in our hearts.

> *[14] Stand therefore, having your loins girt about with truth, and having on the breastplate of righteousness; [15] And your feet shod with the preparation of the gospel of peace; [16] Above all, taking the shield of faith, wherewith ye shall be able to quench all the fiery darts of the wicked. [17] And take the helmet of salvation, and the sword of the Spirit, which is the word of God: [18] Praying always with all prayer and supplication in the Spirit, and watching thereunto with all perseverance and supplication for all saints;*

Lead the Way, Lord

Her hair was a pale yellow like early morning light; it fell in ringlets on her shoulders. She had been picking blackberries all morning, sweat trapped a few strands of hair to her forehead and her fingers were stained with maroon juice. Her bucket was half full, their aroma tickled her nose and she pushed deeper into the briar. As she did, she looked down and between her feet the head of a snake as big as her fist lay in the cool of the bush. The copper-colored head and reddish-brown cross bands alerted her immediately that this snake was a copperhead. In a moment the young girl sprang back, landing on her bottom in the grass, her heart thumping in her ears. A wash of relief passed over her.

As this child entered the blackberry briars she was careful as to where she stepped. She did not push into the briars, nor did she run into the patch, instead, she was careful as she entered, careful where she stepped.

Often I find myself wandering and wondering through life, wishing I knew what God's Will is for me. Which way do I go, what should I do? Questions that I am sure plague more than just me.

In our hearts and minds we have desires. Desires like looking for a new job, entering into a new relationship, maybe starting a new business. Whatever it may be, committing it to the Lord first is the initial step.

Commit your works to the LORD Proverbs 16:3

The LORD gave you desires and affections. He gave you a mind, so think of how you might achieve your goals by using Biblical wisdom. No matter what it is that stirs your heart; submit it to God's will.

You cannot predict the next five minutes and trying to do so only leads to wasting time, and leaving you always frustrated. Allowing God to direct your steps leads you to realize His Will for your life.

The steps of a good man are ordered by the Lord:
and he delighteth in his way. Psalm 37:23

The Golden Lasso of Truth

Casting down imaginations, and every high thing that exalteth itself against the knowledge of God, and bringing into captivity every thought to the obedience of Christ;
2 Corinthians 10:5

Donning my robe like a cape and adjusting my paper tiara with the magic marker star in the center, I crept down the hallway to hide. There I waited in the dark suppressing giggles. As soon as my brother got close enough, I jumped out and wrapped my bathrobe sash around him.

"Oh no, Wonder Woman and her golden lasso of truth!" He wailed and fought to free himself. "I cannot resist the lasso of truth."

"That's right evil doer; tell me what I want to know!" I announced with great triumph! He crumpled to the floor, yelling of his inability to resist the power.

Lately, I have been reminded of the golden lasso of truth. I was really upset the other day. My mind was filled with thoughts, doubt and fear that swirled like an eddy in my mind. Whispers of failures past and possible future flops plagued me. I was worked up to near panic. I retreated to a quiet place and there I prayed. Through my fractured thoughts I brought my fears and doubts before God.

As I have written before, Fear is not of God. It is a principality and its little cohort Doubt can really undermine your confidence. Not just in yourself, but in God, His Word even the people in your life. That is exactly what he wants to do. How does he do it? With lies the only thing he has to work with. It is a very old but proven tactic and he and his minions have been doing it since the beginning.

Satan may have a tired repertoire, but it is just as effective today as in the beginning of time. He is planting doubt in the minds of men and women concerning the accuracy of the Word of God, suggesting that God does not really mean what the Bible says. He goes as far as making you question yourself, how you interpret God's Love and sacrifice and your perception of how others feel or think about you.

> *Now the serpent was more subtle than any beast of the field*
> *which the LORD God had made. And he said unto the woman,*
> *Yea, hath God said, Ye shall not eat of every tree of the garden?*
> *² And the woman said unto the serpent, We may*
> *eat of the fruit of the trees of the garden:*
> *³ But of the fruit of the tree which is in the midst*
> *of the garden, God hath said, Ye shall not eat of*
> *it, neither shall ye touch it, lest ye die.*
> *⁴ And the serpent said unto the woman, Ye*
> *shall not surely die: Genesis 3:1-4*

Did you see what Satan did in those few verses? He planted the seed of doubt in Eve. He in essence said, "Are you sure that is what God said? I don't think that is what he meant. Are you sure you heard it right? You aren't going to die."

The only defense to Satan's lies is truth. Like Wonder Woman's bracelets, we also have a defense and that's the truth. You can combat the fiery darts of the enemy with the Truth of God, His Word and Promises.

So the next time you are fearful, remember God says you are REDEEMED*! "Do not fear, for I have redeemed you; I have summoned you by name; <u>you are mine</u>" Isaiah 43:1*

When you are doubtful, God says you are SECURE! *"Let the beloved of the Lord <u>rest secure in him</u>, for he shields him all day long, and the one the Lord loves rests between his shoulders" Deut 33:12*

The Taming of the Flesh

But I keep under my body, and bring it into
subjection: lest that by any means, when I have
preached to others, I myself should be a castaway.
1 Corinthians 9:27

Bryan had been raucous throughout the morning and frankly the pup was really trying my nerves. He had chased the cats from one end of the house to the other and now they were huddled on the top perch of the cat tree in the corner of the living room. He had drug out every bit of the laundry and lay to waste the bathroom now carpeted with toilet paper.

I decided that he probably needed a walk. Anything to get him out of the house before he finally knocked it down. I had tried to walk him before, but he had proved to be difficult to control on only a leash. A friend had given me a harness to try. This sixty pound puppy was somewhat easy to put into the harness, but the moment the door opened he burst onto the porch dragging me screaming behind him. I struggled to reign in the bucking beast. He twisted and turned on the leash, gnawing on the fabric trying to free himself of the fetter. Finally, in frustration he took off down the road with me flopping behind him like a tangled marionette. I yelled and dug in my heels, but he was bent on running full tilt through the neighborhood. After a couple of blocks, I was too exhausted to continue and allowed him to drag me back to the house.

Bringing our flesh into subjection to God is often like trying to walk an unruly energetic pup. Much like Bryan, our flesh wants no restraints and freedom to run wild. Because of this, we cannot train the flesh to live a Christian life. The flesh and the Spirit cannot coexist. The flesh stands against the Spirit always at war within the Christian.

We were never meant to go into spiritual battle in the flesh. Our conflicts are in the spirit and therefore we must put the flesh under submission to God. Paul tells us in Ephesians that *we wrestle not against flesh and blood, but against principalities, against powers, against the rulers of the darkness of this world, against spiritual wickedness in high places." Ephesians 6:12*

Many times we try to fight in the flesh, depending on our own strength and intellect with a disastrous outcome. There is a consequence to living a spiritual life in the flesh. Both outward and inward struggles will often lead to weariness and ultimate spiritual failure.

Subduing the flesh is a daily struggle. Day-to-day we chose whether we are going to serve the flesh or the spirit. In the words of Paul, we are to die daily. This means that we chose to follow Jesus and His teaching, denying our fleshly appetites. Through prayer, daily Bible reading and ministering to those in need, we strengthen our spirit. Being spiritually strong and focused is a must for the Christian's daily battles.

Cheering on the Team

I was enjoying my Saturday evening with my 3 year old nephew. We had been chasing each other through the house with action figures. I was lucky enough to be Spiderman, he a ninja.

Finally, I had convinced him that we needed to take a break maybe play a game. For the next 30 minutes we sat in the carpet assembling a floor puzzle of the USA. Now, I seemed to have no trouble with the southern states and the upper east coast, but the middle of the country left me a bit more jumbled. Being a helpful youngster, my nephew presented me with the box as a reference and together we pieced each of the mid-states. As I placed each of the bits, my nephew praised me with "Good jobs" and hand claps.

As Christians, we should be as free with our encouragement to others as my nephew was with me.

Words are powerful. You have the power to build up and to rip down one another with just your words. You could chart a new direction in someone's life or send them spiraling in despair. Your encouraging words build up the lives around you.

Life is difficult for all of us. We all deal with finances, job pressures, illnesses, marriage matters and many other issues from day to day. It is your words of encouragement that could make the difference in someone's day. Maybe it will be your words that will give them the confidence or courage to make a difficult decision.

Whatever the situation, you have the power to positively or negatively impact those around you.

Rejected Yet Redeemed

It was Valentine's Day 1976 and I was smitten with a boy named Boyd. I wanted him to know how I felt and I hoped that once he knew he would feel the same. I placed my special handmade valentine in his box nervous, excited and hopeful. The day wore on and Boyd never spoke to me. A day passed and still Boyd never acknowledged me. Finally, on Friday afternoon as we waited for our buses, I mustered up my courage and I asked him if he got my valentine.

"Yeah." He said. His face contorted into a scowl. "Well, what did you think of it? Do you like me too?"

He snickered and looked to his friends, then back to me. "I think when you look like this," He held up a magazine with Farrah Fawcett in a red bathing suit. "I'll like you, but until then you're ugly!"

The boys joined in chanting, "Ugly, ugly, ugly…..." They laughed and passed the photo around. I went back to my seat. Hot salty tears slid silently down my freckled face. One of the boys threw a paper wad; it bounced off my curls into the floor. I put my head down and cried into the crook of my arm as more paper wads hit me and the chant became a roar.

Rejection—An All-Too-Familiar Experience

Rejection is something that each one of us has experienced at different times in our lives. No matter how old or young you may be, the sting of rejection is fierce and lingering. Have you ever felt rejected? Maybe your father was cold and distant. Possibly your mom favored your sister because she was prettier. Were you rejected for membership in a club or circle of peers? Not invited to Prom? Maybe you were passed over for a promotion because someone was younger, possibly better looking? Were you rejected by your children after giving your life to raise them? Maybe your wife or husband left for someone else.

When we chose to trust Jesus and forge a relationship with Him, He accepts us with arms wide open. It is Jesus' acceptance that gives us value. It is from Him that we should derive our self-image.

Do not allow the person or persons who reject you permission to put a price tag on you. God has put His price tag on you. You are worth so much to Him that He came Himself to die for you so you could be His son or daughter, born into His family by faith in Jesus Christ.

> *Now therefore ye are no more strangers and*
> *foreigners, but fellow citizens with the saints, and*
> *of the household of God. Ephesians 2:19*

Guidance in Conflict

I came home tired, hungry and ready to relax. However, the house looked as though a tornado came through. Jackets, backpacks and shoes littered the living room. I huffed as I crisscrossed the floor as if avoiding landmines. However, when I got to the kitchen, I stopped dead in my tracks and stared at the mountain of garbage. It extended well past the top of the garbage can spilt to the floor. I marched to the back of the house shouting for the girls to come out. They did, completely unaware of the impending assault.

My younger daughter said that it was the oldest turn to take out garbage and the reported it was the other's responsibility. Back and forth they spouted out, "Well, I cleaned the bathroom Saturday, ""and I took out the garbage day before!" Back and forth the accusations flew.

That kind of reaction and behavior is not exclusive to my daughter's fighting over chores. Unfortunately, you often find Christians involved in the same pugnacious displays.

Any time we are faced with conflict, it is our natural human emotion to feel anger and want to lash out. We feel fear and want to defend or attack. We feel wronged and want to get revenge. Often this just makes matters worse. I tell you that I just want to get even, make sure that I am proved right.

However, that attitude is not compatible to how God wants us to think.

Conversely, if we tenaciously hang onto biblical teaching, we'll find the power to act rightly. Holding on to God's Word we can avoid behaviors that can be both sinful and self-defeating. There is more than just getting practical guidance from the scriptures, but theology to help shape our thoughts and feelings. It is just as important to find out how to handle a situation as how to think about the church and God.

Just as God and Jesus are as one, we as Christians should also be united in our thoughts with Christ.

The more you look to Jesus, the more you will discover how you are to act in controversial and divisive circumstances. The more you depend upon Jesus, the more you will find unexpected strength to be agreeable, loving, humble, and Christ-like.

Strongholds of the Heart

I was waiting enthusiastically for my fresh brewed hazelnut coffee. Jon had just slid the cup under the Keurig and was about to lock the pod in place when my cell rang. I answered. It was my youngest talking fast and the oldest crying uncontrollably in the background.

"Mom, the cat is sealed up in the wall!! We can hear him!"

"What are you talking about?" I asked, confused and suspecting a joke in the works. "Mom, Vlad is in the wall."

I said my hurried goodbyes and rushed down the street to my house. I entered the back door and my daughter was slumped against the wall, fat hot tears streamed down her face. I quickly began to assess our situation. I called out to the cat and to my surprise and horror he replied with a meow—not from the confines of the wall but rather the bowel of the house.

Earlier in the day, the wall and part of the floor had been torn away due to water damage. Somehow, Vlad had slipped into the hole and was soon closed up. I went outside armed with a flashlight and began to inspect the foundation to see how I could get this cat freed from his prison.

Unfortunately, there was no simple or easy fix, and I returned to the outside with a hammer and determination. I selected a cinder block and began to bang away. Soon, the block began to yield. Into the light Vlad emerged wide eyed and dusty, but no worse the wear.

Breaking down walls is hard work. Whether it is a foundation to free a mischievous kitty or the emotional walls we build for protection. We erect our walls for defense from emotional hurt and sometimes to hide the sins in our lives.

However, walls can cause some serious problems. Over time, they can actually become more of a prison than an act of self-preservation. In fact, the walls that we build into our lives and into our minds are so strong that they prevent us from experiencing all that God has to offer, and they can cause us to become entrapped in our own anger, bitterness, and unforgiveness.

What are the walls in your life? Are there things that you have put in place to protect you? Are the walls you have built preventing you from moving forward and growing spiritually in God?

The Fast and the Futile

The light turned green and the white Suburban in front of me did not move. I gave it a second or two and then I blew the horn, the truck lurched forward. As I followed this vehicle, I watched as it drifted from crossing the yellow line to barely missing the ditch.

All the way down the road it was fast, then slow, weave, brakes, speed up.

Finally, the road opened and I merged with the next lane to pass the erratic driver. As I did so, I stole a glance. The huge Suburban was being piloted by a tiny woman who was very much more interested in her cell phone than driving. This woman was choosing to ignore her responsibility as a driver, of a rather large vehicle, I will add, because she was consumed by her cell phone.

As Christians—and I am speaking to myself too—we are often guilty of rolling through life so self-consumed we miss out on opportunities to touch people in need. We are often blinded by the bills, house repairs, car trouble, love dilemmas, work injustices, grocery prices and the elections that we find ourselves weaving all over the road. We pass by those we could aid. The hungry, lost, lonely, sick and forgot-

266

ten sit along the streets in our lives and often we are so obsessed with ourselves we motor right by them. Our noses stuck in our phones while we tap our feet to Pandora's free music app and Siri reads our text.

We all have a tendency toward self-centeredness. It is our human nature. However, as a born again Christian, we have the Holy Spirit that resides within us.

> ***Hereby know we that we dwell in him, and he in us, because he hath given us of his Spirit (1 John 4:13).***

The big question is, which are you going to allow drive your life? Will it be the flesh or the Spirit?

Out of Bounds

"But of the tree of the knowledge of good and evil, thou shalt not eat of it: for in the day that thou eatest thereof thou shalt surely die."
Genesis 2:17

I was the last to stash my bike in the culvert. I had not wanted to join the others, but they had goaded me until I agreed. I lagged behind as we crossed the field. Watching as the others jumped the creek and crawled under the barbed wire barrier I hesitated. Just a few yards away, the Johnson's pool, like a mirror shone in the midday sun. I was hot and tired; the idea of the cool water wooed me. The others had already entered and I watched as they splashed in the blue oasis.

I climbed the chain-link fence.

The water instantly refreshed me and I dove deep, retreating from the harsh summer sun. Together we swam in the hidden sanctuary and then leaned against the fence, allowing the warm air to dry us. We visited the pool several times that summer.

One day we were overrun by the neighborhood bully, Greg and his friends. They were bigger, older and bent on torturing us. We scrambled to get out of the water and over the fence. From the other side of the creek, I watched as the boys trashed the pool, throwing the lounge chairs, table and plants into the water. I was immediately ashamed. If I had not crossed the boundary, the Johnson's property would have not been vandalized. I never returned.

Boundaries are about taking responsibility for our actions. They are not just for keeping trouble out. Boundaries are for our protection. To keep us from crossing lines we should not. As Christians, we should respect the lines that God has ordained for his children. God has given us free will to choose to live within His boundaries or outside.

Adam and Eve were given only one boundary in the Garden of Eden. The garden provided all that they could desire and only one tree was the man and woman commanded to abstain; the tree of knowledge of good and evil. They had the freedom to remain within God's bounds, but they chose to overstep and sinned.

Their sin is still evident today and we live with the consequences of their choice. When we chose to step outside of the boundaries, our actions touch the lives of all those that we share this world. Some sins last for generations. Alcoholism, adultery, addiction, pornography, molestation, rape, and the list continues. Anytime we chose to step outside the limits that God has set, lives are affected. Sometimes lives are destroyed.

Do you respect the boundaries that God has ordained? Choose today whether you will live within God's Will or out of bounds.

Never Alone

My mom pinned my name to my orange corduroy jumper and kissed me goodbye. As I boarded the bus, I looked back, she smiled and the doors closed. From my seat, I watched as the neighborhood melted away to the main road. Soon I was standing in a crowd of new kindergarteners. We were lined up and marched away to classes.

The room was loud, kids played and I suddenly felt alone. I slipped behind the door and there I stood silent and unseen. The teacher came in; however, I remained behind the door.

Time passed and soon I heard my mom's voice. I peeked out from the door. She was awash with relief as I ran out to wrap my arms around her and buried my face into her middle.

Sometimes we can be in a crowded room yet we feel alone.

Loneliness is something that we all experience from time to time. However, as God's children, we are never alone. The Holy Spirit, the

Comforter (John 14:16) dwells within us, interceding and praying to Lord, even when we no longer have the words to express our pain.

> *Likewise the Spirit also helpeth our infirmities: for we know not what we should pray for as we ought: but the Spirit itself maketh intercession for us with groanings which cannot be uttered. Romans 8:26*

Likewise, God provides people in our lives to help us during difficult times. He uses His children to encourage and lift up one another.

> *Wherefore comfort yourselves together, and edify one another, even as also ye do. 1 Thessalonians 5:11*

From time to time, we all feel lonely. Nonetheless, when we do we need to remember that we are never alone, never forgotten, and always loved.

One to One

Saturday morning I got up early. I showered and then picked out an outfit. I carefully applied my makeup and fixed my hair. I checked and double checked myself in the mirror. I wanted to be my best for my daddy when he came for me. I was early so I went to the porch and waited. Every car that passed by; I eagerly looked to see if it was him.

I was excited just giddy really. In our busy lives, we had tried a couple of times to schedule a Saturday. However, issues, work and weather had gotten in the way. Our plan was to go find him a new cell phone and then have lunch. I had told everyone that I was meeting him. Some people more than once. I really was very happy.

We had a terrific morning. We found him a phone and we enjoyed our favorite meal. Chicken Chimichanga with extra guacamole! We joked and laughed. I sought his counsel and he graciously gave me his wisdom. It is a memory that I will cherish, because I had him to myself. No brother or sister. No grandchildren. No distraction. Just me and my daddy.

Later, as I reflected on our time, I recognized that we should also come before our Heavenly Father with the same enthusiasm. Eagerly we should seek him and put aside our distractions. We should find that quiet one and one time. With confidence we should bring our questions, our concerns to him and then accept the wise counsel He so willingly wants to share with us.

In our hectic world, it is often difficult to cull out a moment of peace and quiet. However, we must find that time. Cancel that event, refuse that invitation, leave the dishes an hour or two more and find that quiet closet. That place where you and your Heavenly Father can be together. Share your day, your worries, your heartaches and your confusion.

> *5 And when thou prayest, thou shalt not be as the hypocrites are: for they love to pray standing in the synagogues and in the corners of the streets, that they may be seen of men. Verily I say unto you, They have their reward. 6 But thou, when thou prayest, enter into thy closet, and when thou hast shut thy door, pray to thy Father which is in secret; and thy Father which seeth in secret shall reward thee openly. Matthew 6:5-6*

Find time for just you and God this week.

The Tupperware Tango

I was washing dishes the other night and I went to put the "gladware" in the cabinet. I actually do not have to the finish this illustration. You already know what I am going to write. You know that when I opened the cabinet door, every last piece of gladware, Tupperware, and plastic butter tub launched into my face. They bounced like ping pong balls around the countertop spilling onto the floor. I wildly grasp at the air in an attempt to catch the deluge and for my effort I managed one lid.

Emma barked madly, Bryan thought it was a game and began flicking the plastic terrors back into play. Miss Dixie's crackling laugh peeled through the house and the assassins watched, smirking. However, my daughters did not even seem to notice.

I was overtaken by sudden chaos. I do not have to type it all out, because you have experienced the same. You too have danced the Tupperware tango.

Many times when I find myself amid the chaos, I am reminded that "*..There hath no temptation taken you but such as <u>is common to man</u>: but God is faithful.*

In this verse, "temptation" (peirasmos) can also be translated "testing." Practically speaking, this term could be translated "temptation and testing." Every temptation is a test; every test is a temptation.

Our lives are series of trials and temptations. And our trials and temptations are not unique. What is unique is how you choose to handle them. You are not the first person to be tempted sexually or financially, nor are you the first person to be facing the trial of cancer the heartbreak of divorce. The key to the verse is "but God is faithful."

In this verse, Paul promises that God is faithful and He will not allow you to be tested or tempted beyond what you are able. Yet, we must draw on God to deliver us. He will give you the strength as you sit in the doctor's office, He will give you an escape route in your temptations.

You have the tools, the resources through Christ to withstand anything that comes your way in this chaotic and unpredictable life. Do not lose heart. Do not allow yourself to feel isolated, believing that no one will understand. No one knows what you are facing, or even how you feel. Everyone has been touched in some way by the same thing that you are facing today. Bring it before God "*who will not suffer you to be tempted above that ye are able; but will with the temptation also make a way to escape, that ye may be able to bear it.*" *I Corinthians 10:13b*

Mother Theresa (1910-1997) once said, "I know God won't give me more than I can handle. I just wish he didn't trust me so much."

Let's Cook Up
Something Good!

I really enjoy cooking. Sometimes when everything is nuts and I need an escape, I pull out the skillet and cutting board. Chopping up veggies rather than chopping off heads is the best route. The other day I found a recipe that I thought was interesting and I wanted to try. I just hoped that I had what I needed in the kitchen. Maybe I should just run on to the store and get the items. I carried my tablet with the list of ingredients and began pulling the spices, vegetables and cans from my cabinets, refrigerator and freezer. I was very excited when I found that I had everything I needed to accomplish this recipe in my kitchen. I did not have to go out for anything.

So out came the cutting board and I began chopping.

As I was chopping onion and soaking in the smell of the garlic as its aroma was being released in the olive oil, I thought about how you and I neglect to see that we too have everything we need within us to accomplish great things for Christ and in our lives.

Everything we need to achieve and overcome is within us. You just have to search it out. Many times, we want the drive through way in our lives. We want all the answers in a nice little package handed to us out the window. However, it is not supposed to be that way.

We all have desires, dreams, fears, worries and situations that we face throughout our lives. Often these experiences can be overwhelming and we begin to grasp at anything to make us feel better. The first thing we seem to forget is that everything we need is provided to us. God has given you the strength to face adversity when it comes and He has given you the talents and the drive to accomplish your desires and dreams. Everything YOU and I need to get through the day, through the nights, the test, challenges, the insecurities is provided. You just have to look for it. Seek the wisdom, for the comfort for the guidance that in the book of Matthew tells us is given abundantly to those that ask.

> *⁷ Ask, and it shall be given you; seek, and ye shall*
> *find; knock, and it shall be opened unto you:*
> *⁸ For every one that asketh receiveth; and he that seeketh*
> *findeth; and to him that knocketh it shall be opened.*
> *Matthew 7:7-8*

We are capable of wonderful things. However, we search in all the wrong places for the strength and the courage to achieve our dreams and our potential. In Christ we have all-sufficient resources. It is through Christ that we experience abundant love and hope of eternity in heaven. The promises of the Bible teach practically to life and godliness, victory over sin, fruit of the Holy Spirit, wisdom and strength to deal with trials and peace that passes understanding. We have it all at our fingertips.

You have everything you need to accomplish anything that you want. So what's holding you back?

Where is Your Hope?

*Why art thou cast down, O my soul? and why art
thou disquieted within me? Hope in God:*
Psalm 43:5

It is 11:23 on Sunday evening and I am sitting in front of my laptop watching the cursor blink. Eagerly it flashes waiting on me to type something. The clock ticks and Monday morning is getting ever closer.

Yet, all I seem to be able to do is to stare at the blinking arrow.

All week I have been looking for a Mustard Seed. Hoping a memory or event will trigger a thought or remind me of a Bible verse or event. I have prayed, read the Bible, talked to friends and waited.

However, nothing has come to me. I keep hoping something will inspire me. I am expecting the words to come and I have been anticipating God's direction.

I have said several times to those close to me, "I don't have a seed this week." "It will come." They reply with gentle encouragement.

Yet, Sunday night is here and I still wait, holding on to hope.

As I read over what I have written so far, I think about Bible verses about waiting on the Lord and holding onto hope in difficult times. About how many live in a state of hopelessness, and how our definition of hope is different than that of the Bible. Man's hope is in worldly things. Most people understand hope as wishful thinking.

"I hope that I win the lottery." "I hope things get better soon."

"I hope I get a raise." And so on.

This is not what the Bible means by hope. The biblical definition of hope is "confident expectation." Hope is firm assurance. As Christians, our hope in Jesus is much more than wishful utterances, it is about expectation and fulfillment of faith. Hope in Christ is the means to trust in, wait for, and to look for fulfillment. When your hope is in Jesus you know that as long as Jesus lives — and he will never die again — and our hope is in him, our hope lives with him.

Where is your hope? Is it in worldly things, people, or money? Our hope should be in the risen savior, Christ Jesus.

God Replace Depression
With Joy

The righteous cry, and the Lord heareth, and
delivereth them out of all their troubles.
The Lord is nigh unto them that are of a broken
heart; and saveth such as be of a contrite spirit.
Psalm 34:17-18

I have dealt with depression on and off throughout my adult life. I am no stranger to the feelings of hopelessness and overwhelming sadness.

Depression comes in many forms. Sometimes we are aware of our triggers and sometimes not. One of my triggers is when I find myself dwelling on the past, such as my mistakes, bad decisions and failings. I find myself saturated in shame and from there I begin my spiral. I worry about my future and my children's life. My head begins to pound and my energy is drained and all I want is the comfort of my bed, pulling the covers over my head and sleeping.

Today, I have been bound by downheartedness. My eyes are raw from salty tears, my head pounds and my body aches. Depression is a very real part of life for us all. It follows some throughout their entire life, robbing the joy of their hearts.

Depression, fear and hopelessness come to all. King David wrote extensively throughout the Psalms about these feelings. He poured his heart out before the Lord in some of the most moving and beautiful Psalms. He also filled the Psalms with his rejoicing and praise as our God lifted him from the pits.

God is still listening. God is still intervening and God is still in charge. Many times we forget the power of God. We watch the news, read the paper and check in to CNN. Life can seem rather pointless when you dwell on all that is wrong in this world. However, we are not spinning all alone on this planet. God is just as much in control as He was when He spoke it into existence.

God does not want you to dwell on the past or fear the future. If you have asked for forgiveness, then God has forgiven you, why do you dwell on it? Forgive yourself and waste no more energy on it.

> **As far as the east is from the west, so far hath he removed our transgressions from us. Psalms 103:12**

Do not fear the future, "**For I know the thoughts that I think toward you, said the LORD, thoughts of peace, and not of evil, to give you an expected end. Jeremiah 29:11**

God has a plan for you and for me. He has a plan for this world. We are not just hanging here, there is a design, and there is a future.

I heard a song in church this morning, it said, "*Lord, replace depression with joy*" Our joy comes from the Lord. Not people, money, station in life, jobs or houses. Our security is not in the threat level of the pentagon, it is in Christ.

I know it seems sometimes hopeless, dark and scary, but God is large and in charge and he cares for you.

Allow the Lord to replace your anxiety and depression with His joy.

Joy Trumps Depression
Every Time

Last week I shared with you my heartache and depression. My heart was heavy and my eyes always moist with perpetual tears. I had thought myself alone.

Who can say what causes us to focus on the bleak and discouraging things around us or why we can find ourselves overwhelmed, dejected and at a loss for hope. However, many of us pass through depression and downheartedness many times throughout our lives.

On Wednesday, a delivery came to my work. It was beautiful flowers. The vase boasted of yellow roses, white lilies and sprays of delicate purple flowers. The smell filled my cubicle with the fragrance of spring, and their beauty coaxed a shy smile.

Who were they from, you ask? The card read, "It will get better. God"

Well, I was crying again, but this time it was with joy. I was not forgotten, neither was my pain beyond God's concern.

Did I find out who the bouquet was from? No, I do not know which of God's children chose to be Jesus' hands and feet for me in my time of need. Over the next few days, I received supporting cards, emails and hugs. I received prayers and words of encouragement. I was honestly lavished in love. God's love. So many people became the manifestation of Christ in my physical life this past week.

We are the hands and feet of Jesus. We are the arms of the Lord when we give a hug. His lips when we smile, a mouthpiece when we share a word of kindness. Anytime you reach out to touch another you are acting as the physical form of Jesus for the needy, brokenhearted, sick and forgotten.

Your hands may crochet a hat for the homeless, you may cook for the sick, you may drive the elderly and you kneel to your knees for many in prayer.

Jesus now sits on the right hand of the throne of God interceding for us. His physical body no longer walks the earth. That is why you and I are called to be the physical manifestation of Christ to those in our life.

Never underestimate what your actions in the name of Jesus do for those hurting around you. I can tell you firsthand, that being lavished by His love through you has broken the bonds of depression that just last week held me captive. Be willing to accept the call to act for our Savior. Share His limitless love with those around you.

Thank you. I will never forget the love that many gave so abundantly in my hour of need.

Heart Strings or Faith

*The heart is deceitful above all things, and
desperately wicked: who can know it?*
Jeremiah 17:9

When I was very young we had some dear family friends. They had a daughter that shared my name and was a year my junior. She had been born with diabetes. It was difficult for this young girl to deal with her condition. Daily she was subjected to insulin shots and she was denied sweets.

Many times when they came up to stay with us or we went down to stay with them in their Atlanta home, the same scenario would play out. The daughter would hide; candy, sodas and anything that she was not to indulge due to her illness. Once alone, she would stuff the sweets into her mouth and guzzle the sodas. Many times their trip or ours would be cut short because the girl would become so ill.

One particular morning the child had consumed some candy she had found in her mother's purse. She had consumed them all and had chased it with a can of coke she had taken from the refrigerator. Her diabetes was so severe that she was immediately ill. It was a terrible scene to witness as she cried and screamed. Her father fought to hold her still so the mother could bury the needle into her belly.

On one such occasion, I stood in the living room doorway agape at what was unfolding before my eyes. The daughter went into a seizure. Her parents struggled to subdue her and my mom rushed to call an ambulance.

Later, as she was taken to the hospital, I turned to my mom and asked, "Why does Missy do that, if she knows it will make her so sick that she could die." I was crying at the thought of her dying.

"Because all Missy can think about is what she wants and not the consequences." She replied.

Have you ever been so deep into a sin that you were unable to see all those around you? Your focus was in what you wanted and the feelings of others were of no consequences to you. Unfortunately, many of us can say yes to this question. I included.

The human heart is the seat of man's selfishness. The heart wants what it wants and does not concern itself with what is right or wrong. This child was focused on her desire and gave no thought to the consequences of her actions. Not only did she disregard her health, she also disregarded the pain, worry and fear that her parents dealt with on a daily basis. All this little girl did was resent and blame those closest to her and that loved her most. Refusing to acknowledge her issues and their repercussion was the child's biggest folly.

Most times, man is the same. We become focused and single-minded. There can be no rest until we have achieved what we want. It is this behavior that estranges people from one another and from God. As long as we are going by feeling and not faith, we will soon meet a terrible end.

I unfortunately know this well. I have chosen my heart before faith. I have hurt people and myself in following the fleshly desires.

We are to live by faith and not the desires of the heart.

Paging the Great Physician!

When you say the word 'dentist,' I immediately imagine Steve Martin's character, Orin Scrivello, DDS, in _Little Shop of Horrors_. Leather jacket, curled lip and travel size laughing gas. He lived to torture everyone that crossed the threshold of his office. Fortunately, for me, my dentist is no way like Orin.

Yet, I seem to harbor the same fear as if he did. I have been nursing a broken and infected tooth for 9 months. Yes, you read it correctly, 9 months. Why, you ask as you run your tongue across your teeth and the memories of your last tooth ache spring to mind. Honestly, I was afraid to deal with the tooth. I did not want to go and have to have it treated. I did not want to miss work, or run up another bill. I did not want to subject myself to the high pitch whirling of the drill, or the needles buried in my mouth making my face droop and my words slur. I simply did not want to deal with it. So I didn't. Each and every day, the infection grew, spreading through my gums into my jaw until I awoke and went to sleep with the constant dull ache. There was no relief.

It is like that when we refuse to deal with sin in our lives. We do not want to have to admit what we have done. We think about apologizing, but the confession sticks in our throat. Maybe excising the sin seems overwhelming. We cannot bring ourselves to call the doctor, rehab or a counselor. We believe we can handle the alcohol we have depended on to numb our minds, pornography to satisfy our desires, the affair that we thought would give comfort, the missing money we hoped nobody would miss, the depression from dwelling on the past. Or our drug habit that bent our minds and left us clueless and hungry for more on our own. Or like me and my tooth, we think that if we ignore it long enough, it will simply heal itself and disappear.

Unfortunately, sin is like an infection. An infection begins with one nasty little bacteria and it multiplies and spreads. So does sin when left untreated. How do you treat sin? First, you acknowledge it, confess and turn it over to the great physician.

After my ordeal was over, the tooth removed the antibiotics kicking bacterial butt, I could not help but wonder why I would allow myself such pain and misery. Was it pride, denial, laziness or fear that held me back? Whatever it was that I allowed, prolonging my pain, was silly and foolish. When the symptoms developed I should have seen the dentist right away. The same is true for sin. When sin enters your life and it does come in many forms and modes, call on the Great Physician right away before it gets a foothold and the opportunity to spread.

Jesus wants to bring you healing. He wants to free you of your sin. Let Him. Allow Him to treat your sin and through Him remove it from your heart. The first step is yours. Get on your knees and make that appointment!

Expectant, Faithful and Confident

> *Behold, as the eyes of servants look unto the hand of their masters, and as the eyes of a maiden unto the hand of her mistress; so our eyes wait upon the LORD our God, until that he have mercy upon us.*
>
> *Psalms 123:2*

Gray pale light filtered through the curtains of my bedroom window. The house was silent. I slipped from the bed, my toes stretching to touch the carpet. I moved to my sister's bed and shook her gently. Her eyes popped open, "Is it time?"

"Almost." I whispered back with a smile. Just then the bedroom door parted and my brother crept in, his eyes shining in the early dawn. Excitement filled the room swirling around us inspiring smiles and little giggles.

Down the hall we crept, my sister dragging a blanket behind us. Silently we filed into my parents room and assumed our positions on the floor just feet from the bed where mom and dad slept. We wrapped up in the blanket and stared at our mom's sleeping face. Not a one of us made a sound or stirred.

In just a few moments, though to us it felt like hours ticking past, my mother moved. We watched expectantly.

Then suddenly, one eye popped open and roved from one kid's face to the next. As quickly as it opened, it sealed again. We exchanged nervous glances and waited.

Again, one eye burst open and studied us. It stopped on each face and snapped shut once again.

"David?" My mother muttered. Her eyes tightly shut, the covers tucked under her chin, she repeated this time louder. "David?"

"Yeah?"

"They're up."

By this time all three of us shivered like tuning forks with excitement. Yet, we continued to wait. Expectant. Faithful. Confident.

Finally, the covers were thrown back and mom and dad gave the signal that Christmas had begun. Running all over each other we took the stairs in a stampede and burst into the living room.

Waiting is hard to do, whether we are waiting on Christmas morning, an answered prayer, a healing, a reconciliation, job opportunity or wisdom in a matter. However, we must wait and we should do so expectantly, confidently and faithfully. I admit that waiting has never been my forte. I do not like waiting on anything.

Many times when we have to wait, we begin to allow our faith to wane and we try to take things into our own hands. God's timing is perfect. Choosing to interfere and impose our own wishes often leads to bad consequences and missed blessings.

Wait upon the Lord confidently. **He will** answer your prayer. Wait expectantly, always ready to receive **His answer**. Finally, wait upon the Lord faithfully. **He will not let you down.**

Masquerade

My daughters enjoy cos-play. Many of you have furrowed brows right now and are questioning what exactly

Cos-Play is. Well, to define it simply, it is dress up for adults, and it is internationally popular. People of all ages go to these Comic-cons. The idea is to dress like your favorite anime, comic book or sci-fi character and assume that role. Wigs, makeup, costumes and props litter my house for weeks before the conventions. My girls take pains-taking time to build their costumes for the day they debut.

Like my daughter's, many masqueraders study the mannerisms and accents of their characters. They work very hard to be as authentic in their portrayal and as true to their chosen character as humanly possible.

However, once they come home from the conventions, they return to their lives' leaving behind the character they had assumed with such passion.

Unfortunately, we too have the tendency to pick up the costume of Christ, play the part and then when the moment has passed return to our own personality. As Christians, we are to assume the character of Jesus each and every day. We do not just masquerade, we are to live it.

When you accept the grace through Christ's death on the cross, it comes with responsibility. Many people want salvation. They want the benefits that come with it but not the accountability. You assume the responsibility to share the message of Jesus with the people in your life. Many Christians forget their responsibility to those around them. They forget that they have taken the name Christian and everything they do is in Jesus' name. Everything they say, where they go, how they treat people, choices they make has Jesus' name on it. When you identify yourself as a Christian, this world no longer judges you by you, they are judging Jesus. They are deciding whether they want to be associated with the name Jesus.

Are you masquerading as Jesus or are you living a life true to His character?

Equal Measure

Give, and it shall be given unto you; good measure, pressed down, and shaken together, and running over, shall men give into your bosom. For with the same measure that ye mete withal it shall be measured to you again.
Luke 6:38

One Sunday evening as my mom and dad were finishing getting ready for church, I had asked if my brother and I could have something to drink. We had been given the ok for tea. My mother makes the most wonderful tea. It is always perfect, never too strong or sweet. When I opened the refrigerator I was disappointed to see that there was not much tea in the jug. Somehow, I had to divide what little there was between us. I took two glasses from the cabinet. One was very slim and tall and the other wider and somewhat shorter. My brother was well accustomed to my tricks, so he demanded solemnly that we were to get equal amounts. I agreed and set the glasses side by side on the counter and began doling out the liquid. I would pour some into one glass and then into the other. My brother was intently watching, his chin resting on the counter, his eyes fixed on my every move.

"There!" I announced, finally draining the last of the tea from the jug. I slid the slim tall glass across to him. He eyed it carefully. Satisfied that they were equal, he lifted the glass from the counter. Just as he was about to drink, my daddy came in the kitchen. Unfortunately, he had been listening and watching at the door. He took the glass from my brother and handed it to me. Then he handed my glass to my brother.

"Hey, why did you do that?" I whined. "You know why."

"No, I don't." I cried back. Daddy shot me a glance and I knew it was in my best interest to let it be.

My brother guzzled the tea as fast as he could in case there was to be another glass switch. He had no idea what had just happened. He did not realize that though the glasses were even, my wider glass held more than his thin glass. I grumbled under my breath, stomped to the table and fought back tears. I had been busted.

How we treat people should be a priority for the Christian each and every day. Do we deal with folks in a forgiving, loving and understanding way? Do we put the needs of others before our own?

In Luke 6, Jesus is instructing those who follow Him to "give" forgiveness and a non-condemning attitude in the same amount we desire to be forgiven. We are to be as merciful as God with one another. That means that forgiveness and love should be a priority for each of us.

Do you give mercy and forgiveness to others as God does for you? Is the measure you use against another the same measure you would want leveled against you?

A Legacy of Glory

We will not hide them *from their children, shewing to the generation to come the praises of the LORD, and his strength, and his wonderful works that he hath done."*
Psalms 78:4

My daughter has been working at a hotel in housekeeping. Every day she comes home with funny, disgusting and outrageous stories of what people leave behind when they check out.

She says, "Mom, there are three types of rooms. First, you have the rooms that are trashed, completely ruined. Beer cans, food and filth. Then you have brooms that are neat and a tip is left on the dresser. Sometimes you get nice notes. One time I had a drink, bag of chips and five dollar bill that said, "Have lunch on me!" And finally the rooms that look as if no one even stayed in them. Those are the creepiest ones."

I thought about that. My daughter sees what people have left behind. A snapshot, if you will, of their lives.

Recently, she was sent to clean out a room of a gentleman that died. She took and packed his suitcase with clothing, a book, some reading glasses and a pad scribbled with notes. She gathered his toiletries and prepared his belongings for his widow to pick up. It was a very sobering day for her, and frankly, it gave me pause as well.

When your time comes, what will be your legacy? What will you leave behind?

We should strive to leave behind a legacy of glory. No, not our glory, but Jesus' glory that is reflected through us. His legacy continues in you and in me. There is no greater legacy than this.

How can we leave this legacy of glory? By living the same way Christ lived through His presence in you. Love one another. Help one another. Reach out to the stranger in need. Feed the hungry, encourage the downtrodden, lift up the weak and show compassion. Accept responsibility. Forgive. Share Jesus with everyone.

What kind of legacy will you leave behind? Will it be lasting? Or will you leave behind only tangible items—buildings, money, and possessions?

In Search of Wisdom

If any of you lack wisdom, let him ask of God, that giveth to all men liberally, and upbraideth not; and it shall be given him.
James 1:15

My daughter was on her first or second day at the hotel she was working when she was faced with something she had never dealt. It was an ironing board. Not many of our clothes these days require much ironing and frankly, my daughter's did not have the privilege to use one.

She tried to close the ironing board, but she could not get it to fold. Twisting and flipping the board she could not figure out how to get it to close. Finally, in desperation, she pulled YouTube up on her phone and searched for instructions on how to fold an ironing board. Unfortunately, however, she could not find one and went on to ask a coworker who was equally puzzled. For over an hour the two young ladies battled the stubborn contraption until finally an older lady schooled them on Ironing Boards 101.

When she related this story to me, I laughed so hard, I thought I would wet myself. She expressed her story with obvious puzzlement and frustration. It was not so much she did not know how to close it;

299

it was more that she chose to consult YouTube. Of all the resources, she chose to reference her phone.

Even in our spiritual lives, we will explore many avenues to gain wisdom and answers, ignoring the first place we should turn. The Bible tells us openly that wisdom and discernment are given freely and liberally if you only ask. Since we do not naturally have the wisdom from above— spiritual wisdom—then we must ask God for it in faith.

Many possess wisdom, but is it of God or man? There is a big difference in God's wisdom and man's. God's wisdom follows righteousness. Man's, earthly desires. Any time we seek wisdom we have to examine whether this wisdom follows God.

Where do you go to for wisdom? Do you seek God's wisdom or man's?

Emma the Terrible:
All Bark No Bite

Study to shew thyself approved unto God, a
workman that needeth not to be ashamed,
rightly dividing the word of truth
2 Timothy 2:15

We have new neighbors across the street. I walked over the other night to introduce myself and share some jam. Nothing says welcome to the hood like fresh blueberry jam! However, in the middle of the chit chat, I heard the familiar yip yap of Emma the Terrible. I turned to see that she had eluded my daughter by squeezing through the screen door. My daughter chased her out on the porch, but Emma shot through her legs after faking left. The little Chihuahua tore down the driveway intent on getting to her mistress. I turned from my new acquaintances and ran for the road, looking for oncoming cars I rushed to get her before she was hit. Without hesitation Emma came across the avenue in a mad dash. Bulging eyes, white needle like teeth bared and fur standing up. She ran past me to the new neighbor and snarled and barked in that ever familiar shrill yip. I scooped her up, while offering my apologies for my fur baby's misbehavior. The lady asked to pet her and as soon as she came near Emma, Emma scrambled to get away from her. Burying her face under my arm, she continued to growl. This is not new behavior for Emma the Terrible, in fact, it is typical.

Emma will bark and snarl, but as soon as someone comes near her she retreats as fast as she started her charge. Oh, she made every effort to convince my neighbor that she was a 150 pound Rottweiler. Emma wanted her to know that she was going to protect, however, when it came time to follow through, Emma just hid and did nothing.

Of course, Emma's behavior is not unique. There are many Christians that also have the tendency to bark and snarl. They boastfully bark about being a Christian yet never seem to get to the action part. When it comes time to get dirty, they retreat. A Christian life is a busy life. It gets dirty sometimes and there are sacrifices. A life of action, not just words. I get frustrated with people that want to boast about their righteousness, sign every petition that comes online or hit share on Facebook, yet when someone is in need they are nowhere to be found. Online petitions do not mean a hill of beans to a family that just lost their house to foreclosure or the husband leaving the hospital without his wife. No matter how many times you hit "Share" on Facebook, it does nothing for the sick neighbor, struggling coworker or hungry child. We simply cannot bark, point and click. We have to be willing to bite into issues too. Be a part of the solutions. We need to trade the megaphone and mouse for a compassionate heart and extend a hand. Words mean nothing unless they are backed by action. Be willing to back up what you verbally claim with action, with love, with compassion and generosity.

Are you a barker spouting empty words, or a biter?

If you read history you will find that the Christians who did the most for the present world were just those who thought most of the next. It is since Christians have largely ceased to think of the other world that they have become so ineffective in this. C. S. Lewis, Mere Christianity

Butterfinger

The child was probably 6 maybe 7 years old. He was a bright young man with dark hair and lively green eyes. Slightly built, he possessed an inquisitive mind and a bit of mischief. It was Saturday and as their ritual dictated he had accompanied his father to the barber for a trim. The weekly trip was more about the camaraderie of the men than actual hair for the father. However, for the son, it was about the prize he would receive if he behaved.

The youngster waited patiently, his hands sweaty in expectation. His feet not yet able to touch the floor, swung back and forth expelling what energy he could. Finally, as his dad climbed into the red vinyl barber chair, he motioned for his son and dug in his pants pocket. With a smile and a pat on the head, he presented the youth with a shiny nickel.

"Thanks Dad!" The youngster yelled over his shoulder as he ran out the door, the bell dangling over the portal announced his departure. Leaving behind the men to continue their political postulating he ran down the sidewalk. The nickel tightly clenched in his fist, his heart racing and his anticipation swelling like shaken cola propelled him ever closer to the general store.

Once inside the establishment, he perused the toys glancing over the army men more than once. Determining he could do without them this week, he set his heart on what he really wanted. He approached the counter; glass jars filled with colorful penny candies hovered at eye level. The counter man leaned down and addressed the lad.

"What can I get for you, young man?

Clearing his throat, he raised the nickel pinched between forefinger and thumb. "A Butterfinger, sir."

"Coming up!" Came the cheerful reply as the nickel scraped across the counter and landed with a clink in the till.

"Let me see your hand, young man."

The boy stood on tip toe and extended an eager palm. However, the man in the dingy apron and a paper cap gripped his hand and with one swift swipe covered the boy's finger in butter.

"There you go!" He beamed down at the child and then began to laugh. "A butter finger!" His laughter roared through the store.

The boy retreated from the laughter and quickly began walking back to the barber shop. The heat of his skin and the light of sun had begun the butter melting. It oozed down his finger and filled his hand. Tears began to swell in the wells of his eyes. Disappointment pierced his heart.

Well, I don't know about you, but I have had my share of disappointment over the years. It is never a pleasant experience to have the hopes and dreams that you have anticipated shattered before you. However, it happens every day to each one of us.

Disappointment is the first seed of doubt. God allows disappointment to enter our lives to see if we will continue to trust Him. Disappointment may seem fairly harmless, yet it is often the tip of the iceberg that will stop our spiritual growth, make us believe we are defeated and make us bitter. If we dwell on the disappointment allowing it to fester in our hearts, it soon becomes discouragement. Discouragement left unchecked becomes disillusionment, then depression and finally defeat.

There is only one cure for festering disappointment and that is thanksgiving. In all circumstances, no matter how dark your situation may be, lift up praise to the Lord. He is the only one that can take the bad things and work them out for good.

> *And we know that all things work together for good to them that love God, to them who are the called according to his purpose. Romans 8:28*

We can thank him for his presence, his love, his blessings and rejoice that he has a plan for us.

> *For I know the thoughts that I think toward you, saith the LORD, thoughts of peace, and not of evil, to give you an expected end. Jeremiah 29:11*

Don't give disappointment a foothold in your life. Lift praise to the Lord.

As the tears spilled over the rim of his eyes a hand caught his shoulder. He turned to see a man in a white apron. The laughing curled lips had been replaced with a kind face. It was not the same man that had been behind the counter. Bending to one knee the man gently wiped the butter from the child's finger and hand. Then he wiped the tears from his cheek. From his pocket he produced a Butterfinger.

Let God help you through the disappointment.

Do You Work for God or Man?

A superior other than my direct supervisor asked me to do something one morning. I was busy. I was working against deadlines and had projects all over my desk. The task I was asked to do was simple and menial. In addition, the person asking could have easily done it. In fact, it would have taken less time for them to do it than to find me and ask me to do it. I will be honest with you; I was not amused.

I left my emails, a person waiting and ringing phone because they wanted it done immediately. I completed the task and returned to find them standing in the same spot at my desk hands on hips. I reported the task complete and they walked away, without a thank you. As I watched them walk away, I was fussing in my mind, I turned to my workspace and began huffing around my cube and sighing loudly. Yep, I was frustrated and just plain mad. Just who did they think they were to stop me, and tell me to do something so trivial in the middle of my work? I had been called away from my job to complete something that did not have to do with my position in the department, or even my pay grade.

As I ranted and slung folders around my desk, a whisper filled my heart. *Who did I think I was to think myself above any task asked of me?* Shame replaced indignation. I claimed to be a servant of Christ. I claimed to live my life as Christ did. Where was my servant's spirit, my joy in helping another? What happened to doing my work as to the Lord and not to man?

Often times, I seem to forget that it is not all about me. The idea that I am to strive to be as Christ like as possible escapes me as I find myself in my "Missy Bubble". I am to work for the Lord. I am to please the Lord and represent Christ. I am not above any task asked of me.

Many times I find myself frustrated at work. Discouraged at times. Overwhelmed and underappreciated. However, it is because I have looked to men for acceptance and worth. Our self-worth is not to be derived from man, companies, bosses or the size of the number on a paycheck.

Work was given by God. ***And the Lord God took the man, and put him the Garden of Eden to dress it and keep it. Genesis 2:15*** God was the original boss. Just as Adam and Eve worked for the Lord, so do we in everything we do.

Your work is a blessing. It is the means provided to you to live. ***There is nothing better for a man, than that he should eat and drink, and that he should make his soul enjoy good in his labour. This also I saw, that it was from the hand of God. Ecclesiastes 2:24***

Rejoice in your work. Give praise that you have work and are healthy and capable.

On hard days, remember that God is the ultimate boss and that you work and answer to the Almighty.

SOAR

The sun's grip had begun to dissipate as the cool of the night chased the last scrapes of pink westward. The heat of the driveway penetrated into the soles of my feet and I enjoyed the soothing spread of the day's end warmth in my flesh. A breeze ruffled my curls and hugged me briefly and continued on through the trees tickling the leaves. A movement in the yard stole my attention and I stood to watch the squirrels as they did their last forage before bed. Above me the birds sought their roost for the night. Swooping from tree to tree with an urgency as the darkness spread across the earth.

I love all nature, but birds hold a special place in my heart. I enjoy watching them, especially when they are in flight. I envy how they hang suspended in the air, soaring high above the world. Confidently trusting and gliding on invisible support.

On this particular evening I spied a red tail hawk. Wings outstretched, she glided overhead trained on the patch of trees behind my house. As I watched, a small black bird, a starling, flapped furiously as it swooped down, striking the hawk. Then another starling attacked the gliding raptor. The hawk's altitude seemed to decrease slightly, she wavered, rocking on the unseen current that she rode, but she continued to glide, her piercing eyes focused on the grove ahead. The smaller foul continued to dive and strike the hawk. However, even under assault, the hawk continued along her course, confident in the air that kept her aloft. She entered the small stand of walnut trees, sending the Starling skittering off, blending into the fast approaching night.

As I watched the scenario play out, I was transfixed by the confidence the hawk had in the current that held her aloft as the assault relentlessly ensued. Though she could have easily been distracted or turned on the smaller foul, the hawk remained on course, focused on the refuge of the grove, her confidence unwavering.

As Christian we are under assault from the enemy daily. Our adversary's emissaries dart in and out of our lives, easily distracting us, however, we must stay the course. As the hawk trust the invisible support of the currents that she rides upon we too need to trust in the Lord though we cannot always see His hand in our lives and in the trials we face. He is quite literally the wind beneath our wings the unseen force that holds us above. However, until we trust in Him, keep focused and stay the course, we will always be falling to the trappings and distractions of the world below.

Set your affection on things above, not on
things on the earth. Colossians 3:2

Do not allow the temptations and heartaches of this world to distract you from Jesus. **You will** be tested, **you will** face trials and temptations that you never imaged, but keep to the course. Trust His love

311

and strength to keep you soaring. He will not allow you to fall but will lift you up as on the wings of eagles.

Soar!

The Echo

*This shall be written for the generation to come: and the
people which shall be created shall praise the LORD.
Psalm 102:18*

I stood on the edge of the quarry. The world was still and quiet except for the droning of the cicada and buzz of a famished mosquito. An angry orange sun blazed behind the trees, reluctant to stand down for the cool night. I sat down and scooted up to the edge. Peering over, my eyes followed down the rock wall to the still dark water below, I felt my stomach roll and the blood drain from my face. I moved back a bit and rested my eyes on the mirror finish of the manmade basin. Nothing stirred, and I wondered if there was life below that glass finish.

As I waited for my family to catch up, I pushed around leaf litter to find pebbles, rocks and nuts to throw into the cavernous pit below. I sat pitching most anything I could lift into the water. I heard my name. It echoed in the great crater, racing around rock walls and dispersing through the trees. Again "Missy" rang out and the sound bounced around repeating my name. I laughed, cupping my hands around my mouth. I shouted, "Over here!" My words rebounded around the rock face of the quarry.

I heard the dry leaves crunching and through the tangle I saw my parents and brother approaching. For the next hour, maybe longer, we sat on the quarry edge shouting into the man made gorge; phrases, songs and my dad's Goofy impression. I laughed with complete abandon and my amusement peeled through the rock confines repeating my joy like waves down the ravine. It was a good time and a cherished memory.

Jesus' love is like an echo—a two-thousand-year-old echo that still resounds today in the hearts of Christians. The Good News that was imparted to you, you now pass on. In essence, you and I are the echoes of Christ. As we witness to those around us, the Good News is passed to the coming generations.

Does your life echo the Good News of Salvation through Christ Jesus? What we do in our lives, echo into eternity.

Car Trouble

These things I have spoken unto you, that in me ye might have peace. In the world ye shall have tribulation: but be of good cheer; I have overcome the world.
John 16:33

My daughter had her first bout of car trouble this week, a really good first bite of life. I have had so many car issues in my past, I understand automotive dilemmas very well. So much so that I am barely fazed by them now. However, my poor first born was dipping her toe into that well of life's woes. She was wringing her hands, bouncing between tears and bursts of anger, and was bent all out of shape.

Do not tell her, but it made me kind of giggle. No, not in a mean way. Not a *"ha-ha"* way, but in the way you do when you know someone is about to get a big surprise—something really good. My daughter was getting a real dose of life, and the opportunity to see God at work. That's when God shows up and shows out for His children in times of troubles and woes.

Her grandfather stepped in and called the mechanic and tow truck. The problem was isolated and fixed the same day. We went to pick up the car and as it often is, the bill was all the money she had. But she paid it, on her own.

There she sat in her car tearful. "Mom, I'm broke. I don't get paid for two weeks." "Yes, but you are forgetting the good things." I said with a momma's smile.

I just love the looks you get from your offspring
when you are trying to help.

"What is good about all this mom?" She gestured as she threw up her hands. "My car broke down and I am broke!"

"Yes, but what about the wonderful things that happened? Your papa got the car towed and into a shop the same day. You had the money to pay for it and you have a good job and will get paid in two weeks. You had family that rallied for you! You had the means to pay your own way. You have a home, there will be food and your needs will be met. You are ok."

"Yeah, I guess."

"Today, you received blessings in your life and you have chosen to dwell on the bad. Your blessing heavily outweighed the problem. After all, the only problem was the car broke down. Everything else was blessings."

I will admit I am bad about dwelling on the bad things. However, when you pull back and really take in the whole situation you find that you are being covered in blessings—blessings that overcome the problems.

God is there with you in every situation. He is showering blessings on you. Do not pour all your energy into the problem so that you are blinded from the blessings. The problems and trials of this life have been overcome by the shedding of Christ blood. Keep your eyes on the cross and not on the problems.

Live Free

A few weeks ago I was sharing with a young woman. I was telling her about my life before I made a full commitment to Christ. Her jaw dropped and at some points she giggled. Finally, she said, "I just can't imagine you doing anything like that! There is no way you did those things." She said shaking her head in disbelief.

"That is because you have only known the redeemed Melissa. " I replied quietly filling with relief that the old me was gone for good.

On my drive back home I was going back over the conversation in my thoughts when a realization hit me like a slap to the back of the head. I realized that though I shared some really terrible things that I had done, I had not experienced the shame when I was relaying my stories. In fact, it is like remembering a movie or book, it was no longer me. The person that had committed those sins lives no more. Not only had I received forgiveness and salvation from Jesus' sacrifice, I had also been cleansed of my guilt and shame.

I can tell you that the realization in that moment filled me with excitement and tears flowed. I had lived for years with regret and shame and during those years I had worked through my way of thinking and prayed for grace to accept the full measure of salvation. This realization brought freedom with it. I was free finally of the past.

Many Christians live with shame and regret. They live defeated lives because of guilt. Though they have asked for forgiveness and have accepted Christ sacrifice they still hold to the shame. Somehow in our minds we think that if we let it go that we are not truly sorry or repentant. We tell ourselves that we can never be fully forgiven, that we do not deserve to fully experience the cleansing power of the blood that was shed on the cross. Nothing could be further from the truth.

> *"How much more shall the blood of Christ, who through the eternal Spirit offered himself without spot to God, purge your conscience from dead works to serve the living God?" Hebrews 9:14*

Hebrews 9:14 clearly states that His sacrifice purges your conscience from dead works. That means that not only has the sin itself been forgiven but the shame associated with it has been purged. Still, it can only be purged if you release it. Guilt and shame have bored into your mind and there Satan has a stronghold over you. His goal is to continually condemn you for a sin that is forgiven. He does not want you to experience the full freedom of salvation

If anyone in the Bible had a right to hold on to the shame and regret of his actions it would be Paul. For years he pursued the Christians. Torturing and putting to death hundreds. In his letter to Timothy Paul writes, ***I thank God, whom I serve from my forefathers with pure conscience... 2 Timothy 1:3a***

Paul accepted salvation and surrendered his shame. Without a clear conscience and surrendering not just the sin, but the regret and shame, you cannot fully enjoy freedom. Paul served God and preached the gospel with full freedom.

If you still hold on to regret, shame and guilt you are not living the life of freedom that Jesus' sacrifice provided to you.

Live Free.

Jump into the Word

Emma the Terrible has been sick lately. She has developed seizures, a condition very common in Chihuahuas. Emma is on three medications, and one is a steroid. If you thought Chihuahuas were hyper and downright nuts, you ought to see Emma on steroids. No cat, no bird, no one walking by the house, nothing and no one is ignored. She bounds through the house barking and leaping on and off the furniture. She races through the yard and under the fence to chase squirrels up the neighbor's tree.

She is like a tiny furry tornado raging through the neighborhood.

Emma already has a very healthy appetite, but the medication has really boosted it. This morning as I pulled out the two 10 gallon buckets, one for cat food and the other for dog, Emma was barking and running in circles, she was ready for some breakfast.

I pulled off the lids and gathered the bowls. Lining them up on the counter, I began to fill them with wet food to be mixed with the dry. With scoop in hand, I turned to see Emma in the dog food bucket, literally standing with all four feet in the food bucket. How she had been able to get into the pail, I have not the foggiest, but she was all the way in and devouring all she could as quickly as she could. She was not satisfied to wait on a portion. She wanted it all.

If only you and I had the same insatiable hunger for the Word of God that Emma does for Kibbles and Bits. I'm not talking about Sunday morning snacking as you follow along while the pastor speaks, or reading through a few verses, I am talking about getting into the Word. Really diving in and savoring every word. Taking time to understand why certain words were used, why things are repeated and even the punctuation. That is where the real meat is, in the deliberate, meticulous study of the Word verse by verse.

God's Word is a sufficient resource. Are you having trouble in your marriage, in your singleness, in debt, relationships, maybe in your employment? The answers are in the Bible. If you want a happier life, you need to fill your heart with the Word. Not just read it or snack on it, but savor it. Make it part of you.

Thy word have I hid in mine heart, Psalms 119:11

God has provided all we need to know in His Word. We are not meant to stumble around through life; wisdom, encouragement, understanding and knowledge are found in the Word. I encourage you to get out your Bible, pull up the Bible app, get on your Kindle, whatever media you choose and get filled up on the Word of God. Jump into the word with all four feet and see what God has for you in His Holy Word.

What Influences You?

The teacher called me to the front of the class. She stood with the paddle in her right hand.

"Turn around Missy. I said NO talking." She punctuated her sentence with a crack of the paddle on my rear. The sting of the paddle was lost in the heat of my embarrassment. "I'm going to send *another* note home to your mother."

Oh please anything but that. I inwardly pleaded as I made my way back to my desk to bury my face in the crook of my arm. Hot salty tears flowed and my nose stopped up. I felt the eyes of the class on me.

I dreaded going home that day. I would have to hand my Mom the letter written in my steno pad by the teacher, outlining my breech of the rules. Once home, I tried to plead with my Mom, explaining that it was not just me, but Angie Reynolds was the one that started it. I was only laughing at what she said. I was not talking, she was. My plea bought me no mercy. I had broken the rules, had been paddled and had a note sent home...again for talking in class. I was in big trouble. Blaming it on Angie would not help me. I knew how to behave in class. I had allowed myself to be influenced by Angie.

More than once I found myself in trouble being asked by my mother, "When are you going to learn to stay far away from Angie Reynolds?"

The influences we choose in our lives are very important. Many times we do not choose wisely and base our decisions on surface qualities. Even as adults we are not very good at choosing the company we keep. We find ourselves in relationships, sometimes even marriages, we should not be in with people that do not share our values. People that use and drain us for their benefit without thought to anyone else. We go to places we should not be, expose ourselves to people that spew negativity. Allow ourselves to be swayed from what we know is right and what is in God's plan for us.

If you are dealing with some depression, maybe anxieties and confusion, take an inventory of the people and the influences you are allowing into your life and home. If the influences in your life are contrary to the teachings of Jesus and the Bible then you will experience conflict in your spirit. Surround yourself with likeminded people, people that lift you up and are interested in the best for you, friends that get on their knees for you. Be ever watchful of the influences in your life, weak and corrupted characters can erode the ground you stand upon.

Ring for Assistance

*Ask, and it shall be given you; seek, and ye shall
find; knock, and it shall be opened unto you:
For every one that asketh receiveth; and he that seeketh
findeth; and to him that knocketh it shall be opened.*
Matthew 7:7-8

Friday, 2:36am

I was awakened by the tinkling of bells. I sat up and heard it again. I know this sound well; it's Big Bryan our American bulldog mix at the back door ringing the bell to let us know he needs out. I slid from the bed and stumbled to the back door where he sat obediently waiting on me. I unlocked and opened it and he took off down the steps. Knowing he might be a moment or two, I stumbled back to my bedroom and stretched out, waiting and listening for him to give me the bark. Moments passed, and I drifted between this world and the realm of wonderful slumber. Amid my floating I heard the tinkling of bells. It must be a dream, I thought, because Big Bryan is still outside. I heard it again. I padded back to the door, and there sat Vlad. His black fur blended in with the night. Only his green eyes shone. Upon seeing my approach, he took his paw and batted the bells. Then he looked back over his shoulder at me. "Meow." He plead. I scooped him up, and in the dark face to face he let out another "Meow." Then he purred and rubbed his face on my chin.

I opened the door and allowed him to walk along the railing of the deck as I waited for Big Bryan to make his way back.

In the chill of the night air, I watched Vlad pace the railing as he lifted his nose to breathe in the sweet cool air. His purr in the stillness seemed as loud as a motor. Occasionally, he came to me and rubbed his soft warm fur on me—gave me a loving head butt and returned to his enjoyment of the quiet darkness.

As I watched the feline, I thought about how Vlad was confident, even though he was a cat, that if he rang the bell he too would have the door opened to him.

In Matthew 7:8, the scripture says, "***For <u>every one</u> that asketh receiveth; and he that seeketh findeth; and to him that knocketh it shall be opened.***" It does not say, only the Jew or only the rich, the educated, or the master. Rather it says ***every one.***

I was curious that the Bible used *every one* rather than *everyone*. So I looked the difference. In the use of the compound *everyone*, it is used to refer to all the people in a group, but when written as two words it refers to each individual who makes up a group, therefore it means each person.

When you ask, when you seek, when you knock, whether Jew or Gentile, young or old, rich or poor, master or servant, educated or not the door is opened. You are not just welcomed, but are invited to knock.

<u>Every one</u> is received at the throne of grace when they repent and ask for forgiveness given only by the sacrifice of Jesus' blood. Won't you please knock today?

Wake up to the Son

I was leaving for work the other morning and as I was pulling the door closed I paused. I stood with the door ajar, looking into the living room motionless in the early morning gray. The house was quiet except for the droning of the air conditioner. My daughters slumbered in their beds; the pets had been fed and were curled up in favorite spots throughout the house resting. Even the birds had nestled their faces in their down. I paused because I wanted to go get back in my bed. I wanted to join them. I wanted to snuggle in warmth with my favorite elephant blanket with Emma tucked under my arm. I wanted to sleep and allow the day and life to carry on while I slept, oblivious.

There are many Christians sleepwalking through life. Maybe the prolonged struggles with trials, trouble, illness, and financial struggles have created bitterness toward God. Maybe they have been victim to the deceitfulness and malice of sin. Whatever it might be these folks are sleepwalking through life slowing choking on a life filled with worldliness and loss of faith. They have fallen asleep spiritually.

Spiritual sleep is when the heart grows indifferent to the things of God. The spiritual senses have become dulled by the weight of worldly things; God is no longer the Christian's focus. Slowly the believer sinks into dark slumber, allowing the things of God to fall to wayside as they become more engulfed in the night and the trappings of the world and the flesh.

As I was studying scripture for this piece, I found Ephesians 5:14. It says **Wherefore he saith, Awake thou that sleepest, and arise from the dead, and Christ shall give thee light.**

At first I assumed that the end of the scripture "and Christ shall give thee light" referred to understanding. I decided to dig a bit deeper. The proper translation actually declares *Christ shall <u>dawn</u> upon thee.*

Throughout the Bible, prophecy is looking forward to Christ and is compared to a "shining light in a dark place" (2 Peter 1:19).

In Revelation 22:16 Jesus is "the bright and morning star". Literally the Word tells us to awake and arise and meet the dawn. He is the dawn of your long night. There is pain, worry and trouble in the darkness, but Christ is the daylight, he is the light of the new day.

Slumber no longer in the darkness of this world, awake and allow Jesus to "dawn upon thee". Stand in His light.

Wake up to the Son.

"Sink Hole"

Humble yourselves therefore under the mighty hand of God, that he may exalt you in due time: Casting all your care upon him; for he careth for you.
1 Peter 5:6-7 (KJV)

I was washing dishes the other night getting my chores done before bed. My mind was a million miles away as I washed. Warm soapy water and the smell of Dawn dish detergent soothed me. Washing, rinsing and stacking over and over again. I was soon to the end of my task. I placed the last of the dishes in the sink and reached for the sponge. I submerged my hands into the soapy water and then very unexpectedly, the sink, dishwasher and dishes disappeared. I leaned forward, peering in the hole before me and in the cabinet below, my sink sat cockeyed resting on an assortment of cleaners and odds and ends, soapy water like a mini Niagara ran out from under the cabinet door and pooled around my feet.

For a few minutes I just stood there, hands soaking wet, soap bubbles all around me. I was in such a state of shock that I just stood there. Water dripping off my elbows, my mouth hanging open I stared in disbelief.

Sometimes everything seems pretty normal, mundane you may say and then life sends you a curveball and everything seems to collapse.

We all have those times when life and plans seems to fall through – perhaps problems in relationships, work (or finding work), finances and health issues. It is in those times that I find myself beginning to spiral, questioning 'why' and upset at God when I don't find answers

God graciously wants us to open up about our feelings. He wants us to share our thoughts (the Psalms are full of people doing just that), However, we need to keep in mind that getting caught up in the 'why', doesn't do you or I any good.

I always want to understand why. Why me? Why is it this way? Why?

You can go through hundreds of scenarios trying to find the why. Often that exercise is fruitless. Know that your suffering is in no way in vain. Our God is a purposeful God.

Sometimes when we suffer unexpectedly, God may be reaching out to others through us in ways we might not even be aware of. Through Jesus we have an eternal hope to share, whatever our circumstances. This is your opportunity to share Jesus in a very personal way. How you exhibit your faith may be the difference between someone choosing God or rejecting.

Falling Short

Over the Labor Day weekend, I traveled with a precious friend and her son to Kentucky. We had a really good time and saw some amazing things. One thing that sticks out in my mind was the tomahawk toss. We were visiting Fort Boonesborough. Oh yes, you are correct—the settlement in Kentucky established by Daniel Boone. One of the attractions was tomahawk throwing.

With a quick signature on a waiver form I was given carte blanche to wield a hatchet.

The gentleman in charge of the tomahawk throw was very kind and informative. He instructed me on how to stand, how to hold the hatchet and how to give it just the right pitch to nail the target. My first time up, the instructor stood next to me adjusting my stance, and the position of my wrist. Finally, he gave me the go ahead and I released the weapon. It spun, hitting the target almost dead center. I squealed as is my custom when I am delighted. The instructor laughed and handed me my next hatchet.

I ran the instructions back through my mind, tossed the tomahawk. It hit the ground before the target with a thud. I reddened with embarrassment.

Over and over I tried and despite my first hit, I missed again and again. The tomahawk fell short. After a few disappointing tries the instructor came back to my side and again worked with my stance and form. I hit the mark.

Try as we might, we too cannot hit the mark on our own. ***For all have sinned, and come short of the glory of God***

I looked up the actual definition of sin as used in the Bible. The word comes from the Greek, ἁμαρτάνω. Transliteration is hamartanó (ham-ar-tan›-o). It literally means to fall short or miss the mark of a target. In the Greek, the word is symbolized by an archer missing the target.

There is nothing that we can do. No deed or action that will cover our sins and make us righteous before God. The only way we can come before the Father is first by the Son. Jesus' sacrifice blots out our sins and shortcomings. With him we are made righteous. Without the covering of our sins by Christ blood we will always fall short.

Spirit Flight 055

I boarded Spirit flight 055 bound for Chicago and settled in my seat, 26A, against the window. I looked out over the ground workers quickly loading luggage. I was excited and a bit scared as well. As I gazed out the window I thought of what my weekend away would have in store for me. In the middle of my daydream the flight attendant, touched me on the shoulder.

"Ma'am", she began with a smile. "Would you mind moving to the seat directly behind you so that this family can sit together?" A husband, wife and two small children waited for my reply.

"Of course." I responded and moved to 27A. I resumed my thoughts as I watched the flurry of activity.

Several minutes later a young man tapped me on the shoulder. "Hey, that's my seat. You gotta move."

"The flight attendant moved me to this seat." I began. However, the guy was uninterested in what I was saying.

"Well" He began shoving his boarding pass at me, "it's my seat." He glared at me.

By the time we began our take off, I was sitting between two large young men. Earphones in, they both had immediately gone to sleep. The one to my right snoring, the other with head back and mouth agape. I sat upright, my arm folded over my lap. One man's elbow was digging into my ribs, and the man to the left's leg weighed on my leg.

I sighed. ***I can do this. It's just two hours***, I gave myself a bit of a pep talk.

Moments later, the attendant passed and did a double take. She came back to me and leaned in, "What happened?"

"27A was his seat." I thumbed to my left. She nodded and walked away. In a flash, she returned. "Can you come with me, ma'am?"

"Ah, ok." I stammered. I followed her down the aisle way to an empty seat. It was one of those large seats, the ones without the knee-bumping seats in front. It was wide and comfortable. I settled next to the window, stretched out my legs before me, and relaxed.

She smiled. "Would you like a beverage? It's on the house. Maybe a snack?" "A Sprite would be nice."

"Right away." She touched me on the shoulder, "Thank you for your kindness in moving. I am sorry that you got moved so much. I especially appreciate your attitude."

With my beverage in hand, I looked out the window just as the sun broke the horizon. A smile spread across my face. God was watching over me. I offered praise as the sun grew stronger and brighter.

This was going to be a great weekend.

Sometimes, I grow weary at being kind. I get my feelings hurt, a lot, because I try to put others before me. Often the thought whispers, "why? They do not appreciate it. They wouldn't do it for you." It is the world that we live in and it has not changed since the beginning. People are still worried about taking care of themselves and not about each other.

However, do not stop. Continue to humble yourself and think of those that you encounter daily. That guy with two items and you have a full cart—let him go first. Maybe on the highway on the way home, that car that's been sitting for a while trying to get in traffic, let them in front. Pick up that mail from the mailroom for the lady that has been so busy all morning she has not had the opportunity to pick it up. Think of how you can help others, not just how you can help yourself.

What a world this would be if we all thought of the needs of others before ourselves. I believe there would be less need and more joyful people.

I also wonder what if Jesus chose not to pay the price for you and I with His blood? What if He had only thought of himself and did not go to the cross? He looked past the shame, pain and death to see how His actions would benefit a world lost, a world dying. Your actions influence. Your actions touch lives. Never tire in doing what is right because it is not in vain. One day you will see the fruit of your sacrifice. You may not realize it in this life, but you will be justly rewarded in God's time.

> **Humble yourselves therefore under the mighty hand of God, that he may exalt you in due time 1Peter 5:6**

Planes, Trains and Automobiles

One of the many things I found fascinating about Chicago was the various modes of transportation. Whether by bus, train, cab or foot you can get anywhere relatively easily. I used my phone constantly to navigate to the next bus stop or train station. All I had to do is follow the little dots on my screen and I would soon be where I wanted to go. Jumping from bus to train by little more than a few hundred yards proved a bit tricky at first, I appeared to have a trouble in my directions. Confusing my East and West, resulting in my friend and I walking in the wrong direction. Using the landmarks, we soon got back on track and to the next connection.

I thought about my own life and how I had confused my east and west in my walk with Jesus. There were times that my disobedience or rebellion led me off the path and in areas I should not have been. It is easy to lose sight and get confused. However, just like the Chicago Transit Authority there is always another chance; another bus or another train. No matter how far off course you may get in your life, be assured there is always a chance of redemption.

Jesus is your landmark, and should always be your center. People, spouses, jobs, money and anything that you have come to depend on will ultimately fail. Jesus is the only hub that you can depend on to always be strong and dependable. ***The LORD is my rock, my fortress and my deliverer; my God is my rock, in whom I take refuge, my shield and the horn of my salvation, my stronghold. Psalms 18:2***

If you are in a place in your life where you think that your chances have passed you by, that there is no redemption, forgiveness, mercy or peace obtainable, think again.

> ***"Even now, declares the LORD, return to me with all your heart, with fasting and weeping and mourning." Joel 2:12***

It is not too late, never too late to turn to Jesus.

Court Appearance

A few weeks ago, I had to go to court concerning the accident. While I waited on my case to be called, I listened to the judge pass down his rulings. Case after case was called. The judge asked questions and the accused answered. The judge weighed the responses and passed judgement.

One young man was called. He came up front and stood before the podium. Behind him was his mother, girlfriend with their child on her hip, grandmother and other family members and possibly a neighbor!

The judge asked the young man who all these people were and if they were material to the case. He began rattling off relationships of the entourage that flanked him. The judge interrupted and commanded that they all sit down.

This was between the judge and the young man.

This scene put me in mind of my own impending time to stand before Christ. I will stand alone to answer for my sins. I cannot blame it on others in my life. Or my circumstances, my finances, my education neither ignorance. I must take full responsibility for it all. It was a very poignant moment of reflection. Am I living a life I should? Does my life reflect a life lived for God?

However, on that day when I stand before the throne, I have the assurance that the price of my sin has been paid by Christ blood. ***In whom we have redemption through his blood, the forgiveness of sins, according to the riches of his grace; Ephesians 1:7.*** Yet, though I know I that I am redeemed, I want my life to be a life that Jesus can look on favorably. I want to do my best to uphold His commandments and share the gospel to all that will listen.

Are you living a life of responsibility and accountability? Have you accepted Jesus as your Savior?

Living Well for Jesus

No discipline seems pleasant at the time, but painful.
Later on, however, it produces a harvest of righteousness
and peace for those who have been trained by it.
Hebrews 12:11

I have a friend I walk with once a week. She is one of the most disciplined people I know. It goes beyond her devotion to exercise; it is part of her finances, her house cleaning and helping others in need. Even down to keeping her car neat and regularly washed! She lives her life in a disciplined and responsible way. I admire her control and her constant and unwavering devotion to every aspect of her life.

Last night on our walk, we stopped to do "squat" exercises. I certainly did not execute the moves with grace, but I completed them. Once I got home and climbed out of the car, my knees and legs began to scream at me. As I struggled up the steps to the porch I really wanted the pain to stop.

There are two ways that could happen. One is to quit and never do another squat. *(Tempting)* The other is to continue to do those exercises until my knees no longer hurt and I gain some flexibility. It would take control and dedication to see it through. I want to get in better shape to be healthy. In order to do that, I need to employ some discipline, self-sacrifice and commitment. Often we want something but the idea of becoming disciplined and being willing to sacrifice seems too huge to tackle.

Unfortunately, this extends to our Christian walk as well. Many Christians are not disciplined in their relationship with Jesus. *(I am speaking to myself if I am speaking to anyone)* We are sometimes unwilling to turn off the TV and make a phone call or visit a sick or shut-in member. Maybe we do not make it to church every week because of other things that come up. Maybe we do not pay our tithes, unwilling to part with our cash. I could go on with examples. The issue is that these actions come with sacrifice and discipline. The Christian life is not to be a life where we sit around nor is it a life where we think that we should be lying about on easy street because we have been extended grace through Jesus' sacrifice. We are to be sharing, loving, tithing, visiting, praying, teaching, learning and exhibiting all the qualities of Jesus. We need to be committed, disciplined and willing to make the sacrifices to touch the lost in our world. Our actions and dedication should be seen by others in our lives.

I want to live a life that never leaves anyone wondering about my relationship with Jesus. In order for my life to reflect Jesus I have to be willing to push aside the easy and comfortable and embrace discipline and commitment. To be bold and not fearful in declaring Jesus as my savior and the savior of all that accept Him. One of my goals for my life is that it is a life that Jesus can use to touch people.

A fulfilling and joyful life in Christ means sacrifice, means accepting responsibility and means being disciplined and pious. These are not popular traits in this world, but they are traits that can lead to a life well lived for Jesus.

God's Word Does
Not Return Void

> *"For as the rain and the snow come down from heaven, And do not return there without watering the earth And making it bear and sprout, And furnishing seed to the sower and bread to the eater; So will My word be which goes forth from My mouth; It will not return to Me empty, Without accomplishing what I desire, And without succeeding in the matter for which I sent it.*
> *Isaiah 55:10-11*

This week I offer the 200th Mustard Seed. I don't know what I am most amazed over, the fact that God has given me material to author 200 or that you have stuck with the Seed.

When I was asked to write a monthly devotional for the college, I never dreamed that it would still be around five years later, be a weekly devotional and have over 600 readers. However, isn't that what the Mustard Seed is really about? How God can use the smallest, most insignificant things and utilize them for His Glory to make something special.

The Mustard Seed has become an illustration of how God isn't just around on Sunday or when you pray, but He is present all the time. Within the ordinary and mundane parts of life, He is reaching out to us. All we have to do is have the faith as small as the mustard seed and look for it. Actively expect to experience God in some unlikely places and circumstances.

Thank you for sticking with the Seed. Thank you for boldly sharing them with those in your Life. In order for the good news of Salvation to reach people we have to be willing, bold and faithful to share. When you share a Seed you are sharing Christ. You are the instrument the Lord uses to get His Word out. Isaiah reminds us that God's Word will not return void, but what He intended it to accomplish it will.

My prayer for the next 200 is that it continues to be a source of inspiration, strength and a conduit for the Lord to speak. Continue with me to share the love, compassion and mercy of Jesus.

Rainy Days

The sun was shining, sky bright blue. The weather mild, trees and flowers in bloom. In all a good day. However, in the middle of the daily routine came a phone call. She answered cheerfully. The voice on the other end began to cry. She recognized the voice immediately as her daughter.

"Mom," the little voice began. "I just got robbed."

"Are you okay?" The mom cried. Relief washed over her, her child was alright.

Someone had gotten in the young woman's car when she went into the store and took everything she had. No doubt they had been watching, waiting for the opportunity. Her tips that she had worked so hard for all week and her check card were gone. She had only been in the store three or four minutes. Her daughter was reduced to tears.

Between her heartbroken sobs she asked, "Mom, why do these things happen to me? Why is it always me?"

I do not know about you, but I feel like this young lady. Why do these things happen to me?

Life is not easy. Not one part of it. Not relationships, or careers, nor school or our health. There are daily challenges to just getting through the day. Anything can happen.

However, we do not face these hardships and heartbreaks alone. We have Jesus. Always in our corner, always there to help us walk the path before us. Often, like this young woman, we feel that the world is against us. That others do not suffer, or deal with the issues that we do daily. It is a very clever and from experience, effective way that Satan has to isolate us. That is indeed what he wants. To isolate us from each other and God. If we believe that no one else endures the hardships we do, that no one understands the challenges we are faced with, then we grow more isolated and more focused inward. If your eyes are focused inward, you do not see the needs of others and you certainly do not see the cross.

As Matthew tells us in his book, the sun rises and sets, it rains on us all. You are not alone in your challenge. You have Jesus with you. He is there when the thief steals, there when the doctor has bad news, present when the layoff slips are handed out and holding you when a loved one goes home.

If you are dealing with the rain, Jesus is your shelter. ***The name of the LORD is a strong tower; The righteous runs into it and is safe.*** Psalms 61:3.

If you are not, then bring an umbrella to those in need and bring their focus to the cross. ***Not looking to your own interests but each of you to the interests of the others. Philippians 2:4***

The rain falls on us all, but we are not without shelter. Run to Jesus, reach out to others in need. Share experiences, boast in how Jesus brought you through it. Do not live without hope. Your Hope is in Christ Jesus and you are **never** alone.

Keep looking to the cross.

Cool Water

*As the deer pants for streams of water, so
my soul pants for you, my God.*
Psalms 42:1

One of the things I have learned during my lifestyle makeover the past few weeks is the importance of drinking water. Generally speaking, I do not like water. Silly really to say, but I do not. I like sweet tea, however, that will not get me closer to my desired weight or to a healthier state.

Water is an important part of the workings of the body. Water flushes fat and toxins, combats depression and fatigue, improves muscle tone and satisfies hunger.

Since I have begun my new standard of living I know when I have not drunk enough water. I feel sluggish, I get a headache and I am prone to more cravings. I also find myself thirsting for water. It seems the more water I drink, the more I thirst. Nothing else will do.

The other day at my desk, I turned up a bottle of cool water. It felt good on my throat and squelched my thirsting. As I put the bottle down, the verse from Psalms 42:1 came to my mind, *"As the deer pants for streams of water, so my soul pants for you, my God."*

Just like I crave water, I also crave a closer walk with Jesus. The more water I drink, the more I thirst for water. The closer I draw to the Lord, the closer I want to be. I thirst for the spirit and a deeper understanding and relationship with Jesus.

Throughout the New Testament, Jesus used the imagery of water to describe the spirit, both terms of water's cleansing properties and as a source of power. Jesus chose water because of its very nature. Water is the foundation of life, growth and the universal solvent.

Recorded in John 4:13-14, Jesus says to the woman at the well: ***"Whoever drinks of this water will thirst again, but whoever drinks of the water that I shall give him will never thirst. But the water that I shall give him will become in him a fountain of water springing up into everlasting life."***

The more I drink water, the more I thirst for it. As long as I am on the earth my thirst will continue. However, as I drink from the Spirit I am filled. My mind is cleansed as I read the scriptures and I am filled with the Holy Spirit to give me the strength to face daily trials and draw me closer to my Lord.

The Holy Spirit that dwells within us quenches our spiritual thirst, facilitates our spiritual birth and cleanses us from our spiritual filth.

Are you drinking your fill of the Spirit?

Under the Sun

This weekend, my oldest moved out to her own apartment. I have cried a lot. As tears streamed down my face, my mind was seized by memories. I remember when I looked into my daughter's eyes for the first time. I felt as if I had always known her. I remember the day she slipped from my fingers and took her first steps, when she uttered her first words, her smile as she went to her first day of school. Her hot tears on my shoulder with every heartbreak. Her nervously twisting her hands as she confessed her wrong. And now, the smile as she waved goodbye to me from her new home.

So many firsts and I was privileged to be there for each of them.

Where has the time gone? Twenty two years gone in a blink. My heart aches and I wish I could wind the clock back if only for a moment.

Life is a continual winding path of growth, change, heartache, joy, triumph and yes failures, defeats and consequences. Each of us share in this phenomena of life. We climb to wonderful heights and at times find ourselves staring up from valleys of despair. Life is an unpredictable, fleeting and fragile thing.

Solomon knew this well. A king of great wealth and wisdom, he was not immune from life's ups and downs. Like Solomon, we all desire meaning in life. I relate to the experiences echoed throughout Ecclesiastes. A common humanity emerges as I read through the pages. Like Solomon we attempt to find meaning chasing after pleasures, commitment to a job, and pursuit of intellect. However, in the end, we are unsatisfied. Life is destined to remain unsatisfying if we do not acknowledge God, and place our trust and faith in His able hands.

Many people find Ecclesiastes to be a depressing book written by a bitter old man, but I do not think that is the intention of the writer. It faces the reality of life. Pleasure, materialism, wisdom and money are all folly. Ecclesiastes takes an honest look at life and makes no promises, but rather entreats us to "Enjoy life and fear God". The key to life is not in life itself. True happiness comes from centering our lives on God, and not ourselves.

Enjoy where you are. Be in the moment. Find satisfaction in your work. Reach out to one another in times of joy and pain. Eat and drink and live.

Never take the day for granted, night comes too quickly.

Then I realized that it is good and proper for a man to eat and drink, and to find satisfaction in his toilsome labor under the sun during the few days of life God has given him—for this is his lot" (Ecc 5:18)

The Enemy Within

"Dear Heavenly Father, I thank you for this day and ask that you forgive me of my sin. Today, I had unfavorable thoughts about a coworker. I blurted out some terrible language because someone cut me off in traffic...

Thinking of driving made me remember I need an oil change. I cannot get an oil change until I get paid. Thinking of getting paid reminded me that I need to pay the house payment. Thinking about the house made me think of how messy it is and that made me think of the yard sale that my friend invited me to participate in and that made me wonder if I should sell those pictures. Wonder how much I could get for them...

I do not know if the example above happens to you when you pray, but I find myself plagued with distraction. I will begin to pray and suddenly my head will itch, my knee will protest and then my mind floats away. I have trouble getting comfortable and I begin to think about everything I need to do and everything I forgot to do. It is a maddening string of interference.

We are all in a constant battle with the enemy within, our flesh. Our very bodies resist when we humble ourselves and begin to communicate with the Father. Our minds lose focus and we find ourselves chasing rabbit trails.

The daily battle of spirit and flesh can be tiresome and frustrating. However, there is something worse than this war, it is no war. So, though you become weary of the war within, Praise God! Serenity in sin is death. Take heart if your soul feels like a battlefield at times, this is a sign that the Spirit is indwelt within you.

Being a Christian does not mean you do not have bad thoughts or desires, but as the verse above declares when you walk by the Spirit, those bad thoughts and desires will not come to maturity. The verse's main point is not war, but victory through the spirit.

> *But thanks be to God, which giveth us the*
> *victory through our Lord Jesus Christ.*
> *1 Corinthians 15:57*

Staying Within the Lines

The assignment was to turn in a coloring sheet of Minnie Mouse for the girls and Mickey for the boys. The winner would be judged on staying in the lines, color choices, and neatness. The winners would lead the class to the lunchroom, restrooms, recess and lead the prayer and the pledge for a whole week rather than the rotating days we usually did.

I chose my colors carefully, laying them out on my desk. I began to color. I observed the Disney standards in coloring Minnie's outfit and chose coordinating colors for the flowers and just the right yellow for the smiling sun. I was careful to not go out of the lines. I was the last to turn in my work and I thought it was perfect. There was no way I would not win.

The next morning as I walked down the hallway the pictures of the coloring pages were displayed on the walls. I scanned them until I saw the little blue ribbon. However, the ribbon was not affixed to my page, but to another little girl's. Disappointment washed over me. My cheeks began to burn and my vision blurred with the building tears. I had worked so hard. I was so careful. I followed all the instructions yet I did not win.

That entire week as I followed in line lead by the coloring winner, I became more discouraged. The next week, the same scenario, and again, I poured everything into making the coloring page as perfect as possible. However, it was for naught. Again, I did not win.

By the fourth week, I quit trying. I slapped on some crayon and scribbled my name and turned it in. Before I could get out to recess the teacher called me to the side, she was holding a few papers.

"Missy," she began. "Are you feeling ok? Is everything ok?" Perplexed, I answered. "Yes ma'am. I am fine."

"I ask because your coloring page this week is not what you usually turn in to me. It is messy and outside the lines."

I looked at the page and shrugged. The stinging pins and needles began on my cheeks and my eyes began to fill with hot tears.

"Honey," She dropped to one knee. "You are not in trouble. I am just wondering why you didn't try on your work. This isn't like you."

Between sobs and hiding my face, I answered. "I tried really hard. I was careful not to go outside the lines but I didn't win. I tried every week, but I didn't win."

"So, you didn't try this week?" She quietly asked.

I nodded my head and my crying erupted again. The teacher gathered me in her arms to console me. Pulling me to arm's length, she smiled and said quietly, "Missy we cannot win all the time, but that doesn't mean that we do not do our best. We always do our best. And we also always do what is right whether anyone notices or not. You know that turning in this knowing that you didn't do your best is not the right thing to do."

I nodded. "I'm sorry." I whispered as I studied my shoes.

"It is ok. But from now on, Missy, always do your best. Always do your best no matter what. Ok?" I nodded.

"Now, Missy, I want you to do it again. This time do your best."

So, I did my absolute very best, but I did not win. I did not win for five more weeks. However, I began to enjoy my coloring assignment. I no longer worried about whether it would win. Every week, I turned in the best work I could, but not to win. Finally, my name was called and a little blue ribbon was placed on my coloring page. I proudly led my class that week.

-For in due season we shall reap, if we faint not.

Apologies and Forgiveness

It was a simple envelope with my name printed in blue taped to the storm door. I peeled it from the glass and stared for several seconds recognizing immediately the unmistakable hand. My daughter watched me with curious eyes as I walked to my bedroom. Sitting on the bed, I stared at the envelope lying on the comforter as if at any moment, it was going to leap on me. I felt the eyes from the doorway on me and turned to give a reassuring smile. She disappeared down the hallway. Lifting the envelope I tore it open and read the neatly written words. The author was requesting 30 minutes of my time to talk and a number to text if I would agree. If they did not hear from me, they would take that as their answer. I replaced the card into the envelope and stared out my bedroom window.

It had been over a year since I had spoken to this person and in that time my pain and hurt had festered into anger. This anger had rooted in my thoughts and even as far as my dreams. It had become a source of distraction and sin on my part.

Weeks before the letter had been attached to my door, I came to the realization that in order for me to have peace, I needed to forgive this person fully. I needed to no longer wait for their apology, but release them and in doing so, myself. Now, as I stared out of the window I pondered the idea of talking with them.

I lifted the phone and texted.

Forgiveness is not easy. It seems to go against the very nature of the human. In order to know the full power of grace and the mercy extended to us, we need to be willing to extend the same to those in our lives that have hurt, betrayed and wronged us. We must give unconditional forgiveness as God's Grace through His Son's sacrifice gives to us.

Forgiveness and peace come at a price as we have to surrender and pardon. By surrendering ourselves to releasing another for what they have done to us whether deliberate or accidental, we open the way for us to demonstrate Jesus' love for others. What good is a forgiven life if we are unable or unwilling to share forgiveness with others?

The next evening we met and with humbleness, this person apologized and asked me to forgive them. This act took great courage, humility, and obedience. As forgiveness is not easy to extend neither is having to say you are sorry. I applaud this person for their courage and willingness to obey God.

Through obedience and courage, we both were privileged to see Grace and Mercy demonstrated.

I was humbled by this experience. Reminded that God has forgiven me repeatedly for my wrongs. How as a follower of Christ, one that has experienced His Grace not forgive another? Being witness to the courage and humility that they came to me with, I was inspired to take a hard look at my own heart. Is there anyone that I owe an apology? This experience has shown me the importance of forgiveness, both to give it and to receive it.

Search your hearts.

Spirit Infusion

*For as many as are led by the Spirit of
God, they are the sons of God.*
Romans 8:14 (KJV)

A couple of friends and myself enjoyed Memorial weekend in Murphy, NC. While touring the shops in town we came across Blue Ridge Olive Oil Company. Within, numerous casks of olive oil and Balsamic vinegar lined the store. Names such as Cinnamon Pear, Dark Chocolate, and Mango neatly labeled the stainless steel drums. Soft light and jazz filled the shop.

We were greeted by two very pleasant ladies that invited to try all they offered. My friends eagerly tipped bottles that poured tiny drops into their little sample cups. While they indulged in the unique occasion I strolled up and down the aisles marveling at all the diversity of sweet and savory offerings however, I did not partake. To be honest I just could not get past the idea that we were tasting oil and vinegar. What was the big deal? Oil is oil, and vinegar is, well, vinegar.

Finally, I could no longer resist, curiosity had captured me. Hesitantly, I lifted the small plastic cup to my mouth and waited for the droplets of vinegar to hit my tongue. Apprehension lingered as the little drop slipped between my lips. However, the sharp acrid taste I was acquainted with did not greet me, but rather a sweet and deep flavor.

To say the least, I was surprised. The fruit and herb infused offerings continued to surprise and delight me.

On our drive home, we discussed the trip and in particular the balsamic. The employee had explained that the light balsamic were due to being fermented for no less than 12 years in stainless cask and the dark counterparts were aged in oak and other wooden barrels. The detail in the infusion of the flavors down to the regions they were harvested played a distinct and important part in the flavor of the vinegar and oils. I will admit, I was very ignorant of infused oils and vinegar but found this occasion very exciting. I will never look at oil and vinegar the same.

Over the next few days, I thought about how the oils and vinegar were changed, improved and enriched by the process of infusion of flavorful ingredients. We are much the same. Once you allow the Holy Spirit to be infused within you, you become so much more than you ever were before.

What you allow to influence you will flavor the kind of Christian you are.

Are you infused with the Holy Spirit? Does He dwell within you and does His influence flow from you?

Bumper Crop

This week's adventure was a morning picking blackberries in North Carolina. I say adventure because if you have ever picked blackberries you know that gathering the juicy treat comes with a price. Briars, ticks, and chiggers are the hazards you must wade through, not to mention the mid-summer heat. We were fortunate that the sky was overcast and that the high elevation provided a cool breeze. However, the briars stood ready to defend.

Attired in jeans, big boots, and long sleeves, I stood at the base of an embankment and marveled at the massive cluster of blackberry bushes. They were interwoven into a thick mat of briars. Vines bowed to the ground by the weight of berries. Thousands of red and black fruit hung in bunches more like grapes rather than berries. I had never seen bushes so burdened. As my friends and I went to picking, the rhythmic sound of berries plopping into buckets echoed up and down the lane.

If you are familiar with growing seasons you may be a bit surprised that we were blackberry picking in June, because blackberries are most common mid to late July. Despite the date, we spent the morning reaching into the thorns to pluck juicy, ripe fruit. As we picked we chattered about the abundance. We all agreed it was the plentiful rain we have been receiving that had encouraged this "bumper crop". As we worked our way through the briar we became quiet, concentrating on our task. During this silence with only the drone of summer insects and conversation of the birds, my mind drifted to thoughts about the berries and the rain. I thought about how the bushes had endured the rain, severe storms, and angry winds and despite it, bore abundant fruit. However, as I thought further was it despite the tumultuous weather, or because of it?

We all face storms in life and some things can only be improved by opposing winds. The storms are intended to strengthen our character and faith. When we stand to look into the dark clouds of an approaching storm, do we hold to our faith, or do we let our fear like the wind sweep us away?

The berry bushes produced an abundance of fruit because of the storms. We too have the opportunity to bear an abundance of fruit when we weather the storms of life by holding on to our faith in Jesus. The storms we face are often painful, disheartening and frightening. However, if we turn to Jesus and focus on Him we can weather the storm and emerge out of the squall better, strengthened and rooted deeply in faith.

> *But the fruit of the Spirit is love, joy, peace, longsuffering,*
> *gentleness, goodness, faith, Galatians 5:22*

Out of the Ruins

Sunlight peeked through the thick canopy of trees that shaded the ruins, making a kaleidoscope of color on the walls of the burned out mill. I walked along the walls, peering through doorways and windows at the rushing water beyond. The broken and decayed columns reminded me of broken teeth in a terrible grin. I lined up the fortification on my phone's screen and began to snap shots of the ruins of Sope Paper Mill.

Scrolling back through my phone I studied each shot. I tried to imagine what this building must have looked like before Sherman and his men laid waste to it in the Union march from Atlanta to Chattanooga. I thought about how all this had been taken in an inferno one summer night in 1864. For 153 years, this structure has been eroding away, returning to the dust that it came.

As I studied the ruins, I thought about how often I focus on the past. I find myself tumbling thoughts and dwelling on former sins. Looking back on mistakes is as fruitless as expecting the old mill to produce paper again.

I thought about Paul in the Bible. A former persecutor of Jesus, he could have revisited his past ruins and mistakes, however, he tells us in Philippians 3:13, to ***"Forgetting what is behind and straining toward what is ahead."*** We can do nothing for yesterday, but we can move forward doing our best daily to represent Jesus and love each other.

Do not allow the past to keep you from the future.

I Will Run My Race

Do you not know that in a race all the runners run, but only one gets the prize? Run in such a way as to get the prize.
Corinthians 9:24 (NIV)

Twilight retreated into the pines of Still Hollow Nature Park. I stood alone on the edge of the pavement watching the hum of activity. The loudspeaker blurted out instructions and music bounced in the air. Soon the announcements and music ended. A hush descended on the crowd. A low murmur of voices buzzed as the runners lined up at the start. A digital clock counted down the time before the race would begin. A chilly breeze wafted through the contenders, raising chill bumps on my arms. With the breeze came the tingle of restrained excitement. I breathed it in and felt it spread throughout my body. I pinned my number to my shirt and retied my shoes, tucking the laces. Nervously, I walked to the starting line and took up position in the rear.

Contenders of every age group and level of fitness filled the narrow starting gate. I saw a woman in her seventies adjusting her belt. It was lined with small water bottles reminiscent of hand grenades. I smiled at the image. A small blonde boy not yet ten excitedly stretched, his father leaned in giving last minute instructions. A middle aged man weaved through the crowd. He took up a position near the front, his face was solemn and his eyes dark.

As I was drawn further into the electricity that whirred in the air, I thought about all these people. I realized that this was not just one race but 270 personal races. 270 different reasons and 270 different goals.

The clock continued its count down and a young woman sang the national anthem. Silence fell over the crowd, everyone turned to face the flag, hands raised over hearts. Her voice rang through early morning, sweet, strong and clear. She concluded, the silence of the runners hung suspended for several seconds. Then the blast of the air horn ripped through the atmosphere and the race began. I passed under the starting line, a thrill rushed over me. I smiled, I was really part of this. I found my pace and focused on the trail ahead.

We all run a race and each one of our races is as unique as each athlete. Paul, throughout the New Testament, used the runner, boxer, and wrestler as an illustration of the Christian walk. It is not for the fainthearted. It takes discipline, commitment, courage and devotion.

I am ashamed to say that for most of my life, I have not run my race for Christ. I have not stepped out of the comfort zone I have burrowed myself so deeply within. I have not invested in what God has given me to further His Kingdom but rather stood on the sidelines watching. Spectating, but never participating because of my lack of faith in what I could do if I trusted Christ.

No more. I will run my race *in such a way as to get the prize.* I do not believe it will be easy, nor do I not expect many failures, but I do intend to run this race before me the very best I can.

Never Doubt the Power of Your Gift

> *Each of you should use whatever gift you have*
> *received to serve others, as faithful stewards*
> *of God's grace in its various forms.*
> *1 Peter 4:10 (NIV)*

When I was in high school, I took a career aptitude exam. These tests are to give an idea of what your strengths are and what job you might be best suited to. My test returned Museum Curator. Without a doubt, natural science, art, artifacts, and world history are some of my favorite things. When my Biblical Archaeology magazine comes in the mail, I run to hide in my room, devouring the articles and pictures from cover to cover.

This past week I went to a Biblical Archaeology and History convention. Prominent men in the fields of archaeology, anthropology, theology, and history filled 2-1/2 days with wonderful presentations, videos and scientific information. It was a weekend that I truly enjoyed. I got to geek out.

During this time, I listened jealousy to each of these academics describe their life's work. I hung on every word as these explorers shared exciting, sometimes dangerous adventures. These men had truly found their purpose and place in life.

Later, as I prayed, I asked God to reveal my purpose. What was I supposed to do? What was the purpose of the next chapter in my life?

"Write." Echoed in my head.

I sighed, "Yes, Lord, but what do I write? Who do I need to contact? Tell me, Lord, what do I do? Is there something else I am supposed to be doing?"

"Write." Repeated in my thoughts. "Just write."

Finding purpose sometimes is just doing what you love, sharing your talents and passion with others. Often, we, and I mean me, want step by step instruction. We want some grand scheme laid out before us. More often than not, it does not happen that way. Many people spend years searching for their purpose. They are so busy looking for it that they walk right by it. They discount this special ability or desire planted in their heart. We should never doubt the power of a gift given by God.

You have a desire in you. You may have the desire to teach or maybe to build. Maybe you find nothing more gratifying than raising a beautiful garden. Whatever your passion, God planted it within you, and it is the means by which you can glorify Him. Every time you exercise that passion, you are worshiping the Lord. Your specific passion, that thing that you think of when you awaken and fall into slumber, is your special gift. It is how you touch others for Jesus. It is the means that you bring pure worship to the Lord. Never doubt the power of the gift God has given you.

May He grant you according to your heart's desire
and fulfill all your purpose (Psalm 20:4)

Never the Last Resort

Pray continually.
I Thessalonians 5:17

At some point, and I am not sure just when, I have become a mentor to some young ladies in my life. They come to me with all sorts of issues. The other day one of these precious young ladies was sharing her indecision about an opportunity that had presented itself to her. I knew that I had not been the first person she had come to, and she had shared some of their insights. After she had related all her concerns and doubts, she asked my thoughts.

I smiled and then said, "Have you prayed about it?"

Deer in the headlights...

"Well." She stammered. "No. Not yet." She thought for a minute and then added. "But I'm going to."

I do not know about you, but I have been in that position many times before. I have run to friends, coworkers and sometimes strangers asking for opinions and thoughts. Just like this young lady, I often forgot to take the situation to God first.

Prayer is not the *last resort*, it should always be our first thought. Taking everything before the Lord should be the way we begin to handle a situation or work through an issue. Then comes the patience. Yes, that terrible word, patience. Once you bring something before God, then you must give Him time to answer, time to give direction and time to bring the situation in focus.

Paul reminds us succinctly in I Thessalonians 5:17 to pray and pray continually. When you face issues, who do you go to first?

He is Trustworthy

I have known all week that my offering would be about prayer. In fact, I was going in an entirely different direction until I had a conversation with a friend. She had been praying about something she wanted and had approached it in prayer. However, she did not have her prayer answered as she had hoped. So, she began to inspect her life, as many of us do, to see if possibly she might have had some sin or in some way was not in line with God's Will. That is when she had her epiphany she freely shared with me over dinner.

When we pray, we should do so by praying for God's Will. She had prayed for His Will and not her own. Because of this, she had realized that what she had prayed for was not what He wanted for her. Now, this unanswered prayer had become a blessing and a show of how God gives us good things. God can see what is coming up in our lives. He knows that buying that car from that particular dealer is not prudent. Maybe purchasing a house right now could be detrimental because you may lose your job. Or maybe there is just a better deal ahead. Possibly that job you want so badly, or mate is not what He has planned for you.

Choosing God's Will over our own is tough. In the past, I have prayed, and I did not ask for His Will instead, I barreled through with only my will in mind. I received what I had asked, but I was in no way pleased once I did.

It is hard to choose God's Will over our own, especially when we want something so badly. However, we can submit to God's Will because God is trustworthy. We know God's love is pure, and he desires to give us good things. Having faith in this, we can trust Him to answer our prayers in a way that benefits us.

> **The LORD will indeed give what is good, and our land will yield its harvest. Psalms 85:12**

Spiritual DNA

Washing my hands the other day, I looked up into the mirror. Suddenly my reflection bore an uncanny resemblance to my mom. A few days later, as she and I dined, I noticed maybe for the first time how she had come to resemble my grandmother. Because I am her daughter, I have inherited many of her traits and her of her mother and so on. Often people have commented that my daughter's look just like me. Because of inherited DNA, we physically resemble our families. But what about spiritually?

On my drive home that night, I wondered if I resembled Christ in any way. Physically I look like my mother, but spiritually are the traits of God the Father and Jesus my Savior seen? Once we accept Christ, we became born again. Renewed. Being adopted into God's family, therefore, spiritually, we are remade. As we chose to follow Him and strive to tell others about Him, our traits should mirror His.

Words are just words, but if our actions and the way we live our lives reflect Christ, often that is the best and most convincing of witnesses.

Does your life resemble Christ? Can those in your life quickly pick up on your relationship to Him? This week take time to look at your spiritual reflection.

What is your Spiritual DNA?

Links in a Living Chain

The rain had finally tapered off and I was beginning to dry. Still shivering, I hiked down the pathway on my way to check point four. Ahead I saw several of my fellow hikers standing around, two on their phones. My pace quickened. *Had something happened? Was someone hurt?*

As I got closer one broke from the group and approached me. "Do you have your ViewRanger on?"

"Yes." I pulled my phone from my pocket. "What's wrong?"

"The markers indicate we go to the left but there is a huge creek there and it is really raging."

I walked with her, passing the little gathering, I peered down the path and a creek probably eight feet wide rushed over the rocks. It looked as if it were boiling. The water churned and so did my stomach. I looked at my phone and the arrow pointed to the left. One of the hikers hung up her phone and addressed us.

"They say that yes this is the way were are to go. Yesterday before the rain it was just a trickle. Others have crossed it. It's a bit slippery they said."

We discussed the best approached and finally it was decided we would make a chain across and get everyone safely to the other side. There was one gentleman in our group and without pause he crossed over, gripped a tree, turned back and extended his walking stick for the next person to grab. Arms linked we stood planted in the creek bed, cold water numbed our legs.

One by one we crossed and continued down the other side.

As I stood in the creek, water rushing up to my knees, my mind swirled with thought. I worried about getting swept down, I worried about falling, or causing the others to fall. However, there was one thought that continued in the back of my mind. *I was a link in a living chain.*

As I pressed on, I thought about the living chain and how each one of us is part of it. Our connection to Jesus is by way of a living chain. Jesus came and taught the disciples and the people, in turn they taught others. Apostles spread throughout the world to share Jesus with everyone they met. We are also part of that very same chain. I was taught about Christ by my parents who in turn were taught by theirs and back through the generations. It is now my time to teach others of Christ, to form more links. This chain that you and I are part of stretches all the way back to the cross. A living chain of links connected one to another through millennia.

You are part of a chain of love, redemption, and salvation. What are you doing to strengthen your link? Are you actively sharing Christ with others? Are you extending the links in the chain?

Beauty from Brokenness

"Behold, I am making all things new."
Rev. 21:5

Though the rain had stopped, the sky hung low and heavy. I was nearing check point four. The trail cut through dense forest and thick scrub. The canopy blocked what little light there was from penetrating the wood floor. I emerged into an area that took me by surprise. The canopy disappeared and a large expanse unfolded before me. Trees lay in piles like funerary pyres. These trees that once stood stretching toward the sky were now scattered like matchsticks, splintered, bent, naked and twisted on the forest floor. Over the pathway, their skeletons created a dark and dreary archway. An archway of death and decay. I stopped and looked up and down at the long, wide scar left by the tornado. It reached up over the ridge beyond my sight and below, disappearing into thick underbrush. I stood in amazement, taking stock of the destruction.

Bending slightly, I entered the gloom of the archway. The quietness was eerie, even the insects and birds were observing silence in this wooded graveyard. Not a sound penetrated the bubble of hush that spread across the scar. The smell of wet, rotten wood tickled my nose. I felt like an intruder trespassing on something private. Silent eyes followed me.

Emerging from the giant's belly, I blinked as my eyes grew accustomed once again to the gray light. Looking back a pang of sadness lingered. Then l I noticed a flower. It had sprung out of a rotting pile of wood. It was so bright against the dimness I had just passed. Perfect petals stretched out to display the flower's delicate beauty. My eyes stretched beyond to see the mushrooms, lichens and moss spread like a colorful quilt. New green leaves and vines were intertwined in the broken dry limbs. They spread out their vining and carried with them life. I touched the carpet of bright green moss, soft under my fingertips and traced the petals of a little pink bloom that with her sisters adored the stump of a snapped oak. A creeper tangled in the dead limbs dripped with white flowers that filled the air with gentle sweetness. Tears clung to my lashes as I gazed at the beauty that grew out of destruction. The fresh, vibrant colors touched my lips with a smile where before I had trembled in sadness. Though the wood was broken, life still thrived. Beauty rose out of the brokenness.

Jesus came to a broken world. Broken marriages.

Broken families. Broken relationships. Broken dreams.

Broken lives.

That is really what His story is about; bringing life to what is broken. Jesus came to heal and redeem. He took on the brokenness of the world and in exchange we have gained freedom.

Are you broken? Through Jesus there can be beauty.

Weary Travelers

"I will refresh the weary and satisfy the faint"
Jeremiah 31:25

I had passed checkpoint four and was headed to the finish line. With only seven more miles to go, I began to allow myself to relax. In doing so my pace slowed. It appeared I was not the only one that had chosen to relax. I began to notice the trail becoming more crowded. I had gone hours without seeing another hiker at different points during the day, but now I had them in front and behind me. One thing we all had in common was our plodding posture. We had been hiking since six am, in the dark, rain and gloom. In silence we trudged along in single file toward our common goal. I noticed that we seemed to be following the hiker in front of us. We no longer consulted our GPS or even looked for marker flags we just followed the one ahead. This was a very different attitude than how we started out earlier that morning.

I think that happens to Christians eventually in their journey. We grow weary. The path gets monotonous and one tree looks like another. In the beginning of our walk with Jesus, we are excited. We have a desire to search out the scriptures, share salvation, work in the ministry and teach. But as time passes, we begin to get tired and become weary. Before we know it, we are just following each other in the motions. Our message has been rejected more than accepted, and there seems to be fewer victories. However, that is the time to really get in the scriptures and on our knees.

If you are experiencing a lull in your spiritual life, now is the time to get on your knees and seek Him. When we become weary that is the time we have to really reach down inside and find the strength that is waiting.

"I will refresh the weary and satisfy the faint." Jeremiah 31:25

The Finish Line

According to my Garmin I had completed 24 miles. The finish line
was just 2.7 miles ahead. Beyond through the dense foliage the sound
of Bluegrass music traveled between the trees. Knowing that the finish line was so close gave me comfort and I quickened my pace.

I was tired, hungry and in pain. My feet were tender and sore. My legs
heavy and achy. Each step brought a grimace. I sunk my pole deep
into the soft soil and continued to climb. I will be honest. I was frustrated with all the hills and steep rocks I could see ahead, I just wanted
to get to the finish line. I began to grumble because the final leg of the
challenge was hilly and rocky. I had hoped the end of the trail would
be easy. My legs were heavy and I just could not lift them. I tripped
over the loose rocks and roots. Using the trees, I steadied myself.

Finally, I made it to the Wish Mile. One mile to go. Along the path hanging from the trees were little stars. Each star had a child on it. A child waiting on a wish. I stopped to look at the smiling faces. It was a good reminder
of why I was on this trail. I was here to make a difference in the lives of
these children and their families. It was not about me. Taking one off the
tree, I put it around my neck and marched on. I had a bit more to go.

The trees parted and rock steps lead to a bridge. I emerged from the thick foliage to the twang of the banjo and cheers. I walked across the bridge, its twinkling golden lights glittered and the smell of food wafted from the tents. My face broadened into a smile. Beyond at the end of the bridge were my dearest friends and my daughter. They were cheering, clapping and waving.

The landing was filled with people, complete strangers, cheering for me. Fellow hikers embraced me along with some I did not know. I fell into their arms and hungrily soaked up their praise, love and warmth. I looked back and watched as more hikers crossed the bridge to join the celebration.

That evening as I lay in a hot tub of water soaking my sore feet and legs, I relived that moment again and again. I imagine that is how it will be when we enter the Kingdom. When we have met the trails, climbed the hills, scaled the rocks and finished the race. Our loved ones and all of those in the heavens will cheer for us. When we think back, all the pain, disappointment and loss will mean nothing. What will matter is that we fought to the end. We picked each other up along the way and we kept our focus on what we are really doing here in this life. It is about the struggle, the faith, the love and victory. I would have never made it through this trial without Jesus or all the people that rallied for me. Those that donated money, their time and love. Those that prayed and those that offered advice.

The trail never gets easy. We are to continue to climb and overcome up to the very end. We can do so through Christ. One day, we will cross the bridge and meet our Lord and Savior on the shore.

Until then, continue to climb. Never stopping until Jesus' face we will see.

Are You Giving the Very Best?

> *Therefore, I urge you, brothers and sisters, in view of God's mercy, to offer your bodies as a living sacrifice, holy and pleasing to God—this is your true and proper worship.*
> *Romans 12:1*

The blaring siren of the fire truck echoed down the shabby street of the small neighborhood. The little girl climbed up on her bed and peered out from between the curtains. The engine, with lights spinning, was outside her apartment building. Several uniformed men disembarked, one carried a black garbage bag. The three men headed up the steps and into the building.

Moments later a heavy knock thundered.

First, she heard the creak of the door. Then indistinct voices. The child strained to listen to what they were saying. Her mother called her name. Obediently, she came out into the front room. Absently, she stood, pulling at her blonde locks. A man in uniform stepped close; he smelled of aftershave and sweat. He dropped to one knee and peered into the shy child's face. "Have you been good this year?" He asked quietly.

She looked to her mother who returned an uninterested gaze. Nodding, the little girl pulled more furiously at her hair. The man reached into the bag and rummaged a bit and then with a big smile presented a Barbie. Taking the doll, the girl gazed in disappointment. The doll was naked and dirty. The platinum locks were matted, and wildly framed the doll's face. Tears began to swell.

The child moved to hand back the toy, but the fireman pushed it gently back, "Oh no, sweetheart, this is yours." He stood, nodded to the mother and with the others disappeared out the door.

Returning to the sanctuary of her room, the girl sat on the bed, the doll beside her, and stared at the "gift." The tears that had threatened to flow did, and she buried her face in the pillow to muffle her sobs.

When I first heard this story relayed to me, I became angry. Why would someone offer this dirty toy to a child as a Christmas gift? As the lady told me the story, the memories triggered more tears. Even after 40 years, every Christmas she re-lived the disappointment and confusion of being offered a ratty old doll. The pain of feeling as though she was not worth having a new doll continued to haunt her.

I knew that this story was a Seed. Earlier today I wrote out a simple outline of what I thought this story illustrated. So moments ago I sat down to write about how we need to be sharing the world's greatest gift of Jesus, and I realized that was not what I was to share. So I began to pray and search the Bible. My search led me to Malachi 1.

In Malachi 1:8 we read, ***"And when you offer the blind as a sacrifice, is it not evil? And when you offer the lame and sick, is it not evil?"***

Malachi was addressing the priest, those that were responsible for sacrificing the animals as atonement for the Israelites' sins. The Lord commanded that only an unblemished animal, healthy and clean would be acceptable for penitence. However, the priest had devised that by taking the perfect healthy animals offered by the people and selling them, they could substitute lame and sick animals and make a profit for themselves.

We do not offer blood sacrifices as they did in the Old Testament. Under the New Testament Covenant, we are to offer ourselves as a living sacrifice to the Lord. We must give Him our all. We should strive to provide the very best we have. Not our leftovers. Give the very best of us to Him. Give our best to those in our life. Do not give what you have left over, what is worn out and dirty.

God gave you His very best, His very own son. Is it not just as evil today when we do not give God our best?

Are you giving your best?

God's Bod

I stood in the middle of the grocery aisle. To the left cookies. Brightly colored packages and tags advertising "buy one, get one free". To the right, the same. I was looking for a particular wafer that is on the allowed list for my weight loss program. Near the bottom, modestly decorated were the approved treats. They were not buy one get one, they were not on sale either. They sat on the shelf in patience repose. I chose the particular flavor I wanted and held them close as my eyes wandered up and down the aisle. My gaze stopping occasionally on a favorite. I looked down at the package and smiled. These were my choice. They were healthier and would not deter my weight loss. I decided in that moment I would not allow myself to be derailed by the momentary gratification. I left the aisle renewed.

When I began this weight loss and fitness journey I had in mind only selfish motives. I wanted to wear cute clothes and be more attractive. However, this lifestyle change has been much more. I have learned about my failings, my weaknesses and my relationship with Jesus. I have also recognized my lack of self-discipline and resolve.

How can I be committed to and steadfast in my relationship with Christ, if I cannot control my desire to eat? If I cannot turn away from foods that are not good for my health, how can I possibly stand up against the enemy?

I also come to understand and appreciate as never before the gift and sanctity of the human body. Many times we speak about how this vessel, this body will pass away. That is true, it will. However, it will be resurrected, glorified and reunited with your soul. This body that we give little thought to at times, is the vessel given to us not just on this earth but in eternity.

While studying for this Seed, I came across this commentary on Chapter 6 of 1 Corinthians. These statements changed my perspective of the human body.

> *It is an honour to the body, that Jesus Christ was raised from the dead; and it will be an honour to our bodies, that they will be raised. The hope of a resurrection to glory, should keep Christians from dishonouring their bodies by fleshly lusts. And if the soul be united to Christ by faith, the whole man is become a member of his spiritual body. (Matthew Henry's Concise Commentary)*

Your body is the vessel that your soul travels through this world but it also the vessel that you will retain in Heaven. Though glorified and made perfect, it remains the same body.

Your body was created in the image of God so that you may glorify and worship Him. Your body is the temple that the Holy Spirit resides within. I want to glorify God with my body. I want to be healthy so that I can be a useful member of the Body of Christ. What kind of home are you offering to the Spirit? Is it filled with trash? Is it run down?

Living Renewed

You were taught, with regard to your former way of life, to put off your old self, which is being corrupted by its deceitful desires; to be made new in the attitude of your minds; and to put on the new self, created to be like God in true righteousness and holiness.
Ephesians 4:22-24

I held up the blouse and tried to envision myself in it. My contemplations were interrupted by a timid voice. "Can I help you find something?" I turned to face a young woman carrying a load of hangers.

"No, I replied, I'm just browsing." "For yourself?" She stepped closer. "Yes." I replied.

"Well, this is the plus size section, you will probably want the women's or juniors. Down that way." She motioned to the other side of the store with her head. Then smiled.

I had just been thrown out of the Plus size department.

"Oh, thank you." I replied and glanced at the blouse I had been looking at. It was a 2X. I slipped it back on the rack and casually made my way to the Women's section, stopping to pretend to look on my way. Once in the women's section, I pulled out a sweater from the rack, gray with a beautiful neckline. It looked so small. I held to myself and looked into a nearby mirror. Looked like a pretty good fit. I felt my cheeks redden with a wash of embarrassment and some bewilderment. Why had I gone straight to the plus sizes as soon as I came in the store? Why did I still perceive myself as overweight?

After I left the mall and was driving home, I thought about that incident. I realized my body has changed during my weight loss, my mind has not. I have lost 67 pounds but in my mind, I am still where I was when I began this journey.

We are the same in our Christian walks. When we chose Jesus as our Savior, we were changed. The old man is shed and we put on the new man. That change begins in the mind. You are no longer a condemned sinner, but are forgiven and saved. Many times, even as Christians, we continue to stay in the past. We hang on to the sins and the wrongs we have done and that others have done to us. That is where we continue to live. However, that is no longer who you are or where you belong. Release your shame and your guilt. It is not yours to carry. Cast it on the cross. You are a new man or woman through Christ. However, that change begins in your mind. You must begin to see and identify with the renewed and redeemed self. No longer the sins, the hurts, or the injustices of the past.

> **Therefore, if anyone is in Christ, the new creation
> has come: The old has gone, the new is here!
> 2 Corinthians 5:17**

Isn't it time to begin living renewed?

Sideways

so that from the rising of the sun to the place of its setting
people may know there is none besides me. I
am the LORD, and there is no other.
⁷ I form the light and create darkness, I bring prosperity
and create disaster; I, the LORD, do all these things.
Isaiah 45:6-7

This morning, I slid on the ice. My car went sideways, missing cars in the turn lane by just a hair. I took my feet off the pedal and rode out the spin. The car came to a stop, and I moved on. Behind me, another car hit the same patch of ice. I watched the car spin, scraping a couple of cars waiting in the turn lane and then finally resting on the curb.

I drove on, giving thanks to God for protecting me.

Sometimes life goes sideways. One minute you are cruising down the road and the next you are spinning out of control. I learned long ago in driving that you do not panic, you ride it out and resist the urge to steer or slam on the brakes. Unfortunately, I have not come to that point in my life.

I want control of my life. I want to do the steering and stop it when I do not like the way it is going. However, it just does not work that way. Learning to trust fully has been and continues to be the hardest thing for me to do in my spiritual and physical life.

Part of walking with Jesus is relinquishing control and putting all your trust in Him. That is easy to say when everything is going according to your plan, but not so much when things go sideways.

No matter what happens, God is ultimately in control. Whether it is sickness, finances, jobs, relationships, or governments. That is hard to swallow sometimes. However, we are not without a voice. We are encouraged to bring these things to the Lord through prayer and we are told not to worry.

> *Do not be anxious about anything, but in every situation, by prayer and petition, with thanksgiving, present your requests to God. ⁷ And the peace of God, which transcends all understanding, will guard your hearts and your minds in Christ Jesus. Philippians 4:4-7*

God is in control and He has a plan.

> *For I know the plans I have for you," declares the LORD, "plans to prosper you and not to harm you, plans to give you hope and a future. Jeremiah 29:11*

There is uncertainty in the world. We do not know what the weather or other governments will do, but we do have the assurance in God's word that whatever might happen in the World, He is ultimately in control and He has a plan.

Is your trust in Christ or is it in you?

To Commit or Not to Commit The Real Question

> *For it is not the hearers of the Law who are just before*
> *God, but the doers of the Law will be justified.*
> *Romans 2:13*

I passed the plate to the young lady. She eagerly took a bite. She looked back at me in surprise. "Oh, that's good! Is it on your diet?"

"Yes," I smiled.

"Is all the food this good?"

"Yes, it is all really good. I enjoy it a lot." I dug my fork into my own plate, savoring the flavors. "Don't you miss the other food, the junk food and pizza?" She asked between bites.

"At first, but not as much now. Also it doesn't taste as good to me anymore."

"Really?" She pondered as she ate. "Isn't it hard? I mean having to stick to a plan when everyone else can eat what they want?"

"It's an easy plan really. I assure you, I do not suffer. I can eat anything I want, but I choose to eat this way. It is about discipline and commitment. Knowing what you want."

"Hmm." Was her only reply. I could see her mind working. She was weighing the cost of commitment. *Could she be disciplined?* She was asking herself. Was she willing to make the sacrifices and deny the flesh?

After a few moments, I added. "If you are interested I will sponsor you."

"I don't have the money right now." She quickly countered.

I thought for a moment. "I'll cover the cost for you." A thoughtful silence. I waited.

"No, that's ok. I think I will just kind of follow what you're doing on my own. I may join later." She smiled at me.

Do you just follow along with others, or are you committed to the plan? Many people just follow, living quiet, and in all respects, good lives. They are truly good people, but they lack the commitment to Jesus. Commitment is hard for people, whether it is to a diet, a relationship, job, or living for Christ. With commitment comes accountability and responsibility. I think that scares some people. Or maybe they worry they can never live up to expectations once they accept.

God isn't looking for perfect people. He is looking for the broken and burdened. There is no expectation beyond committing to Jesus. The rest, through God's Grace, will be given.

Christ covered the cost of salvation with His sacrifice. There is nothing else for you to do other than to accept His offer.

No Expiration Date

I fell back on my bed and stared at the ceiling. I was simply exhausted. Not physically, but emotionally. My heart hurt. My soul wept.

"Lord," I said, "this just stinks."

I let out a long sigh and turned on my side. My mind was popping with thoughts. My worries and the worries of the people on my prayer list. Why were so many dear, God fearing people suffering and in pain?

As I lay there trying to make sense of the senseless, I repeated. *"Lord this just stinks."*

I was reminded of the story of Lazarus.

Lazarus was a good man. A follower of Jesus; he fell ill and died. Jesus was away at the time and the sisters Mary and Martha had sent word for Jesus to come quick to save their brother. However, Jesus did not come straight away. I often wondered why he did not. Why had Jesus waited four days?

If Jesus had come sooner, Lazarus' healing would have been great but would it have been perceived as a miracle to those watching? Possibly the people would have attributed the raising of Lazarus to he had fallen into a coma and simply awakened if it had been within a day or so. Maybe some would believe that Lazarus had just been playing opossum. Whatever those around might have been thinking, Jesus knew exactly when it was time to intercede. Jesus waited frankly until it got really stinky. Really bad.

When he said, "**Roll back the stone**", those around said, "**Oh no, Lord by this time he stinkth**." Jesus wanted there to be no doubt that Lazarus was dead.

Sometimes things really stink in our lives. The doctor says there is no change, the child continues to rebel, the bills mound up, anger still stands in the relationship and you got passed over again at work. It stinks, but maybe, just maybe, it has to get really smelly so that when Jesus takes it and makes everything right there will be no doubt to you or those watching that it was Jesus.

Nothing is ever too far gone for Christ. Take the most putrid situation to Him. He'll tell you to *roll back that stone*, he's got this.

Often we think things are so far gone that nothing can be done. Someone has strayed too far. Nope He can bring them back. Too many hurtful things have been done and said. Nope, Jesus can mend it. There is nothing too stinky for Jesus to make right.

Do not give up. Pray. Believe. Wait expectantly. It is coming.

Change is Happening

*Now faith is the substance of things hoped
for, the evidence of things not seen.*
Hebrews 11:1

A coworker stopped by my desk the other day.

"Wow," she began. "How much more have you lost now?"

My shoulders drooped, and I sighed. "No more. Can't get past the 68 pounds I have lost."

"Really? You look smaller."

"Scales haven't budged."

"Well," she said with an encouraging smile. "You look great, and smaller. Your body is just adjusting. The scales might not show it but there is certainly change happening."

We chatted a few minutes more about kids and life and she returned to her department. I returned to my work and I thought about what she said. *"The scales might not show it, but there is certainly change happening."*

I found much needed encouragement from this. Not about my continued weight loss but about some situations in my life that weigh heavy on my heart. I awake in the night two or three in the morning my mind already working, questioning, worrying and then my imagination fires up and my thoughts excite my anxiety. I wipe that away and I pray. I pray until sleep reclaims me. Morning comes and the problem has not changed.

Or has it?

Often we give up when the scales do not move. As humans, we need a measurement a matrix of change that we can look at. Something tangible so we can have proof. However, there is no matrix for faith.

I want to encourage you as this precious lady encouraged me. I know that you have a burden. It could be finances, or your children. Maybe your job, health or just life decisions. Whatever it may be, continue to take it to the Lord. Continue to pray. **Do not be anxious about anything, but in every situation, by prayer and petition, with thanksgiving, present your requests to God. (Philippians 4:6-7)**

Just because you do not see measured change, does not mean that it is not happening. Quite the contrary. If you are doing what the Word instructs and believing fully, **change is happening**. The Father is working on your behalf. He is changing and softening hearts. He is making a way financially to meet your needs. He is healing.

Do not look to the scales for evidence of change, but have faith and KNOW change is happening.

The Bible: It's in There

I stood staring at the rows of spaghetti sauces. Name brands, no names, and lesser names, you name it, a whole lot of sauce was stacked on those shelves! I was reading the ingredient and nutrition facts. I was endeavoring to make an educated and healthy choice. I wanted to know what was in the jar that I was going to be serving to my family.

Have you ever noticed how many ingredients are unpronounceable? Some do not appear to be real words. These multi-syllable words are the names of chemicals that are added to our foods to "enhance" flavor and shelf life. What is really interesting is that this information is listed for us yet we do not know what those words mean. We have no idea what is included in the food that we are introducing into our bodies. Most often we are more concerned about the flavor and frankly the price. Only the surface and immediate gratifications of spaghetti sauce is the concern.

We are unfortunately the same with our understanding and knowledge of the Bible and the character of God. We take it at a glance, but few of us really dig and study to truly understand what that Holy book has to teach us. What wisdom, guidance, comfort and strength are we missing out on because of ignorance? What insights to the very character of God are we rejecting by choosing not to study and know His words recorded for us.

It is this lack of knowledge that leads to the destruction of Christians. The physical, spiritual and emotional destruction of God's people. We are ill-equipped to handle the daily trials and pitfalls of life. We do not know the power we possess within the mere whisper of Jesus' name. Why? Because we lack knowledge. We are ignorant of our true identity. We rely on the world and its people to define us, mold us and inspire us. We trust the labels and take it in by mouthfuls.

Shouldn't we be digging into the Word of God to learn all that we are and possess? Shouldn't the Word be our guide, our source of understanding and comfort?

Are you just looking at the outside of the Word or are you truly examining what is contained within? Got questions, heartaches and in need of wisdom? Try the Bible, it's in there.

Come and Drink

> *But whoever drinks the water I give them will never*
> *thirst. Indeed, the water I give them will become in*
> *them a spring of water welling up to eternal life."*
> *John 4:14*

I walked down the hallway and up the ramp to the water fountain. I was surprised to see several people waiting. I fell in line and watched the clear liquid splashing in each cup or bottle. I listened to the chatter of my coworkers and smiled at the quips. I thought about how fortunate we were that we have water flowing clean, clear and cool. It gushed in an unending stream. Filling cup after cup. Just there for the taking.

Holding my empty bottle, the story of the woman at the well sprang in my thoughts. (John 4:1-42) Like the people of the day, we each had brought vessels to carry our water back to our respective desks. One even had a coffee pot. We each waited our turn for our share of the filtered refresher. Without a doubt, we all would return for a refill.

The woman at the well came late in the day to fill her jugs. She came late because she was despised by those in her village. She wanted to avoid their stares and judgment. She quickly followed the lonely path to the well. The hot midday sun had heated the sand, it scorched the bottom of her feet. Sweat beaded on her brow, but her tongue was parched. She had been waiting all morning to come for her share.

I imagine she was more than just surprised when she came into the cleaning and found a man there. A Jewish man with kind eyes that he did not divert when she emerged from the pathway. Instead, his eyes met hers with a compassion she had never experienced. He was poised on the bricks that lined the rim of the well, his hands folded in his lap as if he indeed had been waiting for her. He addressed her kindly and asked for a ladle of water. In return, He offered her a gift. Living water. She did not have to wait in line. Instead, He waited for her.

You do not have to wait for His forgiveness or salvation. You don't have to wait until you feel worthy or ready. He is waiting for you by the well. Waiting for you to come and drink.

Grace Biscuits

I do love a good bargain. So, of course, the other day when I came across some dog biscuits on clearance, I did not hesitate to purchase them. I got three boxes for the price of one. With this excess in dog treats, I was very generous in doling out the bone shaped delicacies.

Every time Emma the Terrible and Big Bryan went out to potty, upon their return they were given a bone. On the second day of this new routine, Big Bryan went to the back door and rang the bell.

Dutifully, I let him out. I had just shut the door when he barked and scratched. I opened the door and he came in stopping by the table with the treats on it. I reached into the box and gave him one.

Moments later, the bell rang out again. I looked around the house to the back. There Big Bryan sat waiting. As he heard me approach, he stood and rang the bell again. I opened the door, he exited and as soon as the door was shut, he barked and scratched.

This went on the rest of the evening. Some of his request I ignored. But to be safe, I let him out occasionally. Almost every time, he would return immediately to the door, bark, scratch and reenter pausing near the little table.

By day three Emma sat next to him, exiting and reentering eager to claim her bone. By day four, my daughter complained of loss of sleep because of Bryan ringing the bell in the middle of the night.

Like him, I do enjoy the odd midnight snack.

I was amused at how quickly these pets had figure out the plan. Purely motivated by food, each exploited the opportunity to the max.

They just kept coming back for more and I, having an excess of the little tasty treats, was very indulgent in handing them out.

As I lay in bed the other night, I thought about those little Grace Biscuit I was giving so freely. I also thought about how eagerly my pooches gobbled them up. Immediately, I thought of the verse in Romans. **What shall we say then? Shall we continue in sin, that grace may abound?**

And abound it does, for each of us. However, grace is no excuse to think that we can just go through life doing as we please with the thought that we are forgiven and our actions rendered null and void.

On the contrary, our actions, choices and how we conduct our lives impact all those around us in ways we never consider. Where it is true, grace is available and never-ending, it is also our responsibility to live our lives as Christ would and did.

Paul I believe says it much better than me.

What then shall we say? Shall we continue in sin so that grace may increase? By no means! How can we who died to sin live in it any longer? Romans 6:1-2

Focus Wheel

Standing in the clearing, my father scanned the trees with his binoculars.

"There!" He exclaimed. "Oh, he's beautiful." He said as he passed the binoculars to mom. A quick succession rang out in the woods. *"Rap, rap, rap"*

I want to see, I exclaimed pawing at my daddy for the binoculars. He bent, slipped the strap over my head and handed them to me. They were heavy and my little arms quivered under their weight. I struggled to lift them and daddy helped me hold them to my face. He guided up toward where the sound had come.

"Do you see him?" He whispered. "No. Everything is blurry, Daddy."

Daddy turned the wheel on top of the binoculars and suddenly a black and white woodpecker with a brush stroke of red atop his head came into focus.

"Wow." I breathed. The leaves and trees were so close. It was as if I could reach out and pet the colorful percussionist. "What is that?" I asked, poking the little wheel with my finger.

"It's the focus wheel. You turn it until you can see." "It makes blurry stuff better?"

"Yes." He smiled at me touching my cheek. "Makes blurry clear."

Recently, I lost my focus. My sight became fuzzy and blurry because I was focused on the situation and not the Cross. I was really in my "Missy Bubble". All I could see was all the problems, all the issues, but not the solution. That happens sometimes. Maybe to you too.

A friend of mine helped to turn the Focus wheel for me. She came alongside me and told me some things I needed to hear. She laid it out in plain English. It stings when someone has to address you about your behavior, but thank God for them! I am thankful I have people in my life that love me enough to help me regain focus. As Christians, we are a family, therefore we have a responsibility to **gently and with kindness** give each other a nudge when we stray. That can be a scary position. Often we refrain from addressing another because we fear their wrath. However, our love for a brother or sister— and most importantly—their eternal soul, must be our first and only concern.

On the flip side, we should have humility and be able to humble ourselves to accept correction from those in our lives that we know love us and Jesus. Sometimes we need help with the *focus wheel*.

Living at the Corner of Priceless and Cherished

> *For I know the plans I have for you," declares the LORD, "plans to prosper you and not to harm you, plans to give you hope and a future.*
> *Jeremiah 29:11*

It was six days before I was to be out of my house. I needed to be out before the new owners took possession. However, finding a place to accommodate two dogs, a cat and parrot is not too easy. Nor is finding a place that does not take your life savings to move. I had been waiting to hear about a particular place that accepted the animals and installment payments on the deposits. At the last minute, it fell through. The office manager said they just couldn't sign off on my application. I was devastated. Consumed by a huge tsunami sized wave of fear. It was Thursday, and the move really needed to happen over the weekend. I was packed, but I had nowhere to go. It was beginning to look like my furry kids would have to find shelter elsewhere. Frankly, I was wondering where my daughter and I would shelter. I will not lie, I was scared. I was spending most of my time pacing around, wringing my hands and lamenting *"What am I going to do?"* It was at that time my sister in Christ tweaked my *focus wheel* from the problems back to the Cross. I was worrying myself to death and asking God and frankly anyone within earshot what was **I** going to do? The problem was **I** kept saying what **I** was going to do. Not what was God going to do. So I stopped asking myself that and instead, I asked God what was His Will in this situation. I told Him I trusted that He was going to work everything out to my advantage.

The next day I received a call from an apartment complex. I had sent out several email inquiries, and she was calling to see if I still was looking for a place.

"Yes, I am." I answered.

"Well, that's great. I was calling because we are running a 24 hour sale." "Ok, tell me more."

"If you can get your application in, pass all the checks and take possession immediately, we will waive all fees and all that will be due is prorated rent."

I asked a few questions as this needed some clarification. No pet fees, no administration fees, no deposits, nothing would be required? I was shocked. I went through my list of needs, including asking about whether there was access to a washer and dryer. Mine had died a couple of weeks before, and I needed a new set but it would take time to save. She cheerfully answered, "All new units have washer and dryer provided in them."

I looked heavenward. Could this be true? A washer and dryer provided?

"Ok, I said. I am very interested." She emailed the rental packet, and I got started on it right away. I had it back to her within the hour.

Two hours later she called me back. "Melissa, you went through faster than any application I've ever done. We would love for you to come pick out your new home."

"Ok, when?"

"Well, in order to get all fees waived everything has to be completed within the 24 hour window."

I drove straight over.

She led me to a golf cart and said, "Let's look at this one first. It's my favorite. I think you will like it too."

As we took off, I silently prayed for discernment and wisdom. I asked God to let me know if this is where I needed to be. Was this His Will?

The cart slowed and the young lady swung right. The street signs read, *Priceless and Cherished.*

I smiled and laughed out loud.

"What's funny?" My chauffeur inquired.

"Oh, the street signs. I'm going to be living at the corner of Priceless and Cherished."

That is exactly where each of us live daily as His Children. To God, you are priceless and greatly cherished. He loved you and me so much that He gave His Son so we may have eternal life.

When things are piling up around you. When people hurt you. When the money is not there. When the kids are acting crazy. When the boss passes you over. When the doctor has bad news. When the divorce papers come. When pain seems unbearable. Remember where you are living. Remember that you are priceless and cherished by God. That amid all the heartbreak and problems that steal your focus, shatter your heart, and keep you up at night, He is working. He is working to provide you with everything you need. He has a plan to prosper YOU.

I learned an important lesson. It isn't about what I can do but about what God can and will do. It was a lesson in faith and trusting His timing.

It was also seeing demonstrated how much He cherishes me. My worth to Him. Live your life daily at the corner of Priceless and Cherished.

Momentum

I stepped out on the porch, locked the door and turned to descend the steps. I stopped short. Rain gently fell, the world was wrapped in gauzy gray. The driveway was ankle deep in water. The constant rain had flooded the yard and where the driveway ended and the yard began was obscured. I pulled up my hood and balanced on the bricks stacked around the flower bed. Avoiding the huge puddle I got in the car and started it.

I live in a school zone. Constant traffic up and down the road all morning. Sometimes a line of cars stretches the entire road. This morning in the cold, steady rain, traffic had slowed. I would not be able to back out of the drive easily, so I decided I would back into the yard and pull directly out into traffic.

Because of the water that stood on the front of my property, I knew that I would have to pick the right area to back into. I steered the car down the driveway and turned the wheel to enter the soggy grass.

The car backed into the yard; a fury of ripples spread out around me. I felt the rear sink a bit, I tapped the brakes slowing the car but not stopping my momentum. I quickly shifted. The car lurched and freed me from the muck. I pulled forward and out into traffic.

Momentum is the difference between getting stuck and moving through the muck. Now and then I feel like I am surrounded by a sea of problems. It feels like the water is rising, threatening to envelop me. I'm struggling to just keep my head up. It is times like this that I feel tired. I am weary of the never-ending issues that rain down. When this happens, it is tempting to just stop. Pull the covers over my head and hide. However, that is what our enemy wants us to do. He wants you to become so overwhelmed that you quit. He wants you to believe you are drowning, sinking in the muck.

So what to do? Keep moving forward, continue to follow Jesus right through the center of the muck and mud. He will lead to higher ground. And when it gets really deep and your feet get stuck, reach up, Jesus will lift you and carry you through.

Do not let the enemy stall your momentum. Continue moving forward.

Seek Renewal

Therefore we do not lose heart. Though outwardly we are wasting away, yet inwardly we are being renewed day by day. [17] For our light and momentary troubles are achieving for us an eternal glory that far outweighs them all.
2 Corinthians 4:16&17

Big Bryan, is not adjusting to life in an apartment very well. Before he would ring the bell, someone came, opened the door and let him out to romp and play in the yard as long as he wanted.

Unfortunately, Bryan can only go outside on a harness, tethered to either my daughter or me.

The other morning in the chill of the predawn hours, Big Bryan decided he was not going to go easy out into the courtyard. He bucked, spun around, bit at the leash and finally flopped on the ground. He emitted a long, exasperated sigh. No matter what I offered, no matter how hard I pulled, Bryan was going nowhere. He just laid in the grass facing away from me staring.

I feel very bad for Big Bryan. I also understand how he feels. Things are not going the way he wants. He had no say in the situation. One day he was loaded in the back of the car and brought to a new home.

No yard, no laying in the grass and rolling in the dirt. Just scheduled times to go for walks. So he did what most of us do when things do not go our way. He pitched a fit, showed out and then just flopped down.

Often, we get put in situations in our lives that we did not choose. They are not what we want. And so, like Bryan, we buck, bite and finally just stop and flop. However, Paul tells us in 2 Corinthians that is exactly what we should not do. ***"Though outwardly we are wasting away, yet inwardly we are being renewed day by day."*** Despite what the circumstances, instead of allowing ourselves to waste away, we are to call upon the Lord and allow Him to renew us daily. Through this renewal, we find strength, clarity and perseverance to get through the trial that has been set before us. Bucking and running ourselves into exhaustion and depression does not help. Nor does it allow us to grow in our relationship with Jesus.

If you are facing circumstances that are draining and sapping your joy, turn to the Lord and allow Him to renew you. Instead of focusing on the situation, focus on the Cross. Continue to seek His Will. By doing this you will have the strength and wisdom to get through.

At the Car Wash

*Not by works of righteousness which we have done,
but according to his mercy he saved us, by the washing
of regeneration, and renewing of the Holy Ghost;*
Titus 3:5

My car is a mess. Since the move and rushing about from one place to another I have not had time to clean it out or wash it. It is so bad that someone I work with commented to someone else that, "They don't know who that car belongs too but it looks like they are living out of it."

So yesterday I made a point to schedule time just for cleaning my car. I had been parking beneath a pine tree at the old house and sap had coated it. So I stopped by the auto car wash with a baggie of quarters. I started at the top scrubbing down the car with pink foam that generously spurted from the ragged brush.

I scrubbed and scrubbed, each rinse revealed more of the bright white paint. However, I would have to start scrubbing again, the sap was really stuck on. As I began to rinse for the last time I heard the buzzer. It was to let me know that time was running out. My daughter took the baggie to put in the last of the change. However, we did not have enough to prolong the rinse cycle. So there my car sat in the stall, pink foam sliding down her sides.

There was only one thing to do.

We jumped in the car and headed down the street to the automatic wash. As we sped down the boulevard pink trailed us. A glob hit the windshield of the car behind us. I pressed the gas pedal a bit harder.

I paid the machine, pulled around and was guided to line up on the track. I put the car in neutral took my hands from the wheel and relinquished control. Once out of the other end of the tunnel my car gleamed a snow white again.

As I was sitting in the car during the automatic wash, I thought about how often we think that we can clean up the dirt and grime of our lives on our own. It is true that we can scrub and we can vacuum, but in the end, we need help. We mean it, we really want to be clean. We really want the alcoholism, the foul mouth, the extramarital affair, the lying the…well, whatever it may be. We want to be able to come clean.

But we cannot.

It takes Christ to make a total change in the heart.

Is there a part of your life that needs some cleaning up? Take it to the Lord. Turn it over and let Him remove the guilt and shame. Stop trying to do it all yourself. He is there, ready, willing and able.

Heart Construction

Since I have moved across town, my commute has changed. I now pass through the center of construction. Everyday traffic slows to a 35 mile an hour crawl. Orange and white barrels direct traffic down ever changing lanes and exits. Concrete walls are erected and removed overnight. It can be quite vexing at times.

As our city grows, adjustments have to be made to accommodate. With people relocating to our city and our million visitors each year, we have to undergo some structural changes. No one enjoys the stop and go of road construction. The dust, uneven payment and disinterested stares of workers seemingly on a perpetual break. Traffic cones and flashing lights funneling commuters through the bottlenecks.

Just typing this description has raised my blood pressure.

In many ways our journeys through life are much the same. We encounter detours, closed roads and reduction of speed along our way. It is equally vexing and challenging. In order to grow in our journey with Jesus, we have to be open to change. Our hearts and attitudes need occasional upheavals to encourage growth, faith and strength. We have to embrace the changes and focus on the ultimate outcome.

Once the construction is completed, traffic will move smoothly through the city. Extended lanes will give this major artery ease. The barrels will eventually disappear, the dust will settle and traffic will return to normal. In fact, it will be better.

If you are dealing with some heart and life construction, take heart. Focus not on the current state, but look forward to the eventual out-come. You are undergoing these upheavals and changes so that Jesus can grow you. Growth cannot be accomplished without change.

The Best is Yet to Come

"But as it is written, Eye hath not seen, nor ear heard, neither have entered into the heart of man, the things which God hath prepared for them that love him."
1 Corinthians 2:9

I was driving home around dusk one evening. It was that time of day just at the fringe when the light is extinguished and darkness envelopes. Ahead I saw movement and slowed. It was a deer, spindly legged, it's fur blending into the impending darkness. The green glint of her eyes shone as brightly as my headlights. Seeing my approaching lights, she bolted and ran up the embankment onto the off-ramp. Startled by the lights of the freeway, she turned and ran back into the median. I slowed and so did the cars behind me. Someone blew the horn and she bolted again, this time into my lane. I slammed on my brakes and swerved. She turned back and up the embankment, she glided again. She sprang over the guardrail and melted into the scrub.

I continued my drive home, slightly nervous, fearing another would run out on the roadway. As I drove I thought back on the delicate creature, the wide eyes, flaring nostrils and heaving chest. I thought of the fear and the confusion she was experiencing. I felt bad for her. How lost and frightened she must have been with the feel of asphalt beneath her hoofs, sudden blare of the car horn and glare of headlights.

I do not know about you, but often this world and all that I see and experience at times leaves me confused, anxious and scared. There are times I just do not know which way to go, what to believe, or what I should be doing. It is easy to get wound up in the lights and sounds.

As much as that sweet creature did not belong on the asphalt, we do not belong to this world.

Even though we are in this world as Christians, we are not of this world. Our home, our inheritance is Heaven. This world is full of bad things, sickness, death, suffering, and heartbreak, but you and I have the assurance that there is a glorious Kingdom awaiting us.

I know at times you feel as confused and scared as that deer, but do not fear. Focus on what is ahead. This is not all there is for us that believe. We have the best yet to come.

Heart Examination

*But a man must examine himself, and in so doing
he is to eat of the bread and drink of the cup.*
1 Corinthians 11:28

Fixing up my new space has been fun. Picking out colors, arranging furniture, and making everything just so. The other day I brought home a full length mirror for my bedroom. Leaning it against the wall, I let the pets out of the crates. Big Bryan flew out of his kennel and ran immediately to the mirror and a box I brought into the living room.

His interest peaked, Bryan circled the box, I could hear him breathing in and then snorting out as he gleaned every bit of olfactory information these new items had brought with them. In his distraction, he had not noticed the reflection in the mirror. Movement captured his attention, he raised his eyes. Face to face with his unexpected reflection, he fell back on his hind quarters, a startled bark escaping him. He ran behind me. One eye peered out from around my legs.

I had to laugh. Big Bryan is such a sweet dopey dog. After regaining his canine composure, he tentatively approached the mirror again. He was not sure what it was but his curiosity won out and he continued his examination.

Sometimes after some self-reflection, we too are startled by what we see. Throughout my journey with Christ, I have had to turn inward and examine my heart. What are my motives? Why am I doing what I do? There were times what I saw was very ugly.

Self-introspection is intimidating. However, in order for any of us to grow as Christians and simply as good, kind and caring people, we have to take time to examine our own hearts and motivations. We also have to have the courage to change. Most times that is more difficult than facing the flaws we possess. To change ourselves and to forgive others, to erase prejudices and to allow healing, all of this takes courage and dedication.

I challenge you to take a peek inside your heart. Really examine what you harbor and then bring it to Jesus. Drop at the foot of the cross and allow Him to help you unburden.

Isn't it time for a good Heart Examination?

A Deliberate Choice

Seek the LORD while he may be found;
call on him while he is near.
Isaiah 55:6

Something caught my eye. Hanging in the trees, several feet above the asphalt in a harness, slowly twirling in the breeze, was a man. I watched as the crane lifted him higher into the dense foliage. Only his red hard hat was still visible between the leaves. The tree bent to the wind and then righted itself until the next breeze rustled through the branches. It waved back and forth, the sun dancing on each leaf. I heard the high pitched whir of the chainsaw peal through the atmosphere. I heard the whine bog a bit as the saw's teeth munched through the old tree. Moments later, a crack, and then the branch as big a bus was lowered to the asphalt by another crane.

As I sat in my car enjoying the sunny day and my lunch, I wondered about that man. Every day he goes to work trusting in harnesses, ropes, and people to convey him up and down to cut limbs from lofty heights. If those lines broke, or a limb kicked back or if someone made an error, his life would be in grave jeopardy. However, he was as relaxed as me. He seemed unphased as he dangled several feet above the ground.

I find it interesting that people are more comfortable trusting in ropes, elevators, car brakes and medications rather than Christ. If you can see it, feel it or if everyone else does it then we are good with it. People will telephone a psychic, try to contact ghosts, play the lottery, or talk to a bartender but refuse to even entertain the existence of God. Or acknowledge the sacrifice of His son.

Why? Because Faith in the unseen goes against the very nature of man.

Choosing Christ as your Savior and placing complete trust and faith in Him is a decision. It is not a feeling. It is a deliberate choice. A choice that must be renewed daily.

The tree cutter chooses each day to strap on the harness and give the thumbs up to the crane operator. Daily, shouldn't we suit up in Spiritual Armor, make a conscious decision to live in faith and then do it?

Today, where are your faith and trust residing? Is it in people? Maybe money? Perhaps your job? Choose today and every day to place your faith in Christ Jesus.

> *9 If you declare with your mouth, "Jesus is Lord," and believe in your heart that God raised him from the dead, you will be saved. 10 For it is with your heart that you believe and are justified, and it is with your mouth that you profess your faith and are saved. Romans 10:9-10*

Are You Living for Jesus?

> *And he died for all, that those who live should*
> *no longer live for themselves but for him who*
> *died for them and was raised again.*
> *2 Corinthians 5:15*

In Mexico, the sun is hot and the roads dusty and rough. I was ready to get out of the van. I had bounced around the back of the conveyance long enough. We had been traveling for two hours over bumpy roads with only scrub brush, litter and an occasional village as a view. Finally, the dust settled and the van door smoothly rolled back. I stretched my back and surveyed my surroundings. Before me palm trees, and lush, dense vegetation loomed above. Elephant ear plants massive and emerald green towered above our little group as we made our way down a dirt pathway that bisected the living boundary. Above the bellowing call of Howler monkeys announced our arrival and the screeching of unseen birds blared from the treetops. Joining the cacophony, cicadas droned from the surrounding jungle. The denseness of the foliage brought a cooling breeze that I happily welcomed. I walked the narrow corridor with each step, my excitement heightened. It was a relatively short passage, and as quickly as my eyes had adjusted to the dimness, our little group of travelers passed through the wall of trees to a clearing. It was like walking through an unseen veil, time travel if you like, as I gazed at the Mayan Ruins of

Kohunlich (KOE-HOON-LEECH). Spread over 21 acres, temples, citadels, courtyards and a palace were elaborately situated.

Level, perfectly manicured lawns sprawled. The entire site was bathed in the golden light of the retiring sun. Long shadows stretched melting into the jungle beyond the hidden city.

I stood, awed.

I climbed the steps of the palace and scanned the other ruins. Closing my eyes, I imagined what this magnificent thriving city must have looked like over 3000 years before. The buzz of life and the colorfully painted buildings I imaged, began to come alive on my mind's stage. I thought about the people. They had lived, loved, fought, suffered and died in this isolated oasis nestled in the thick subtropical landscape. It was a surreal moment. In the passage of time, we are no more than a blip. I entered the hall of mask and gazed at the 8 foot tall masks, grotesquely displayed with fierce eyes and lolling tongues. What were they representative of? Why such ferocity? I pondered these thoughts as I traced the carvings with my eyes.

Our guide led us to the ball field. It was a swatch of thick grass between two walls leaning at 45° angles. Our guide, a proud Mayan descendant, told how the game was one of ritual and not entertainment. He passed a heavy ball made of sap that bounced easily. Though the rules and the exact logistics of the game are mostly unknown, it is believed that the winning team's captain was sacrificed at the end of the game. Not the losing team, as first reasoned. Why would the winner be sacrificed? Because to be a sacrifice to the god was an honor, and these athletes were competing for the privilege to die for their god. In Mayan creation mythology, the gods had to die for life to be created. In essence, the shedding of the god's blood brought life to man. Therefore, the Mayans believed they had to repay that blood sacrifice several times a year to ensure fertility of the land, the people and crops. It was the demand of the gods.

I thought about this on my way back to the van.

Our Lord and Savior shed His blood to give us eternal life. He asks not that we repay Him with our blood but that we live for Him and share His Love with others. His sacrifice does not expect repayment but is given through grace for our redemption.

These people thought it an honor to die for their gods yet many of us have difficulty in living for ours.

Are you alive for Jesus? Does your life celebrate His sacrifice and love?

Banish Fear

Scuba diving has been on my bucket list long before it was called a bucket list. So when the opportunity arose to dive while on my cruise, I dove for it.

Honduras, according to Captain Mike, is one of the "hot spots" to dive. In fact, Isla Roatan is well known in dive circles. That fact in itself made the possibility even more appealing. I was very excited that morning and eager to do something I had only dreamed. We boarded the boat, met Captain Mike and swiftly left the pier for the dive shop.

Crisp, yellow sun danced on the aqua blue waves of Mahogany Bay. Salty ocean air tickled my nose and seasoned my lips. Along the horizon we saw other dive boats, fishing boats and cruise ships. It was a very busy though fare. We became acquainted with the others on the excursion. A few were from our ship.

I could feel the excitement from the participants. I wondered if they too were experiencing jitters. Did they also have that little tremor? You know the one you feel deep in your belly when you can barely contain the erupting excitement? The boat pulled aside the wooden dock and three young island men appeared from the small hut set back in the palms. Offering bronzed, strong hands they helped us from the boat to the dock. Introductions all around were followed by signing forms and flipper measurements.

I continued to simmer with excitement.

Ang and I sat in the boat as it bobbed rhythmically on the lapping waves. We had been through the class, fitted with BD jackets and weight belts. Now we waited our turn to enter the blue expanse.

Flippers protruding before me, I shuffled to the boat's aft. With the rocking of the boat shifting the weight of the tank, I was unsteady and unnerved. I followed the instructions given and leaped into the churning depths.

There is a lot to remember when you are struggling in open water. Inflate BD, clear ears, stay vertical, breath in and out in the regulator only and do not drown. I hit the deflate button on the BD jacket and in a fury of bubbles I began to sink beneath the water's surface. Expectedly, my ears felt the pressure change, and as I was instructed, I cleared my ears.

Now it was time for my skills test. I was to remove my regulator, blow bubbles out of my mouth and reinsert the mouthpiece.

Attempt 1- FAIL *Resurface* Attempt 2-FAIL *Resurface*

Attempt 3-Success but then panic

Resurface

Final attempt- Deflate BD, sink beneath the waves, clear regulator, and ears.

Success!

The weighted belt drew me further into the depths. Around me nothing but blue. I immediately wondered, *what lurked behind the blue?* My tremors of excitement were becoming a simmering fear.

Clutching the rope that stretched between the world above and the world beneath I felt the sea exert her pressure. My lungs felt compressed, my ears began to ring. Above me the sun's light and warmth faded. Nothing but blue closed around me. Cooler water rose from beneath me spreading ribbons of cold around my legs. It traveled deliberately, steadily up my body. The pressure increased and my ears hurt, sharp stabbing pain in the left. I waved to the instructor, pointed to my ears and he did the sign to clear them once again. I tried to relieve my discomfort. No luck, the piercing pain continued.

My body continued to sink with the weight around my middle.

Between the pain, fear, fading light and creeping cold, I began to panic. I tried one more time to clear, pinching my nose and swallowing, but this time the mask creased and the ocean flooded into my mask. Instinctively, I held my breath. The instructor tried to calm me, but panic was driving now. Hand over hand, I pulled myself up the rope kicking with all I had. A flipper came off, but I barely noticed as I clawed my way back to air, light and warmth. I broke the surface and tore the mask and regulator off. I greedily inhaled all the air my lungs could hold.

When I look back over my life at my many failings and spiritual pitfalls there is a common denominator, fear. Fear robs us of joy and peace. It causes us to buckle under the pressure and settle for less than God's best for us. I allowed my fear to take over and I reacted in panic.

Others on the excursion completed the test and descended to 40 feet and glided along the sandy bottom. They trusted the process, themselves and the instructor. They did not let fear rule the situation.

Fear is an ugly force. It can exert pressure on you and whisper things in your mind. Allowing it a foothold, it conjures up imaginings and doubt. There is no place for fear in a Believer's heart.

I wish this story ended with me gearing back up and with determination descending to 40 feet and swimming victory laps around the coral bed but it does not. Instead, I climbed back on board defeated, disappointed.

Fear keeps you trapped. Keeps you from opportunities and experiences. Fear does all these things, but you do not have to allow it. Ultimately, fear answers to you. Reject it, rebuke it and never let it rule you.

Trust in Him and deny fear.

> **For God has not given us the spirit of fear; but of power, and of love, and of a sound mind. 2 Timothy 1:7**

Jesus Is As Close
As a Whisper

In the same way, the Spirit helps us in our weakness. We do not know what we ought to pray for, but the Spirit himself intercedes for us through wordless groans.
Romans 8:26 NIV

Fluffy white clouds lazily floated on an invisible river under a blistering sun. The temperature was nearing 100 degrees, and I was feeling every one of them. I stood under the only shade tree with a cluster of equally hot and sweaty tourist. I listened to the young man recite facts and answer questions that I am sure he has heard hundreds of times. As my eyes blurred with my sweat, I noticed that this young man was as dry as my throat. Not one bead of sweat clung to his rich brown complexion.

After our guide completed his presentation, we made our way between two decayed buildings at the foot of El Castile, poised atop a ridge, it stood tall and proud looming 130 feet. To imagine this building had stood almost as long ago as our Savior's Ascension was surreal. I stood for a moment and looked up at the apex. I snapped a few pictures and then I began the climb to the top.

Until you begin to climb the steps, you have no idea how big they are. Our tour guide had explained that the steps were intentionally large, so that the average 5 foot tall Mayan would be forced into a posture of supplication as they climbed the steps. If I had to use my hand to climb the steps at a height of 5'6, I imagine that some of the ancients literally had to crawl. The steps radiated with the sun's heat scorching my hands. I grimaced when I realized that their bare skin had been in direct contact with the hot surface of stones as they crawled.

I made it to the first level and turned to look back at the courtyard that stretched before me. The king's palace sat opposite roped off. It was under excavation and tourist were not allowed to scale it. Open doors and windows on the top of the palace like missing teeth in an ugly grin, looked back at me.

We had made about a third of the way. I used my hand to hold my hat to my head and looked up at the other two-thirds. A small gecko darted between two stones. The sun continued to beat down.

Following a pathway, we came to a staircase that snaked up the side of the temple. It was narrow, without guardrails and I gripped the stones to steady myself. Large birds circled over the jungle, crying out or maybe laughing at the white sweaty tourists. The sun burned hotter on my shoulders and sweat continued to race down my skin. A grassy landing opened up and my companions and I stood gazing up at intricate carvings on the wall face of the temple. Fierce figures with protruding tongues and intense eyes stared at the horizon. We continued up another set up steps that skirted just under the figures. I looked down at the ground below me and hugged the smoldering rock face closer. This staircase lead to an alcove. I exited the single file line of tourist and stood in the shade of the stones and enjoyed the coolness. Then it was back to climbing and after only a few steps I stood at the top of El Castile. The sun reflected off a slab of polished limestone that adorned the top. Before me the Belizean jungle shimmered in the haze of sun and sweat. At one time this sparsely settled area had been a major civic and ceremonial hub. Bright green grass divided the buildings that sprawled over the site.

Between the heat and my fear of heights, I was ready to find my way back to earth. I began the journey back down. I was glad to set my feet back on terra firma. I would have made a really bad Mayan. I just don't think I could climb up those steps to harrowing heights for ritual. Fortunately, for all of us, He is not looking for us to do such things. We only have to call out and Jesus is there. Always beside us no matter where we may be. Our prayers do not have to be shouted in the sky from the top of a temple or blood spilled to get His attention. In fact, the Holy Spirit that dwells within each believer is in constant prayer for us.

Even when you don't know what to say. You are at the end of your rope, face down in tears of despair, the Holy Spirit is communicating for us. Romans calls it "wordless groans" on our behalf. Our Lord is always with you and He is always conscious of your needs, your heartbreaks and worries.

We do not have to climb to towering heights, all we have to do is whisper the name of Jesus.

Whispers of Millennia Past

Our van ride had been mostly uneventful. We sailed down a deserted freeway cut through thick scrub that grew close to the edge of the pavement. Beyond, hills, emerald green raised up out of the dry landscape.

Together with our fellow travelers, we listened to Alexandria as she educated us on the Mayan culture. She was a beautiful young woman. She had dark brown hair that bounced in a ponytail on the back of her head. Her eyes, almond shaped and as black as onyx were set in a very pleasant face. She proudly shared her knowledge.

Once at our rendezvous, Alexandria, who wore a bright yellow long sleeve shirt and carried a pole with a picture of a blue jay on it, shouted instructions

"Keep your eye on the birdy!" She barked. "And keep up!"

She rushed us through a line that stretched through a pavilion down a walkway, and through the market. I had to almost run to keep up. As we walked down the corridor to the site, hawkers rushed to meet us. They yelled out prices of their wares and table after table displayed all manner of carvings, textiles and colorful blankets. At first, I tried to be polite but as I fell further behind the little blue jay, I soon stopped my apologies and raced, dodging peddlers to catch up. The stream of tourist slowed into a bottleneck. Crowds following guides like new ducklings left the pathway and flooded the city of Chichen Izta.

I stood before the stunning Kukulkan Temple. The jewel of the Mayan. Fierce effigies of the Flying Serpent creature adorned every side of the stone pyramid. White fluffy clouds glided across the blue sky, casting momentary relief from the sun. The breeze selfishly refused to blow. The humidity clung to my skin and sweat began to bead across my nose. However, I did not care, it was this site that had inspired this adventure. I had wanted to see this temple for years. I had read about it and watched more documentaries than I should admit. This was the moment, the big climax of my Mayan Adventure.

The 75-foot temple rose up in the center of the city. It stood, a lone sentinel in the jungle gleaming. Silently it stared back at us. It is without a doubt an impressive monument. Each stone had been cut and fitted perfectly to create one of the most impressive step pyramids in the world. An actual calendar, with four sets of ninety-one steps plus the top step, made 365 days. Fifty-two sunken stones woven into the masonry on each level represented the weeks. Down one side of the pyramid, adjacent to the ball field were carvings depicting the sacrifices after the sacred ball games. Ballplayers became executioners as you followed the story to its bloody conclusion. At the top of the pyramid, five small serpent heads lined the edge. One was broken. Giant snake heads protruded from the bases of the four staircases. Their mouths agape in silent warning hisses.

I stood amazed.

Unfortunately, our adventure ended abruptly. I reluctantly left the park, saddened I had not been able to see it all. I followed the little blue bird back to the van. My mind still focused on the wonders I had just seen.

I settled into my seat and waited for the last of our group to load. I thought about what I had experienced. For all of Chichen Itza's grandeur, for all the stone temples, intricate carvings, acoustics, and architecture, the people that built it are gone. They were assimilated into the Spanish. Today small rural areas continue to speak the ancient language and observe the religion but little else. Monuments, stories of unwavering bravery, and amazing knowledge of astronomy, and stonework are all that remain. Anthropologist and archaeologists work to understand the culture and offer a hypothesis of how they rose and fell within the last millennia. That is it. Nothing more. Just whispers from millennia past.

There is no difference for you or me. Our houses, businesses, monuments, stories, and culture will someday be gone. Peter tells us that we are just like the grass. Here for a season, gone the next. All you and I have is now. Tomorrow is not promised, yesterday faded. Just this moment, this day.

What will I do with it while I have the opportunity? How will I choose to impact those around me? How will I choose to serve God? Will I serve the poor, lift up the brokenhearted, encourage the weak and feed the hungry?

All you have is this moment. What will you do with it?

Oh, That Cat

I was cleaning up around the apartment the other morning. As I loaded the dishwasher, our cat Cleo hid under the door and when I was distracted. She shot out and attacked my ankles. I screamed and almost dropped a plate. Upon my shrill reaction, she dashed out of the kitchen and crouched behind the garbage can. I continued my task with one eye on her and she kept one eye on me.

After the kitchen was straightened I retrieved the broom and dustpan. I began sweeping up. I had a neat little pile of all the crumbs and little bits that find their way to the floor. I turned to reach for the dustpan and when I turned back, Cleo had dove into the neat stack and was batting the debris around.

"Oh, that cat!" I bellowed. Ears folded and eyes like pools of black ink, she dashed between my legs and out of sight.

I swept again, this time I had the pan close at hand.

On to the living room I got my duster and ran it across the TV. In a flash the feline sprang and in midair caught the duster. Startled I let go of the handle. Her feet hit the floor silently and she was off, ears pinned back, tail straight up she ran with the duster clamped between her teeth.

"Oh, that cat!" I yelled again and followed her down the hallway.

Cleo relentlessly stalked me through the rest of my chores. She attacked the broom and refused to release it. I stood with her dangling off the bristles. She stared at me with her eyes glinting, bottomless pools of predator instinct. She growled to let me know she was not going to give up the prize. I gave the broom a couple of good shakes but she still did not relent. I gave up and moved on to other things. I was keenly aware of her presence as she waited for her next opportunity to pounce. We watched each other intently.

Sometimes I feel stalked in my day to day life. I am just trying to get through the day and problems and issues crop up to distract me, frustrate me and plague me. I think most can relate. I might go as far as to say that issues and difficulties seem to worsen as you try to do good things. I think Peter and the folks he was writing to understood. They were trying to live holy lives and share the gospel and they were enduring Roman persecution. Peter's letter reminded this flock what was to be done. Be alert, be sober, resist evil and stand firm in your faith. He also reminded us that all believers are suffering throughout the world. They too have car trouble, marriage trouble, bad diagnoses, job loss, bankruptcies, betrayals and heartbreak. However, we persevere, keeping our eyes on the cross and holding firm to faith and hope.

But in your hearts revere Christ as Lord. Always be prepared to give an answer to everyone who asks you to give the reason for the hope that you have. 1 Peter 3:15

Come What May,
Enjoy the Sunsets

The chores were done, the house was quiet and I had a book I really wanted to get started reading. I went out on the balcony with my iced tea and began to submerge myself in the story. After a while my attention was coaxed away by the blood orange hue of the setting sun over the mountain. I watched as slowly the color faded and deep blue filled in the craggy rock face. The encroaching darkness revealed tiny dots of white winking at me. I smiled. The chirping birds were quietening down for sleep, the evening air was cool, my dogs were stretched out on the deck and the cat curled in the chair opposite. I was in that moment content and at peace. I relished the moment.

Unfortunately, it was for only a few brief moments. Barging into my peaceful thoughts the nagging reminder that not all was well in my life. There is an issue that brings me pain and hurt. A disappointment that wakes me in the night. I looked out over the treetops, my smile melting. My thoughts consumed with this pain.

Isn't it interesting how we can allow one thing to ruin everything good in our lives? Joy drains and we allow ourselves to sink into despair. All our energy and focus is detoured and all we can see, think about is that one thing.

I thought about this during my morning drive. When we allow these circumstances to drain our joy and take our focus from the cross we are doing a great deal of harm to ourselves. Life will never be just perfect. There will always be something that burdens your heart. I questioned, why does it have to be that way? I imagine that if everything were perfect, I would spend less time on my knees. If everything were perfect where would my faith have an opportunity to grow? If everything was just so, how would I have a testimony?

I have turned this situation over to God several times. I find myself taking it back and fretting over it. I have given it to the Father and so now I must leave it with Him. I cannot allow it to steal my joy, but daily anticipate through faith that He is handling it. I will continue to pray and believe that He has it in hand, but in the meantime, I will enjoy the sunsets.

Choose Wisely

I recently finished a 21 day food challenge. This challenge consisted of a list of approximately 100 approved for weight loss foods. Of these foods the object was to choose 21 and only 21. This would be your bank of food for 21 days. If you deviated you had to go back to day one. All the foods listed were good for weight loss and provided nutrients and low caloric values.

I finished the course in the 21 days. Last night I was reflecting and thinking about my choices. I thought about the criteria I used to choose my 21 foods and how they fit together. I had looked at many different principles. Nutrients, caloric value, availability, cost and naturally, flavor. I spent quite a bit of time working that list over. I realized that I had spent much more time on that list of foods than I did on other decisions in my life.

Our lives are one choice after another. From the mundane, such as what to wear, to marriage, careers and most importantly, who we serve. There are many choices we face daily, and as 1 Corinthians 6:12 tells us, all things are permissible, but not all beneficial. We have a free will, and we may choose any path we want. Unfortunately, I believe many of us choose unwisely and without proper thought.

Daily you are given a vast array of choices. None of these should be taken lightly. Take time to evaluate and weigh your choices. Many times, we may not get a second chance.

Choose wisely.

You've got to Love First

*"A new command I give you: Love one another.
As I have loved you, so you must love one another.
35 By this everyone will know that you are
my disciples, if you love one another."*
John 13:34-35 (NIV)

Ah, summer! The smell of Hawaiian Tropic lotion, sweet juicy watermelon, lightning bugs with little yellow lights dotting the evening sky, long tall glasses of lemonade and cannon balls. Yes, you read it correctly, cannon balls. Cannon balls in the deep end that sets the whole pool to rocking. That sends little kids off their floats and mommas fussing because they got splashed! Repeating cannon ball dives that keep the pool water choppy and the deck perpetually wet. That's how to do cannon balls.

This past fourth that is what I was doing. I got to the pool first and I broke that still mirrored blue with a perfect cannonball. I sank deep into that cool blue oasis, a flurry of bubbles around me. I did a couple more. Soon my youngest joined in and together we got the water swaying. My oldest daughter showed up and that pool was rocking. We had the swimming pool to ourselves for about an hour and it was a great afternoon full of laughter, fun and cannon balls.

As one, we can make an impact, but when we join together, we can make a bigger impact. I am often frustrated by how many Christians are unwilling to join together to spread the love of Christ. How many are unwilling to follow the "new commandment". It seems that we let the differences get in the way. Where it is true that different denominations, regions and culture have different doctrines and views, still our common goal is the saving of souls and the love of Christ. The rest is just manmade opinion. There is only one truth. God is love and loved us so much so that He sent Jesus to atone for the sins of an entire world.(John 3:16) Not just some of the people or just certain dominations or ethnic groups or regions but all people.

In John 13:34-35, you may notice that it seems a bit redundant. Three times, Jesus says "Love one another". In my studies, I have come to realize that when points are repeated, it means you need to get it. As well, when Jesus said to love one another, he didn't just mean those in that room. He meant everyone.

We are to love one another. That is the new commandment. We are to share the love of Jesus. Not condemnation. Not judgement. Not prejudice. Just love one another unified.

Want to make a big impact for Jesus? Then love one another. No matter who they are or where they came. The best way to demonstrate Christ love, is to love first.

New Wineskin, New Wine

> *And no one pours new wine into old wineskins. If he does, the new wine will burst the skins, the wine will run out and the wineskins will be ruined. No, new wine must be poured into new wineskins"*
> *(Luke 5:37-38).*

I made some decisions this week about some things that I want to accomplish in the next few years. These are not new goals. Instead, they are old goals that I have yet to realize. For years, these items have been on my list, but I have allowed circumstances and situations to derail me. Just as I made up my mind to follow through on the first of this list, a situation popped up. I began to allow myself to get distracted, and in just a few minutes I had begun to talk myself out of following through. In just a short time, I had already retracted my plans and was convinced that this new situation would not allow me to finish this goal. I sat alone, disappointed.

As I was talking with the Lord, later on, I realized that I was just following my Modus operandi. For my entire life, my MO had been to allow circumstance and situation to hinder my progress. It is now or never to make a commitment to following through. I realized I was trying to put new wine in old wineskins. So, I read up on that particular parable, looking for wisdom.

The parable of the new wine in old wine skin is recorded in three of the gospels. Matthew 9:14-17, Mark 2:18-22 and Luke 5:33-39. Because it is mentioned three times by three separate writers, I think there is definitely a lesson just waiting to be learned.

The parable was spoken by Jesus to rebuke the accusations of the Pharisees, that he and his disciples were not as pious as the Pharisees. Jesus was anything but conventional. He ate with tax collectors and sinners. Spoke to women and lepers and according to these Pharisees, he was not fasting enough. Unfortunately, these men that had devoted their lives to being scholars and experts on scripture and God, just could not get past what they thought was Jesus' flagrant disregard for the laws. The legalistic approach was all they knew. If the Pharisees were going to be able to embrace Jesus as Savior, they would have to let go of the legalistic way they viewed their relationship with God. They were so inundated by rules and laws they had lost the relationship. Jesus was offering freedom from the legalism and a relationship of grace and love. Unfortunately, they were unable to relinquish their old ways of thinking. Jesus never broke the laws, he just followed them as they were intended. Not with legalistic focus, but with love.

I cannot continue to use my old way of thinking to accomplish my plans. Obviously, my old mindset has not worked. If I am going to do something new, I need to renew my thinking. I do not want to miss out on realizing these goals because I am unable to change my MO. I got my new "wineskin" and I followed through on the first step to completing my goal.

Do not allow yourself to miss out on God's gift of love and redemption because of old ways of thinking. Do not be denied realizing a desire or a dream. If they are not working out or coming to fruition, then examine your MO.

Get a new wineskin and get ready to make new wine.

Izods, Levi's and Wimzees

Jesus Christ the same yesterday, and today, and forever.
Hebrews 13:8

As I was walking across the parking lot into the office this morning, I realized that I was wearing an outfit that was quite popular in my junior high days. Middle school for you younger readers. One Christmas, my mom and dad got me the peak of 7th grade fashion. A beautiful green Izod, yes with emblem. A pair of Levi jeans with white tag and kelly green wimzees shoes. Or "wimpies." as my brother called them. I even had the ribbons for my belt. I thought I was the bee's knees and let's face it, I was.

As I made my way to my cubical, I continued to enjoy the fond memories of that year and I pondered on how things change, repeat and recycle. What's in this summer will be forgotten the next. Izod, Levi and Wimzees are just one of the many brand names floating out there. They no longer are coveted items nor do they command the attention or income they once did.

Even churches go through trends and branding. I see churches taking denominations off their signs and replacing them with more trending names. No longer are hymns sung, but new praise songs, and new VBS programs are marketed each summer.

Buzz words and terminology in media, business and our teenagers are coined. A constant wave of new fads and fashion seems to rule day to day life. I heard higher waisted jeans are back. Even this year's new diet will lose footing to a new easier, faster version.

Thankfully, God is the same yesterday, today and tomorrow. His love never changes. His justice constant. His grace never-ending. His patience longsuffering. His mercy rains down.

You may not be able to keep up with the buzz words the ever changing politically correct titles, skirt lengths, "in" colors and 7th grade fashion, but know that Jesus is the same every day. He is your anchor in this turbulent fickle world.

Head over Heels

I relished the early morning chill as sweat beaded on my skin. Thin rays of pale sunlight like fingers slowly reached through the dense foliage making yellow and green between the trees. It was as if I was looking through a kaleidoscope. My calves ached from scrambling over the rocks jutting out the trail. Ahead the white marker ensured us we were on the right path. I followed the group, breathing heavy, trying to regain my breath. With the worst behind us, I relaxed, found my pace and followed. The path was covered with smooth varying shapes of rocks that rolled under my feet. I continued up the incline.

The trail made a dogleg and ahead a tree clung to the edge of the mountain. Knobby roots reached back into the hillside. The roots made natural steps and steadying myself by leaning on the tree, I hopped over the roots. I fully expected to land on solid ground. I fully expected to continue my pace, but that is not what happened. Instead, my right foot landed, folded outward and pitched my body out over the trail's edge. As I fell I waited for the landing and it seemed to take forever until my shoulders hit the rocky ground. My legs rolled up and over me. I remember that moment of realization when I recognized the bright orange shoestrings rolling overhead as mine. Gravity and momentum drew me head over heels down the bank. Dirt, branches, rocks, and debris joined me. I grabbed frantically for anything but my body continued to roll. Finally, and I do not know how I got my feet in front of me. Ahead of me, a large tree lay. I extended my legs. Finally, the ride was over and I lay in the cool, damp dirt staring up at the kaleidoscope. Beyond my fellow hikers yelled asking if I was ok. I sat up gave the thumbs up and yelled back I was fine.

The ride down had been fast, but the journey upward would not be the same. I reached as far back as I could, drew my legs up and dug my heels into the soft dirt. Lifting my rear, I began my slow return to the trail and toward my fellow hikers.

It is unfortunate how quickly we backslide in our Christian life. One poor choice, one careless word or one night of indulgence can send us spinning head over heels. Anyone of us may fall into temptation and sin. These failures can wound our souls cause the weak believer to stumble and strengthen the plans of the enemy. Therefore, all of us should take heed lest we fall. Often we believe that because we are going to church, reading our Bibles and paying our tithes we are above the temptation. It is this attitude that leaves us vulnerable.

Despite our shortcomings and backsliding, Jesus' promise is secure and He makes good on these promises by welcoming us in His arms of grace. Though you may backslide, it is never beyond God's grace and love.

Walking Through Manna

Have you ever prayed and over time began to wonder if you will be answered? Maybe you have been praying for days or even weeks. Maybe you have been praying for years.

I wonder how many answers to prayers I have missed because I was anticipating an answer that conformed to my notion of how it should be answered.

When Moses and the Israelites were in the wilderness, the people had many complaints. One complaint was that God had removed them from Egypt and their fires, where they had pots of meat and bread to sate them. After 400 hundred years of praying and anticipating freedom from captivity and slavery, they were upset with how they had been released. Somehow the grumbling of their bellies canceled out that the prayer had been answered. They were free.

However, all they did was complain and whine because of the hardships they faced.

As I was studying this week, I found myself reading the Exodus story. The Israelites named this substance, described to resemble coriander seed, manna. Manna means, "what is it?" I can imagine the Israelites strolling through the manna. They are looking up in the trees all around the camp for the promised bread. All the while they are walking all through the answer to their request. Manna was not the loaves of bread they had expected. Instead, the tiny seed like substance had to be gathered, ground and made into a porridge or cakes. God provided the element they needed to prepare bread.

Often, the answer to prayer is not the baked, sliced and packaged product we think it should be. Sometimes, it is the pieces you need to achieve the request. If God did everything for us, what would we learn? Without a doubt, God could have left loaves of bread outside every tent, but in the end what would it have accomplished? Just like children with parents that indulge and spoil, the Israelites would not have respected, obeyed and loved God. We are the same. Sometimes the answer is not packaged, it is the needed ingredients.

Are you missing the answers to prayers because you are trying to identify them in the way you think it should be answered? Are you walking all over your manna?

In Isaiah 55:8, we are told,

> *"For my thoughts are not your thoughts, neither are your ways my ways," declares the Lord.*

We cannot anticipate what form the answer will be by relying on our own thoughts, but we must pray for discernment and grace to recognize the answer when it is given.

I'm a Crack Pot for God

For God, who said, "Let light shine out of darkness," made his light shine in our hearts to give us the light of the knowledge of God's glory displayed in the face of Christ. 7 But we have this treasure in jars of clay to show that this all-surpassing power is from God and not from us.
2 Corinthians 4:6-7 (NIV)

My daughter called me at work the other day to reluctantly inform me that her cat had knocked off my ceramic cross. The cross had broken in half, and little pieces had showered the kitchen floor. When I got home, the cross was on the counter. It was listing forward and had several pieces missing. My daughter had attempted to fix it with some glue. Unfortunately, the cross was beyond repair. I was sad thinking about throwing away this decoration. It has been so long since I obtained it, I really cannot remember where it came from or from whom. For the time being, I decided to leave it where it was. A few days later, as I was cleaning the kitchen, I heaved a sigh and reached for the cross to dispose of it. However, before I did, I noticed how the fading sun that was streaming in the windows was coming through the cross. Orange sunburst passed through the cracks and holes. The cross glowed.

Often, I think I cannot be utilized by God because I do not have it together. I have issues and problems galore. However, God prefers flawed, worn out, and broken people. When you are flawed and broken, you must fully rely on Him. It is His power and not on your own that brings glory to Him and allows those around you to see the light within.

This broken piece of ceramic also reminded me that Jesus, who was broken on the cross, was the ultimate example of how God uses brokenness to heal and redeem.

You do not need to be perfect for God's use. He is more than satisfied to take you exactly where you are. In debt, not a problem. He can use that to teach obedience and discipline. Carrying around scars of past relationships? He can use that too. Now matter what has wounded you, He can heal you and use you to help and bring healing to others.

We are all "cracked pots" and we all have purpose and use.

Representing the Crown

Now if we are children, then we are heirs—heirs of
God and co-heirs with Christ, if indeed we share in his
sufferings in order that we may also share in his glory.
Romans 8:17

I woke up feeling terrible this morning. Headache, tired, grumpy and I was not into going to work at all. I laid in the dark willing myself to get up and get ready. Finally, I reluctantly slid out of bed and into the shower.

Words can be powerful and I decided to use mine this morning to boost myself up. So I began declaring that I was feeling better and praising the Lord. I hummed hymns as I packed my lunch. I prayed aloud as I dressed. As planned, my spirit lifted and my physical issues began to alleviate.

As I drove in to work, I continued my affirmations.

"I am the daughter of the Most High God, the Almighty, the great I AM. I am a Princess!" I declared aloud. "Yes, I am a Princess!" I announced with enthusiastic pride.

Do you know what that means to be a Princess? Whispered in my thoughts. I fell silent as I pondered this.

Do you know that the life of a true princess is not one of excess, tiaras and bonbons? A true princess is loyal to the crown and an ambassador for the king. A true princess does not belong to herself. Her life is a life of duty and responsibility.

The Queen of England receives more than 70,000 invitations a year from around the world. Of course, it is impossible for her to attend them all. Because the Queen cannot fulfill these requests alone, she depends on her court. Princes, princesses, dukes and duchesses attend these functions on her behalf.

They represent the crown.

Many times, just like I did this morning, we claim the kingdom and our inheritance, but what about our responsibilities, our duty to God and the lost? It is easy to go around calling yourself a princess, an heir, and a child of the king, but what about the obligations of your position? While we have a great inheritance, and are indeed co-heirs with Christ, we also have a duty to share the gospel. Romans 8:17 reminds us that in order to share in the glory, we need to share in the suffering. We are to be working, sharing, loving and reaching out to the lost on His behalf.

How do you represent the Crown?

Jam Session

I have another item to mark off my list of things I want to learn and experience. You may laugh when you read it, but I was very excited about it. I learned how to make jam, jelly and syrup and then how to properly can. I also made vegan breads with everything raw and natural. Before you are bowled over with too much awe, I did not do it alone. No, there were five of us, one generous teacher and four eager pupils.

My sweet neighbor and I drove to meet my friend, our tutor for the day and a couple drove up from outside Atlanta. We went through the usual pleasantries you do when you meet new people and then our instructor divided us and we set upon our task.

As I read the recipe, gathered the ingredients, two other ladies measured and mixed. Beyond in the kitchen the Jam was heating up. Blueberries, strawberries and grapes simmered.

We laughed. We spilled flour all over the table and grappled with fractions as we tripled the recipe. We talked about our children. Shared favorite recipes and reminisced about moms and grandmothers in the kitchen. We shared ourselves with one another as we toiled.

The smells in the house were divine, the early sun, pale yellow, streamed through the kitchen window and our chatter seasoned with laughter peeled throughout the house. It was a good time. We sweated as we stood outside on the porch next to the water bath and with great attention filled the piping hot jars with the rich, sweet gloopy jam. It was hard work, but the reward outweighed it.

I got more from my day than just a cabinet full of delicious breads and glorious jams, jelly and wild violet syrup. Yes, you read it right, sweet, aromatic *wild violet syrup*. I got a glimpse of community and cooperation. As I stood at the laptop reading the recipe aloud, I looked out at those working together beaming with smiles and enthusiasm. Just an hour before, we did not know one another. Yet now we were elbow to elbow in mashed bananas. We were a diverse group. Representing two states, different ethnic backgrounds, different denominations, and differing tax brackets. All the usual things that historically have divided people. However, this Saturday in early June, all those things were the absolute outermost in our minds. We were taking the bounty the Lord had given and together we were making something sweet and delicious to enjoy and share with our families and friends.

So often we divide ourselves from one another because we are focused on all the wrong things. Money, power, skin color, dominations, and regions are just the seasonings we bring to the mixing bowl. We should be focused on the task ahead of us. Time draws near for us all. Let's concentrate on working together to share God's Grace to **all** those we encounter.

Bon appetite!

No Peanut Butter Before Its Time

I love peanut butter. Not as much as chocolate, it is true, but peanut butter is some really good stuff. Creamy, nutty, melt in your mouth yumminess. The other day I pulled my jar from my desk drawer and unscrewed the cap. I was ready for the sweet and salty afternoon snack. Peering into the plastic container, my heart dropped. Clumped in the corner, huddled a tablespoon size of my nutty passion. I took my pretzel rod and slipped my hand into the confines trying to scoop a bit. Try as I might I just could not reach the last little bit. All I got was a perfect peanut butter ring around my fist.

Sigh.

Well, I thought, I might need something a bit more styled for peanut butter retrieval. Back into my drawer I pushed around the mustard, ketchup and salt packs to discover my plastic cutlery. Ah, a spoon, just what I needed. I crammed my hand back into the jar, intent on liberating the last holdout.

Forefinger and thumb tightly pinched the plastic utensil. I would have my peanut butter!

Snap.

The plastic broke. The spoon head lay in the bottom of the jar. Its tip buried in the butter viciously teasing me. I heaved an unhappy groan and replaced the cap. No peanut butter for me today. I would have to wait to get a new jar.

Have you ever wanted something so bad you could just taste it? It is right there on the tip of your spoon, but no joy. No peanut butter for you.

I do not know about you, but I do not like to wait. Maybe you are like me and you are having a hard time waiting on something you have earnestly and faithfully brought before the Lord. Do you sometimes feel that maybe God has not heard you? Nothing in my life is rarely as hard as waiting on the Lord to answer. However, what I find tougher is not trying to make it happen myself. Sometimes I just want to run ahead of God and take it on myself. Just march right in spoon in hand and take it, manipulate it, coerce it or prod it.

Many times, I have done just that. Oh yeah, I have pulled up my sleeves, tucked in my shirt straightened by back and marched right in. Unfortunately, every time, my actions led to pain, disappointment, tears, frustration and sin.

God hears you and me. He hears and he cares for us all. He also knows what is best and when is the best time. If we take it upon ourselves we cheat ourselves of the blessings the Lord has for us. His timing is perfect.

Often, I tell my daughter who has recently gone weary waiting on something she desires. "Honey, you can only see today. Now. But the Lord sees way, way down the road and He knows when is the right time. If you really want this, and it is really important, then wait on the Lord."

God indeed hears your prayers and he has YOUR best interest at heart. Trust Him, He will not fail you.

> *Therefore, I will look unto the Lord; I will wait for the God of my salvation: my God will hear me. Micah 7:7*

What Do You Seek?

*And ye shall seek me, and find me, when ye
shall search for me with all your heart.*
Jeremiah 29:13

I had just poured a hot cup of coffee and then diluted it with sweet creamer. Sipping it, I peeked out the window to see the squirrels and birds gathering their Saturday morning breakfast. Through the blinds a slow moving car stole my attention. It paused outside my house and then crept on down the street. All morning long, I found myself peering out to see cars slowing, stopping and then moving on down the road. I went outside to peruse my yard and look over my house. What could be drawing these people's attention? While I was standing in the yard, another car slowed, the window came down and someone's hand poked out clutching a phone. I turned to walk toward the car when it pulled off. What in the world was going on in my yard? As the morning progressed more and more people crowded the sidewalks. People I did not recognize from the area. Now people and cars seemed to be pausing at intervals up and down our street and at my home.

As the day progressed, I found out what was the interest in our little corner of East Ridge. Pokémon. Yes, our little street appeared to be teeming with the animated creatures just hanging about waiting to be captured and stored in cell phones. Essentially, this game places the pocket sized monster characters in the real world, as long as you have the app and stare at your screen through the camera lens. This Saturday people crawled the streets, playgrounds and businesses in the pursuit of Pokémon.

You will be interested to know that 9.55 million people are playing Pokémon Go daily in the United States **alone**. (source: The Wrap) That is 5% of the population. I am not talking about kids either, this number is for Americans over the age of 18 years of age. Would you like some more statics? While 5% of our countrymen are combing their neighborhoods for animated creatures daily, less than 19% of Americans are attending church once a week. (source: Churchleaders. com) It appears as a whole we have our priorities askew.

> *Seek you the Lord while he may be found, call you upon him while he is near. Isaiah 55:6*

Throughout the Word we are called to seek the Lord. This invitation is to all people, but it comes with a warning. *"Seek you the Lord while he may be found"* The promised blessing is not unconditional. *"Call upon him while he is near."*

In the parable of the ten virgins (Matthew 25). Some of the virgins were not prepared, the Bible calls them the foolish ones, they did not have the oil for their lamps. While they were gone looking to purchase oil, the bridegroom came and those (the Bible denotes as the wise ones) that were prepared went with him to the wedding banquet, while the others were left behind. Later the foolish virgins arrived and *said "Lord, Lord, open the door for us!" But he replied, "Truly I tell you, I do not know you..."* (Matthew 25:11-12)

We do not know when our time here on earth will end, whether we are called home or he comes on the clouds to take us. However, we should be prepared. Shouldn't we be seeking His face rather than chasing the latest fad, style or Pokémon? What do you seek?

Seek Ye the Lord

I stood hunkered over, focused on the red headed kid with the ball. I switched my eyes from him to the tall kid with a crew cut. I felt the adrenaline surge from my feet to the top of my head. I rocked in anticipation, ready to dart left or right to dodge the red ball. The boys passed the ball between their hands and jumped at me, faking an assault. Just as the red headed kid moved forward to spike me, I was knocked in the head by another ball. It came from the left, from a place that I had not anticipated. As soon as the rogue ball hit the mark a deluge of rubber inflated bombs hit me. I fell and sprawled out on the gym floor. Unprovoked, I was nailed one last time in the gut. It took my breath. I rolled to my side, holding my midsection.

Life is often like that. You are prepared for some things. You are watchful, and you know what to expect. But then out of nowhere, you get hit by something unexpected. It takes you down, and once it does, you seem laid open for repeated assaults from all sides. I have felt like that for the past month. I just keep getting hit and cannot seem to get back up. One issue after another. Financial, health, relationships, and the list goes on. For every step forward, I slide three back.

I know that many of you understand that feeling. Most, if not all of us, have had seasons in our lives when everything hits at once. There is so much we do not know where to turn and often are continually disappointed because nothing and no one can seem to help.

It is these times, I should focus my eyes on Jesus. I should place all of my trust in Him. He will deliver me.

I know that in my head. I know that in my faith, but it is my flesh that just wants relief. It is my flesh that wants my back to stop hurting. My flesh wants the aggravation of insurance companies and doctor bills to end. It is my flesh that wants and needs physical comfort. My flesh needs the spoken words of affirmation and compassion.

I have realized that has been my whole problem the past few weeks. I have been looking for comfort in the flesh rather than in the spirit. Instead of seeking God solely, I have been seeking resolution in the flesh as well. Searching for someone to help fix the situation. Someone to comfort me and let me know it will be alright. I have been in constant frustration and anger because I have been looking for the answers in all the wrong places and from the wrong people.

Through all troubles, tribulations and trials, our focus should be on the only one that can and will give us strength to endure what this world throws at us. Often we forget that as the pain and disappointment mounts. However, we must turn our eyes to Him.

I know that this week, I will train my eyes on God. I will wait upon Him in anticipation of Him moving in my life and this situation, making a way for relief and peace. If you are in a difficult time in your walk, I encourage you to focus on the only One that can deliver us in hard times. If you are enduring frustration and anger, you may want to see if your trust and faith is in God or in another person.

People will let us down, but God will never fail us.

Patience is not for the Fainthearted

7 Be patient, then, brothers and sisters, until the Lord's coming. See how the farmer waits for the land to yield its valuable crop, patiently waiting for the autumn and spring rains. 8 You too, be patient and stand firm, because the Lord's coming is near.
James 5:7-8

Mom and dad had just left. My brother, sister and I had been charged to stay in the den until their return. I watched them pull out of the driveway, and peering out the window, I waited until the taillights disappeared down the road. I checked on my siblings and returned to the living room. I slid the brightly colored box from the back of the tree—I had placed it in just the right place for a moment such as this. I slipped the knife in smoothly and silently cut through the tape. Finally, the end was free and I turned it up to peer into the wrapping. A wide smile extended across my face. It was indeed what I had wanted and hoped for. I carefully folded the paper. I was cautious to make sure that it was exactly as before and I re-taped it with care. I did the same with every package with my name on it. I slid the boxes back into the pile and strolled to the den, still wearing my Cheshire grin.

A few weeks passed, and finally it was Christmas morning. My siblings scrambled to the living room tripping and pushing one another. Unfortunately, I did not share in the enthusiasm and excitement. I found my spot next to the tree and as my family passed out the gifts, I knew each one handed to me. I even knew some of the other gifts for brother and sister. I had revisited the tree to peek into every package. My impatience had influenced me to ignore the rules of waiting. I had, in effect, cheated myself of the joy of Christmas. My inability to exercise patience had robbed me of the magic of that morning.

Patience is not a virtue of mine as demonstrated in the above illustration. In fact, ask anyone in my inner circle and they will tell you without hesitation waiting is not something I do well. However, do any of us? Whether it is Christmas morning, or prayers answered, waiting for what we want, for a situation to be resolved or a conflict abated, waiting is simply hard to do. In the past few weeks, I have been going through a lesson in patience. I <u>have not</u> enjoyed it. However, as I mature in my walk with Jesus, I am learning to relax. To calm my unruly flesh and walk in spirit. Oh, my toddler flesh rises, but each time I learn to indulge it less and look to God for my strength.

Patience is important in your relationship with Jesus. Throughout the Word, we are instructed in patience, instructed to wait upon the Lord. Why is patience so important? When you take a step back and allow God to work in your life, allow Him to move your mountains, you get a front row seat to the beauty of His love for you and His majesty and sovereignty in everything. To see His hand move in ways you could have never anticipated. He softens hearts, He heals sickness, He makes a way when you think you have nowhere to go. He places His saints in your path to teach. He sends His love to you at just the right time. Your trials, your troubles, the heartaches and the suffering are not in vain.

They are segues for the Lord to show up and show out. For you. To show you that He is always there. Always in your corner and always in control when you feel like you're spinning out of control.

If you chose, as I did on that Christmas morning, to make things happen you miss out on the splendor of God at work. You cheat yourself of blessings. Opportunities to grow, and sadly, the occasion to strengthen your relationship with Jesus. You miss the privilege to experience a love that has no equal.

If you are struggling in a difficult situation, ***"Be strong and take heart, all you who hope in the LORD" "Psalms 31:24*** and ***"Trust in the Lord with all your heart, and do not lean on your own understanding" Proverbs 3:5 Yet the LORD longs to be gracious to you; therefore he will rise up to show you compassion. For the LORD is a God of justice. Blessed are all who wait for him! Isaiah 30:18***

Always Go with Plan G

Trust in the Lord with all your heart, And lean not on your own understanding; In all your ways acknowledge Him, And He shall direct your paths.
-Proverbs 3:5-6

I am getting ready for a trip this weekend. It is a big deal for me. I have always traveled with others in a group. Places like the Smokey's and the beach. However, this time my friend and I are stepping out and heading for Chicago for a few days. It is a big, busy city and I am a slow-going Tennessee girl. It will be a new experience for both she and I.

As with all trips there is planning, financing and details. With recent situations, the accident and having to buy a new car, some of these details have run a bit short in the wallet. I have been praying that the Lord will provide the funds. Every day, I pray and wait expectantly.

A friend of mine asked me if I had gotten my funds together for my trip. "No", I said, "I am waiting on the Lord. He will provide what I need."

She looked at me quizzically and then with hesitation said, "Do you have a plan B?" "Nope", I smiled, "don't need a plan B, going with Plan G."

I so understood her inquiry. Many times, I have prayed about a situation or need and then I formulated my Plan B. Sometimes C and D! We are always trying to keep a bit of control in all the situations in our lives, aren't we? Just in case, we need that Plan B.

The failure of Plan B is that we are not trusting in God fully. We are still holding on to our own understanding, and capabilities to save ourselves.

Learning to trust in God fully is in no way an easy task and I struggle with it daily. However, every time that I held on, stayed focused on Him, wonderful and miraculous things have happened. He has revealed Himself to me in ways I would have never imagined. Holding on and trusting that God is working through your situation brings with it more reward than just what you had requested. The experience brings stronger faith, a closer walk with Him and perseverance in a cold unforgiving world.

There is only one full proof plan, that's going with Plan G. Trusting in God Almighty. Hold on. Do not let go. ***Seek the Lord and his strength, seek his face continually. 1 Chronicles 16:11***

Are you Willing?

I have been speaking with a friend that has been such a wonderful inspiration to me concerning my writing. She has been encouraging me to complete a book that I have had an idea for quite a while. I start and then stop, distracted by daily life. I get started again, only to become derailed with another issue. Then I begin to doubt whether I can complete this book. Then I worry that I have do not have the talent or knowledge to write this book. The more I allow myself to dwell on the things that I could fail, I miss out on precious time I could be writing.

During one such conversation she reminded me that she believed I had been given the gift of writing and therefore I was expected to use this gift to glorify God. I thought about this statement and I prayed about it. As I prayed the story of Esther came to my mind.

If you keep quiet at a time like this, deliverance and relief for the Jews will arise from some other place, but you and your relatives will die. Who knows if perhaps you were made queen for just such a time as this?" Esther 4:14

Esther was created at a specific time in history to save the Jews. She was created to be beautiful, but it was much more than her beauty that besotted the King. She was endowed with characteristics and talents that impressed the king. However, with all she needed given to her, she still had doubts. She worried about not being able to fulfill her mission. As well she feared for her safety.

Often, we are guilty of the same thing. We are given specific talents and opportunities to share Jesus with others but we withdraw. Afraid we are not capable or that we cannot fulfill the task. There could be nothing further from the truth. You have been endowed with talents and abilities, you have no reason to doubt your skills. All you have to do is be willing.

We are all given talents that are specific for God's plan. However, just like Esther, you and I have a choice and a free will. If you chose not, another way will be found, however, you will not enjoy the blessings. Would you want that blessing to pass away? You have been created now in history for a specific purpose, a plan. Do not let it slip away from you. Do not fear, but place your trust and your belief where it belongs, in God. Every day, ask, "Lord, where am I going and what I am doing to bring you glory? Father, how can I use my talents and assets to further the kingdom?"

God is looking for the willing to fulfill His plan. Are you willing?

Get Up Off Your Samsonite

> *I must work the works of him that sent me, while it*
> *is day: the night cometh, when no man can work.*
> *John 9:4*

I drove past a bus stop yesterday. It was not for a city bus, but rather a travel bus. I noticed as I sat at a red light, that all these people were sitting on their suitcases. They just sat there, playing on their phones and staring off into their thoughts. As I took in the sight, it made me think of how some Christians are doing the same thing.

Many Christians today seem to be sitting on their luggage and waiting on the bus to Heaven. We hear so many claiming that *'Jesus is coming,'* and, *'Time is near.'* Yet a good deal of those same have packed it in and are sitting on their suitcases just waiting on Jesus to return. Now is not the time for Christians to be sitting on the Samsonite, it is time to get up and get to spreading the Word. Put your luggage up, you have work to do! Jesus is not here yet! There are people dying and going to Hell right now and they live in your neighborhoods. They work with you. They check out your groceries they change your oil and they are hurting. They need hope in this world. They need Jesus and the only way they will hear about Him is if you tell them.

Yes, this world is in trouble. Yes, there is corruption, murder and unspeakable things happening all around us. However, you as a Christian have a responsibility to this world. Jesus said,

> ***A new commandment I give unto you, That ye love one another; as I have loved you, that ye also love one another. By this shall all men know that ye are my disciples, if ye have love one to another. John 13:34-35***

Notice in these two verses that *"love one another"* is repeated three times. It was repeated so you would understand the importance. We cannot afford to just quit. Now more than ever, we need to be loving the unlovable. Feeding the hungry. Clothing the naked. Bringing warmth to the cold. Sharing Christ. The night has not come and there is plenty to be done.

It is still day so get up off that Samsonite!

Governing Authorities

> *Let everyone be subject to the governing authorities, for
> there is no authority except that which God has established.
> The authorities that exist have been established by God.*
> **Romans 13:1**

Years ago, I was placed in a job that had become vacant. The person
in that role had been fired and the company needed someone to fill
in quickly while a replacement was found. I was to be the interim as
they interviewed. I really enjoyed the job and I applied for the position. I thought it was a slam dunk. I knew that I would have the job.

As they started to comb through applicants, I waited for my turn.
Yet, I was never scheduled for an interview. Finally, I went to Human
Resources and inquired. I was told that the job required a four-year
degree and therefore I was not eligible for consideration. I was angry,
hurt, offended and confused. If I could do the job, and was, in fact,
doing the job, why could I not be considered? The application process continued and I continued to do the job, however, not joyfully.

One day, the HR director came into the office to introduce the candidate that had been chosen. He was a nice enough young man, fresh
out of college and thrilled to have the position. His eyes gleamed with
eager excitement. I began to clear off the desk when the HR director announced in front of the entire department, the new employee

and me, that I would be training him in the position. I was not only training this young man for the position I wanted, I was training my new supervisor.

I would love to tell you that I handled it with grace and dignity, but I am afraid I did not. Instead, I grumbled, fussed, cussed, whined and threw a tantrum, or maybe two. I, in no way, conducted myself in a Christian way. I was also not very nice to the new guy.

Sometimes God puts people in our lives in a seat of authority. And sometimes, that is hard to handle. However, we are to be submissive to these individuals, and treat them with respect.

In the book of Romans, we are reminded that the person that is in authority, was established in that position by God. It is a reminder that God is in control of every aspect, including who is your boss. As a Christian you are to recognize their authority and respect it.

It is at times a bitter pill, but know that there could be many reasons why this person has been placed in that role. Maybe so that you can learn something or maybe so you can be a positive and Christ-like example.

Do you respect the authorities in your life?

God Chip

Ye are the salt of the earth: but if the salt have lost his savour, wherewith shall it be salted? it is thenceforth good for nothing, but to be cast out, and to be trodden under foot of men.
Matthew 5:13

I have been experimenting with food dehydration. It is a wonderful way to preserve food and frankly yummy too. My latest experiment has been with zucchini and squash. I love potato chips. I mean a true torrid lifelong affair! Sour cream and onion, barbeque, jalapeño and ranch, oh and the truffle ones. Salty, savory crunchiness! So, I thought, *what if I took zucchini and squash and made healthy chips with all my favorite flavors?* And it was this thought that started the chip rolling. Sounds relatively easy. Slice veggie, place in dehydrator, set timer and carry on. Seems reasonable. Right? Not so much. There are a lot of things to consider. Thickness of slice, spices, time to dry and temperature.

There is a lot to consider in our walk with Jesus too. What are the right conditions to be a crispy, crunchy God chip? Do we take time to pray, study our Bible, and truly live a life of love and truth? Are we eager to satisfy the hunger of the world? Or are we cold, limp Christians?

Making the perfect chip takes all the best ingredients, seasonings and making an appetizing Christian does too. I talk to several non-believers and they almost all tell me the same thing about the Christians they have been exposed. Their stories are in no way appealing and frankly, some redden my face with shame.

The Word tells us how we are to be to those we encounter. ***Let your speech be always with grace, seasoned with salt, that ye may know how ye ought to answer every man. Colossians 4:6*** The word says *how ye ought to answer every man.* Not just who fits in the group or who is socially acceptable.

Many times, you may be the only representation of Jesus to the people in your life. Do you want to be flat and tasteless or do you want to be boldly flavored with the Holy Spirit?

Divided We Are Conquered

This past week, the 45th president of the United States was sworn into office. Riots, marches, looting, and division ensued. Men and women divided. Blacks, whites, Hispanics, all races divided. Republicans and democrats. The American people divided. Hatred spewed. Anger acted out. A country ripped apart.

It was this moment that made my heart ache. I also felt the chill of dread because I know that our enemy is having his way by creating derision and division. Divided we will surely fall.

I will admit I was dejected and my hope for our people wavering... until.

I visited a new church this week. A last-minute decision. What I saw and experienced gave me hope.

A woman, Caucasian, middle aged, stocky, blonde, and well-dressed, had come to the front. It was evident this woman was burdened. Her face was swollen from hot tears shed in despair. The pastor approached her, and prayed for her, his voice low and his words earnest as he entreated the Holy Spirit to come. The pastor hugged her and she walked past. Shaken from the experience, she made a few steps and faltered. A young, lovely African American woman in jeans and a polo quickly came to her and steadied her. The middle-aged woman collapsed on the altar. Her body shook with sobs.

At this point, the young woman could have easily returned to her seat. No ill would be thought of her. She had after all come to the woman's aid and prevented her fall. She had shown concern and care. However, this beautiful young woman knelt next to this lady. I did not sense familiarity between them. The young woman rubbed her back and shed her own tears as she prayed for the troubled woman. The older woman turned to embrace her comforter. Her embrace was accepted without hesitation.

I stood, watching, the song of praise fading with the sights and reality around me. My full attention was focused on this unlikely pair. Sitting on the carpet, oblivious to the congregation, to the music or anything of this world, the young African American woman cradled the other. She rocked her as a child, fully embracing her, stroking her hair and praying. She allowed the woman's hot tears to flow on her as she buried her face in the younger's neck. It was for me a beautiful and moving moment. A moment of renewed hope.

There was no white or black in this embrace. There was only two people, one sharing the burden of the other. Interceding for another in need.

No politics. No tax brackets. There was God's people doing what Jesus commissioned all of us that call Him Lord to fulfill. To love. To comfort. To share.

We may not agree on who is in power. We may not see eye to eye on some issues, but our priority is to love one another in an unloving world.

United we stand, unbreakable and strong.

These Boots Aren't Made for Zipping

I lay on my bed, both legs sticking up in the air. I had tried unsuccessfully to zip up my boots. The zipper was up the back of the leg. When I reached down to zip the boot, I fell forward. I had tried sitting, standing, propping my leg up on the counter, even getting my youngest out of bed to assist. Finally, I thought I might have figured out how to zip up my boots. Gravity might just be my friend this time.

Gripping the crochet hooks hanging from the zipper tabs of my new black riding boots, I pulled.

I would wear these boots today!

I pulled on the crochet hooks again. My stomach muscles screamed, and my lungs strained for air, but I gave the hooks one more tug. I am pleased to report that my boots were zipped! Success, but it took some doing.

Exhausted, running a bit late and sweaty browed, I grabbed my purse and headed to the car. On my way to the car, I felt a sharp pain. The zipper on the left was rubbing into the back of my ankle. I ignored it. By the time I got to work I was limping. The zipper was munching away on my ankle. Throughout the day I adjusted the boots and did everything I could to avoid the sharp pain of the zipper digging into my flesh. By the time the day was done, I could not wait to get out of those boots. As I sat staring at the raw and painful skin over my heel I thought that I really should have tried them on before I bought them.

Have you ever been so focused on what you wanted that you were willing to do most anything to see it happen? However, you never considered whether or not you should do it or if you were prepared for it?

Me too, and not just with really kickin' boots! Often times, we concentrate our focus on what we want and what we want is not always good for us. Careful consideration and prayer should be the first thing we do whenever we embark on a new endeavor. Allow the Lord to guide you. With His guidance, financial loss, relationship issues, hurt feelings, and maybe even mangled ankles can be avoided.

Enter into every new endeavor with prayer and careful consideration.

Rest in the Reign

I am not saying this because I am in need, for I have learned to be content whatever the circumstances.
Philippians 4:11

I was driving home from work, tired and frustrated. The traffic stopped just below the tunnel. Rain fell, quiet and cold slowing the traffic to a snail's pace. The sky was gray hanging over the city in a white gauze. I sat in my car inching my way up the hill. As I waited, I stared out the window at a little area with goats. A tight fist of adult goats were huddled in a lean-to to escape the rain. As they stood in the shelter they gazed down at the line of cars puffing exhaust. My attention was quickly stolen by three little goats. Tiny and unsteady they were running all over the enclosure chasing one another. These three little baby goats were undeterred by the rain, fog or the traffic. They ran around on wobbly legs fueled by interminable energy. Running up and down the ramps; they played with little care of anything around them. As I watched I soon found myself laughing. Those little goats; fearless and carefree melted my traffic irritation away.

As I watched these little knob kneed kids run about, I thought about how we should also be content even in difficult times. The rain may have made things messy and more treacherous to us, but it was only weather to the little ones.

Rain comes to us all, in all seasons of our lives. Like Paul writes in Philippians, we need to be content in our circumstances at the time. Without rain, crops and flowers do not flourish and without rain in our lives, faith and trust is not nurtured.

Circumstances and weather are always changing, learning to be content and trusting in Jesus to see us through is the only constant we can count on.

If you are in a rainy season in your life, trust in Jesus and *rest in His reign.*

The Great Commission
is to Us All

John had checked the locks and peeked in on the kids and now he was slipping under the covers to warm himself next to his wife. He quickly fell into a peaceful slumber. Sometime in the night he was awaken by the sound of breaking glass. Peering out his window, he saw that the neighbor across the street house was on fire. Flames leapt skyward, he stood watching. A chill, maybe from the cold reaching in through the window, engulfed him, he returned to his bed eager to warm himself.

The next morning as John left for work he saw his neighbors standing in front of a smoldering pile of wood that had once been the neighbor's house. He stepped up between Joe and Bill and inquired.

"Could the fire department not get to it?" "They never came." Joe whispered.

"No one called." Bill added.

"What do you mean *'no one called'*?" Marveled John, "Didn't you call Joe?" "No, I was watching a movie." Joe looked down at his hands.

"Bill?"

"I didn't want to be nosey. Get into their business. Anyway, I thought you would have called John." "Why me?"

"Your kids are on the same ball team, aren't they?"

"Yes, but it was cold. I was tired. I just thought someone else would do it."

We are often guilty of this kind of reasoning as Christians too. We think that the responsibility lies with just the pastor or maybe just missionaries. We do not want to jeopardize our comfort, or maybe we think that if we share Christ with another that we are being judgmental or interfering in their lives.

However, that is not what Christ commanded of his disciples and followers. As Matthew tells us, Jesus said ***make disciples of all the nations, baptizing them in the name of the Father and of the Son and of the Holy Spirit,*[0] *teaching them to observe all things that I have commanded you.***

As a Christian, a disciple and follower of Jesus, you are to share this miraculous and wonderful blessing with all those in your life. Do not assume that someone else has already reached out. Boldly share Jesus with all in your life. You may be the only person that does for that one soul.

For His Glory Only

> *Do nothing out of selfish ambition or vain*
> *conceit. Rather, in humility value others above*
> *yourselves, not looking to your own interests but*
> *each of you to the interests of the others.*
> *Philippians 2:3*

I waited in line at the grocery. I had a cartful. Behind me a young man stood, holding a dozen eggs and a loaf of bread.

The person in front of me finished loading their cart and left. I turned to the young man, "Would you like to go ahead. I have several things, I hate for you to have to wait on me." I ended my inquiry with a smile.

The young man eyed me suspiciously, his brown eyes moving from me to my cart. Leaving him to mull it over, I began to unload my cart on the belt.

After a few seconds, he addressed me. "Well, if you are sure...." "I am." I smiled.

Shyly, he pushed past me and scanned his two items. I continued with my task. He took his receipt and walked away.

As I scanned my items, I thought about that young man. His hesitancy to accept an act of kindness bothered me. However, it occurred to me that many people rarely witness kindness, especially kindness without recompense.

We live in a world that teaches a "me first" mentality. When we accepted Christ as our savior, we became responsible for sharing the word and emulating Christ in our daily lives.

As Paul told to us in Philippians, we are to think about others and place their needs above our own. We are to treat others as Christ did and like Christ does, without looking for reward. In fact, be prepared to receive nothing in return.

Do it not for yourself, but for the glory of the Lord and not your own.

Always Looking to Jesus

When I got home yesterday, there was a twenty foot furrow across my front yard. The sewer company had finally come to fix the line. I felt a wash of relief. However, this wash of relief quickly drained as I noticed the sound of rushing water. I crept to the end of the porch and looked down into the ditch.

Sticking out of the side of the trench wall was a hose and from the hose, gallons of water gushed in an arch.

I spent the next 3 hours waiting on the porch for either the sewer or water company to come and fix the issue. While I waited, gallons of water flooded the trench and soaked my already soggy yard. A growing puddle engulfed the lawn.

As I waited, I thought this must be a Mustard Seed and quickly scrolled through my phone to verses about fountains, floods and water. I found several. However, they just did not strike me as the focus of this event. The issue was fixed, and I went about my nightly duties still trying to figure out what a broken water line had to offer as a Seed.

By the next morning, I still had nothing but that nagging feeling there was something in this event. What I did realize is that, often times, we immediately focus on the situation rather than on God. I was so sure that the water break was the focus that I never looked elsewhere. However, we should be looking past the situation and directly to the cross.

Jesus himself, when faced by agonizing death on the cross, looked past the situation to God. He knew that soon he would be in his rightful place in heaven. He also knew that by this sacrifice and enduring the torture of the cross, you too would have a rightful place in heaven.

By focusing on Jesus rather than the situations and circumstances, you can face and overcome all things through Christ.

Life is Short, Wear Your Glitter

> *When Jesus spoke again to the people, he said, "I am the light of the world. Whoever follows me will never walk in darkness, but will have the light of life."*
> *John 8:12*

I was dressing for church and I couldn't decide which pair of shoes to wear. Still in the box was a new pair I had caught on sale. They were so pretty: black, with little beads that reflected the light. I put them back in the box. I did not want anything to scuff or mar them. As I looked between the shoes, my eyes came back to rest on those new shoes. I wanted to wear them, but then again I did not want anything to happen to them. Safely tucked in their box, they would remain shiny and new.

Later, as I got into the car with my friend, I said almost apologetically, "I decided to wear my new heels. Do you think they are too glittery for Sunday morning?"

She laughed as she replied, "No girl, life is short, wear your glitter!" Life *is* short.

I thought about that statement throughout the morning. What good could those shoes do in the closet, in a box, out of sight? I think that Christians have the same mentality when it comes to sharing the gift of salvation. They want to keep it hidden away, afraid to get it out and risk some scuffing up.

I get it. There was a time when I did not want to share salvation with others. I was afraid of the ridicule, the judgment, failure and looking foolish. But what good is my testimony if I just keep it to myself?

What good can I do if I fear getting out of the box and into the light? I cannot glitter for Christ in the dark.

We should take every day and shine for the Lord. Christ is the light of the world and you should be reflecting His Glory in your life. Glittering at home, in the workplace, with your friends or even when you are just at the store. We are presented with opportunities daily to show the love of Jesus to those around us. Do we choose to be the reflection of Christ? Or do we stay in the dark, afraid of getting scuffed up?

Life is short! Are you only wearing your glitter on Sundays, or every day? Shine on!

Living by Faith, not by Feelings

> *Therefore I do not run aimlessly; I do not fight like I am beating the air. No, I discipline my body and make it my slave, so that after I have preached to others, I myself will not be disqualified.*
> *Corinthians 9:27*

She walked ahead along the path leisurely taking in the beauty of the wooded trail. Calling back over her shoulder she asked, "You okay back there?"

I strained to hear her question. My heart pounded in my ears fiercely drowning out the drone of the bugs, the song of the bird's and her question.

"What?" I called out between labored breaths. "I said, are you ok?"

"No. This death march has caused me to have shin splints, my knees are hurting, my chest is tight, I am sweating, my head is throbbing, and I am tired," I shouted back, struggling to transverse the incline. She disappeared around the next turn. I wanted terribly to stop and sit but I knew that I had to continue. I had to ignore the aches and the pains. I had to not go by how I felt, but rather continue in what

I knew my body needed to burn excess calories and improve my health. Plus, I did not know the way out!

As I continued to struggle to catch up and match her pace, the verse from Corinthians swirled in my thoughts. ***I discipline my body and make it my slave...*** The more I study and read the letters of Paul, the more I realize that this great man, an apostle of Christ dealt with the same issues I do today. He also struggled in the flesh, and he understood the importance of control and discipline.

A few weeks ago, I wrote about how our minds drift and our very bodies resist when trying to pray. As I walked on, I thought about how much we struggle in the flesh in many different ways. When we say fleshly desires, we seem to automatically think of carnal sins, but our struggle in the flesh extends so much further. I give up to my flesh considerably more than I first thought. I let how I feel dictate how I react to situations, reacting to others, getting the house clean, getting on my knees, getting off the recliner and how I exercise. I am guilty of living by my feelings and not by faith.

As people of God, we are to be in control of our bodies and our thoughts. No wonder many non- believers say pass to living a life in Christ. Is my faith something that someone else would want? I speak of faith. I write of piety and loving one another but does my life, my choices, my reactions back it up? I am disappointed to say that in many areas of my life I fail miserably. I allow my feelings to rule.

This lifestyle quest that I have placed before myself has taught me much. Not just about food and portions, but about where I am lacking in my character. I am overweight and out of shape because I chose to be that way by giving in to my fleshly desires. I am learning that eating correctly, exercising regularly and keeping busy is as much for the soul as for the body. When I speak to someone about living for Christ, making sacrifices, placing others first; when they look at me do they believe that I am doing the same? To be honest, I would have to say probably not.

Living by feelings is the way the world lives. As a follower of Christ, I should be living by faith. Doing what is right in every aspect of my life. Not falling into the pitfalls of feelings. I may feel like having another plate, but is that what my body needs? I may feel that a person is attacking me so do I react in kind, or do I, in faith, address them in love and forgiveness.

...So that after I have preached to others, I myself will not be disqualified. I do not want to be disqualified because I chose to allow my feelings to get in the way of living in faith and sharing the gift of salvation to others. I want my faith to be something that others see I take seriously and want the same in theirs.

Old Dogs, New Tricks

> *Like a city whose walls are broken through*
> *is a person who lacks self-control.*
> *Proverbs 25:28 (NIV)*

There is a little bag of Fritos in the snack basket. Oh, that salty crunch, yum. However, Fritos are not on the approved food list for this week, or any other week for that matter. Every time I walk by, I hear, *"That one little itty-bitty bag won't hurt my overall diet."* However, I know that if I partake in that little snack that it will do more than slow my weight loss it will erode my will power. I know what will happen, I will eat it, revel in the momentary pleasure of it and then I'll start kicking myself, I'll be ashamed and discouraged. In my discouragement, I will end up devouring more foods that are not good for me. This lack of control will lead to destabilizing my insulin and I will feel sick, discouraged and hopeless. Instead, I chose to exercise discipline and focus **not on what I think** I am missing out on, but what is my gain.

> *No discipline seems pleasant at the time, but painful. Later*
> *on, however, it produces a harvest of righteousness and peace*
> *for those who have been trained by it. Hebrews 12:11*

Discipline and self-control are choices. I am a free agent. I have free will. As a young woman self- control and discipline were far from me. I was bent on pursuing every avenue of pleasures and willful disobedience to God and all authorities in my life. It did not take long for my life to spin out of control. My walls broken down, I was overrun.

Unfortunately, it took years for me to accept that the repercussions were due to my choices and my choices alone. Living a life that is responsible, self-controlled and disciplined is no easy task. It's hard and at times unpleasant.

Through this journey, the Lord has opened my eyes to how I got to where I am. My lack of discipline in consumption of food led me to being overweight and on the threshold of medical issues. It was my choices that lead me here, and it will be my choices that will lead me out.

Often, we cite circumstance, people, money, and luck for why we are where we are. But truthfully, you and I are where we are because of the choices made. I continue to learn about myself on this journey. The restraints I believed were placed on me were really placed there by me. Not people in my life. Not the circumstances. Not the amount of money I was earning. It was my choices. In any circumstance, you are free to make the choice. Even if that choice is just in your attitude.

Examine your life. Are there issues in it that need to be addressed?

It is never too late to make a change. Take it from an old dog, learning some new tricks.

Choose You this Day
Whom Ye Will Serve

> *But if serving the LORD seems undesirable to you, then*
> *choose for yourselves this day whom you will serve, whether*
> *the gods your ancestors served beyond the Euphrates, or*
> *the gods of the Amorites, in whose land you are living. But*
> *as for me and my household, we will serve the LORD."*
> *Joshua 24:15 (NIV)*

This week, my friends and I headed three hours west to Ethridge, Tennessee, to visit Amish Country. There are approximately 1500 Amish in the Ethridge area. Descendants of the Swartzentruber settlements, they are primarily farmers but also produce beautiful furniture, quilts and baskets. They live without electricity and running water, and they do not drive cars. Children are educated until the 8th grade and from the time they are 4 or 5 years old participate in daily chores, farming, and caring for younger children. All the people are simply dressed, women in long below the calf jumpers over long sleeve blouses of blue and plain bonnets. The men in denim pants, blue shirts, denim vest and brimmed straw hats.

We had the privilege of touring the settlement in a horse drawn carriage. As I swayed with the motion of the wagon, I was mesmerized by the scenery, as far as eye could see blue skies, and emerald crops stretched to the horizon. Every couple of miles we passed white farmhouses with laundry flapping in the constant warm breeze that wafted by heavy with pungent odors of sweaty horses and fresh blooms. I fell in love with the simple beauty. As we rode, bouncing across potholes, the driver relayed facts of Amish life. The Amish have many traditions that seem strange. However, there was one tradition that continued to revolve in my mind well after we had returned home.

When the Amish turn 16 years old, they are given freedom to leave the settlement on the weekends and experience life in the English world also known as the "Devil's Playground". This period is called the Rumspringa, (literally means "running around" in Pennsylvania Dutch the language of the Amish.) The Amish believe that choosing to follow Jesus should be a voluntary choice of an adult. After a period, the teenager chooses to pursue life in the English way, or stay. If the child chooses the English way, the family has a funeral for them and they are no longer spoken of. If the child returns, they become candidates, and if selected, enter an 18-week program. The candidate is given a final chance to change their mind. If they commit, they are baptized and become a member of the community. From that time forward, they agree to reject the Devil, the world and live in obedience to the Church's ordnung (order).

All of us go through much the same challenge in our lives. We may not be turned out at 16, but at some point in our journey, we must choose who we will serve. We all come to the fork in the road and the moment of decision waits. Will you decide to accept Christ, His teaching, and then live accordingly? Or will we choose to follow the gods and trappings that are offered in this world?

I urge you not to wait but ***Choose You this Day Whom Ye Will Serve.***

An Omer for Every Man

As I have shared before, this lifestyle journey that I have embarked on has really taught me more about my character and relationship with Jesus than anything else. During this program, I have learned some things more important than food combinations and calories; I have recognized behaviors that lead to this weight.

One thing I have come to realize is that I am fat because I take more than my fair share. It was a sobering moment when I heard those words. It was like another tumbler fell and I was closer to cracking the code. It is easy to take more than your share in this world we live. It is a world filled with decadence and temptations. Overindulgence and gluttony from everything to upsizing that value meal, all you can eat buffet and getting that fully loaded new car. We have so much and we want more. It's just part of human nature. In the book of Exodus, the Israelites were complaining of hunger and wishing they had just died in Egypt rather than being free. Isn't that just like a human, we rather be in captivity getting fat than enjoying freedom in the Lord.

> *And the children of Israel said unto them, Would to God*
> *we had died by the hand of the Lord in the land of Egypt,*
> *when we sat by the fleshpots (pots of meat), and when we did*
> *eat bread to the full; for ye have brought us forth into this*
> *wilderness, to kill this whole assembly with hunger. Verse 3*

Sounds like some folks got a bit spoiled and comfortable relying on the captors. So God sends them Quail for meat at night and manna in the morning for bread but there is a stipulation.

> *Gather of it every man according to his*
> *eating, an omer* for every man,*

Everyone was to gather according to their fair share. However, there were some folks that were afraid they might not get enough and did not trust that God would make good on His word, so they gathered more than an omer per person. You might remember what happened.

> *Notwithstanding they hearkened not unto Moses; but some*
> *of them left of it until the morning, and it bred worms,*
> *and stank: and Moses was wroth with them. Verse 20*

That's right, what they gathered beyond the measure commanded, rotted and filled with worms. When we live a life of gluttony, wanting more than our share, rot sets in. It destroys our bodies, minds and souls.

I have realized that for me this goes beyond filling my plate a second time, it is in my material possessions and my attitude. Beyond just measuring out my food, I have begun to take inventory of my material possession and how I choose to use the excess I may have. I have begun to clear out closets, cabinets and drawers. Instead of saving that $10 for a drive through stop, I realize I need to be handing it to those less fortunate and in need.

We live in a world of decadence yet; there are many that suffer hunger, cold and homelessness. I am making sure from this point on that I do not take more than the share allotted to me, because if I am taking more than my share that means I am taking someone else's.

Take a moment this week and ask God where you may be taking more than your share and how you can contribute to those in need.

An Omer for Every Man.

Trail Master

Pale yellow light filtered through the trees casting long, searching fingers into the thick foliage. I stood on a rock overhang, and I looked out over Chattanooga. A gray fog covered the valley like cotton candy in a bowl. A cool breeze ruffled my loose curls and then gusted through the trees that stretched skyward. I followed the playful gust with my ears as it passed from one tree to another, rustling the leaves, making them giggle. Wave after wave of giggling leaves circled me, lifting my hair and refreshing me. I listened as the birds chattered, sharing the neighborhood gossip. June bugs droned and water dripped from the rocks. I closed my eyes and listened to the orchestra on the mountain side.

Taking another chug of my water, I stepped back onto the trail and continued the steady climb. As I walked alone in the morning I took in the beauty and allowed my mind to rest. I continued for half a mile and then ahead the trail split. One continued along the same path that I had been on and the other turned sharply back left to climb the mountain side. It was a steep incline.

As I neared the divide, I wondered, which way should I go? As I neared the split, I saw a pile of white dust. It was flour. Flour that the Trailblazer trainer had dropped to let those that followed know which way they should go. I looked back to the left and three spaced piles of flour glowed on the worn trail. I turned sharply left continuing along the new trail.

Occasionally, I saw other hikers. Some had maps, others were following those in front of them and still, others moved confidently to their destination. Again, the trail became quiet and I continued following the path. As I walked I thought about our own lives the paths that each of us follows. The inclines, the rocky portions the thick mud and obstacles. I thought about how we all travel our paths. I pondered on my own wrong turns and those times in my life that I chose not to follow my Lord and where He would have me go. I also thought about the times I had taken the path He had illuminated for me. Many times, it had been hard, but Jesus never left me to walk that path alone.

I continued the trek and at every fork, there were glowing piles of flour leading me higher and to my goal. When I emerged from the foliage into the parking lot the trainer and other hikers cheered me. High fives all around!

I stood looking over the entire valley and at the rolling mountain tops. The fog had burned off and now the mid-morning sun showered down warm yellow rays. I had made the 5-mile journey. Though for most of it I walked alone, I was never truly alone. The trail master showed me the way. Following the flour markers, I had made it to the top.

Jesus tells us, "I am the way, the truth, and the life: no man comes unto the Father but by me." (John 14:6) Jesus has shown us the way and prepared the way for us. Just like the trail master left flour markers, Jesus lights our way. It is up to us to choose to follow Him or our own way.

Setback to Comeback

For though the righteous fall seven times, they rise again,
Proverbs 24:16

It was Friday morning, my scheduled weigh in day. I set the scales down on the floor, drew in a deep breath and stepped on the platform. I stared in disbelief and hopped off the scale as if it had suddenly become hot. I waited for the digital numbers to fade and gingerly stood once again on the scale. The same numbers appeared, flashed twice and then held steady. I was up 1.5 pounds.

A wash of disappointment coated me. I went to sit on the side of the bed and stared at my hands. Tears swelled until I blinked and then two hot tears slid slowly down my cheeks. I had tried so hard. I had refused dessert and breakfast out. I thought I had done everything right yet the scales offered a different account. I fought back additional tears and carried on getting ready for work.

Throughout life, we face failures. I dare say that most of us have suffered several bitter disappointments. Those moments when we know that we had given all we had to give and for whatever reason it just was not enough. It is often hard to swallow. Life is tough at times and those times tempt us to throw in the towel.

Can anything make the difference?

I like the story of the fishermen in Luke 5. Simon and the others had been out all night and morning fishing and they had caught nothing. They had quit for the day; the Bible says they were washing their nets to put up. Simon and the men were done, they were literally hanging it up.

In verse 4 Jesus told Simon to go out deep and drop their nets. Simon was fast to reply that they had worked all night and caught nothing. However, Simon said to Jesus, because you asked me to I will do it.

Simon went out, dropped his nets and the catch was so big the nets began to break and he had to call in assistance! So, what was the difference?

Jesus was in the boat.

Nothing can have more influence on your success than having Jesus in your boat. You will have failures, disappointments and setbacks, but get back up, invite Jesus to join you, and try again.

And continue to try until you have success!

As I approach the fifty pounds lost mark, I know that I have had this success because I first dedicated my weight loss to the Lord and when I am weak, I bring it before the throne.

Through Christ my *Setbacks are Come backs*!

The Glory that Awaits

Tired, sweaty and sore, I stood and looked down into the gorge. The sun shone on me and I closed my eyes lifting my face to meet the rays of warmth. I returned my gaze to the mountains stretching in the distance. It had been a long hike. My clothes clung to my sweaty skin; I mopped my face with my bandana and reflected on the trail behind me. There had been many steep inclines and loose rock making my journey difficult. I was tired, hungry and eager to sit down. While I rested, I nibbled on a protein bar.

I stood preparing to begin the trek back down the 4 mile trail. However, before I did, I took time to stand and let my eyes stretch as far as they could in the mid-morning sun. I took in the fresh air and absorbed the tranquility of the moment.

The course had been difficult. There were steep hills, deep gorges, rockslides, downed trees and gnats however, at that moment when I reached the trail's end and looked out over the beauty, the difficulties I had just come through seems to melt away. It is replaced with awe and satisfaction.

We all face obstacles, but we push forward, following our path to the end. One day, we shall leave this world and step into Heaven. The pain, heartache and pitfalls of life will melt away when we see His glorious face. No longer will we ache from the falls, our bodies will no longer rebel with muscle pain nor will be inflicted with illness. In Romans, Paul reminds us that our suffering here cannot compare to the glory that will be revealed to us in time.

I know that we are all facing heartache, illness, disillusionment, fear, pain, and uncertainty. Do not let these obstacles keep you from pushing on to the glory that waits.

Press On

*I press on toward the goal to win the prize for which
God has called me heavenward in Christ Jesus.*
Philippians 3:14

I double checked my pack, took my phone off the charger and made sure I had my headlamp. For months I had been training for this day, this very moment. I knelt at the foot of the hotel bed and began my prayer. A prayer of thanksgiving for this opportunity, strength of body and protection, not just for me, but everyone that would be out on the trail. I stood, grabbed my walking stick and headed out to roll call.

It was raining, cold and black as pitch as I began the first leg of the challenge. My lamp barely penetrated the darkness. Below the rush of water mingled with the sound of rain against my hat and rain jacket. Only a half mile into the hike, I felt warmth on my face and wiped it away. In the beam of light from my headlamp, I looked at my hand. Sticky red blood covered my palm. I had to go to the side of the trail and deal with a nosebleed. Hikers passed me, and I realized that I was losing precious time, and my place. Nose packed, I headed up the hill. I looked ahead and behind, but could no longer see the bobbing headlamps in the darkness. A pang of fear shot through my gut.

In the darkness, rain, and fog, I had trouble seeing the route markings and found myself at a rocky dead end, backtracking I glimpsed the little yellow flag and trekked. I could only see a few feet; the light bounced back off the fog. I found the next marker and started an incline. Water washed fiercely down the side of the mountain, rolling over the rocks in the pathway. I planted my stick and stepped on the closest rock. It shifted, and my foot slid into the water, and I went down, landing on a rock, my jacket ripping and the contents of my pocket washed away. Tear swelled. My glasses had been in that pocket. I hoisted myself up from the rocks and scrambled to get across. Using my flashlight I searched, but I could not find them. I continued up the path that leads to the staircase said to be 600 steps to the overlook. By this time the darkness seemed to press in on me. I felt it crush, my chest becoming heavy. Alone in the predawn hours, packed nostrils, soaked and missing my glasses, I climbed. Rain, now pelting me sideways, joined with the wind as if to push me back. I continued. I fixed my gaze on the spot of light that hovered on each step ahead of me, and I sang. Over the cacophony of rain and wind, I sang out, "This Little Light of Mine." All threes verse, over and over until I stepped on the final landing.

I had made it to checkpoint one. I was late, frustrated and a part of me screamed to tap out. I opened an electrolyte gel and filled my mouth with the sickly sweet taste of artificial tangerine. Washing it down with water from my camel, I set out for checkpoint two five miles ahead. Two miles in, according to my Garmin, my ViewRanger alarm went off. Somehow, I was off course. Using the map on my cell phone, I tried to find where I might have missed a turnoff. I held the phone in the light from my lamp. I walked back slowly, watching the little arrow spin, hoping that it would point me in the right direction.

Anxiety began to swell with the tears. I was alone, behind schedule, without my glasses and soaked to the bone. I questioned if I was to continue. Was I even supposed to be here? A flood of tears started again. I leaned against a tree and began interrogating God. Why was He allowing all this adversity? I had trained for months. I had pushed myself more than I have ever pressed myself physically. I had developed discipline and was committed to seeing this through. I had dedicated each hike to God; I had humbled on my knees to ask for Him to protect and bless this day. Why was this going all wrong?

Only the continual percussion of rain was my reply. I attempted to dry my tears on my wet sleeve and walked until I found the correct turn obscured in the darkness and fallen leaves. I followed the path, only a couple of feet ahead of me illuminated. I made it to checkpoint two, still behind time. I ate a sandwich, warmed myself in a waiting van for a few minutes and headed to checkpoint three. I knew that if I did not increase my speed, I could face disqualification. On leg three, I ran. I have never run that far before. My walking stick tucked under my arm, I ran and as I did a realization came to me. The understanding I immediately knew I had to share.

You may plan, study, train and do everything right. You may be doing something noble and grand. You've prayed and given Glory to God, and it still may be wrought with issues. It rains. Wind attempts to blow you off course. You lose your way. But you keep pressing forward. You keep your focus on the light and follow, trust and believe because even in the darkness and rain, you are never alone. Even with loses, bloody noses and obstacles, He is there and will never leave you. Hard times and challenges befall us all. Just because you have done everything right, you will still face adversity. Do not lose hope or faith in Jesus but press on.

NO Eggnog for Us

My friend climbed back into the car. She sighed loudly and looked at me. "It is Christmas Day, and no one has eggnog?"

"Who would have guessed!" I replied.

"Is there anywhere else we can check?" She asked. "Let's just drive down the road and see what is open."

Unfortunately, we returned home empty-handed and disappointed. We had visited five convenience stores, the Family Dollar and one liquor store, and there was no eggnog in town. It was apparent: eggnog is an item that needs pre purchasing.

Later, after everyone left and I was cleaning up, I thought about our little quest. Running up and down the road, stopping at every open venue. We were out looking for something when it was too late to be found.

Several people will wait until it is too late to seek Christ. Throughout the New Testament, we read warnings that we should not tarry. We do not know how much time we have. Tomorrow may be too late.

Please do not wait until it is too late to seek Jesus. Seek Him today, "For now is the day of salvation."

CPSIA information can be obtained
at www.ICGtesting.com
Printed in the USA
LVHW040916300920
667476LV00001B/16